PRAISE [illegible]

Midnight Duet

"*Midnight Duet* [is] a gender-swapped *Phantom of the Opera*—which means the heroine, delightfully, gets to play the villain's role. Erika Greene is ambitious, brashly confident, hedonistic, sharp tongued, and sexually demanding . . . The electricity between Christof and Erika is instant and explosive."

—*New York Times*

"Charmingly bonkers."

—*Kirkus Reviews*

"Comfort delivers a high-heat, high-volume contemporary romance . . . The spicy sex scenes titillate, and the plot is leavened with humor and unabashed silliness."

—*Publishers Weekly*

"Scorchingly hot, delightfully snarky, surprisingly sweet . . . this fun, bonkers, gender-bent modern take on *Phantom of the Opera* is everything I didn't know I wanted."

—Cathy Yardley, author of *Role Playing*

"*Midnight Duet* delivers on its delightfully bonkers premise! Funny, sexy, and heartfelt, it takes the archetypes we think we know—the Broadway diva and the arrogant rock star—and reveals humans who learn, grow, and love."

—Eden Appiah-Kubi, author of *The Bennet Women*

"The steamy romance novel pipe organists have been craving."

—Jennifer Bardsley, author of *Talk of the Town*

"*Midnight Duet* is the steamy romance musical theater geeks have been waiting for. Leads Erika and Christof have sizzling chemistry, and a cast of outrageous side characters kept me laughing until the last page. So much fun!"

—Addie Woolridge, author of *The Bounce Back*

"Jen Comfort takes two larger-than-life leads, incendiary sexual tension, and a hilarious scene-stealing supporting cast and dials the amp all the way up to eleven in *Midnight Duet*—a romance that's dramatic, campy catnip for theater lovers and angst lovers alike. It's a horny romp that also accomplishes a heartfelt exploration of loneliness, growth, and belonging—ultimately unbreaking two broken people who realize the power of letting go and letting others in."

—Jen Devon, author of *Bend Toward the Sun*

The Astronaut and the Star

"An elegant balance of similarity and difference."

—*New York Times*

"A stellar debut full of horny heart and humor."

—*Library Journal* (starred review)

"The fun, original premise of Comfort's debut—which pairs a NASA scientist with an up-and-coming film star—will draw readers in . . ."

—*Publishers Weekly*

"A goth, bisexual astronaut takes on the task of training a himbo actor for his role in an Oscar-bait space movie . . . Fans of grumpy-sunshine pairings will revel in the banter and chemistry between these two . . ."

—*Kirkus Reviews*

"*The Astronaut and the Star* was a feel-good romantic comedy that had plenty of heart, entertaining banter, science-y goodness, and an opposites attract couple who will quickly win your heart."

—Harlequin Junkie (Harlequin Junkie Recommends)

"A unique, fun, and steamy romantic comedy filled with space science."

—Nerd Daily

"*The Astronaut and the Star* is sure to be on everyone's keeper shelf. A goth ice-queen astronaut meets a sweetie pie himbo actor, and the result is all pointed jabs and heart-melting heat. I loved every page of this fabulous grumpy-sunshine romance."

—Victoria Dahl, *USA Today* bestselling author

"A slow-burn, funny, and sharp romantic comedy. Jen Comfort brings new meaning to grumpy-sunshine romance. A must-read."

—Meghan Quinn, *USA Today* bestselling author

WHAT IS *Love?*

OTHER TITLES BY JEN COMFORT

Midnight Duet

The Astronaut and the Star

WHAT IS *Love?*

JEN COMFORT

This is a work of fiction. Names, characters, organizations, places, events, and incidents are either products of the author's imagination or are used fictitiously. Otherwise, any resemblance to actual persons, living or dead, is purely coincidental.

Published by Montlake, Seattle

www.apub.com

ISBN-13: 9781662516443 (paperback)
ISBN-13: 9781662516436 (digital)

Cover design and illustration by Sarah Horgan
Cover image: © Nadia Chi / Shutterstock

Printed in the United States of America

For my mom, who still crushes a game of Trivial Pursuit

AUTHOR'S NOTE

A few trivial matters . . .

This book is not about *Jeopardy!*

That said, this book's fictional game show, *Answers!*, shares striking similarities to America's Favorite Quiz Show, and I have been a *Jeopardy!* fan for a very long time. While I intend this book to be a loving, "inspired by" sort of tribute, I've changed quite a few things for both legal and plot reasons.

Along those lines, I don't recommend using this book as a study guide for how to prepare for *Jeopardy!* But, since that conceit formed the basis for this plot, I do go into more detail about my research on champion study techniques in the afterword—in case you're inspired to try out for the show after reading this.

No guarantees that you'll also meet, beat, and fall in love with an attractive rival if you make it on *Jeopardy!*, but no guarantees that you *won't*—it's happened before!

A note about untrivial content

This book briefly introduces an aging parent suffering from memory decline. I don't enjoy writing angst, so I don't delve deeply into those waters here—but this is a topic some readers might not be in the right space to read at all. If you want to avoid only the specific chapter where the character is introduced to minimize the angst as much as possible while still enjoying the rest, you can skip chapter 20. I've tried to include context clues in subsequent chapters so you won't have missed too much.

Chapter 1

IN THE DICTIONARY: BETWEEN *LOATHE* AND *LOVE*

Answer

Most Vulcans ascribe to this strict system of reasoning, from which we can deduce Vulcans must be good at sudoku.

Question

What is logic?

Before.

Theodore "Teddy" Ferguson III fell in love with Maxine Hart the day before she crushed his intellectual prowess on national television.

Had he known his fate, that cold March morning in Culver City, he'd never have locked gazes with the big-eyed redhead when they'd both reached for the last powdered chocolate doughnut in the *Answers!* greenroom.

Had he known she'd ruin his waking life and haunt his dreams in explicit fashion, Teddy would have abandoned the doughnut—and the game show on which he'd set a winning-streak record for the past seventy-one games.

Instead, he'd have taken a rideshare directly to the airport, where he'd have boarded a flight for Ushuaia, Argentina. From there, he'd charter a boat to Antarctica, where he would begin a new life in the only location where he might not be recognized as the infamous *Answers!* champion—and Oxford-educated professor of geography and geoscience at Princeton University—who had lost to a woman who'd identified *ice cream truck researcher* as her profession during the interview segment.

This was, technically, an exaggeration, since *Answers!* only aired in 30 of the world's 195 countries. But the point was, Maxine couldn't humiliate him in front of millions of viewers if he lived at the South Pole. And Teddy would sleep well at night, never to be haunted by the knowledge that kissing Maxine tasted like Juicy Fruit—specifically, isoamyl acetate, the primary flavor ingredient found in jackfruit.

But Teddy was only a trivia genius with a mind like a steel trap; he was not an oracle.

He didn't have a clue what he was about to go through.

"Did you know it's titanium dioxide that makes them so white?" Teddy asked the mystery woman, nodding at the doughnut they'd both reached for. Her hand hovered next to his own, frozen two inches above the prize.

The truth was, Teddy was sick of powdered chocolate doughnuts. But he wasn't eating them for pleasure—he was eating them out of caution. He'd eaten one before winning his first game, and since Teddy ascribed to the religion of "better safe than sorry" with zealous devotion, he'd decided the wisest procedure was to mimic each action he'd taken prior to that first win. Every day. For three straight weeks.

Overly cautious? Perhaps. Successful? Unequivocally.

Surely, that's why his heart had stuttered to a stop as their eyes met, only to restart with alarming fervor. Letting this pretty newcomer take his doughnut could be disastrous. Deliberate sabotage, even.

Teddy fought the urge to lunge for the pastry. It's not like he was superstitious (how pedestrian! He was a *scientist*; he'd gone to *Oxford*). And this woman gazing at him with doe-eyed innocence couldn't possibly know his fate hinged on this simple doughnut, because episodes of *Answers!* were filmed months in advance (taped at a rate of five games per day, three days a week), and players kept to a strict code of secrecy until episodes aired. Today was Tuesday, so this fresh batch of hopeful trivia adepts hadn't sat in last Thursday's audience, watching him trounce their peers in back-to-back tapings.

His pulse calmed. Logic prevailed.

Neither this doughnut-poaching woman nor any of the other contestants mingling in this greenroom had any idea that Teddy currently ranked as the second-best player in all of *Answers!* history—and the only player currently ranked higher than Teddy hadn't played a competitive trivia game in three decades.

He was a wolf hiding in a flock of sheep, and this woman was a particularly fetching ewe.

Perhaps that was why Teddy had forgotten that nearly every version of the aforementioned fable ended with the wolf's demise.

She blinked at him. "Titanium dioxide, huh?"

Teddy grinned, the confidence of having gone undefeated for so long empowering him to flirt, when five weeks ago he'd have, at best, awkwardly mumbled an apology. "Don't be alarmed. It's a completely natural mineral, often used in sunscreen."

(For Teddy, the relaying of trivia *was* flirting.)

Her eyes were moss green and enormous, like one of those deer cartoons from the sixties. He memorized the rest of her like she was a composite of facts he'd need to recall on demand (and he would—but involuntarily, in his vividly explicit dreams). Tall. Pale skin. Pointy nose. Wide mouth. Wild mane of inferno-red curls. And, oddly, a full reptile-print pantsuit in the same green hue as her eyes. A name tag stuck to her lapel declared her "Maxine ♡."

She smirked, her gaze flicking to his own name tag.

"The *third*, huh? And a posh English accent? Well, aren't you fancy." Was that a tinge of Brooklyn in her smoky voice? He'd have to hear it again—

Without breaking eye contact, she picked up the doughnut and swiped it down her nose, leaving a streak of white in its wake. "There. Now I won't get a sunburn from the stage lights."

He felt his smile wither.

Maxine (with a heart) bit a hunk off his doughnut and chewed. Then, her face twisted. "Oh, I forgot. I hate chocolate."

"You—*what*?"

"*Chocolate*," she enunciated. (Brooklyn, without a doubt this time.) Her gaze was serial-killer calm. As if in slow motion, he watched her flippantly toss *his* lucky doughnut in a nearby trash can. "By the way, most major doughnut companies dropped titanium dioxide from their ingredients in 2015. I subscribe to the Dunkin' Donuts fan club newsletter. See ya out there, champ!"

She stalked off, leaving him staring into the depths of a sloppy wastebasket. He glanced over his shoulder, assured himself no one was paying him particular notice, and retrieved his mangled prize. It was halfway to his mouth when he stopped himself. He stared at the mystery slime coating the doughnut's left flank.

Get ahold of yourself, man.

Teddy let the doughnut fall back into the bin. When he glanced up again, *she* was watching him.

Her smirk bloomed into a smile full of pointy canines and neatly rectangular incisors. It chilled his blood. Heated his skin. Made his brain tingle, in the way only really, *really* brilliant bits of trivia did.

Somehow, she must have caught wind of his record-setting run, and now she was trying to rattle his composure. The brazen gall of it! Who did Maxine (with a heart) think she *was*?

Existence would be unbearable until he learned the answer.

He sidled up to her at the coffee station. “I see you’ve been informed. How?” Keeping match results hush-hush was a long-standing code of honor among staff and contestants on the *Answers!* game show, and he wanted to know who’d dare betray this sacred institution.

Maxine made theater of carefully selecting a stir stick. She inserted it in her coffee, gave it a thorough mixing, and took a delicate test sip. “Mmm. Tastes like victory,” she murmured.

“Was it Bryan? Was he the one who told you?” *Bryan.* That toadstool. He’d been especially sour after his match yesterday, hadn’t he? You never could trust a Dartmouth man.

“No clue what you’re talking about, bud.”

He cast a sidelong look to ensure no one was eavesdropping and lowered his voice to a whisper. “My record . . . *winning* streak.”

Her fawn brows popped up in a facsimile of surprise. “You want me to believe you’re on a winning streak? A record-breaking one?”

“Don’t play coy.”

“You. The man I just saw trying to eat a doughnut out of a trash can. *You’re* a champion *Answers!* player.”

He gritted his teeth. “I eat a powdered chocolate doughnut every morning before taping.”

“And now you don’t have one.” She gasped. “Oh, no. What are you going to do? Are you going to . . . are you going to *lose*?”

His spine stiffened. “I am not.”

“Oh, silly me. I forgot you probably won’t play against me today.”

It startled Teddy when his stomach dipped in disappointment. *How odd.* “Why not?”

“I’m just an alternate. I’m scheduled to play tomorrow. But Ingrid over there has a case of the baby barfs, and she might have to postpone.” Maxine nodded toward a blonde woman emerging from the restroom, her skin tinted the same shade as the room’s green walls. “Though between you and me, I think she’ll rally. She told me she’s in a women’s rugby league. I’ll bet she can handle a little discomfort.”

Teddy's nose twitched in irritation, but he caught it before it showed on his face. A sick competitor was hardly any fun to beat. He'd be deflating her dreams when she was already suffering, and what was the fun in that? No, he'd been winning so easily for so long. He was bored. He wanted—*needed*—a vicious fight.

Could this woman before him be the worthy challenger he'd been waiting for?

"Where did you study?" he demanded. His brain flipped through its trove of data. If his teenage years growing up in New Jersey had taught him anything, it was that denizens of the New York City boroughs were ferociously loyal to home. "Columbia, perhaps? Cornell?"

"Why does it matter?"

"Educational background is an objective measure of aptitude." He shouldn't have to state the obvious.

"Sure, it is."

The way she looked like she was stifling a laugh made him want to defend his entirely reasonable question. "I'm trying to determine if you're as much of a threat as you say you are."

"You want to know the truth?" Maxine crooked a finger.

Teddy didn't remember making the conscious decision to lean in. But, suddenly, he was close enough to count her individual eyelashes as she lowered her gaze to his throat. She smelled of something faintly tropical that he couldn't quite place, and he had the irrational urge to press his thumb against her glossy lips and measure if they were as soft as they looked. His pulse thundered under his skin.

"The thing is . . . ," she murmured, and Teddy knew in that instant, without a shred of doubt, he'd follow that velvet-washed voice into the depths of hell.

"What?" His voice came out scraped raw with desire.

"I'm worse."

Teddy jerked back. He had the terrifying sensation of having picked up a rock, only to find a snake clinging to its underside.

Maxine's victorious expression made it all the more humiliating. She knew exactly what kind of effect she was having on him.

His cheeks prickled with heat, and he glanced around the room to see if anyone had noticed him falling prey to her strange brand of hypnosis, but thankfully, the other contestants were busy studying or nervously chattering among themselves.

Maxine had made him feel like a fool, and that could not stand.

"I've already won seventy-one games," he warned her in a low register he hoped conveyed the gravity of his threat. "There is only one man on earth who has performed more impressively on this show. What makes *you* think you have what it takes to defeat me?"

"Oh, Theodore."

"Teddy," he corrected. Maybe too quickly. "I go by Teddy."

"Cute."

"Many great men—"

She was already walking away.

He caught up with her again as she settled at one of the round tables scattered around the room beneath wall-mounted televisions airing the network's other shows and framed photos of previous *Answers!* sets. "Berkeley, then," he continued guessing, as if she hadn't rudely dismissed him already. "That's where you attended university." Of course, she'd be a Berkeley girl. With that hair and the outfit and that *attitude*—

With a secretive smile, she swirled her coffee, pressed the pad of her fingertip to the top of her hollow stir straw, and brought it to her mouth like it was an eyedropper. When her glossed lips closed over the end of the red stick to suck the coffee out, Teddy's abdomen clenched. She made the innocent action seem . . . provocative.

"You seem unsettled. Was it something I said?"

"Of course n—" His voice caught. He tried to swallow, but his mouth had gone as dry as the Antarctic (largest desert on earth, by geological definition).

"Coffee?" She held out her cup.

Teddy ignored it, forcing the words out on a rasp. "Just tell me where."

He sounded desperate. He didn't care. The idea that she knew something he didn't was unacceptable. It tormented him. He had to *know*. Not only the particulars of her schooling—everything about her. Who *was* she? Was she as smart as she claimed to be? What would her nails feel like digging into his scalp when he splayed her over the mahogany desk in his home's study and—

Teddy swiped a hand over his face, as if that would cleanse him of the highly inappropriate thought.

Alarm sirens blared in what little remained of his reasonable mind, but he ignored them. Vaguely, he was aware he should be reviewing American presidents' wives' maiden names and Latin word roots—both areas he'd missed during his flash card practice last night. But Maxine interested him a thousand times more.

She was the only trivia puzzle he wanted to solve right now.

The contestant coordinator entered the room and called his name along with two others to go to be fitted with microphones for the first match. They hardly mattered—neither name belonged to Maxine.

The woman in question raised her cup in salute. "Go get 'em, Theo."

"It's *Teddy*."

Her terrifying smile was back. "Come to the hotel bar tonight after taping. If you're still around after today's matches, you can buy me a drink, and I'll put you out of your misery."

Did she mean she'd finally answer his question . . . or something more sinister?

"I'll be there."

She dared to *wink* at him. "Better win a lot of money today . . . I have expensive taste."

Teddy found her at the dimly lit hotel bar that night, already sipping from a glass of glinting amber liquid. It matched the light-struck bits on her halo of curls. Her dark coat was draped over the stool next to her. She'd waited for him, like she'd said she would.

The tightness in his belly eased. Then it twisted again, into anticipation.

He wove through the lively crowd.

The show put all the contestants up in the same midpriced hotel within shuttle distance of the studio, so he and Maxine weren't the only ones who recognized each other. But most of the players he'd beaten today had already gone home in shame, and the rest were newcomers, having been flown in for the next day's tapings. Only a few of his former foes lingered in the crowd, nursing their disappointments over house red wine and well cocktails.

"He'll take one of these, Harris," Maxine told the bartender when Teddy reached her, gesturing to her own drink. "And you can put both on his tab."

Teddy settled into the leather stool next to hers. "Presumptive of you. I prefer red wine."

"I know. The Bordeaux, right? Same glass every time, for almost three weeks? How superstitious of you." She winked at the bartender.

"It's not superstition. I simply don't see a need to risk disappointment by alternating my selection."

"Oh, but risk is the spice of life." A sly smile settled over her lips, as if she had already determined he was the kind of man who drove exactly the speed limit. (Which he was.) But she only raised her glass. "To your wins today."

So, she'd watched all of them. "To my wins."

She watched him sip his scotch, rolling the honey sting around his tongue as peat stripped his wine-attuned palate of reason. "Do you like it?"

"It's . . . excellent," he admitted.

"Good. In victory, you deserve whisky. In defeat, you need it."

Who was this woman who paraphrased Napoleon and had the confidence to taunt him?

"You've seen me play several near-perfect games today, so why do you believe you can defeat me tomorrow?"

Instead of answering, Maxine drained her drink in one go, set the glass down with an exaggerated sigh of satisfaction, and ordered another. He drummed his fingers on the bar. The new drink appeared, and she swirled it in the low glass, sampling the aroma like he wasn't even there.

Teddy leaned forward. "Maxine."

She glanced up and seemed surprised to find him there. "Right, sorry. ADHD. I get lost in my thoughts sometimes. I was just thinking about how weird your accent is. You use this super-ritzy British vernacular, but every now and then you pronounce words like a basic American bro."

Basic American bro? He knew his expression reflected the horror he felt by the way Maxine's eyes lit up.

"My family moved to Princeton when I was nine for my father's academic pursuits, and I didn't return to England until I went to university at Oxford. Does that satisfy your curiosity?"

"Not at all. My curiosity is insatiable."

"You were saying something about tomorrow . . . ?" he prompted.

"*Tomorrow . . .*" She paused for effect. "I'm gonna humiliate you so bad you'll cry onstage."

"Bad*ly*. It's badl—" It came to him: where Maxine had gone to university.

He'd pondered this puzzle during the fifteen-minute breaks between tapings. During the lunch break. Even during gameplay, when he should have been focusing on the board. He'd missed ringing in on what had turned out to be a valuable Daily Duplex question because he'd been considering whether Maxine might have attended an institution overseas. Perhaps that was why she'd thought he wouldn't guess.

But now Teddy realized he'd been assuming logical parameters she hadn't set.

"Nowhere," he said. "You didn't go to university at all, did you?"

"This is going to come as a traumatic shock to a fancy professor like yourself, but I don't need an expensive diploma to be good at trivia. There are other ways to learn stuff, you know."

He wanted to crow with delight. For all her coy taunting and overconfident assertions, she was—"An uneducated nobody," he marveled.

Her little smirk shrank, and he knew he was right. Guessing a correct answer always gave him a burst of satisfaction: he was intelligent, and there was no problem in the world he couldn't solve with enough research and thought. But it still seemed as if the lights in the room had dimmed a bit.

Which was when he realized how his words had sounded. "I didn't mean—"

"You're sure you're smarter than me, aren't you?"

"Well . . . yes." Was he supposed to lie?

Her sneer told him: yes, he was.

"Ms. Hart," he explained gently. "I am an associate professor of geography and geoscience at—"

"Oh, I know. Everyone knows. Princeton. You did your undergrad at Oxford. Generations of distinguished scholars in the Ferguson family line, blah, blah, blah. Did you know the sound techs have a drinking game based on how often you bring up one of those facts in your contestant-interview segment?"

This wasn't going well. "I did . . . not."

Perhaps elaborating on his elite pedigree was not the fastest way to endear himself to women in bars. And he *did* want to endear himself to her, he realized. But he'd clearly hurt her feelings with his *uneducated nobody* remark, and he didn't like the way it had snuffed out her spark—her fighting spirit. It was what drew him, like a moth to her flame. He wanted to set it alight again, even if it meant she hated him.

Maybe that's why he said, "You're rather confident for a Brooklyn girl with no formal schooling. What makes *you* think you can beat *me*?"

She speared him with her eyes. Teddy had never been so relieved to see a woman furious with him.

The room brightened again.

"I watched how you play. You run down every category from left to right, betting the same amount for every Daily Duplex, always betting just enough on the Final Answer question to hedge against the competition but not a dollar more. From a technical perspective, you play consistently and you're rarely incorrect."

"And? What's the problem with that?"

She licked her lips like a cat scenting a mouse in the floorboards, and Teddy's pulse shifted into a higher gear. "You really want to know?"

"Regale me."

She scooted her chair closer, gesturing for him to lean even farther in.

He did. He hadn't learned his lesson.

"You play like a little bitch, Theodore."

"A *what*?" His voice rose an octave.

"You heard me." Maxine tossed back her drink again and plunked the glass on the bar with a flourish. "That's your weakness. You're a superstitious coward who doesn't take risks. And tomorrow, I am going to annihilate you. I'm going to crush you so hard you'll be on your knees begging for mercy before the Final Answer round."

"Metaphorically, I assume."

". . . yeah. Sure."

Not a single proper rebuttal found its way to his lips. She couldn't possibly be serious . . . was she?

Did he *want* her to be serious? Because the thrumming in his low belly made him think he really did—parts of him, anyway. What was wrong with him?

She unwrapped a stick of gum, releasing a burst of tropical scent into the air, and folded it neatly into her mouth. Then she hopped up from the stool, slinging her jacket over her arm. "Thanks for the drinks, champ."

Maxine was already slipping through the crowd before Teddy registered what had happened. Feeling like a fool, he fumbled for his money clip, tossed what were probably far too many bills onto the counter, and hurried after her.

It wasn't hard to spot her by the elevator bank, with that red hair glowing like an Olympic torch.

When Maxine saw him, she raised a brow but thrust her boot out to stop the elevator doors from closing. "Well, aren't you forward," she remarked, eyeing him up and down in a way that made Teddy feel instantly too warm. "I don't usually take dates back to my room after the first drink, and definitely not ones who've insulted my intelligence, but you *are* wearing glasses and suspenders, which I find very slutty on a man. My virtue is real negotiable right now."

"I . . ."

The doors closed on them. Maxine pressed a floor, then blew a tiny bubble with her gum, waiting for him to continue.

Pop.

He managed to gather himself. Supply some flimsy reason for why he'd chased her down, beyond irrational obsession. "I demand you elaborate. Why on earth would I wager beyond what's necessary? That's incorrect strategy."

Was that an *eye roll*? How dare she roll her eyes at thirty years' worth of data analysis on the most statistically beneficial way to win on *Answers!*?

"Strategy is a rule book for good boys like you. I don't like rules. They're boring."

The doors opened, and the smell of pool water hit him. It was enough to make him wrest his attention from Maxine's mischievous cat gaze and to realize that they'd somehow ended up at the rooftop pool. The lights were out on this level, so it was dark, save for the reflection of Los Angeles's city lights turning the hazy night sky purple. Through the closed glass doors to the patio, he could see that the glowing aqua pool was still and the lounge chairs were neatly stowed.

"We've come to the wrong floor," he observed.

"No, we haven't." Maxine stepped out and beckoned for him to follow. For some unfathomable reason, he did.

"It's closed." He pointed at the enormous sign posted on the door, warning guests about seasonal maintenance.

Maxine swiped something in front of the sensor above the handle, and it unlocked with a chirp. She swung the gate open. "Oops," she said, biting her lower lip coquettishly. "Didn't see the sign."

Curious, he tried waving his own room card over the sensor. The panel light flickered red at him. "How did you—"

"Coming?" Maxine let go of the handle, and the door began to close behind her.

He caught it before he could think twice. His heart was racing far too fast. The scotch—it had to be. The liquor had clearly gone straight to his head.

"I don't have my swim shorts."

"Better turn back then."

He didn't. Instead, he followed her out to the pool.

Chilly air buffeted him. He'd left his overcoat in his room.

"Let's get in. The water is heated." Maxine tossed her suit coat onto a stack of lounge chairs and kicked off her boots. Before he knew it, she was unbuttoning her high-collared blouse, and he wrenched his gaze away the instant he caught a flash of creamy skin. Teddy's father had taught him to be a gentleman.

He focused on the haphazard trail of clothes she'd left behind, imagining the silk of her blouse sliding over his fingers—until he heard a quiet splash, followed by her squeak of delight.

When he glanced back, she was floating in the pool, bare limbs distorted below the water line. She still wore her underthings, he noted with a guilty release of held breath, and they were vibrant green against her near-translucent skin. Tiny whorls of steam followed her as she swam out to the middle of the pool. Her long legs kicked out, slow and mesmerizing. When she reached her destination, she turned around to face him. "Come on! It feels good, I promise. Unless you're afraid of getting in trouble."

It was a challenge. And Teddy's pride took umbrage.

He stepped forward. It wasn't until cool water closed over his calf that he realized he was still fully clothed, poised half-in, half-out on the top step of the pool's shallow end.

What the hell am I doing?

"Why, my dearest Lord Ferguson, I believe this is a shoe-free pool," Maxine warned, expression devilish with glee. "I didn't know you were such a bad boy."

He ignored the heat prickling up his neck. "I am most certainly *not*."

"What a shame."

He glanced around, trying not to betray his trepidation. What harm could this possibly bring, really? A scolding from the hotel staff? There was a clause in the *Answers!* show contract about not competing against anyone he had a personal relationship with prior to taping, but they weren't doing anything that could jeopardize his run; it was only a swim. And it *was* chilly.

With as much dignity as he could muster, he perched on the stack of loungers to untie his soggy dress shoes, then slid them off and neatly stowed them beneath the chair. He'd begun unrolling his socks when he felt her gaze on him. He slowed, suddenly self-conscious.

"You're so . . . precise," she observed. Her tone was playful, but there was something else there, too, and it made him acutely aware of the slide of his sock down his calf. The way the wet merino rasped over his ankle bone and whispered along the sensitive underside of his foot.

He swallowed and rushed the other sock off, trying not to think. About anything. All he knew was that he couldn't bear undressing further. She'd already stripped him naked in other ways; the fabric over his chest was the only armor he had left.

When he padded over still fully clothed, Maxine raised a brow. "You're going to get your fancy pants and shirt all wet."

"I have others." He sat carefully on the pool's edge, easing his lower calves into the water. Lukewarm heat closed over his legs, even as goose bumps broke out over the rest of his body. Best to get in entirely, before he froze—or lost his nerve.

"Now I know you're rich." Her tone was light, but there was bitterness underneath it.

Well, he *had* won over $2 million in aggregate over the past three weeks of filming. But the truth was, Teddy simply wasn't thinking about clothing while in her presence.

He was hardly able to think about anything at all.

He slid all the way in and let the water close over his head. When his feet hit the bottom, he opened his eyes, blinking at the sting of pool chemicals. Maxine's ghostly limbs floated mere meters away, where the pool bottom dipped into the deep end, treading water with languid ease. Her underpants were the color of absinthe; lace, with little black bows affixed to each hip. He wanted to—

He squeezed his eyes shut. But the reverse image was imprinted on the back of his eyelids.

When he surfaced, scraping his hair out of his eyes, Maxine's tinkling laughter floated across the water. "Isn't it great?" The topic of his wealth had been dismissed.

He looked down at the transparent white fabric stuck to his chest. "I look ridiculous."

"Mmm." It might have been agreement. He couldn't tell. Maxine floated closer. Her red curls were still dry, clipped to the back of her head. He wondered what they'd look like down, floating in the water around her like a mermaid's. "Sometimes you have to look ridiculous to have a good time. And that's what we're here for, isn't it? A good time?"

It wasn't clear to him whether she was referring to their current trespass in the hotel pool, their choice to compete on a game show, or their participation in the whole of human existence.

"Perhaps that's what you're here for, but this is not a game to me, Ms. Hart. You should know I take this trivia competition quite seriously." Teddy wasn't accumulating wins solely to pad his ego. He had a purpose, and it was one that meant something dear to him—and his father.

Teddy did not like the thoughtful look on her face as she sank into the water up to her chin. "You seem like the kind of man who takes everything seriously. Don't you ever get bored?"

Until today, he'd have answered without hesitation: *I'm perfectly content with my solitary, predictable life.* But a man who'd never seen the sun didn't know to miss its warmth, and the thought of never seeing Maxine again made him shiver.

"Perhaps after I defeat you tomorrow, you'll better appreciate the merits of such diligence and caution."

"You're sweet, you know that?"

"This warning is for your own good." He tried to impart gravity in his tone. It didn't work—Maxine drifted closer. Teddy had the distinct impression he was crocodile food. He rushed to add, "Managing expectations is integral to avoiding disappointment."

She drew up to him and placed her hands on his shoulders to anchor herself. Her cheek brushed his as she leaned to whisper in his ear, and her soft breasts pressed into his chest. Her flesh was hot, the water was lukewarm, and he was dying. His throat closed in an inhale.

She whispered, "I'm going to eat you alive."

God, I hope so. "You underestimate me," he forced out.

"Prove it."

"I intend to."

"No. Right now." She pulled back. Her lips were parted, her pupils dilated. It wasn't only him. He wasn't imagining this. Maxine felt the rush of battle too. "Prove it," she repeated, but this time her voice was breathy.

He shouldn't do this. He really shouldn't. He'd only just met this woman. And he had to compete against her tomorrow, in an effort that would require emotional detachment and complete, utter focus. But her lips glowed pale peach from the pool lights, and her bare skin pressed against his through his wet shirt, and above all—*above all*—she'd challenged him.

No one ever challenged him.

So, Teddy kissed her.

His lips found hers, and he tasted tropical fruit and chlorine. Her mouth was soft, and it moved gently against his. It was lovely and unremarkable—until he felt the hands on his shoulders glide up his neck to cup his face. Her lips parted.

And everything changed.

Teddy had experienced kisses before. Mediocre kisses and passionately brilliant kisses. He'd kissed women, and he'd kissed people who were not women. He'd been in a long-term relationship in his late twenties, and he'd had his share of casual dating and one-night stands. He was not exceptionally worldly, but he was not particularly virginal either.

But Teddy had never experienced a kiss like *this*.

Maxine kissed him like they were at war and their mouths were the battlefield, and it changed his world. Everything he thought he knew about love (a slow-burning, respectable, reasonable thing) was suddenly wrong, every unassailable truth about the universe flipped on its head.

Because in that very moment, Teddy fell helplessly in love with Maxine Hart.

And suddenly he—the man who had won seventy-six consecutive trivia games on the basis of his sheer accumulation of knowledge—wasn't sure if he really *knew* anything at all.

At the thought, terror froze his spine into a rigid line. Like generations of Fergusons before him, Teddy had spent his entire life pursuing knowledge for the noble sake of it. He prided himself on his intelligence and scholarly accomplishments. So if he wasn't a man who *knew* things, who was he?

He didn't know. This woman was dangerous. An unpredictable variable that could upend his entire life.

The only thing he was utterly certain of was that if he let this kiss continue for a second longer, he wouldn't be able to stop.

Teddy jerked away, backpedaling through the water. "I should go."

At first, Maxine only blinked at him in lust-glazed confusion. As if she were translating his words from another language. Then her eyes narrowed, the rejection clearly registering. "You're fucking kidding me."

Teddy hoisted himself out of the pool, water pouring from his soaked clothes. "It's late. We have to be at the studio tomorrow at seven," he reminded her.

"Coward."

Teddy winced. Not because the accusation stung—though it did—but because she was right.

And he didn't know what to do about it except run away.

After.

The following day, Teddy lost to Maxine.

He lost so badly that he was embarrassed to show his face in the hotel bar after the show, though he did anyway, hoping she'd make an appearance—to gloat about her victory, if nothing else. Except he'd only waited in miserable, self-pitying despondency for a woman who never appeared. Teddy was too proud to seek her out in any other way, after how thoroughly she'd beaten him.

It had nothing to do with the shame of having retreated from their kiss like a gutless fool, having approached the abyss of love, only to peer over the edge and decide that perhaps it was a bit too risky. Teddy was logical. Reasonable. Every impulse checked at the gate and properly queued for consideration.

He simply hadn't had time to *consider* Maxine Hart.

When the episode aired three months later, article after article declared him thoroughly, and resolutely, *eviscerated.* Maxine had eaten him alive, like she'd promised. His brain had been so thoroughly scrambled by her deliberate attempt at distracting him with seduction the night before (or so he'd convinced himself) that he simply could not buzz in fast enough. When he had managed to ring in before Maxine, he'd stumbled over answers he'd once known cold. And for the first time in his entire record-breaking run, he'd gone into the Final Answer round in second place, though still within striking distance of Maxine. Except she'd got the answer wrong. He'd got it right. He should have won, but he hadn't—because Teddy had bet conservatively, not trusting himself to answer *anything* correctly after what she'd done to his ego in the first two rounds.

If only he'd bet more.

If only he'd taken the risk.

If only he'd stayed after the kiss.

If only.

Instead, Maxine went on to set a record-breaking score total of her own. By the time she lost in a narrow match, she'd edged past Teddy's total cash winnings record of $2.6 million—in half as many games.

But if there was one thing in this world Teddy could not bear, it was defeat.

He vowed to avenge his loss . . .

And thus, the greatest rivalry in the history of trivia was born.

THE SINGLE ANSWER ROUND

Chapter 2

TERMS OF ENGAGEMENT

Answer

From the Latin for "to speak," it is used to refer to a meeting between hostile parties, often to negotiate a cease-fire or prisoner exchange.

Question

What is parley?

A year later.

Maxine slouched low in the barstool and tugged her sweatshirt hood farther down her forehead so the pair of trivia geeks moseying up to the bar wouldn't recognize her.

It didn't work.

"Heyyyyyy, kiddo. I thought you weren't coming out tonight," came Rabbi Cohen's warm voice. "How are you feeling?"

Maxine faked a Tiny Tim cough. "Terrible. Death is imminent."

Rabbi Cohen nodded, expression grave. "Better get a whisky from Dino before you pass on, right?"

"One last taste of this mortal plane."

Dino, the grizzled owner of the eponymous Brooklyn dive bar where Maxine and her trivia team had spent many a weeknight, gave Maxine a skeptical look. "One? You've been *tasting this mortal plane* since—"

"Fifteen minutes ago," Maxine finished with a warning look at Dino. She raised her glass. "I'm savoring it."

"She couldn't resist celebrating her annual-tournament win with us!" Marlon jumped in front of the rabbi to drape his upper body along the bar facing Maxine. He rested his cheek on his fist and grinned at her. "I can't wait to see Teddy Bear's face when you crush him *again*."

Dino warned, "Off the bar, Marlon."

"I'll have a Chardonnay, Dee-Dee."

"Call me that again and you'll be pissing Chardonnay out your earholes." Dino whipped a dish towel in Marlon's direction, missing Maxine's bespectacled friend by the space of a fly. Dino hadn't survived the Bosnian War and thirty-plus years of Mets fandom to have his bar top be disrespected by a twenty-four-year-old planetarium tour guide.

Marlon rolled his eyes and begrudgingly slid his body into the seat next to Maxine's. "Why are you up here? Let's go to our table in the back so we can see the screens better. Front-row seating for your *victory*." He nudged her playfully.

Maxine wished she really were dying, like she'd claimed in their group chat earlier that day. It would spare her the humiliation of watching her teammates discover that she'd not only lost the annual tournament on *Answers!*, where former champions from that year's regular season competed against each other for bragging rights and a substantial cash prize, but she'd lost to *Teddy*.

Teddy: her nemesis. Her mortal enemy. Her white whale.

Exactly one year and three days ago (but who was counting?), that man had kissed her like no man had ever kissed her before . . . and then he'd run away like she'd thrust a clipboard in his face at a grocery store and asked if he could spare a minute to save endangered succubi. (*Every day, toxic masculinity destroys 10,000 acres of their natural habitat!*)

How dare he, the spineless jerk? *She'd* chosen *him*. He should have been flattered!

It also stung because her romantic liaisons didn't usually run away so quickly; it usually took 'em a few weeks before they discovered her delightfully unique personality wasn't an affect she could take off along with her makeup. Guys or girls, it didn't matter—Maxine was whatever the opposite of an acquired taste was to her paramours.

As if Teddy's chickenshit bolt into the night wasn't insulting enough, he'd come back eight months later to humiliate her in the annual tournament, and hadn't once brought up their kiss in any of their brief backstage interactions. He clearly hadn't been pining for her, or lying awake at night fantasizing about what would have happened if he'd taken her back to his hotel room and really gone *all in*. Which was rude as hell—and that's why he could shove the $250-thou tournament prize he probably didn't even *need* up his generationally rich butthole.

Maxine popped a stick of gum into her mouth and mumbled, "You guys go. I'll join you in a bit."

Her friends finally ambled off, and as soon as they were out of sight, she motioned for Dino to close out her tab. She couldn't stop everyone from watching her epic loss, but she sure as shit didn't want to be here while they did.

Her team, the Factual Fanatics, normally spent their weekly trivia sessions at Dino's practicing for games on the cutthroat Tuesday bar-trivia circuit, but for six straight months leading up to the annual tournament, they'd spent all their free time helping Maxine train to defeat her greatest foe on *Answers!*

Except Maxine didn't exactly do *training*, per se. She credited her regular-season run to being faster on the buzzer than everyone else and betting it all on every Daily Duplex. But there was no getting around it: the annual tournament required actual studying. Sure, she had an insatiable appetite for knowledge, and her brain was like a limitless-capacity sponge, absorbing information from podcasts, video games, books, internet memes—you name it.

Just don't name *memorizing lists of facts*, because Maxine did not do that.

Her ADHD brain simply refused to work that way. And if she tried to force-feed it information like years of public education had tried to do to her, it would only fall right back out days later.

Which was why trying to "study" hadn't helped—in fact, it had seeded doubt in her own intelligence. How was she—a public school dropout—supposed to compete at an elite level when she couldn't remember which river ran through Mali?

In the end, she'd lost so badly that she'd been in the red going into the Final Answer round, which meant she hadn't even had a chance to wager on the last question of the game. It was the most humbling moment of Maxine's life—and she'd grown up scouring crusty casino floors for spare tokens.

She'd let the Factual Fanatics down. She'd let millions of viewers down. Worst of all, she'd let her own pride down. For exactly nine months, from the time she'd first beat Teddy in the regular season to the time she'd lost to Teddy in the tournament, Maxine had really believed she was hot shit. That she was smart enough to hang with the big boys and girls and their big, gothic-font diplomas. Like, *Not only can I compete with these prestige-educated smart-asses, I can kick their asses! So now who's the "troublemaker who has no respect for authority and whose only contribution to English class is occasionally commenting, 'Wake me up when Dickens gets an editor'"?* (Suck it, Mr. Maroni.)

That the different way she learned was *good enough*—no matter what every one of her childhood teachers had said.

And then she'd let Teddy gloat over his revenge victory while she moped in a cab ride to the airport, because she'd been too pissed at herself to even shake his hand after the show, which was the part where she'd let herself down a second time.

No one knew she'd lost yet except Maxine, the other contestants on the show, and her sister, Olive, who had been sworn to secrecy. But after the final game of the tournament aired tonight, everyone would know.

Problem was, Maxine's attempts to get drunk enough to be totally cool with that weren't working.

Dino raised his bushy brows when he saw her gathering her bag to leave. "Where you going, kid? Show's about to air."

As if on cue, the recognizable opening notes of the *Answers!* theme song played over the speakers, and there was a smattering of applause from patrons. One didn't come to Dino's at 7:00 p.m. on a weeknight and expect to see sportsball on the big-screen TVs. The people crowding into the back barroom were here to watch a game show.

"Dino, I'm done with trivia. Officially retired," she announced. "Tell everyone. No more competitions for Maxine Hart."

Not even the one she'd turned down two weeks ago. *Especially* not that one.

"I'm not even going to watch *Answers!* anymore. This tournament was my swan song. Which—fun fact—is sort of a misnomer, because most swans don't sing. They hiss or whistle. But there's a specific type of swan—the whooper swan—with an extra loop in their trachea. And when whooper swans die and their lungs collapse, their final breath gets forced up their extra-curly windpipe, and it makes this sad, musical whistle—"

"You're not dying," Dino reminded her. He was used to Maxine's tangents; trivia was one of her two love languages.

Trash talk was the other, though that honor was reserved for people she *really* liked. Not that she didn't like Dino—it simply wasn't smart to insult the guy who poured her whisky, even in jest. She'd be drinking nothing but Jäger for the rest of her days.

She popped her bubble gum. "I'm dying metaphorically. It's the death of my ego." She leaned forward to whisper, "I lost."

Dino gave her a look. "Yeah, no shit. Now how about you *get* lost with that attitude. You've been moping here since three, and this bar is for contenders, not little girls who give up after a fight doesn't go their way."

Maxine sighed. "I appreciate the tough love, Dino. But it's over, so stop trying to convince me. There's nothing in this world that will ever draw me back into trivia competitions. I'm going to do something else with my life. Something useful. Volunteer with orphaned raccoons. Teach small children to drive monster trucks in televised combat. Donate my organs to science . . . y'know, whoever will have me."

"You want to wash dishes?" Dino offered begrudgingly. "Ricky quit on me. Said he's getting a goober car now."

"Uber," Maxine corrected absently as she considered Dino's offer. Maxine had worked the dish pit before. She'd also been a hairdresser, a skydiving instructor, an assistant at a perfumery, a lifeguard, a bespoke tailor's assistant, a haunted-subway tour guide, a Krav Maga stuntwoman, and an ice cream blogger. And that was only the first two pages of her résumé. There were thirteen other pages, dating all the way back to her first "real" job at seven years old in Atlantic City, which had involved holding seats at slot machines for the all-day gamblers while they went for bathroom breaks—one dollar for fifteen minutes. Maxine's side hustle had ensured she and Ollie always ate, even on the days Mom lost big.

Maxine's lack of workplace longevity didn't come from delinquent performance—on the contrary. She simply got bored when she got good at a job, which usually took about three months, at which point she'd quit and move on to something else. Where was the challenge—the *fun*—in doing something she'd already mastered?

The only thing that had ever held her interest was trivia. There was always more to learn. But now, Teddy had stolen that joy from her.

Besides, she didn't technically *need* the work after her *Answers!* wins. Even after the steep taxes on the payout, she'd been able to pay off Ollie's student loans and still have a nest egg left over.

"Thanks, Dino, but I've still got my tutoring gig, remember? I mean, I don't get paid for it, but it's still a job. Technically." Besides, who else was going to teach neurodiverse kids that learning didn't have to be boring? Definitely not the public school system, which, as far as Maxine was concerned, was designed to suck children's souls out to make space for robot parts. "Those kids are the only other thing that I've ever cared about. And they're all I have left now that Theodore Ferguson III has ruined my life."

Behind her, the thud of the winter vestibule door sounded, and Dino nodded at the newcomer. He turned back to her. "It's not like you haven't lost a game before, Max. What do you have against this guy? He break your heart or something?"

"Teddy?" Maxine sputtered. "Don't make me laugh."

"He's a looker, that's for sure."

"Maybe if you're into privileged, uptight academics who think everyone outside their ivory tower is unworthy of their company. Maybe if you're into English-sounding posh boys who probably iron their socks before bed every night and cut their bland-ass potatoes into tiny, bite-size pieces. Maybe if you're into precisely coiffed golden hair and perfectly symmetrical faces and princely cheekbones and aristocratic noses that scream, 'I've come from fourteen generations of selective breeding—'"

"Fifteen, actually," said a crisply accented voice behind her.

A voice that haunted her nightmares—and her fantasies.

Maxine froze. Behind the bar, Dino had suddenly made himself extraordinarily busy polishing a glass.

Through gritted teeth, she accused Dino, "You sold me out."

Dino raised the glass to the light, inspecting it for invisible smudges.

"Fifteen generations," Teddy repeated. "That's as far back as the Ferguson family record takes us, though I have no doubt it goes further."

Maxine refused to give Teddy the satisfaction of whirling in surprise. "I knew I sensed a bit of prehistoric peasant in you." She busied herself rummaging through her purse until she found her winter gloves. Only after she'd taken her time sliding each glove on like an elaborate reverse striptease did she turn to face her adversary. "If you came all the way up the Jersey Turnpike from Princeton just to gloat, prepare to be disappointed. I'm not staying to watch."

"I've already had three months to gloat, and to be quite honest, it's growing dull." Teddy drew up alongside her. "Though now that you mention it, I could be persuaded to savor one more gloat."

His cheeks were ruddy from the frosty air outside, his tortoise-shell-framed glasses lightly fogged at the bottom, and his golden-wheat locks glittered with melting snowflakes. But that was the extent of his dishevelment. His tweed overcoat was lint-free. His black cashmere scarf arranged in an editorial knot. His lush hair was parted just so, slicked back from his face and held in exacting place with hair gel that Maxine knew from up-close experience smelled like vetiver, rosemary, and citrus. He looked like he'd been caught posing for *GQ* between an invite-only lecture at the museum and evening tickets to the symphony.

One more gloat. That absolute dickweed. Maxine wanted to rip his scarf off, mess up his hair, and leave sweaty handprints all over his lily-white dress shirt. That would teach him . . . something.

She gave him a forced smile. "Dino? Get the fancy professor man whatever he wants, on my tab. I did win more money than him, after all."

"Well, if you don't count the tournament." Teddy returned her smile with a false one of his own.

"Shh, Theodore. No spoilers." Maxine nodded in the direction of the back room, where the episode's first round had begun.

"*I'll take Cry Me a River for a thousand,*" came Maxine's voice from three months ago.

"*The answer there is . . .*" Dr. Loretta Love, the show's infamous host, trailed off in a way that everyone knew could only mean one thing. Familiar trilling synths echoed from the speakers, followed by whoops and cheers in real time from the Dino's audience. "*. . . the first Daily Duplex clue! You found it early, so you don't have any money yet, but you can wager up to a thousand.*"

"Max heart!" Marlon crowed at the TV.

"*Maximum wager,*" television-Maxine echoed.

Without looking, Maxine knew her on-screen self was giving the camera her signature move: shaping her hands into a heart and pushing it forward, as if she were giving her heart to the audience.

She always went all in on the Daily Duplexes. It was the strategy that had beaten Teddy the first time and won her over $2.6 million. But it was also a fast way to tunnel into a negative score if she got the answer wrong.

Maxine didn't need to stick around to witness this train wreck again; once was enough. Without another word, she pushed away from the bar and stalked toward the bathroom hallway, fumbling for the crushed box of cigarettes in her pocket as she went.

Maybe Teddy wouldn't follow her if he thought she was going to the bathroom.

Maxine continued down the narrow hallway past the bathroom, then glanced over her shoulder before slipping through a door marked "Employees Only." An interior stairwell took her up to the second floor, where Dino kept his office. Toward the back of the building's narrow footprint at the end of the hallway, Maxine knew, was a cluttered storage room that boasted a big industrial window over an old leather banquette from before a long-ago remodel. Perfect for gazing out over the picturesque maintenance equipment and weed-dappled cement in the backyard of the adjoining building. There was also a pretty decent view of downtown Manhattan, and a girl didn't grow up in Brooklyn without being a little romantic about the big city.

She'd clambered onto the banquette and wrenched the ancient window open when Teddy pushed into the room. Maxine waited for the sound of the door closing behind him before she glanced over her shoulder.

"Well, aren't you forward," she mumbled around the unlit cigarette between her lips. If he recognized the callback, she couldn't read it from his expression.

She hadn't turned the lights on, and Teddy's tall form was only visible in the orange glow filtering in from the streetlights outside. Shadows played with the sculptural lines of his face as he inspected the stacks of sloppy manila folders, the broken barstools, and the dusty pinball machine in the corner.

"You're not very stealthy, if you meant to hide from me."

Maxine shrugged. He was right. "What do you want?"

He approached, his steps slow and heavy on the creaky wood floorboards. A thrill went through her. She suppressed it, instead distracting herself by riffling through her coat pockets for a lighter.

"I spoke to Nora today," Teddy said. "She said you turned down her invitation."

So that's what this is about—the Ultimate Answers! *Tournament.* Nora was the show's new producer: a media-savvy ratings shark who had been brought over from a reality-TV network when *Answers!* had been purchased by a streaming service over the summer. Even the world's most popular trivia show could be bought on the cheap if your old executive producer had been charged with a federal crime for tampering with contestants. Some exec had engaged in nepotism lite and slipped his goddaughter into the contestant pool—which was a huge no-no, but an extremely boring way to tank one's career and narrowly dodge a year in prison. Thanks to the Van Doren trials of the 1950s, the merest whiff of game show rigging had serious criminal consequences.

To "reinvigorate the brand," Nora had concocted some ridiculous *new* tournament, featuring the top-ranked players from the show's entire history . . . and a record-setting grand prize of $2 million, thanks to deep-pocketed sponsors.

As hard as it had been to pass up a chance at that much cash, Maxine would rather be eaten alive by rabid seagulls than experience the humiliation she'd just gone through at the annual tournament. Besides, she didn't need the money now.

Not that it wouldn't be nice to have.

With a prize like that, maybe she could kick-start her pipe dream. Use it as seed money for that school for neurodiverse kids she'd always wanted to open—

And how are those same kids going to react when you lose again? All she'd end up doing was proving to everyone, including herself, that she wasn't good enough. That her thirty-six-episode run was a halcyon combination of less-experienced opponents, fast buzzer timing, gutsy bets, and sheer luck. When she went up against the best players in the game . . . players who actually knew their shit? Maxine couldn't cut it.

Firmly, she told Teddy, "I'm done with trivia competitions." Maxine gave up searching for her lighter and tugged the cigarette free of her lips.

"Why?"

"None of your business."

"Fair enough." He closed the last distance between them; then a tiny flame appeared in front of her face. Teddy held out a blocky lighter, its silver body etched with a fancy coat of arms.

"Thanks." She begrudgingly let him light her cigarette—and then let it dangle out the window between her fingers. Catching his quizzical look, she explained, "Oh, I don't smoke. I just like the smell."

Maxine demonstrated with a deep breath, inhaling the eau de Brooklyn fragrance of winter air mixed with city stank and that glorious whiff of secondhand smoke. If she closed her eyes, she could pretend she was in an Atlantic City motel, watching *Answers!* on TV while Ollie did homework and Mom counted the tokens left in the Care Bears lunch box. Good times.

Funny how nostalgia glossed over the rough edges.

"I want you to reconsider."

"Why?" Maxine blinked up at him. "Last I saw on The *Answers!* Fan website, we're basically tied at the top as the second- and third-ranked players. Since the first-ranked contender retired decades ago, you've got a clean shot to victory with me out of the picture."

"That's the problem." Teddy lowered himself to the empty side of the banquette she crouched on, the old leather creaking under his weight. Teddy was more solid than he looked in those nicely cut suits of his.

Soaked white fabric clinging to his firm chest—

Maxine forced herself to look out the window. Focus on the present, and not the lust-drenched memory that had entertained her for way too many nights over the past year.

"You don't want a clean shot, is that it?" Maxine asked. "You like when I make it hard for you?"

"Exactly." Teddy shifted, trying to find a dignified way to sit, even as he sank into the ancient cushion. He seemed to settle for awkwardly crossing his right ankle over his left knee. "I play significantly better when I'm faced with a worthy opponent."

Worthy. Best to not think about how that made her chest glow warm. "I get it, trust me, I do. The thrill of the chase is good stuff . . . best drug there is, next to coffee. And really, *really* good sex."

Teddy cleared his throat. If it weren't so dark in here, she'd swear he was blushing . . . which made continuing to tease him a tempting prospect.

Except the last thing she needed was more temptation, especially as far as Teddy was concerned. "My answer's still no."

"Tell me you don't want a chance to avenge your loss."

Her spine stiffened. "I lost because I misplayed. Not because of *you.*"

Definitely not because his indifference to her had unsteadied her self-confidence—her firmly rooted belief that she was *awesome*—and that Teddy had lain awake every night just like she had, reliving their kiss and extrapolating scenarios in which he hadn't stopped but had instead hauled her out of the pool, plunked her on the ledge, and drowned himself by free diving between her thighs. (RIP, noble aquanaut; you died a hero.)

He raised his hands in surrender. "All right. I won't tell you what Nora said, then. I'm sure you don't want to hear it."

"You're right, I don't," she lied.

"Final answer?"

Maxine stubbed out her cigarette—hard. "What did Nora say?"

"That you and I are the greatest rivalry in the history of *Answers!* That I should try to convince you to compete because I can't bring in the viewer numbers alone."

Why hadn't Nora said any of this to Maxine on the phone? Probably because she was a bloodthirsty reality-TV sorceress who knew how to get a rise out of people. And it didn't take a genius to figure out that no one got a rise out of Maxine like Teddy did. From Teddy's unbearably smug expression, he knew it too.

Well, screw that—no one got the upper hand on Maxine Hart.

She brought herself to eye level with Teddy so she could stare right into his baby blues. Close enough to smell the vetiver.

"This is about the kiss, isn't it?" she asked.

Teddy's inhale was audible. "What?"

"Come on, Theodore. Tell me the truth. Why did you run away?"

He shot to his feet. "I believe it's against the rules to have a personal relationship with another player prior to taping."

"Sure, but only for regular-season episodes. Tournaments are another ball game." Maxine stood too. He didn't get to look down on her—he'd already done enough of that. "And it only counts if you get caught."

A flush colored his cheekbones. "It was a conflict of interest—"

"Bullshit. If that was really the reason, we'd have been in the clear the next day after I beat you. But you never even tried to find me. I think your poor, fragile ego couldn't handle the thought of losing to an *uneducated nobody*."

Teddy went still, and there was a long silence as they stared each other down, his expression changing from flustered innocence to something far more interesting—anger.

"You're right," he said finally, but his tone wasn't conciliatory. "I didn't like losing very much at all."

"Ha! I knew it."

"You *humiliated* me! What did you expect? That I'd run into your arms afterward?" He began to pace the small area. "I had half a mind to suspect you'd tried to seduce me to throw me off balance."

"Oh, that's rich," she scoffed. "You're really going to try to blame *me* for your loss? Once a coward, always a coward."

"And you wouldn't know anything about cowardice, would you?" He stepped forward until he was close enough to kiss, and lowered his voice. "Losing doesn't feel so good, does it, Maxine? Discovering you aren't as infallible as you thought you were, in front of millions of viewers . . . well, that's a bitter pill, isn't it?"

"I'm a big girl. I handled it," she snapped.

"You wouldn't even shake my hand afterward."

"I had to catch my flight."

"Did you? It seems to me like you're the one who ran away that time. You don't like losing either."

Maxine licked her lips, her stomach fluttering. She opened her mouth to deliver a scathing comeback.

Nothing came out.

"Come back and face me." Teddy continued, "I might have taken the title last time, but you still hold a higher winnings record. We're even. But you know the rules . . . we're both disqualified from playing the regular season again, and the annual tournaments are limited to the victors who've won five or more games that season. The Ultimate Tournament is the only way we can compete against each other on *Answers!* again. The only way to know for sure. If you give up now, we'll never find out who's better."

"Are you sure you can handle finding out?" she heard herself say, when what she'd really meant to tell him was, *Fuck off.*

His winter gloves were still on, she realized, as his hand came up to cup her cheek. The leather casing was buttery soft, his touch warm against her air-cooled skin. His thumb traced a reverent path down to her lower lip and pressed the soft flesh. His eyes were hooded, expression deliciously shadowed. "I'm unsure I can handle the alternative."

Against her will, she pressed her face into his touch, her own eyes falling shut. Kissing Teddy right now was a terrible idea. What kind of message would that be when she still planned to send him away empty handed?

Her lips parted. *Maybe just one . . .*

In a voice so low she could barely hear it, Teddy said, "I'll see you in Los Angeles."

The heat against her cheek disappeared. By the time her eyelids fluttered open, Teddy was gone.

Chapter 3

CINEMATIC CRIMES AND PUNISHMENTS

[Dr. Love: We're looking for the movie title.]

Answer

Tommy Lee Jones tries to stop Ashley Judd from killing her husband—again.

Question

What is *Double Jeopardy*?

Maxine did everything in her power to forget her unexpected rendezvous with Sir Teddy Righteous, the Bane of Her Existence.

Maxine began the process by drinking herself into a state of incomprehension that very same night. No one at Dino's questioned this, because they'd all watched her catastrophic loss on television. A girl who blew her substantial lead by blanking on the final question, thus losing an entire championship tournament—and a quarter million sweet, sweet prize dollars—deserved a whisky shot or ten. On the house.

When Maxine woke up in her Sheepshead Bay apartment the next afternoon, she threw herself into her work.

. . . which didn't, technically, exist.

And it's not like she planned to actually finish repainting the walls of her apartment (currently: emerald in the half she'd started three months ago, sage in the unpainted portion), or fold any of the towering piles of clean laundry that she'd created (she didn't mind throwing her laundry in the machine—it was folding and then reuniting those items with her dresser drawers that made her want to shrivel with agonized boredom).

Besides, she didn't have time for repetitive chores. She was very busy. Lots of important stuff to do. Such as . . .

Maxine ferreted through her brain for an excuse, then pulled out her phone.

"Why are you calling me? I told you, three to seven are my study hours," her sister said by way of greeting.

"Just checking in. I thought eight to midnight were your study hours." Maxine popped her wireless headphone in her right ear and pressed play on her game controller. On screen, her fighter rotated slowly in the character-selection screen.

"Yeah, those too."

"Nerd."

Olive's tone was aggrieved. "I'm in *med school*, Maxie."

"Yeah, you're welcome. I'm checking in on my investment." Maxine swapped her fighter's outfit to a flashy white-and-silver getup. Too much? She tilted her head at the screen, considering. *I could totally rock a white-and-silver outfit situation like this when I win the Ultimate* Answers! *Tournament . . .*

Not that she was considering competing just because Teddy had called her a coward. But if she *were* going to fly out to LA just to teach him a lesson? Boy, would he be sorry—

Nope. Not falling for it. Not even thinking about it.

She swapped back to the blue reptile-print costume. Not much topped the blue reptile. But if she won five more online tournaments on the "mortality" difficulty level, she'd get the *lime-green* reptile print, which, she'd decided, was exactly what her fighter, MAXDEATH!!!!, was missing in her virtual life. (Any similarities to the outfit she'd worn the day she met Teddy were only a coincidence.)

"I thought you were tutoring in the afternoons again. Don't you have something better to do than bother me?"

She *had* been tutoring . . . until her only remaining student, Tyler, decided he was really into soccer now. Maxine reassured her sister. "I promise, I'm keeping busy. But we're not here to talk about me. Let's talk about why you're studying all the time and not banging hot doctors all over campus." On screen, MAXDEATH!!!! executed a roundhouse kick combo into her opponent's face.

"First of all, because none of us are doctors yet?"

"What about your professors? Any McDaddies in homeroom?"

"*No.* And don't call my instructors *McDaddies*. That's weird and gross and super outdated."

Maxine's fighter moved into close quarters and queued up her special aerial attack, only to be ambushed by her opponent's own aerial. Maxine stifled a curse word that her sweet, innocent, twenty-six-year-old baby sister shouldn't hear. "Are you at least going to parties and trying drugs?"

"No, I'm not trying *drugs*. Can I go now?"

"What the hell am I paying for if you're not even trying drugs?"

"Look, I'm hanging up—*oh*." There was a long sigh on the other end of the line. "Maxie, I'm sorry. I forgot your episode aired last night. How'd it go over with the trivia team?"

Maxine shrugged, even though her sister couldn't see it. "Fine."

"It must have been painful to watch."

The pity in Olive's voice made Maxine want to retch, and the hangover didn't help. "No big deal. It's not like I didn't know how it ended." She spammed the attack button with vigor. Her opponent was down, and that was how Maxine liked it. Time to send him ungently into the good night.

"Teddy's a really tough opponent." Olive clearly meant to be soothing.

Maxine's fighter straddled her pathetic excuse for a sparring partner, placed her claws over his ears, and ripped his head off to hoist aloft until his spinal column waved behind her like a party streamer. An exaggerated fountain of blood pooled around MAXDEATH!!!!, dousing her in victory.

She said curtly, "Teddy's a stuck-up prick who spends too much money on perfumed hair products."

"Oooooh. How do you know what his hair smells like?" Olive's singsong tone was a faint echo of the little girl Maxine had half raised, but it still made her smile. There were only two warm spots in Maxine's cold-blooded heart, and one was reserved for her sister.

The other spot was for snakes, which were cool as shit.

"He had the nerve to show up at Dino's last night, supposedly to recruit me for some ultimate tournament, but really because he wanted to rub it in."

"He wanted to rub *something* in."

"There it is. I knew there was proof we were related."

Olive *tsk*ed. "You shouldn't have used your super-seduction powers on him right when you first met. Now he's going to be obsessed with you forever. You have to stop leaving a trail of lovestruck casualties in your wake—it's just cruel at this point."

"My victims all deserved it," Maxine mumbled without conviction. The truth was, her vixen persona was a front. If she told her little sister that all those affairs had ended when Maxine's undiluted personality inevitably became a little *too much* for the other person, Olive would worry.

"Don't you ever want to have a real relationship? You know, fall madly in love?"

"Ew, no. You want me to end up like Mom?"

"Shit, Maxie. I forgot to send you Mom's lucky token for the tournament."

"That's definitely why I lost. You're a bad baby sister," she said, even though Maxine wasn't superstitious. Luck was all about your odds, and odds could be calculated.

Olive whined, "I'm sorry!"

"*Not* forgiven. Straight to jail. Disowned immediately."

"That's why you have to compete in this new tournament. So I can make it up to you and get back in the will."

Maxine paused at the game's title screen. Suddenly, she wasn't in the mood for a bacchanalia of bloodshed anymore. She was more in the mood for wallowing in bed and occasionally brushing her hand across her cheek while pretending it was Teddy's hand instead. Which was disturbingly unlike Maxine, who made a point to be certified Cool, Hot, and Unsentimental (TM)—since feeling shit meant having to regulate it, and her brain didn't exactly do that well—and the fact it was *Theodore Ferguson, Lord of Starched Buttholes*, that her sentiments had latched on to was even more disturbing.

"So when's this tournament?"

"For me? Never. For everyone else, it's in five weeks. But they want us out in LA this weekend to sign paperwork and do promo stuff."

"This weekend, as in tomorrow? I mean, you could probably still catch an early-morning flight out of Newark, or something."

Technically, Maxine was only a ten-minute taxi ride from JFK, but Olive knew she'd had a vendetta against that airport ever since the incident with her emotional-support ball python, Miss Cleo-asp-tra, who was still traumatized by the experience.

"No. I'm not going. There's nothing in this godforsaken universe that will convince me to return to the scene of the crime, where my ego was brutally executed in front of a jury of millions of viewers."

"What about revenge?"

Maxine's finger hovered over her controller's power button. *Revenge* . . .

"After all, you murdered his ego first," Olive reminded her. "Which means you can do it again. And you know the best part?"

She licked her lips. "What?"

"You can't be tried twice for the same crime. It's—"

"Double jeopardy," Maxine and Olive said in unison.

So tempting . . .

But the siren call of the risk-reward schema was all too familiar. Hadn't she learned her lesson? She'd risked it all on *Answers!* the first time because she'd wanted to prove she could—and win a better life for herself and Olive. But she'd already gotten that in spades.

Then, she'd gotten greedy. Not for money, but for glory. Almost tying for second place of all time should have been enough to soothe whatever emptiness in her psyche needed validation—that she was *smart* enough and *worthy* enough—but apparently not. Even with more money and recognition than she'd ever dared dream of, something was still missing. And continuing to chase whatever that was would probably bite her in the ass.

Maxine had spent the three months since her dramatic loss in the annual tournament trying to figure out what was wrong with her. Was this just the way her brain was built—to always crave more of a good thing? Would she never be satisfied?

It was a real fear. One that was starting to keep her up at night. Look at what had happened with Mom, a textbook gambling junkie in thrall to the dopamine mob boss in her brain. Her addictions had led her down a long dark tunnel, chasing light at the other end that only she could see. And she'd dragged her daughters along with her, from one casino to the next, progressively seedier, gambling hole.

Maxine had thrived in that underworld—who needed structured school and rules when you could be earning cold, hard cash in a variety of side hustles by age fifteen?—but Olive had started to wither away. Her sister was a valuable seedling languishing in a bed of hardy weeds. And unlike Maxine and their mother, whose brains seemed to take the concept of living as a personal challenge and could weather nuclear winter in a trash bag if they had to, Olive's brilliant, neurotypical brain needed the light; the steady sureness of authority and consistency and dependable adult role models.

So, at eighteen, Maxine had left Mommie Dearest behind in hell, slung Olive up on her back, and clawed them a path to the surface. She'd gotten her GED, acquired a "real job" to satisfy the government, and lobbied for full custody of Olive.

But now her little sister didn't need her anymore. Olive was a grown woman with fully paid tuition to med school and a bright future, their mother had died a decade ago in a shocking twist of luck, and Maxine had enough money that she could happily while away the rest of her days paying rent on the same cozy one-bedroom she'd lived in as a kid and ordering takeout for every meal. She was free to do whatever she wanted with her life.

Problem was, she hadn't figured out what that was yet. That annual-tournament loss had set her back on her ass—hard—and now she was afraid she'd fail at anything she set out to do.

But what if she did compete this one final time? And what if she *won*?

This was her last chance to prove to the world—and herself—that an *uneducated nobody* could outcompete the greatest trivia champions in the world. Show all the neurodiverse kids out there that losing a round didn't mean losing the whole match.

And really, who was to say that her purpose—the thing she was meant to do with her life—wasn't winning this Ultimate *Answers!* Tournament, requesting her prize money to be paid out in singles so she could roll it into a 500-foot tube, and then *shoving that tube up Teddy's tightly clenched ass*?

"Did you just sigh dreamily?" Olive asked. "You must be thinking about Teddy."

"Yeah, thinking about him losing." Maxine powered off the controller. "On second thought, maybe I *will* compete in this tournament . . ."

Chapter 4

CROSSWORD CLUES (7)

Answer

These types of crosswords are unique in that the clues are the puzzles in themselves.

Question

What is a cryptic?

Very early the following morning, Teddy was on a flight out of Newark to Los Angeles to sign paperwork and film promotional material for the *Ultimate* Answers! *Tournament*. Though he'd done his best to muster enthusiasm for the challenge without Maxine's participation, this was the first time he'd embarked upon an *Answers!*-related trip with such utter lack of anticipation. He was feeling so lackluster about the entire scenario that he hadn't even brought study materials to cram during the flight, as was his usual modus operandi.

Not a second wasted that could be spent learning trivia—that had always been his motto. He'd run previous tournaments on a strict diet of protein shakes, six hours of sleep per night, and an intense desire for victory.

But what did it matter now? This time, he intended to sleep on the flight and wake up looking refreshed for the cameras.

He had already disinfected his first-row business class seat, queued up five hours of white noise on his noise-canceling headphones, completed his six-step skin-care routine with bottled water in the lavatory, and begun his crossword when the lead attendant announced the plane doors were closing.

And then chaos erupted in front of him.

"Wait!" a woman's voice cried out.

Startled, the attendant backed away from the door, allowing a redheaded tornado to stumble onto the plane, gasping for breath.

Maxine.

She straightened, centered herself in the aisle, and addressed the crowd of gawking passengers. "Phew. Almost missed it. Traffic in this city, am I right? This is what I get for not flying out of JFK."

The attendant cleared her throat and gestured to Maxine's three overstuffed bags. "Ma'am, I don't know how you got this far, but you're allowed one personal item and one carry-on—"

Maxine waved the attendant away, her gaze searching, then finally locking in on Teddy, seated right before her in the first row. Her eyes narrowed in a way that made his pulse race in dread—at least, he hoped it was dread, and not something concerning, like lust.

He'd spent quite a bit of time eradicating his unhealthy obsession with this woman. After many, many months of forcibly blocking her from his thoughts, he was safely recovered and now thought of her as no more than a respected equal in the trivia sphere.

His dreams of her were now strictly platonic.

The acts he performed on himself in his morning shower had no relation to her whatsoever.

And it had been a full five weeks and six days since he'd queued up his curated porn compilation of redheads.

Recovered. Healthy. Professional respect.

"Oh, these aren't all mine. One of these is my husband's," Maxine said.

Husband. Teddy's soul sublimated into the stuffy cabin, undoubtedly spraying everyone in business class with aerosolized disappointment. When had she gotten married? Surely, he'd have heard; he'd requested a push notification—

"Right, Teddy Bear dearest?"

She leaned in close, and for a lightning second—in which Teddy's heart came to a full and lethal stop—he thought she intended to kiss him.

But she only said in a low voice, "Do me a solid, buddy. I know you only brought one bag."

How did she know that? "I see you've deigned to compete in the tournament."

"Only if they don't kick me off this plane, *Theodore*."

Teddy gritted his teeth. "You're breaking the rules, and I don't intend to be an accomplice to—"

"Please?"

"Absolutely not. And may I ask how it came to be you *just so happened* to book a seat directly next to mine?"

"People like me. You should try it sometime."

"You bribed the desk agent."

Maxine pouted. "Look, I'll play the in-flight trivia game with you and let you win."

"I don't need to be *let*—"

"Prove it."

"My win record stands, I need prove nothing to you."

"Sure you don't, hot stuff. Oh, sorry, I meant *Doctor* Hot Stuff. Did I get your title right, *Mister* Record Winning-Streak Man? Or is it *Lord* Oxford Comma? *Baron* Textbook? *Duke* Nukem—"

They were beginning to draw attention. And Teddy despised attention. "Just sit down."

Maxine straightened, a triumphant smile on her face. "Thanks, babe!"

"And don't distract me. I have a rigorous study schedule to maintain."

She said in a conspiratorial tone, "I could use a little rigorous maintaining myself."

"Sorry, what?"

"What? We're married, remember? On our honeymoon, actually." Maxine heaved a fluorescent-lime duffel into the overhead compartment, cramming it alongside his compact Samsonite. Then she announced to the cabin at large, "Gosh, I hope the pilot doesn't hit any turbulence. I put all my sex toys in there, and I think some of them have lithium batteries in them."

With that proclamation, Maxine plopped into the aisle seat next to him.

"She's joking," Teddy reassured the other passengers, including the attendant, who only seemed to relax slightly as she retreated to her cubby. Through clenched teeth, he added to Maxine, "You *are* joking."

Maxine snapped open the laminated safety card with an air of massive grievance. "The average vibrator has a lithium-ion battery of, like, eighteen watt-hours, and the FAA only bans lithios over a hundred watt-hours."

"Thank you, I'll file the energy specifications of sex toys in 'Categories that will never appear on the show.'"

"Or you could file it under 'Things Teddy will never need to know because he's never going to bang another living being with that metaphorical bow tie around his ball sack.'"

"What is the ball sack in this allusion? My pedagogical pride?"

"Bingo."

He crossed his arms. Maxine was intentionally trying to rattle him because that was her primary methodology for gaining the upper hand, and he refused to allow it this time. "I'll have you know there are many

Answers! fans who delight in my vast array of knowledge and who are very impressed by my Oxford diploma."

"Really?"

"Yes, really." He didn't like how defensive he sounded. What Maxine thought of him shouldn't matter so damn much—but it did. "Sophisticated intellectuals who value my devotion to the pursuit of education at the highest level, and who appreciate my rational play style."

"Oh, so you think my play style is irrational." Maxine's eyes narrowed at him over the top of the safety card. "Maybe I accidentally won two and a half million bucks, then. Maybe I tripped and fell on all those Daily Duplexes I used to keep doubling my score."

"I'd argue a good player should be able to win without collecting a single Duplex."

"So now you're suggesting I'm not a good player?"

"I'm suggesting there's a more respectable way to play. One of the many things taught in higher education is the pursuit of intellectual integrity."

She muttered something under her breath that sounded rather like she was mockingly parroting the words he'd said.

"Very mature."

"What? I'm an uneducated street rat—you can't expect me to be *mature*."

"Rats are highly cooperative, intelligent creatures who can memorize a route in a maze after only a single pass. They would thrive in the upper echelons of scholarship." He gave her a meaningful glance.

"God, you're such a snob."

"Say what you like. My last win proved my point," he said, hoping that would end the discussion. Best to not let her know she still had the power to unsettle him, or she'd use it relentlessly.

The plane taxied down the runway, and Teddy returned to his crossword, trying to reclaim his mental peace.

Clue: "Heat, in a literal sense (5)."

He filled in the *A*, but its peak spiked out the top of the box. He gripped his fountain pen harder, trying in vain to smooth the edges of the *R* and *D*. The *O* was a half-moon mess, and the last *R* was barely legible.

"Seven down is idée fixe. Obsession with an accent. Très cute."

He slapped a hand over the paper. "A crossword is meant to be a solitary activity."

"But you put a little dot next to that clue. You didn't know it."

"I would have arrived at the answer."

The look she gave him was suspiciously pitying. "We both know the romance languages are not your strength."

She was not wrong. "You're entirely wrong."

"You missed that $800 clue about Shakespeare inventing the word for a certain reptile based on its Latin name. Remember that?"

"No, can't say I do." *Lacerta. El lagarto. Alligator.* He'd rung in reflexively, because the category was Amphibians and Maxine was one question away from running the entire column, and he'd had to break her momentum. And when he beat her to the buzzer, she'd made this *sound*, this audible whimper of dismay—

"You blanked. You didn't know your Latin."

"Erras."

"Recte sum."

This was ridiculous. Five minutes, and she'd already goaded him into arguing like ancient Roman schoolchildren. Teddy tore out the crossword puzzle from his workbook and thrust it at her. "Have at it, then. Bequeath your unparalleled brilliance upon us all."

He did not like the way her eyes lit up as she gleefully snatched the paper, like he'd just gifted her a bouquet of green dianthus. He had an entire booklet of crosswords, and he'd only given her one to buy himself a window of peace. If he were actually going to offer Maxine a gift, it would be something far more impressive than a single crossword.

An all-expenses-paid vacation to Challenger Deep, for example. A one-way flight to Mars. A portal to another dimension.

Anything to be relieved of his addiction to her.

Maxine hunched over the crossword, and Teddy yanked his eye mask down so he wouldn't have to see her little pink tongue sticking out between her teeth while she went to work. The mask wasn't good for anything else at this point. There was no chance of falling asleep on this flight.

The very second Maxine had appeared, his brain had gone haywire, and it didn't appear his body had any better sense either. She scrambled him like an X-class solar flare assaulting his interior electrical network. What had he been *thinking*, insisting she compete in this tournament? Had he forgotten the catastrophic effect Maxine Hart had on him?

Or had he—and this thought was even more apocalyptic—secretly craved that feeling of devastation, with all the addictive impulse of a cat discovering the existence of cheese?

Dear god.

He'd made an enormous mistake. Teddy rarely made mistakes—except where Maxine was concerned. And clearly, he'd let his latent obsession with her overshadow his sense of self-preservation.

There was no other way out of this: he *had* to stifle his attraction to Maxine at all costs.

Winning this tournament was vitally important, and this time, it *was* about the money.

Unbeknownst to anyone, Teddy had already spent his previous winnings. He didn't regret what he'd spent it on, but he hadn't planned on becoming so . . . dissatisfied with his life.

It was a feeling he hadn't been able to shake, and it had begun exactly one year and five days ago. Ever since meeting *her*, he'd been craving something irrational. *Don't you ever get bored?* she'd asked, and it had burrowed under his skin. Over the next few months, the infection had spread. Then one morning, he'd woken up with the ludicrous urge to resign from his comfortable associate professorship and embark upon an unprofitable creative journey that would shame all fifteen generations of Fergusons before him with its utter impracticality, and the more he tried to ignore this desire, the stronger it became.

Except Teddy couldn't resign from his job. Despite Maxine's assumptions about his inherited wealth, the truth was that his father had relinquished his claim to the Ferguson coffers on a matter of principle, which Teddy wholly supported (one's integrity mattered more than money). Except now his father's health was declining, the cost of his medical care was increasing, and it was Teddy's duty as his parents' only child to foot the bill—because if he explained he no longer had the money for it, he'd have to explain how and why he'd spent his winnings.

Which was why Teddy needed to win this tournament. Then, and only then, could he satiate his desire for frivolous dreams.

But he'd somehow forgotten how dangerous Maxine was, and that was a very concerning problem. Her mere proximity threatened his sanity.

His very soul, even.

There was even a small, but alarming, chance that he wouldn't survive the experience at all.

While Teddy slept, Maxine methodically worked her way through filling in his entire dorky little crossword book with incorrect answers.

There had been exactly one seat left on the plane when Maxine booked it three hours and forty-five minutes ago, and it was the seat in business class that happened to be next to Teddy's. Not like he'd believe her if she told him that. Theodore Ferguson III apparently subscribed to the fervent ideology that Maxine's entire purpose in life was to ruin Teddy's.

How conceited! How *absurd*! As if she'd waste precious brain cells thinking about Teddy when he wasn't around. How classically masculine of him to imagine the solar system revolved around his sunshine ass.

How could he think she'd *wanted* to spend five and a half hours next to the man who'd intellectually curb stomped her on national TV? Not only did Teddy represent the greatest failure in her life, but he was also the physical embodiment of everything her "grew up trash poor in Brooklyn" self hated most: generational privilege, wealth, and elitism.

That's why she tormented him.

Because she'd never been sure if Teddy's narcissism made her want to laugh or vom, so she'd settled for the third route—the low one, where she fulfilled his expectations by annoying the ever-loving fuck out of him. Then, at least, she could treasure a shred of utopia every time his sculpture-perfect face twisted with misery. At this rate, he was either going to age twenty years in a single week, or he was going to spend half his *Answers!* winnings on Botox injections, and thinking about this future cosmetic suffering really took the sting out of how unbelievably insulting it all was.

She still wished she were sitting next to anyone else in the world, though.

It wasn't the first time Maxine's toxic relationship with procrastination had screwed her over, but since things usually worked out more often than they didn't, she had no plans to change.

One could argue there were a ton of challenges to having ADHD in a world designed to reward tedium and consistent focus. Maxine preferred to instead dwell on the mega-sweet advantages it gave her.

Such as the creative problem-solving ability that came from easily connecting seemingly unrelated thoughts from her brain cloud.

Or the ability to thrive under pressure.

And above all, the almost childlike ability to derive intense joy from very simple things.

Like how Teddy lightly snored.

It sounded like a cat softly purring, and it was deeply undignified, so she'd recorded a sample on her phone to play back for him when he woke up. Teddy discovering a personal imperfection he had no control over would drive him batshit. Maxine had never felt so much serenity in her life.

Vandalizing Teddy's crossword book only killed an hour. Maxine drummed her nails on her tray table, half listening to her podcast about ant colonies. She thought about browsing through Teddy's expensive-looking leather satchel to spy on what kind of study material her archnemesis planned to defeat her with, but decided sacrificing her dignity in such a way was pointless. It wasn't like she was going to try and out-study him. Eventually, the adrenaline rush from the last-minute decision to compete followed by the mad dash to the airport wore off, and Maxine fell asleep to the rhythmic *prrprrprr* coming from Teddy's weirdly attractive throat. And since she absolutely loved sleep more than anything else in the world, Maxine was out cold until Los Angeles.

She was rudely awakened by something soft and heavy plunking into her lap.

"Come on, then. If we hurry, we can stop at the hotel to drop off our bags before we head to the studio."

Blearily, she forced her eyes open to find her duffel on her thighs and Teddy's herringbone-clad crotch at eye level with her right cheek.

And what a crotch it was.

The nice flat front of his tailored pants lay smooth against his pelvis—except for a very classy and subtle hint of morning wood. And although Maxine generally preferred not to think about Teddy at all, it's not like she hadn't *wondered.* Teddy was—objectively speaking—sexy as shit. In a really starchy way that made her want to slap his smug smile off his face while she fucked the daylights out of him, but sexy nevertheless.

Maxine's body, still half-trapped in sleep mode, had suddenly gone awfully hot and tingly. But then, she was always horny when she first woke up, and there was a dick in her face. It's not like Teddy was special.

"Maxine," he prompted impatiently, and her brain finally caught on to the fact that everyone else in the rows behind them was trapped in the aisle behind Teddy.

"All right, all right. Everyone needs to cool their tits, it's seven in the goddamn morning."

"It's actually quarter to eight. We've been delayed on the runway, and now we're short on time, so let's get on with it. We need to be in the studio by nine."

Maxine groaned. She tried to stand, but the seat belt was still buckled, so she only flopped around like a fish.

"For the love of—" Teddy reached down into her lap to unclasp the seat belt for her, and the act made his hand brush against her stomach, and that made a bolt of lust shoot down her spine so fast she saw stars.

It was with the greatest effort in the world that she managed to collect her other two bags and stumble off that plane with any semblance of dignity at all. She followed Teddy through the airport in a dazed thrall, her brain fully offline, until she registered they were waiting for a rideshare together.

"I can get my own car," she grumbled.

Everything sucked. The Los Angeles light was too bright, and even though the sun had barely risen, she was sweltering in her long emerald wool coat.

Her mouth tasted like how subway water smelled.

A headache poked at the backs of her eyeballs.

And Teddy still looked disgustingly attractive, and she didn't want to be in an enclosed space with him a second longer because her body was colossally confused about whether it was acceptable to be turned on by him.

He frowned down at her. "Don't be ridiculous. We're going to the same place. Aren't we, *wife*?"

Maxine was starting to feel a little panicky now. Like getting away from Teddy's immediate radius was important for her emotional stability.

She blurted, "I need coffee."

"They have coffee at the hotel." The car pulled up.

"I need it *now*."

Teddy handed the driver her bags, then placed his hands on her shoulders and gently but firmly steered her into the back seat. And for whatever reason—grogginess, practicality, unrepentant horniness, an embarrassing weakness for being manhandled by someone who was actually taller than she was—Maxine went along with this with the docility of a cow to slaughter.

"Really not a morning person, are you?" he said once the doors were shut around them. He drummed a cheerful pattern on his thighs. "Isn't this a delightful piece of trivia. Maxine Hart hates mornings."

"Not as much as I hate you," she told him.

"Is that why you decided to compete? Because you loathe me and want to see me lose?"

"No." She didn't loathe Teddy. In fact—and she'd rather chug a bottle of ant poison than ever admit this aloud—Teddy was one of the few men on this earth who *impressed* Maxine. He was wicked smart and a worthy competitor. And, personality-wise, not a complete piece of human garbage. It was everything he *represented* that she despised; the man himself merely irritated her, and a good chunk of that irritation was because he was determined to be extremely hot in her presence. Big difference.

"Then why?"

What was she going to say? *I need to prove to myself that I can win—not just in regular-season play, but against the best of the best?* He'd never understand.

Guys like Teddy, who'd probably had the world handed to them on a silver platter, didn't know what it was like to grow up feeling unintelligent and unworthy. She had shit to prove to herself—and to all the other kids out there with ADHD who were made to feel like they didn't fit into Teddy's world.

"I was bored. Seemed like a good way to kill a few days," she told him instead.

"A few days in LA, perhaps. But the tournament won't begin filming for five weeks, and any champion seriously hoping to win should have begun training the moment they received Nora's call. Once we return home after the weekend, this is a minimum eighteen-hour-a-day commitment. I can't decide if you're being deliberately flippant about your studying schedule, or if you really don't intend to prepare at all."

Maxine slumped down in her seat and closed her eyes to block out both the light and the sight of him. "Rote memorization's not really my thing."

"You're serious."

"Yep."

"So prior to your winning thirty-eight games in a row—"

"Didn't even crack a dictionary."

"No one uses a dictionary to study for *Answers!*, but that's beside the point. You can't possibly be asserting that you won over $2.5 million without proper education, tutelage, or a single day of preparation, can you? That's impossible."

"Why? Because your fancy-pants schools taught you there's only one way to learn stuff, and that way is boring and uncreative and really designed to turn happy, imaginative kids into obedient cogs in the capitalist machine?"

When he didn't respond at first, she cracked an eye, and sure enough, Teddy was glowering at her from behind his thick-rimmed glasses. It made him look a little mean, like a professor who was incredibly disappointed to have caught you cheating on a test and was about to dole out some serious verbal punishment, followed by a private lesson on the scholarly ethics of getting railed in a plaid skirt and loafers.

Maxine made herself stop looking before she melted into the seat on her way down to the special hell level where they put deviants like her. She wasn't allowed to have sexy fantasies about Teddy, because Teddy was a gigantic intellectual snob who wasn't interested in making any of those fantasies into reality, and what did that say about her standards?

Finally, he said tersely, "Might I remind you this *obedient cog* defeated you in the annual tournament."

"Did you? I can't remember. I've been too busy counting all my money from the time I ended your seventy-four-episode streak."

"It's seventy-six, and you know it."

"Oops, my bad. You know how quickly my uneducated brain forgets useless information."

Thankfully, it wasn't long before Maxine spied a drive-through coffee shop and instructed the driver to pull in. The driver had barely flicked on his turn signal before Teddy said, "Never mind that. We don't have time to stop for coffee."

Her blood boiled. "Don't listen to him! I'll buy your coffee if you pull over."

"And I'll add to your generous tip thrice the beverage's value if you don't," Teddy countered. In a low, terse voice, he said to her, "Timeliness is a measure of one's integrity, and I take it very seriously."

"As if five minutes will make a difference! Admit it, you're punishing me."

"For what?"

"Being too hot and smart."

In the rearview mirror, Maxine could see the driver's brows rise as he assessed his squabbling passengers. Then, he did a double take. "Hey, weren't you on that *Answers!* show?"

Maxine didn't love getting recognized in public—she wouldn't mind being a local celeb, but female-presenting *Answers!* contestants got a lot of creepy crawlers skittering up in their DMs. Contestants like Maxine got it worst of all because there was a specific type of reply guy who saw her "quirky" personality as a measure of her accessibility, and after manic-pixie dreamgirling her into their waifu fantasies, they thought it made her a real "ungrateful bitch" when she didn't fawn over their unsolicited marriage proposals or dick pics.

Little did they know, Maxine was just holding out for the elusive dick pic–proposal combo meal.

She was about to deny her identity when she remembered there was coffee on the line. "That's me! I'll give you my autograph if you pull into that coffee shop right now."

"I, too, was on that show," Teddy said darkly.

The driver's eyes flicked to Teddy's in the mirror. Whatever he saw on Teddy's expression made his face pale. "Sorry, miss. It's his ride, so . . ."

Maxine glared at her opponent, who resolutely refused to make eye contact with her. He crossed his arms and stared at the back of the driver's headrest.

"Theodore," she whispered. "Look at me."

A muscle in his jaw twitched.

"Theodore."

"What?" he snapped, finally glancing her way.

Maxine slid a finger across her jugular, then pointed at him, to make sure he knew his days were numbered.

His lips twitched. "I'm shaking in terror."

New plan: she wasn't just going to beat Teddy.

She was going to *break him.*

Chapter 5

OTHER *L* WORDS

Answer

From Latin for "to read," a story from the past popularly regarded as historical but unauthenticated.

Question

What is a legend?

Every time Maxine walked onto the *Answers!* set, she was freshly surprised at how much smaller it was in person than it appeared on TV.

It was easy to forget because part of her would always remember the way the *Answers!* set had looked the first time she saw it at ten years old, on a screen at some dingy sports bar off the Atlantic City boardwalk. While Mom played video poker and Olive colored in her preschool workbook, *Answers!* held Maxine's attention hostage. The show's soundstage had looked huge and glorious on that screen—a glossy trivia spaceship floating through a grand nebula of integrity garnered from five decades of being broadcast into living rooms across the continent.

That was the *Answers!* set indelibly fixed in her brain.

Twenty-three years later, Maxine had shown up on set as a contestant and learned that the *Answers!* she'd fallen in love with on TV was little more than a syndicated chimera . . . a mirage designed to entice and excite its audience into forgetting about the outside world for eight minutes of revenue-generating commercial breaks padded by twenty-two minutes of delight. Behind the scenes, game show magic came from a precisely coordinated symphony of camera angles, cleverly arranged backdrops, colored LED background lighting, and canned sound effects. Not all that different from the casinos Maxine knew so well from her childhood. The *Answers!* theme song even ran at an upbeat tempo of 132 bpm—just like the dopamine-stimulating music in most modern slot machines.

But that's showbiz, baby. And despite having seen behind the curtain, Maxine still watched the show religiously every night. She was a believer. Always would be.

In person, the studio set was approximately the size of a two-story Duane Reade, except instead of white fluorescents and beige metal racks displaying overpriced bodywash, everything was black and blue hued—matte for the 160-person-capacity stadium seating offstage, and glossy for onstage areas. And hiding beneath that gloss were all the things invisible to the casual viewer's eye. The things only an exclusive club of former contestants knew. Maxine adored this kind of insider knowledge because she'd always had a compulsion to know how things worked. Mysteries compelled her to slice them open and dissect their innards.

Like half a century's worth of scuffs, wear, and black gaffer's tape. Or how barely off screen—directly in front of the raised stage—cameras, audio-visual techs, and partitioned booths for the live trivia-verification researchers and judges vied for limited space. In the far-left corner of the stage, a sixteen-foot jib crane—used to capture sweeping full-set shots—lurked like a dormant sauropod. The ceiling was a gridded jungle gym of aluminum-alloy trusses, lighting fixtures, and speakers. And then there were things only contestants on the show saw—the video-clue screen next to the game board, the electrical access doors on the flip side of the podiums, the gear-controlled box risers contestants stand on to ensure they're all the same height for the cameras.

Maxine had rarely needed a riser, because she was five foot ten, plus three more inches in boots. Though, she distinctly remembered how they'd adjusted hers when she'd played Teddy. Yet another ding on her ego he was responsible for.

The man in question stalked ahead of her into the studio with his precise, long-legged stride and apologized to one of the contestant coordinators for being late. Maxine intentionally took her time sauntering in after him, lest the other contestants think they'd arrived together.

Well, they had. But not like *that*.

One of the coordinators recognized Maxine and silently ushered her toward an empty seat in the bottom row of the audience seating—directly next to Teddy (ugh). Fortunately, he didn't bother to acknowledge her, so fixated was he on the bombastic woman with a platinum mullet and a New Zealand accent who had already begun addressing the gathered contestants. Maxine recognized Nora, the new showrunner, from her live postshow podcast videos.

"Hey, Paul," Maxine whispered to the contestant coordinator who'd seated her—a big-bellied, mustached Black man with a fondness for Hawaiian shirts and gossip. "How was the honeymoon?"

Paul beamed at her. In low tones he replied, "You remembered? The Galápagos were incredible, of course. You sweetheart. You always were my favorite."

"You say that to all the contestants."

Barely moving his mouth, Paul murmured, "Not all of them." His eyes rolled toward the bronzed, square-jawed bulldog of a man three seats down, who wore a grim frown beneath his heavy brow and salted golden hair.

Sikander Shaw. Ranked sixth overall. Former Olympic gymnast (2004, no medals) who'd gone on a twenty-two-day streak six years ago. He'd made minor news two years ago for punching a man in the freezer aisle of a Sam's Club. His play style was vicious, and he was almost always first to ring in on tough clues, but his overconfidence had backfired on him in his final game. Since Maxine played similarly, she'd have been inclined to like him, except he was reportedly rude to the staff on set.

After Paul promised to smuggle her coffee from the commissary, he also offered to hang up her coat, but Maxine declined. As always, the HVAC blasted ice-cold air into the windowless space because the show's host, Dr. Loretta Love, ran hot and she refused to perspire in her signature *Dynasty*-era suits that sported shoulder pads stacked as high as Maxine on a Saturday at half past four. Loretta wasn't here now, but the crew kept the studio on permafrost year round out of respect. Or fear.

Probably both.

Nora's voice rang out: "And thank you for joining us, as well, Maxine."

Even from the front row, Maxine could feel every head turning toward her, so she swiveled in her seat and gave her fellow contestants a cheerful "'Sup!"

Nora continued, "I'm sure you all recognize Maxine Hart, our third-ranked contestant of all time by total games won."

Maxine raised a finger. "Second, by total cash winnings."

There was a smattering of applause, some more enthusiastic than the rest.

Below the sound of the applause came Teddy's terse aside: "In regular gameplay only."

"Which is the metric that matters," Maxine said through her smile.

"Is it?"

"We'll find out, won't we?"

Before she turned back around, Maxine scanned the audience. She'd already guessed who most of her competitors would be, and sure enough, all but one of the top-twenty-ranked contestants of all time were in attendance. A few were people Maxine had met during the annual tournament three months ago, but most were top-scoring contestants from the past two decades, whom she'd only seen when she'd watched their runs on TV. The only missing player was Hercules

McKnight, a legend who still held an indelible lock on first place—and no one expected him to be here. He'd retired from trivia twenty-five years ago and had repeatedly told the media he'd never compete again.

Not a single one of the competitors in attendance was anywhere close to Teddy or Maxine on the scoreboard, by any metric. Between the two of them, they had a lock on the number two and three spots for number of games won (Teddy), money earned (Maxine), and Coryat score (a tie). Mostly used by hard-core fans and bookies, the Coryat score measured both a player's accuracy and buzzer speed as a percentage of questions answered correctly out of the number for which they'd successfully buzzed in. Trivia land's version of a batting average.

As far as Vegas odds went, Maxine and Teddy were neck and neck for the title. Of course, anything was possible in *Answers!*, but as long as both Teddy and Maxine made it past the first two rounds—which should be easy, barring any dramatic upsets—it would be between her and him.

Finally, she'd have her redemption. Her validation.

The only contestant Maxine hadn't expected to see among the contenders was Zola Mattick, a College Tournament champion from two years prior. Maxine's fellow Brooklynite had competed on behalf of Medgar Evers College. She'd dominated the tournament—and become an internet sensation for having the brass tits to call Dr. Love on an incorrect ruling (and she'd been right!)—but since Zola hadn't played during the regular season, she wasn't listed on the leaderboards. Zola was now twenty-three years old, though, at five foot two with her overlarge glasses and her fluffy, tightly-coiled black hair styled into two signature pom-poms atop her head, she was likely to be carded for many years to come. Despite hailing from the same hometown, Maxine had never met Zola in person, but she *had* tutored Zola's brother, Zakai, for a few years. They'd bonded over the shared experience of being out-prodigied by a younger sister.

Unable to help herself, she whispered to Teddy, "Zola's here. She must be the winner of the Fan Favorite contest."

Teddy's lips pressed together. "She's a masterful player."

Maxine pretended to pout. "I thought I was the only player you were afraid of."

"Don't be absurd. I'm not *afraid* of you."

"You will be."

Teddy gave her a wary sideways glance.

Maxine stifled a laugh, and it came out as a snort. From the corner of her eye, she saw a familiar face take notice. Tarrah Prince winked at Maxine.

The ER nurse had placed third in last year's tournament, so she knew Teddy and Maxine well. Tarrah was a curvy, burgundy-haired, half-Korean and half-white bombshell who didn't have great buzzer timing and was only ranked tenth overall, but she'd managed to get lucky on key clues and had a deep array of knowledge. More important, Tarrah had a low tolerance for bullshit and a high tolerance for potent potables, and Maxine liked her a lot.

". . . updating *Answers!* in a sexy, fun, fresh direction," Nora was saying when Maxine tuned back in. "There's no question we're a mainstay in living rooms across the globe, but they're *dated* living rooms with cable boxes in them, and cable is an endangered species. I'm not letting this show go the way of the Chinese paddlefish. Really cool creature, by the way. A shame it hasn't been spotted since 2003. But I digress . . ."

Maxine raised a brow. *So, she's one of us.* A true-blue trivia nerd. It was more than Maxine had expected from someone who'd made her name with the dystopian game show *Baby's Got Back Payments*. Maybe there was hope for *Answers!* yet.

"After this, we're going to have Paul and his team take you through paperwork, then we'll get you in hair and makeup to film some one-on-ones with Loretta. Real softball questions, but we're going to make it playful, make it fun. Drum up a sense of excitement. Play up old rivalries . . ."

At this, a roomful of eyes landed on her and Teddy.

". . . refresh viewers on who you are, and so I want those of you with compelling backstories to really lean into it, give the fans someone to root for . . ."

Her phone buzzed, and Maxine tried to discreetly slide it out of her jacket and glance at the screen without making it obvious that she wasn't paying much attention to Nora's speech.

Tarrah: Notice there's only 20 of us?

Maxine hadn't bothered to count, but Tarrah had a better view and was rarely wrong. *Answers!* tournaments usually featured a bracket-style climb to the top; three players to a game, with the winner advancing to the next round. Twenty-one players in the quarterfinals, nine in the semifinals, and then the remaining three facing off in the final match.

Maxine: Are they changing the format?

Tarrah: LOL. Nora said format's same as annuals. U not paying attention. Distracted by someone? 😘

Maxine: not this again

Tarrah: K and I broke up btw, if ur still in denial maybe I'll see if Prof Mapquest wants to show me some maps

Tarrah: take me over the international date line

Tarrah: show me his longitude

Maxine: 😫

Tarrah: locate my marianna trench

Tarrah: oh shit

Maxine frowned at her screen, then stole a glance at Tarrah. But the other woman's attention was fixed on the stage, where Nora stood with the smug expression of a game show host who'd just made a dramatic announcement. Gasps and polite applause rose up around them, but Maxine was entirely lost. She glanced at Teddy for a hint of what she'd missed, but he wasn't looking at her. He'd gone as stiff as a day-old corpse, those nice, big, manicured hands of his clasped tightly in his lap.

And then a man walked out from backstage, and Maxine's insides recoiled.

Nora announced, "It's my pleasure to welcome Hercules McKnight as our twenty-first contestant."

There was a burst of eager applause. Everyone was thrilled to be in the same room as an *Answers!* legend.

Maxine didn't bother clapping at all. That fake-tanned douchebag could clap his own ass cheeks together if he needed a warmer welcome; he wasn't getting one from her. Maxine's short-term memory sucked, but her long-term memory could hold a grudge like nobody's business.

She snuck a glance at Teddy, but his expression was still drawn, and his reserved clap was exceedingly British. Was Teddy just nervous about going up against an undefeated player, or was there something more there?

Hercules came alongside Nora and gave the audience a TV-worthy grin. The undefeated *Answers!* legend was resplendent in his signature wine-hued turtleneck and monogrammed blazer, his improbably inky hair pulled back in an elegant queue, highlighting his even more improbably bronzed cheekbones—just like the ads plastered on city buses and subway stations everywhere. "The McKnight Academy: Strengthen Your Child's Mind," his giant head boasted on billboards spotted up and down I-95. In one iteration of the ad, a CGI-rendered version of a shirtless Hercules held aloft two serpents labeled "Boredom" and "Laziness" as if he were strangling them, à la his Grecian namesake.

Ten-year-old Maxine's impassioned letters to PETA failed to generate outraged action against Hercules on behalf of serpent models worldwide.

And it wasn't just billboards; he infested radio, print, and television too. The McKnight Academy was the Visa card of academic advertising—it was everywhere you wanted to be.

McKnight's bogus private school propaganda was never more insidious than during commercial breaks on *Answers!*, when his silken voice promised parents that for the right price, he could shape their little mush-brained toddlers' gray matter into *Answers!*-winning material. Didn't they want their precious Jimmy to win 112 games in a row, like he had in 1993? Didn't they want their precocious spawn to carve out an undefeated spot on the trivia leaderboards? It wouldn't cost much, a trifle, really—just the contents of their savings account. But little Jimmy could earn all that back when he became a doctor, or a rocket scientist, or a record-setting game show winner! Writing Hercules McKnight a fat check was an investment in their child's future.

And if anyone's future was seeing the results of those hopeful investments, it was Hercules's. That man had transmuted his 1993 *Answers!* fame into pseudoeducational gold, and by the mid-2000s, he'd become richer than Mansa Musa himself. You couldn't trip over a wealthy suburb along the East Coast without landing on a McKnight Academy private school.

"Well, doesn't this suck dinosaur dick," Maxine grumbled beneath the sound of applause. She didn't need to look at Teddy to know he'd heard her. "Didn't he resign undefeated?"

Teddy's answer was terse. "Neither of us stands a chance."

Nobody tells me what I can or can't do! Maxine crossed her arms. "Uh, speak for yourself."

"While I admire your charming hubris, Ms. Hart, his gameplay statistics are nearly flawless. It will be impossible to outplay him."

"Well, you can kiss my *charming hubris*, because I'm taking both your asses to the cleaners."

Teddy's sigh rang with pity.

So what if she had to beat both Teddy *and* the most legendary, undefeated player in *Answers!* history? She'd grown up poor, neurodivergent, and *pissed off.* Maxine ate challenge for breakfast and washed it down with a glass of spite. There was nothing she couldn't do with enough embittered feminism and classist rage.

Maxine decided then and there that she wasn't merely going to win; she was going to *slam-dunk* this tournament and leave the inbred intelligentsia crying in the paint. And she was going to do that by . . .

Her rational brain blared alarms, but this wasn't time for self-doubt.

. . . somehow.

She'd beat Teddy and Hercules somehow.

"I'm honored to be back here," Hercules said with just the right balance of humility and good cheer. He made a show of looking around the set. Hercules might look like a Kraft Mac & Cheese Steven Seagal, but you had to hand it to the guy—he knew how to work a crowd. "It's smaller than I remembered."

This elicited chuckles from the audience. Maxine's phone buzzed.

Tarrah: that's what she said

Maxine: . . . about his integrity. Guy's a scam artist. Look up the 2003 Quiz Team scandal.

Hercules continued with a long, ego-stroking, abjectly *boring* monologue, citing his desire to "reinvigorate America's youth by returning to the place where it all began." The monologue conveniently hop-skipped over the fact that Nora had almost certainly guaranteed Hercules a minimum cash payout in exchange for his exalted participation—in addition to the $2 million he'd win if he took the crown.

Because rumor had it—and Maxine *loved* intrigue, so she drank from the rumor mill daily—the McKnight Academy juggernaut was now teetering on the verge of bankruptcy.

Tarrah: All I see is Herc's got a net worth of 100 million??? Girl forget finding where in the world does Teddy's sandy dick go! I'm looking to get bukkake'd in 24k gold, babyyyy

Maxine: bukkake is the noun version of the verb bukkakeru, which means "to rudely splash with liquid" but gold's melting point is like 2000 deg which is basically lava temp

Tarrah: so?

Maxine: so wear protection

Tarrah: nerd

Maxine: eat my nerd shorts

Tarrah: so u want 2 be friends or what? U never hit me back

Guilt needled Maxine. Tarrah had reached out often after the tournament, but she lived here in LA and Maxine lived in Brooklyn and was atrocious at responding to texts. Or remembering to call people back. That kind of behavior tended to make potential friends feel like Maxine didn't care about them, even when she painstakingly entered their birthdays into her calendar reminders and went out of her way to spend time with them in person.

But those weren't the only reasons she hadn't responded to Tarrah these last few months.

Maxine: sorry. I was licking my wounds.

Tarrah: don't be sorry. I get it. I pour alcohol on mine; it's sterile.

It was nine thirty in the morning, but the more Hercules droned on about Hercules, the more a shot of whisky in her to-go coffee cup sounded like a brilliant solution to her problems.

Because the truth was, Maxine had no idea if she could beat the best trivia player in the show's history. She wasn't sure anyone could. He might have conned a generation of starry-eyed parents into investing in his bogus schools, but his venerated run on *Answers!* had been 100 percent real. As a teenager, Maxine had watched those episodes every single time they'd aired in syndication; she'd seen what Hercules was capable of. He was relatively fast on the buzzer, and he wagered like a man who was confident he'd never, ever be wrong—because he never was. Of the 4,440 clues he'd answered over the course of 113 games, he'd gotten exactly six wrong. One of those six was because of a hotly contested mispronunciation error.

The only player close to Hercules's correct-answer rate was the man sitting next to Maxine, whose correct-answer rate was 91.4 percent.

Accuracy had never been Maxine's weapon of choice (61 percent—but who's counting?). She was more of a "buzz first, worry about whether you know the answer later" kind of player. Chaos was her modus operandi: she rang in on everything, wagered wildly, and chose clues like she was throwing darts blindfolded to disrupt other players' momentum (and find the Daily Duplexes before they did). But the real reason Maxine had won thirty-six games in her original run was because she probed at her opponents' defenses until she found their design flaw—then struck without mercy.

And everyone has a weakness, Maxine reminded herself. *Even Hercules . . .*

Chapter 6

FAMOUSLY UNINVITED

Answer

While planning a lavish ball to celebrate his bestselling true-crime novel, this author is alleged to have said about his guest list, "The point and fun of giving a party is about those you don't invite."

Question

Who is Truman Capote?

While the other contestants retired to the greenroom to fill out the requisite paperwork and await their interviews with Loretta, Teddy pulled Nora aside in the backstage hallway.

"I wish to withdraw from the tournament," he said without preamble.

Nora eyed him up and down, her gaze inscrutable. Behind her, he realized with a keen sense of irony, was a wall of photos featuring every annual-tournament winner since the tournament's inception in 1989. "I'm sorry to hear that. Your potential rematch against Maxine is a hot topic on the socials, and there'll be a lot of disappointed fans. May I ask what's changed your mind?"

Teddy cast a quick glance around the hallway, then lowered his voice. "I'm not sure I can compete against Hercules."

"Oh! Now that's just not true, Teddy." Nora's expression was a mixture of relief and warm reassurance. "Granted, Hercules surely remains a stalwart competitor, but we all know anything is possible in a tournament setting—"

"Sorry, that's not what I meant." Teddy cleared his throat. "I meant I may not *be able* to. Legally speaking."

Nora's brows shot up. "Go on."

"You see, I attended the New Brunswick McKnight Academy from the ages of eleven to fifteen. I was a member of their quizzing team for that entire time."

"The New Brunswick . . . is that one of the locations where—"

"Yes."

"Ah, shite." Nora blew a puff of air upward, ruffling her jagged fringe. "How did our legal team not ID this conflict of interest?"

"I transferred to a public school after the scandal and subsequent lawsuit broke. I've never publicly advertised my attendance at McKnight Academy, but if anyone should go digging, I imagine it wouldn't be hard to find. Therefore, it's best if I promptly withdraw for the sake of the show's integrity."

Teddy was proud of himself. He'd rehearsed this speech in his head on his way over to find Nora, and it sounded exactly as regretful as he'd intended.

He was confident that no one could tell from his performance that his intestines were tangled in a writhing knot, and that twin blots of pain had spiked behind each eyebrow. If he were alone, he'd use his thumbs to smooth his scrunched brows into submission. For now, he just had to feign that he was implacable, like he always did.

But to his dismay, Nora looked thoughtful. She tapped a finger against her lips. "I'm going to run this by Flor—she's our chief counsel.

Of course, we've got to be careful, but I'm of the mind that there's quite a lot of gray area here, since you never actually interacted with Mr. McKnight while you attended the Academy. Right?"

"Correct. But—"

"Then you hold tight, Professor. There's hope yet!"

Teddy forced a smile. "Brilliant."

Brilliant.

"Professor Ferguson?" a stagehand called down the hallway. "You're up next!"

And before Teddy could argue further, Nora was urging him along, and suddenly he was back on the soundstage with Claudia from hair and makeup blotting his forehead and a sound tech pinning a lapel mic to his suit jacket.

He felt queasy. "May I use the restroom before I go on?"

There has to be another way out of this.

Paul, the contestant coordinator who had a preference for Hawaiian shirts and (if Teddy recalled correctly) a cat named Mama Mia-ow, glanced at the stage and gave Teddy a moue of regret. "Sorry, sweetheart, we've got a tight schedule, and Loretta's almost done with this one, so you're up in less than sixty. We'll have you in and out, all right?"

He began to reply when a familiar, throaty laugh rang out. The sound of it sent electricity over his skin, and—as if it had magnetized him—he drifted closer to its source. He'd just spent an entire flight in close quarters with Maxine, but in the fifteen minutes they'd been apart, his body had already gone into withdrawal.

A concerning problem for further analysis.

His gaze fell on the stage, where Maxine was being interviewed by a well-preserved woman in her sixties with dark-brown skin, a towering topknot of smoothed silver hair, and an indulgent expression of mild tolerance—a far cry from her usual aura of judgment and disdain.

Dr. Loretta Love was the show's longtime avatar, and as such, she was an international beacon of unfathomable knowledge, an arbiter of intellectual justice, and a woman who could tear down the loftiest ego with a single cutting quip. She'd been hosting *Answers!* since 1990, when her husband—the show's creator and then host—had died of sudden cardiac arrest on set at forty-six years old. After his death, it came to light that Loretta—who had a PhD in chemistry and had met her late husband when he'd been a banquet server at her postdoc celebration party—had been the real brains behind the operation; not only had the show been her idea, but she'd written most of the questions and answers for the first two seasons.

To the *Answers!* community, Dr. Love was God Herself, and to be verbally shredded by her during the "get to know the contestants" segment of each show was akin to a religious experience. The nicest thing she'd said to Teddy during his seventy-six-game run was that if he weren't such an aggressively adequate trivia player, she'd have asphyxiated of boredom after his fifth game. And since to be called *adequate* by Dr. Loretta Love was an unparalleled honor, Teddy's pride glowed whenever he thought of it.

Dr. Love was saying to Maxine, "You have a huge online fan club, in part because you're known for always betting it all on Daily Duplex clues. Do you feel like your strategy will change now that you're up against Hercules?"

"Max Heart . . . we're takin' it to the max every time, baby!" Maxine said, forming her hands into a heart shape in front of her chest. Her gaze lasered in on Teddy where he stood in the offstage shadows. "It'll be fun to have some real competition for once."

"A bold statement."

"A girl's gotta attract fortune's favor."

Loretta arched a brow with the distinct air of someone trying not to appear amused. But Teddy knew from experience how difficult it was to resist Maxine's charm.

A waft of strong cologne was the only warning Teddy had before Hercules materialized beside him. "My, she's got quite the stage presence." The other man chuckled. "But we can't all be selected on the basis of intellectual merit, can we? This is televised entertainment. Hercules McKnight, by the way."

Teddy accepted the proffered handshake, resisting the urge to blurt platitudes at his childhood idol. In the ninth grade, he'd won a signed photograph of Hercules in a Quizzing League match, and he'd had it laminated so he could tape it to the inside of his locker without damaging the photo itself. This was the man who'd inspired Teddy to pursue competitive trivia. The legend who'd set the *Answers!* record Teddy had been trying to reach during his own run.

He wondered if Hercules knew that Teddy had attended one of his schools.

If Hercules knew that Teddy had once worshiped him like a hero.

If Hercules knew that Teddy was partly responsible for the scandal that had led to McKnight Academy's ruined reputation and financial decline.

But none of that mattered. All Teddy could think about was that Hercules had made a slyly derisive comment about Maxine, and that bothered him.

Teddy replied, "I think you'll be impressed when you play against her."

"If she gets that far. Oh, don't look at me like I'm a grievous maligner. I've watched her episodes, and I think we can agree she's got a habit of dressing before sizing her britches," he drawled in his Louisiana accent.

Teddy clenched his jaw so he wouldn't reply with something he'd regret. Just because he'd said something similar to Maxine didn't make it okay for someone else to do so.

"Let's finish on a philosophical note," Loretta was saying onstage. "You've told us already that you hope to win the title to inspire other girls growing up with ADHD, and that this show was very meaningful to you growing up. But you've also said in previous interviews that trivia is, by nature, trivial, and that 'serious players' have forgotten that at the end of the day, *Answers!* is merely twenty-two minutes of nightly entertainment. How do you reconcile those two statements?"

Hercules flicked a business card out between two fingers. He said to Teddy in a low voice, "Should you find yourself available, I'm hosting a salon at my humble vacation villa in Santa Monica tonight . . . nothing formal. Just an evening of wine and conversation with our fellow elite trivia players here."

"Quite the event, for all twenty-one of us."

"Oh no, only a select number. I think you and I both know the vast majority of these players are sacrificial pawns. Tokens, to appease the rabble who think of this as no more than a game show." Hercules's gaze was fixed on Maxine. "No, tonight's guest list is exclusive."

"I see." Teddy considered the smooth card stock. Did he really want to go to an event that excluded Maxine on the basis of her background? It felt . . . wrong, somehow. Not that he and Maxine were *friends*, per se, but he felt a certain loyalty to her. She may be his foe, but she was a foe he considered his equal in skill—even if he didn't approve of her methodology.

"I do hope to see you there. I think we have much to discuss that isn't fit for unfiltered company." After that declaration, he strode off, apparently uninterested in watching the rest of Maxine's interview.

But Teddy was rapt. Maxine's airy cheer had solidified into something more substantial now. Something that felt real.

She leaned forward in her seat, her forest floor eyes glittering. "Trivia *is* by nature trivial, but that's what makes it so fun. Facts by themselves are dry and boring, but trivia is learning made holistic. *Answers!* gives people entry to a world where everything is interconnected. Where each piece of information gets more meaningful when it interacts with other parts of the world."

"How so?" Loretta asked.

"Like . . ." Maxine blew a gum bubble. Even from a distance, Teddy swore he could smell the tropical flavor. "Okay, check this. The fact that there are 52 cards in a standard deck doesn't mean very much. It isn't a very interesting fact on its own. The fact that there are also 52 weeks in a year could be a mere coincidence. Except there are also four suits in a deck and four seasons in a year, thirteen cards in a suit and thirteen lunar cycles in a year, and if you count all the symbols in a deck they add up to 365. So, a *fact* is knowing that there are 52 cards in a standard playing card deck, but a good *trivia* fact is knowing that the 52-card deck's design was based on a calendar year. Trivia takes this boring piece of information and makes it . . . magical. It makes meaning out of raw data, the way statistics does with numbers, except trivia does it with all the loose odds and ends of the universe.

"So, that's why trivia matters to me. Until I saw *Answers!*, I thought learning was solely about rote memorization, because that's what I'd been led to believe throughout my on-again, off-again relationship with our educational system. But *Answers!* taught me that learning was about finding meaning—finding *answers*. That connecting the dots is exciting. It's about finding a sense of wonder in the ordinary. And that was something that even I could do. Something I was passionate about doing."

The frigid studio suddenly felt stuffy. This was the first time he'd heard her articulate her passion for trivia, and never before had someone laid his secret insides out and explained them so succinctly. It should have been a relief, to realize his soul wasn't utterly alone in an ocean of dissimilar strangers.

But instead it made his skin heat with shame.

He wasn't like Maxine. They were as different as night and day in personality, they were from dramatically disparate backgrounds, and above all, she drove him out of his goddamn mind. He was a man who enjoyed routine, and she was chaos made flesh. If he was the embodiment of calming beige, she was a glittering beam of gamma ray—and for some inexplicable reason, he was consumed with the desire to stand in her light until every last one of his cells melted. She was his antimatter, the arrow aimed at his Achilles.

He certainly shouldn't *relate* to her.

Teddy Ferguson didn't pursue higher learning for the sake of . . . *fun*. This was about integrity. Honor. About generations of Fergusons before him who had made their name praying to the altar of intelligence and being summarily blessed for their relentless devotion. And then Maxine beamed at the camera and said, "And that's why I dropped out of high school."

Teddy squared his shoulders and decided he was being absurd. How could he have been ready to forgo an invitation from his childhood hero out of solidarity with Maxine, who probably didn't even want to go to a stuffy "salon" of intellectuals? If there were sides in this contest, surely Hercules's was where Teddy belonged.

Chapter 7

BEASTLY BUSINESS

Answer

In the corporate-takeover world, this term means to make an unsolicited offer so generous and overpriced that it's nearly impossible to refuse.

Question

What is a bear hug?

It had taken Maxine exactly thirty-seven minutes to discover she was the only top-ten-ranked player to not receive an invite from Hercules, and Maxine was pissed—which made her even more determined to attend.

For one, Maxine had a real problem with being told no.

But more important, she needed to get a lock on Hercules's weakness while she still had the chance. This was a prime opportunity.

Maxine knew the ultra-elitist Herc had excluded her because she was low class. But even tenth-ranked Tarrah had gotten an invite, and she'd shown up today in a Wu-Tang-emblazoned bomber jacket. What, exactly, constituted *class* in Hercules McKnight's mind?

"Stanford," Tarrah said with a shrug when Maxine confronted her in the smoking pen outside the studio—a little cordoned-off area in the back lot facing the *Circle of Fate* soundstage, where scummy nicotine addicts could inhale gasoline and eau de dumpster between puffs of death incarnate. "I was on the swim team. Guess it makes me . . . *worthy*." She trilled the last with an exaggerated posh accent.

"Are you going?"

"Shit, yeah, I'm going! You think I want to eat In-N-Out when I could be eating caviar?"

"Don't flaunt your West Coast In-N-Out privilege, it's unbecoming."

Tarrah took a drag from her vape pen. "Don't hate the player, hate the supply chain. Anyway, that man is single and old, and I'm looking to become a tragic widow."

"Old? He's only sixty-two."

"Old enough for a tragic fall," Tarrah said dreamily. She nodded at Maxine's unlit cigarette. "You gonna smoke that or you just accessorizing?"

Maxine shook her head. "I'm craving caviar. Can you clue me in to where Hercules's shindig is tonight?"

"Would if I could. But I don't have an address." She showed Maxine the cream-colored card, which was blank except for a monogrammed *HM* and a phone number. "He said to call when I was ready for a pickup any time after seven, and then show the driver the invitation."

Maxine snapped a photo of the card on her phone and handed it back. Shouldn't be too hard to replicate in the hotel's business center. Instacart some nice linen card stock, and bada bing, bada boom.

"You don't think he'll throw you out?"

Maxine considered it. "Nah," she decided. "I think he's trying to psych me out. Give me an inferiority complex. He thinks he's playing 4D chess, but joke's on him because I only play checkers. And once he realizes that he can't get inside my head, he's going to start to worry about me."

"Hit him with the Uno Reverse play, huh? I knew I liked you." After several moments of companionable silence, Tarrah asked, "So, what's your plan for dealing with Teddy?"

Maxine shrugged. "Same as before, I guess. Snag the Daily Duplexes before he does, and wait for him to choke on his Final Answer bet."

Tarrah blew a perfect vapor ring. "Girl, you know I'm not talking about trivia."

The ring floated past Maxine's nose. Irrationally annoyed, she swiped her finger down the vapor's center, inadvertently turning it into a heart.

"I'm still figuring that part out."

♡

The rest of the morning went by in a blur.

"We're pulling out all the stops for this," Nora told them after everyone had filmed their spots with Dr. Love. "A full-court marketing extravaganza. We're pushing this as the biggest event in *Answers!* history."

There were group photos for social media and print press. Then individual photos. Then individual Hometown Howdy clips—sixty-second cheeseball promos designed to be aired on each contestant's local news stations. They even filmed spots for the tournament's corporate sponsor.

"Don't drink it, these are props," Paul warned them as he scaled the audience-seating steps where the contestants waited, passing out lukewarm cans as he went.

Next to Maxine, Tarrah audibly gulped a mouthful of liquid. "This is foul."

Maxine read aloud from the can's label, "'VitaLager: all-natural, low-alcohol beer infused with holistic vitamins. A subsidiary of Mediana Health Insurance.'"

"Our new target audience is young, hip, and health conscious," Nora explained.

More like Mediana was ponying up the two-mil prize bag. Nevertheless, Maxine and her fellow contestants dutifully beamed at the camera and flashed the buttercup-yellow can, reciting award-winning lines like "Beer smarter, not harder" with all the enthusiasm of medieval serfs tasked with performing a play at their despotic baron's town fair.

Watching Teddy try to sound enthusiastic was the most entertaining part of all. They'd posed him at one of the podiums, as if he were planning to shotgun the can before buzzing in on a question. Despite his having come straight from a cross-country flight, his thick swoop of sandy hair was still precisely styled, and there wasn't even a hint of fatigue in his aristocratic face. He looked like some early-2000s book-cover viscount masquerading behind a pair of glasses.

"Imbibe intelligently," he intoned with an expression of haughty disdain. He refused to say the beer's actual slogan. The incorrect grammar was an affront, he argued.

Finally, they were set free.

"Safe journeys back to your hometowns," Nora told them. "You have five weeks between now and when we begin filming on May eighth to plug holes in your knowledge base, refresh the basics, and zip up that buzzer timing! Remember—it's anyone's game."

Two rows of seating ahead of them, Maxine watched Hercules lean over to Teddy and murmur something in his ear. Teddy nodded, like he'd just been bequeathed vital insider knowledge.

What a heartwarming display of class solidarity.

She cornered Teddy on the way out of the lot, where a shuttle awaited to take them back to the hotel. A cluster of the younger contestants—Zola and the other two players still in their twenties—walked up ahead of them. No one followed them. Teddy and Maxine had been the last to leave because the VitaLager rep on set wasn't pleased with Teddy's script adjustments and therefore wanted him to stay and refilm the ad several more times, and Maxine hadn't wanted to miss a second of Teddy's humiliation.

"Buddy-buddy with the enemy, are we?" she accused him.

"Our fellow contestants are not *enemies*, Maxine. We are trivia enthusiasts participating in a spirited contest of knowledge."

Maxine ignored him. "What did he want? A friendly bonding sesh over your shared inbreeding? Hints on how to take me—his only real *competish*—down?"

He stopped walking and squinted at her in the midday sunlight. Now that the morning clouds had burned off, it was a balmy sixty-six degrees on the well-worn asphalt between concrete buildings, and Teddy had draped his long coat over his arm. His sleeves were rolled up, too, and the light-golden hair on his ropy forearms drew her eye.

It made her wonder if he was furry elsewhere. Did he wax his chest? His balls?

For luck's sake, do not think about Theodore Ferguson's balls. Her body's attraction to him was disturbing enough without imagery.

"Hercules invited me to his estate this evening. I'm being cordial. Are you familiar with the term?"

"Estate?"

"Cordial."

"I love a good aperitif." When he groaned, Maxine asked, "What?"

"I find puns juvenile."

Maxine fluttered her lashes at him. For a guy who loved crosswords, it was awfully hypocritical of him to be annoyed by wordplay—a fact she filed away for her future entertainment. "I love puns. I love them almost as much as I love *you* . . ."

He inhaled sharply.

". . . losing."

He released his breath with a glower.

"To me, specifically."

"You may not have the pleasure, this time."

"Look, trash talk is one of my love languages, but let's get back to you telling me what Hercules said."

Teddy looked more uncomfortable in the sun with every passing second. He shuffled his briefcase into his other hand, and when he swapped his coat to his other arm, Maxine saw a flash of familiar cream peeking out from the inner breast pocket. *The invitation.*

If she could just reach out and snag it—

Teddy took a few steps back, drawing out of the main walkway and toward the shadowed gap between the *Circle of Fate* soundstage and the empty one next to it. "I need to tell you something."

Maxine glanced behind them, but lunch hour was over, and the streets of the buff-hued studio lot were relatively empty. She followed him into the narrow alley full of abandoned set pieces until they found a spot between a stack of traffic cones and a prop palm tree. "Is this where you murder me? Professor Ferguson, in the dark alley, with his massive—"

"Maxine."

"Brain," she finished. Then she gave him a sly smile. "Why? What did you think I was going to say?"

He let out a breath. "You really need to stop doing that."

"Doing what?" She tucked a coil of hair behind her ear and watched his eyes follow her movement. *Oh yeah, he still has it bad.* Maxine felt another tiny pang of guilt and tried to ignore it. *Poor little rich boy has a crush, boo-hoo.* It wouldn't kill him. Hell, it was probably good for him to experience the fine art of not being able to get something he wanted. Disappointment built character. After all, look at her . . . more character than anyone on the dating apps knew what to do with!

So, sure, she'd played a little dirty that first night they'd met. But playing clean was a privilege that girls who grew up poor couldn't afford. Moving up in the world was a pricey endeavor, and so was her sister's med school. You played the cards you were dealt, and Maxine had been dealt a pretty face and cast-iron guts.

She'd kissed Teddy, and he'd lost to her on *Answers!* the next day. Who was to say it was *her* fault he'd played like a lovestruck zombie? And it's not like he hadn't walked away with over two million bucks from his seventy-six-game streak. That, plus a slot on the greatest-of-all-time roster seemed like a decent consolation prize; no permanent harm done.

With one small caveat, whispered the part of her brain that flipped back to that kiss whenever she needed to take her self-pleasure from zero to sixty—fast.

Her physical attraction to him was . . . annoying. Maxine would rather be caught blowing the entire Red Sox roster on a Macy's Thanksgiving Day Parade float than catch *feelings* for Theodore Ferguson III.

"I'm withdrawing from the tournament," he told her.

It was like someone had splashed cold water on her. "What? Why?" It came out more sharply than it should have. Why *was* she upset? She should be happy. One less Teddy meant she could focus exclusively on taking down Hercules.

"I shouldn't say. It's a sensitive matter."

Maxine stepped closer and cupped her hand over her mouth, as if they were kids gossiping in the schoolyard. "Ooh, are you having a torrid affair with Loretta?"

To his credit, Teddy only looked disappointed in her. "Dr. Love is a lovely, accomplished woman who would almost certainly rather have any of the fine denizens of Hollywood over one of the contestants on her show."

"Yeah, but you would if you could, right?"

"Decline to answer."

"A simple yes or no. 'Yes, Maxine, I'd bang Loretta because I'm a red-blooded human and she's got rockin' tits for a sixty-five-year-old.' Or 'No, Maxine, I'm a stuffy, ageist twat, and I hate boobs.'"

"I'm being baited, and I won't respond to it."

Maxine *tsk*ed. "I knew it. You hate boobs. You hate boobs unless you tell me right now why you're dropping out of the tournament."

"Do you really think you can torment me into submission?"

"Will that work? I can give it a shot."

Was that a vein throbbing in his temple or just the way the shadows fell in this alley? Either way, he was five seconds from cracking.

Maxine beamed at Teddy. Teddy glowered back.

Five . . . four . . . three . . . two . . .

He sighed like a deflating balloon. "I was a McKnight scholar during the Quizzing League scandals."

Maxine gasped in delight. "You? You were one of the cheaters?"

"Absolutely not," he snapped.

"Come on, T-Bear, fess up . . . I won't judge you. It's me you're talking to. Maxine Hart. The girl who learned to count cards before she learned to count."

"First of all, that's an utterly nonsensical claim. And second—and I know you'll be disappointed to hear this—I am a terrible liar."

"No one's perfect." She patted his arm, and his bicep twitched under her hand.

He seemed to shake himself. "Several of my elder teammates were aware that our coaches had bribed the judges to supply the clues ahead of time, but I was kept in the dark. They probably thought I'd report them."

"Sounds about right."

"When I overheard two of my teammates discussing it in the bathroom, I was outraged. Cheating is wrong, Maxine."

"So bad and wrong. I, for one, would *never*." She shook her head solemnly. "So what did you do when you learned your proudest accomplishment was a lie?"

"I immediately reported it to the Quizzing League national board, of course. I'd thought it was the right thing to do. But as a result of the investigation that ensued, all McKnight Academies were banned from competing in quizzing events, and the Academy's reputation was thoroughly damaged, which was the beginning of the institution's financial decline."

"Normally I don't approve of snitching, but since it was on McKnight's bullshit private academies, I'll give you a pass."

His expression became a study in blankness. "My father didn't believe me when I told him I had nothing to do with the cheating. I was withdrawn from McKnight Academy and sent to public school to pay penance, where I discovered my intellectual affinity made me . . . unpopular."

There was an odd squeezing feeling in her chest that might have been heartburn from drinking three cups of coffee on an empty stomach, or it might have been sorrow for teenager-Teddy. Maxine wasn't sure what the pang meant, since she'd always tried not to dwell on negative emotions. ADHD might grant her superpowers, but it also meant her brain did a piss-poor job of regulating emotions; bad feelings could balloon out of control fast and swallow her for hours. Maxine knew she could improve on that with stuff like meditation and therapy, but why do something so unbelievably *boring* when she could instead be living her best life by jumping out of a plane or stealing lingerie from Target or spending five hours on the internet learning about hyenas?

"Aw, buddy," she said quietly. Uselessly. She wished she knew what to say to make him feel better, but since she avoided depressing conversation at all costs, all she could think of were flippant jokes. Finally, she settled on, "Want me to shank Hercules for you?"

"Please don't get disqualified on my behalf. Without me competing, you've got a fighting chance to win."

"I'm choosing to generously ignore how arrogant and wrong that statement is because of the overwhelming pity your villain origin story has evoked."

"You're too kind." Teddy rubbed at the twin spots over his brows with his free hand, and Maxine realized he *was* tired, after all. The gesture also angled the arm with his coat draped over it closer to her.

She bit her lip. *I shouldn't.*

"Do you want a hug?"

His whole body stiffened. "What?"

"It's like where two people stand face to face and their arms go around each other—"

"I know what a hug is."

"Well?"

His wintry-blue eyes assessed her warily from behind his glasses. "I'll remind you I'm voluntarily withdrawing, so you no longer need to murder me."

"Oh my god, I'm not a boa constrictor."

"You offered to shank a man a mere sixty seconds ago!"

"To his *face*. Give me some credit."

He set down his briefcase. "Very well. But be quick about it. If we miss the shuttle, we'll have to pay for a rideshare."

"We're rich, Teddy. I think it's our noblesse oblige to support the local economy." She held her arms out wide.

He didn't move.

Fine. She'd do it herself. She stepped in and closed around him like a Venus flytrap. Her arms slid around his biceps, and her palms spread along his back—loosely enough that he could free himself easily, but inviting enough to encourage him not to. He stood there, frozen, with his coat pressed between their bodies. Maxine let her cheek come to rest on his shoulder, because she wasn't wearing her heeled boots today, and that made him taller than her.

How refreshing! Normally, she liked towering over men. You could measure a man's insecurity by how much it hurt his feelings. But Teddy was . . . well, *Teddy*. He didn't need a physical reminder that they were equals, because they'd already established that in front of millions of viewers.

She absently petted the soft fabric of his dress shirt. His back was warm but not sweaty, and firmly muscled around the shoulder blades. His crisp vetiver scent surrounded her. "This is nice."

With her ear pressed against him, his slow exhalation echoed in his chest. "Yes. It's actually . . . quite nice."

"Is it pure linen or a blend?"

"Sorry?" His shoulder blades bunched beneath her hands. "Oh. My shirt."

Maxine pulled back to inspect the weave. "Wait, is this sea-linen cotton? I worked in a tailoring shop for a couple months, and I know how expensive this stuff is. Hot damn, let me get a look at this label." She pawed at where the right side of his shirt had been neatly tucked into his pants, trying to tug the hem free.

"There's no need to—"

"Do you know how hard it is to source this stuff? It really only grows in the Caribbean—"

"Maxine." His hand closed around her wrist, gently but firmly. His voice was a register lower than usual. "Don't begin to undress me unless you intend to finish."

Heat swept over her skin. Her wrist was on fire. Her eyes came up to meet his, and she discovered that ocean eyes could burn too. A challenge.

He always did this, Maxine realized. He acted so stuffy and ornery that she'd underestimate him, write him off as an ascetic. And she always fell for it too. How could a man who went by *Teddy* be a threat to her confidence?

But then he'd just do this *look*. This particular glower. Not his normal glower, which was all lordly and exasperated and involved trying to forcefully make his eyebrows merge, which was probably giving him bitchin' headaches. No, this was a much darker, unequivocally sexy, professorial glower, with narrowed eyes and clenched jaw. It was a look that said, *You're in trouble, Miss Hart.*

And every single time, Maxine's body reacted accordingly, and every time, she'd have the distinct thought: *I bet this man knows how to fuuuuuuck.* And then, because Maxine had never in her life been able to resist learning something exciting and new: *Let's find out.*

"My room or yours?"

Teddy dropped her wrist like it had come alive and hissed at him. "Don't waste your efforts. The tournament is still five weeks away."

"Oh, you haven't seen effort, baby."

"You're right. I haven't."

She was so busy tamping down her sexual frustration that it took Maxine a second to understand he was insulting her.

But she never got a chance to issue a blistering comeback, because Nora materialized at the entrance to their alleyway. "Teddy! Glad I caught you. I've got great news about that little matter we discussed earlier. Spoke to Flor, and looks like you're good to go."

Teddy looked taken aback. "Are you quite sure?"

"Positive," Nora chirped. She didn't seem remotely fazed by Maxine's presence, her proximity to Teddy, or their alleyway location. "So I'll see you two in five short weeks, then, yeah? Fantastic!"

When she left, Maxine and Teddy glared at each other in accusatory silence until it was Maxine who finally backed down. "Guess we're still on for that rematch, huh?"

His jaw worked. "I suppose we are."

"Then you better get to studying. See you later, alligator."

Only after she'd made it out of the studio lot and into her rideshare did Maxine slip Teddy's invitation free from her sleeve and into her palm.

Chapter 8

A HAIRY DILEMMA

Answer

The Rapunzel Number is a mathematical formula that calculates the effects of gravity on this hairstyle, which returned to popularity in the '50s after Sandra Dee wore one in *Gidget*.

Question

What is a ponytail?

Teddy arrived at Hercules McKnight's villa seventeen minutes late and full of self-recrimination. He hated being late, but not as much as he hated the idea he'd been so rattled by Maxine that he'd managed to lose his invitation.

Thank goodness he'd run into Helen Kaur, the pink-haired, septuagenarian former librarian (ranked fifth), in the lobby. Upon hearing his plight, she'd insisted Teddy escort her to the party. "He wouldn't dare turn you away when you're with me!" she'd declared with a swish of her rainbow-fringed shawl.

He'd enjoyed his ride with her, which consisted of a lively discussion about favorite science fiction authors (hers, Le Guin; his, Butler). Sure enough, when they arrived at Hercules's sprawling, lushly landscaped property in a security-gated cul-de-sac, there was no one to stop them from entering through the wide-open door. In fact, as Helen and Teddy tentatively explored the vaulted entry and the airy, tastefully appointed modern living area, it appeared Hercules didn't seem to employ any staff at all, which surprised Teddy. He edited his mental assessment of the man he'd grown up idolizing to include "surprisingly down to earth."

As down to earth as one can be when one keeps a seven-bedroom luxury villa in Santa Monica as a vacation home, Teddy revised again, rounding a corner and finding himself in an open kitchen large enough to host a full catering staff.

His father would have despised this entire place. Dr. Arthur Ferguson scorned what he called *new money.* Gold was meant to be hoarded in the form of books or donated to educational institutions, not spent on decor by people who used the word *decor.*

"Welcome!" Hercules called to them from the concrete patio, which was visible through the sliding glass doors left flung open to the cool Los Angeles night. Hercules was barefoot and wearing a very Californian outfit of denim trousers and a simple white button-down. In the distance, the remnants of a rosy sunset glowed over a panoramic ocean view. Tall onyx-cased heat lamps, which reminded Teddy of a certain space odyssey, cast a flickering glow over the other eight guests who'd already arrived. "Please. Help yourself to the bar. Pour a glass of whatever poison you prefer and make yourself at home."

As Helen helped herself to a glass of dry vermouth, Teddy's attention was locked on the flame-haired figure holding court at the center of the patio in a viridescent jumper. A gossamer cape fixed to the shoulders fluttered in the breeze. She looked like a re-creation of Botticelli's Venus, but if she'd been born of the earth, not the sea. When she threw back her head and laughed at something that handsome fellow redhead Ryan Murray (ranked fourth; made history in 2017 as the first trans man to break the top ten) had said, Teddy stifled the urge to toss Ryan into the infinity pool that edged the patio. Even though he knew Ryan was happily married to his husband of over two decades, with whom he had two children.

Teddy's jealous fantasies were interrupted by Hercules clinking a spoon on his glass of champagne. When the group quieted, he announced in his drawling accent, "Now that we're all present and accounted for—and then some"—a wry glance in Maxine's direction—"I'd like to invite you all to participate in a practice game."

With the click of a remote, a projector illuminated a familiar game board onto a theater-size screen affixed to one of the villa's exterior walls.

"Sizing us up, are you?" Sikander Shaw said in a joking tone. His narrowed eyes weren't joking at all.

Hercules chuckled and raised his glass in acknowledgment. "I won't hold it against you for being suspicious. But truth is, I'm just nostalgic for the game I love. It's so rare I have the opportunity to play against worthy opponents."

"And if we don't feel like participating in this little showcase of yours?" Sikander asked.

"You can play the role of host. How about that, hmm?"

"And how will we know you haven't already memorized all the questions?"

Hercules managed to raise a brow in a way that was both thoroughly amused and wholly condescending. "There are no stakes to this game, Mr. Shaw. What incentive would I have to cheat? But if you're so inclined, please help yourself to that laptop next to the projector, where I've had one of my top McKnight graduates compile over 450,000 questions from the *Answers!* archives into a simulator that will randomly populate this game board by question value. Feel free to refresh the board as many times as you desire."

Sikander seemed assuaged by this.

"Sounds like fun to me! But how are we all going to play?" asked Tarrah Prince, the woman he and Maxine had played against in the final round of the annual tournament. She was dressed as if she were going to a dance club in a miniature white dress, except her feet were as bare as their host's. The sway in her posture said the pink cocktail in her hand was far from her first of the evening.

"Ah, that's the fun part! There are ten of us remaining, so we'll play a preliminary round in teams of two. The bottom-two scoring teams will be knocked out, and we'll advance the winner to play against the remaining two teams."

"Why teams? Why not just do this individually, in tournament style?" This came from Zola, the Fan Favorite College Tournament champion.

Hercules gave Zola an indulgent smile. "Well, we do eventually want to eat dinner tonight, don't we?"

This drew polite laughter, which Zola didn't seem to appreciate.

"Now, shall we play?"

There was a chorus of agreement, but Maxine held up a hand. "Let's talk about this lack of stakes. I propose we add some. You know—for *entertainment* purposes. It's not like we can't all afford it."

Irritation flashed over Hercules's preternaturally unlined face. "And pray tell, what does our uninvited guest consider to be an entertaining wager?" He pulled a slim money clip from his back pocket and withdrew a hundred-dollar bill. "Cash?" When Maxine gave a snort, Hercules held up his phone. "No? Would you prefer Cash App? EBT?"

Helen cleared her throat. "Now, now. That's uncalled for."

Hercules ignored her. "Tell us, then, Maxine. What incentivizes a woman like *you*?"

Teddy opened his mouth to put a stop to this conflict before it devolved into what was surely going to be Maxine-inflicted violence, but then he saw her lips curl in a way that could only be described as *wicked*. And, because Teddy was addicted to Maxine in a figurative sense that he desperately prayed would never become a literal one, the look chilled him and thrilled him in equal measure. It was like witnessing a viper's fangs slowly unhinge from their membranous storage, and

Hercules simply stood there waiting for her answer, blithely unaware he should be running away.

"Hair."

Hercules blinked. "Hair?"

"If you lose, I want your ponytail to hang on my trophy wall."

Hercules's hand shot up to the tail in question. His neck reddened. "That's absurd."

"And if I lose," Maxine continued, "I'll cut off mine. I'm serious! I have my cosmetology degree, and I can do a bitchin' fade. I'm an honest woman. I only dish out what I'm willing to eat."

If Teddy's stomach dropped, it was only because risk-taking made him anxious, even as a bystander. Maxine would be equally striking with short hair; the drastic cut wouldn't tame his infatuation in the slightest.

"Yeah, no. I'm not cutting my hair off," Zola said.

Maxine waved away the concern. "Relax, this is a side bet between me and Herc. Whadya say, big guy? I'm ready to put my metaphorical dick on the table. Are you?"

Hercules looked like he was going to brush Maxine off, as if her challenge was somehow unworthy, and this lack of respect bothered Teddy more than the gambling. So he said, "If I recall, McKnight, you're still undefeated. And Maxine has been beaten twice already."

"Thanks for reminding everyone," Maxine said with a smile that didn't reach her eyes.

"My pleasure," Teddy replied neutrally.

Hercules's gaze snapped between the two of them. "Well, Ms. Hart, your opponent makes a persuasive claim. A gentleman wouldn't refuse a challenge from a lady . . . with one caveat. I'll select the teams."

"Deal." Maxine shook Hercules's outstretched hand.

Hercules smiled. "You'll be with Teddy."

Chapter 9

SENSE AND SENSIBILITY

Answer

Of the five senses, this is the first to develop in mammals, and it is the only sense that can be fatal if missing.

Question

What is touch?

Maxine convened with her reluctant partner in a corner of the patio next to a grill large enough to roast a saber-toothed tiger whole.

The other teams were either doing the same or refilling their drinks—but most of them didn't have hair in the game.

"All right, listen up, this is how we're going to—"

Teddy held up a hand. "No."

"*No*, what? Herc only picked seventh-ranked Zhang Wei over there because he's a beast on the buzzer. Even if McKnight's gotten McSlow, Zhang will make up for it. We need a strategy." Maxine paced as she spoke, adrenaline lighting up her veins like nothing else could.

It also made her impatient, which, combined with Teddy's need to be petty about his win over her, made her fuse nonexistent. It also pissed her off that he looked dorkily handsome in his slate-gray suit pants and matching vest. Teddy's nod to "California casual" was to drape his suit coat over his arm rather than wear it, but he was still wearing an honest-to-god *bow tie*.

And right now, she wanted to cram that bow tie in his mouth.

He said tersely, "You're treating me like I'm your adversary, not your teammate."

"It's my hair on the line. We do it my way."

"You can't defeat the number one–seeded player using the same methodology that lost against the second seeded."

Maxine reached into her strapless bra and pulled out the stick of gum she'd tucked into her left boob cup. She popped it into her mouth and chewed, pretending to consider his words. "Here's the thing. You know your stuff, Theo—"

"Teddy."

"—but you play like Punxsutawney Phil on a sunny day."

His expression darkened. "And you play recklessly."

"Fortes fortuna iuvat."

"And as I'm sure *you* well know, that phrase has been attributed to Pliny the Elder immediately preceding his death during a foolish campaign to rescue his friend from the eruption of Mount Vesuvius. Perhaps it might be better translated as '*mis*fortune favors the bold.'"

Maxine was chewing her gum so vigorously she bit her tongue. She stifled her wince, even as the taste of copper filled her mouth. Through clenched teeth she said, "I guess we'll see."

He threw up his hands. "Fine."

"Fine!" She stormed toward the cocktail tables that Hercules had set up as makeshift podiums.

"Perhaps you can donate your hair to charity," he called after her, stalking off in the other direction.

Was he *abandoning* her? "Is that where you donated your heart, Cowardly Lion?"

Teddy disappeared into the house. *I don't need him anyway,* she told herself.

She picked up the replica buzzer and weighed it in her hands. It was pretty close to the same weight and size as the real thing. Not bad.

Hercules clinked his glass again. "Are we all ready to begin? Up first, Mr. Ferguson and Ms. Hart will face off against team three, consisting of Ms. Tarrah Prince and Mr. Ryan Murray, and team four, consisting of Mrs. Helen Kaur and Ms. Zola Mattick." If Maxine and Teddy won, they'd have to play again to beat Hercules and Zhang in the second round.

Then the *beep-boop-beep* sound effect played, and the projected game board populated on screen. Without warning, Teddy reappeared by her side and unceremoniously plunked two mugs of coffee on their table.

She tried not to feel relieved that he'd come back.

"What are these for?" she whispered as Sikander read the categories aloud. Maxine had already scanned them.

"Drink. Caffeine improves reaction speed."

Maxine slid the mug away. "Not for me." She loved coffee, but she'd already had three cups today on top of the stimulant meds she took for her ADHD, and too much caffeine would make her jittery. Besides, she was amped with dopamine and adrenaline from the prospect of competition, and that combo was usually where the magic happened. That's why some people with ADHD excelled in crisis situations but floundered in calm ones; Maxine would rather defuse a bomb than spend fifteen minutes filing paperwork.

Except Teddy seemed determined to get her wires crossed.

"I'll handle the literature category," he told her.

"Why? Because you think I can't read?" she snapped, not because she meant it, but because she didn't like being told what to do by anyone. Least of all the stuck-up know-it-all who was in the process of rolling up his sleeves to reveal his forearms, which, as everyone knew, was one of the sluttiest things a masculine-presenting person could do. Was he *trying* to distract her?

"Perhaps you can *read* that the category is Worldly Literature, which means they'll be looking for location-based book titles, and as we've previously established, geography is not your strength."

"All that matters is that we ring in before Helen, because you know as a librarian she's going to be all over that category."

"Do *not* ring in unless you know the answer," he warned.

Maxine gave him her best Mona Lisa.

"Maxine—"

Sikander announced that Maxine had the first selection.

"I'll take Worldly Lit for eight hundred," she called out.

"'This fifth novel in a series, which takes place on a train from Istanbul to Paris, introduced readers to what would become the author's signature *Fleming Sweep*, in which each chapter ends with a suspenseful hook.'"

The very second the lamp next to the game board lit up, indicating it was safe to ring in, Maxine and Helen smashed at the clicker.

Tarrah, who held their team's buzzer upside down, glanced around. "Oops, are we starting?" Ryan gently pried the device from her hand and replaced it with her cocktail glass.

"Maxine," Sikander called.

"*Murder on the Orient Express*!"

"Incorrect."

Teddy lunged for the clicker, but Maxine jerked it out of reach. "The Orient is not a qualifying *worldly location*," he admonished in a harsh whisper. "Give me the buzzer."

Helen rang in and gave the answer: "*From Russia, with Love*."

"Correct."

The librarian sighed wistfully. "I used to think Sean Connery was so dreamy! Well, until I learned he was a horrible misogynist."

Maxine whispered to Teddy, "Relax, okay? I focused on *train from Istanbul* and *suspenseful hook*. Easy mistake."

"*Fleming* Sweep? Ian Fleming? Author of the Bond novels?" He was still trying to speak in hushed tones, but his voice strained with each successive question.

"It's one clue! You gotta break eggs to make an omelet!"

They were so busy arguing that they nearly missed the next clue, which was called by Zola. "Groundbreaking Women for two hundred dollars."

"'This daughter of Lord Byron is credited with inventing computer programming when she wrote the world's first machine algorithm in 1843.'"

Teddy knew the answer was Ada Lovelace, but Maxine—who was still indignantly glaring at him about the last question—held the buzzer clutched in her fist. By the time she snapped her gaze back to the board, Ryan had already rung in and answered correctly.

"Stop distracting me."

"Your obstinacy is costing us this game." He knew he shouldn't care—it was only a game, after all—but the prospect of performing so abysmally in front of his peers was killing him.

"Let me *focus*," she hissed, angling away from him.

"Let me *ring in*," he bit out, reaching an arm around her.

She dodged away. "No!"

Ryan called the next clue; neither Teddy nor Maxine paid it a shred of attention.

Teddy jerked at the buzzer cord, causing the laser-pointer-shaped clicker to slide out the bottom of Maxine's fist. Snatching it up off the table, he cradled the buzzer protectively against his sternum. "I'll handle these next few clues—"

"Give it back!" Maxine lunged at him.

Teddy sidestepped—and rammed directly into the cocktail table. It toppled with a crash, sending coffee and shards of ceramic flying across the concrete patio.

The game came to a screeching halt.

"Oh my," exclaimed Helen. The other party guests stared in horror—except for Tarrah, who looked entertained.

And Teddy and Maxine stood there sheepishly, caught midtussle like playground children.

Hercules calmly stepped around the broken mugs and stood the table up. He gave them both a disbelieving look. "Do we have a problem?"

Teddy cleared his throat. "My apologies. We had a small disagreement that got out of hand."

Maxine mumbled "I'll get a broom" before scurrying off.

"Do we need to call the game a forfeit?" Hercules asked.

Teddy assured him they did not. And after he and Maxine, red cheeked with humiliation, cleaned up their mess, the simulated *Answers!* round continued.

And they continued to lose.

Maxine begrudgingly handed the buzzer over to Teddy for the Daily Duplex round, where they barely clawed their way back into the game. But they were down by over four grand heading into the Final Answer question, in which Maxine convinced Teddy to bet all but a dollar on the final category of Pop Music, and she managed to eke out a victory by being the only contestant who knew that Prince had written the Sinéad O'Connor hit "Nothing Compares 2 U."

When Sikander announced a fifteen-minute break between games so players could refresh their beverages and shrimp dip, Maxine pulled Teddy into the library to reconvene.

The library was accessible from a separate set of double doors on the patio, but to Maxine's disappointment during an earlier snooping expedition, none of the books inside it were real. Instead, the floor-to-ceiling bookshelves were filled with empty hardback shells in chic, color-blocked shades of seafoam and taupe that matched the abstract floor rug.

It seemed very strange to Maxine that someone of Hercules's caliber in trivia had zero real books in his home, but who knew? Maybe he was an e-book guy. Maybe he kept a vast library in his Louisiana house. There were a lot of explanations besides suspicious ones. Maxine knew she had trust issues, and all the mystery and true-crime books she listened to weren't much help.

Still, she couldn't shake the feeling. "Is it just me, or is Herc giving off a real Clark Stanley vibe?" she asked Teddy, who had, predictably, also beelined to the bookshelves as soon as Maxine closed the doors behind them.

"The original snake oil salesman?" Teddy tried to tug *Frankenstein* free and frowned when it didn't move. "That's a bit harsh. You know, being wealthy isn't a crime, Maxine."

She muttered, "The shit people do to *become* wealthy usually is."

"Like winning $2.6 million on a game show?" Teddy gave her a pointed look. When she stuck her tongue out at him, he sighed, as if defeated. "You did well there, getting that Final Answer clue."

It was the most lackluster compliment she'd ever received.

. . . it still made her glow with pride.

She turned to inspect the view of white-and-red boat lights dotting the twilit ocean. "Prince is the greatest musical genius of the twentieth century, and getting that answer wrong would be a disgrace to his memory."

"I'll let that egregious slight against Miles Davis stand because we don't have the time to reeducate your misguided taste."

Maxine suppressed a twinge of surprise. Sure, she'd watched him guess all the jazz-related clues correctly during his games, but it still hadn't fully registered that he *liked* jazz. Or any modern music at all. The Teddy she'd built in her mind only listened to overwrought classical music and the sound of his own voice.

"We need to divide and conquer based on our strengths," she told him. "Because we're up against Herc next, and I'm not handing that *Under Siege* knockoff the means to make a cursed doll of me."

"Do we need to worry about John and Jeff?" Teddy asked, referring to the other team. Maxine had to hand it to Herc; it *was* kind of funny that he'd paired up the two blandly interchangeable white dudes. The only difference was that one of them was an accountant and one was an attorney. Even the *Answers!* crew had a hard time telling them apart.

Maxine frowned. "You mean Jake and Jim?"

"I'm certain there's a Jeff."

"How certain?"

He paused. "I'm certain their names both begin with *J*. Do *you* know their names?"

"Of course."

"What are they?"

"*J* . . ."

"Jay?"

"Yeah!" She snapped her fingers. "Jay."

"And?"

She grimaced.

"You've no idea, do you?"

"Wipe that smug look off your face! You don't know either."

Now it was Teddy's turn to grimace.

In that shared moment, two of the world's top-ranked trivia champions reflected on the irony that of all the hundreds of thousands of facts stored in their brains, none of those facts included the names of two of their competitors.

She waved a hand. "They're barely more than henchmen. Sub-bosses at best. Let's focus on the Big Bad." The *J*-names were ranked eighth and ninth, respectively, and had all the wagering gusto and intellectual breadth of a stack of empty pizza boxes. "We need a system for ringing in. I'll hold the buzzer, and you tap the table if you know the answer."

"No. Requires you to look at the table and not the clue, which means you'll lose a split second in switching focus."

"True. And Zhang has the highest attempt-to-ring ratio of anyone here." Maxine paced the perimeter of the circular room, her brain whirring. Teddy idly inspected the globe in the room's center. "Okay, I got it. You put your hand on my arm, and if you know it, tap once."

"That won't work."

"You have a better idea?"

"Let me show you something. May I see your arm?" he asked.

Maxine dutifully came to the other side of the globe and stuck out her arm. Her bare skin looked awfully pale beneath the overhead lights, and part of her brain wandered off to address it—*I should have applied fake tanner. Actually, I should check the expiration date since I haven't used it since last summer. Should I order more now, just in case? Oh shit, I can't remember where I left my phone—*

Teddy's searing grip closed around her wrist, startling her brain into temporary silence.

"Sorry. I run hot."

"Actually, I run cold, so it feels nice." *More than nice.* Heat swept over her skin and made its way to her chest. Her heartbeat revved.

"Close your eyes."

And leave herself vulnerable? "Nice try, buddy. I'm not falling for whatever game you're running on me."

"What on earth do you think—" Teddy's sigh was deeply exasperated. "It's faster to demonstrate this biology lesson than explain."

"Yes, Professor," she grumbled, reluctantly complying.

After a second, she felt the barest of touches on the back of her arm. Goose bumps swept over her skin. Then his touch disappeared. "Was that one finger, or two?"

She willed her voice to come out steady. "Two?"

He touched her again. "Now how many?"

"One?"

"Wrong, both times."

Her eyes flew open. "Are you sure?"

He gave her a look. "Close your eyes, I'm not done."

The room went dark again, and she warned, "If you're trying to make me feel stupid, it won't—"

A finger skimmed her palm, and electricity zinged through her nerve endings, making every erogenous spot on her body light up like a goddamn circuit. She made an involuntary sound that was too close to a squeak for the sake of her dignity, and her eyes snapped open in alarm.

"How many fingers?" Teddy asked calmly.

"One." She tugged her wrist free, clutching it to her chest. "And that's enough. I get the idea." She felt shaky. Unbalanced.

"Your palm has three times more mechanoreceptors than your wrist. The more concentrated your nerve endings are, the faster you can register slight variations in pressure."

"Big focus on human physiology during that geography PhD program of yours, was there?"

"Something like that." His mouth twitched. "I dated a neurobiologist."

"Oh." Jealousy reared up before she could stop it. Another woman's nails tracing the sculpted lines of his naked body—

What the hell is wrong with you? Maxine slammed the door to her imagination shut.

Teddy went on, oblivious: "You're right handed, so during the game, I'll hold your left hand and press my thumb against your palm, and you can buzz in with your right. It's a small advantage, but we'll need it."

Her stomach flipped. "Isn't there another place that's equally sensitive?"

"Oh, there is."

She swallowed. Trying not to visualize—

"Lips," he said swiftly. Whatever he read on her expression was enough to make him back up in alarm. "Lips . . . are the only part close to being that sensitive. But the palm is more appropriate for this setting."

As if in a trance she couldn't break free from, Maxine felt her fingers shoot to her mouth. She ran her index finger over her lower lip. Imagining it was Teddy's touch, and not her own.

Teddy's eyes locked on her movement, and his eyes darkened behind his glasses. The air in the room suddenly felt heavy.

The door to the hallway burst open, and both Teddy and Maxine jerked apart as if they'd been caught doing something illicit.

But it was only one of the brown-haired, medium-size *J* names she couldn't remember. "Oh!" he said, stopping in his tracks. He glanced back and forth between them. "Sorry. I didn't realize, er . . . I was looking for the bathroom."

"Two doors down," Teddy and Maxine said in unison.

"Thanks." He gave them both an awkward thumbs-up. "Huge fan of both of you, by the way. Excited to match up."

"Same," Maxine said.

"You had an impressive run," Teddy added graciously.

J-name took another quick glance around the library—almost as if he was looking for something—before giving them both another cursory smile and disappearing down the hall.

Maxine avoided Teddy's gaze. She said out of the corner of her mouth, "Do you even remember his episodes?"

"Not in the slightest."

She could still feel his phantom touch on her skin. Her body was oversensitized. Overaware of his proximity. It made her want to peel off her flesh and flee into the night. She *knew* she shouldn't have closed her eyes around Teddy. He was dangerous. The only person she'd met who could breach her hardened defenses and unbalance her with a single touch.

And if there was one thing that was nonnegotiable, it was that she needed her defenses. Beyond those ramparts was an insecure, sensitive, glass-hearted mess who wanted to curl into a ball at the slightest criticism. And since child-Maxine had needed to fake being older than she was in order to step into the "adult" role whenever Mom was on a gambling spree, she'd learned real fast that crying and self-pity were not viable options. Over time, she'd developed such a thick skin that barely anything left a scratch.

Now, she had defense building down to a routine. Every morning before getting out of bed, she spent fifteen minutes masturbating, and then another five minutes hyping herself up with superlatives, compliments, and praise until she believed it all with her whole soul. Then, she showered with the most decadently expensive hair products that game show money could buy, ate whatever the fuck she wanted for breakfast, wore whatever made her look hot as hell, and kissed Miss Cleo-asp-tra on her head for good luck. And then she stepped out into the world confident that there was no insult, setback, or rejection that couldn't be deflected with a good old-fashioned Brooklyn *Fuck you, asshole!*

Until she'd met Teddy, no one had ever been able to get to her, because she was Maxine Hart, and she was *amazing*. Everyone who dared insult her was so far beneath her that they may as well be sidewalk scum under her boots.

But oh, did Teddy get to her. He was the only one who'd ever truly bested her, which made him her equal. And since she couldn't pretend he was beneath her, that meant he had the power to wound her . . . and that *terrified* her.

Maxine bolted for the patio doors. "You know what? I've changed my mind. We don't need a strategy. Let's just wing it, okay?"

"What? Where are you going?" His voice followed her. "Maxine!"

She burst out into the night, grateful for the rush of cold air over her skin, and veered right onto a sloping stone ramp through the garden.

She heard him call her name again, but she didn't stop. "It'll be fine!" she hollered over her shoulder. "I needed a haircut anyway!"

The path split, and she went right, into the grove of fruit trees and hibiscus. Solar-powered garden lights glowed at her feet, but it would be hard to see her in the darkness. *Please don't follow me,* she prayed, even though parts of her were lobbying hard for him to do exactly that.

I can totally pull off a short cut and not look like Peter Pan with a perm, she lied to herself. *Sure, I've made the wildly impulsive decision to chicken out of working with Teddy, thereby abandoning what little chance*

I had of beating Zhang and Hercules, but my hair grows fast. I can take folic acid . . .

Another turn, and she found herself at a gazebo. A quiet snicker sounded, and Maxine stopped in her tracks, which was when she registered the smell of Tarrah's weed pen.

"Oh shit, it's the cops!" Tarrah squealed. Then she burst into cackles. "Gotcha! It's just Maxine."

Maxine blinked, willing her eyes to adjust to the darkness.

When they did, she, too, began to laugh.

Because there, silhouetted against the bruised Los Angeles night sky, were Tarrah Prince, Helen Kaur . . . and a giggling Zhang Wei.

Chapter 10

POP CULTURE HEADLINES FROM THE 2010S

Answer

"The Secret Language of Bros" (*Boston Globe*): This animated children's show with the tagline "Friendship Is Magic" finds a surprise fan base.

Question

What is *My Little Pony*?

Maxine walked into Dino's hoisting the plastic baggie with Hercules's ponytail over her head like a sports trophy and was met with a chorus of cheers.

"I return from the battlefront victorious!" she crowed, tossing the bag on the bar top. "Behold, the skin of the Nemean lion."

Dino scowled. "Get that shit off my bar."

Marlon snatched the bag and held it up to the light. He *tsk*ed. "Hercules's got a dandruff problem."

Rabbi Cohen rubbed his bald head beneath his kippah. "Some of us should be so lucky."

Maxine ordered a whisky and reconvened with Marlon and Rabbi Cohen at their usual table in the back. Since it was a Monday and not a Tuesday, there was no bar trivia tonight. Instead, the boys were here to help her train for the tournament.

She had no intention of doing any such thing. But she was here to humor them, and it's not like she had anything better to do tonight. She grabbed one of the battered Trivial Pursuit boxes from the bookshelf behind their table and began shuffling the question cards. They'd already been through all the questions from every edition and expansion pack, all of which Dino helpfully kept in stock for bar patrons, but it was as good a way as any to ID her weak spots. And since she had to do a shot every time she got a question wrong, it was an efficient path to getting blitzed enough to wipe all traces of Theodore Ferguson III from her mind.

"Tell us *everything*," Marlon said.

Rabbi Cohen sipped his pilsner. "And for the record, ma'am, I want you to know we don't appreciate you playing coy with the details over the group chat."

Before she could answer, they began barraging her with questions.

"Was McKnight as intimidating as he looked on TV? What was his house like?" Marlon asked.

"Did you meet Ryan Murray? He was fantastic on his run. What about that Helen Kaur? I bet she had fun hair. Did she have fun hair?"

"Did Hercules miss any questions? He's got to have gone soft. I mean, the Herc I saw on TV was unbeatable. Does he suck now? Is that how you beat him?"

"Kiddo, let the woman answer," Rabbi Cohen said. But before Maxine could say anything, he added, "How *did* you beat him?"

"Wow, guys. *Wow.*" Maxine sat back and crossed her arms. "First of all, rude. I beat Hercules through sheer skill, speed, and mental fortitude."

Her teammates shared a look.

"Bull," said Rabbi Cohen.

"Shit," finished Marlon.

"Watch your language." The rabbi set down his beer and leaned forward on his elbows. "What my young friend is trying to say is, cut the bullshit, Maxie."

Maxine crossed her arms and gave them a sullen look. "Okay, so they paired us up in teams, and Hercules's teammate was blazed off his ass and couldn't ring in fast enough. Teddy and I got a head start—"

"Whoa, whoa . . ." Rabbi Cohen held up his hands. "Back up. You were paired with Teddy?"

"Oooooohhh . . . ," Marlon said in a singsong voice.

"Was there smoochin'?"

Too close for comfort. "Absolutely not. What's wrong with you two? Teddy's my archnemesis, remember?"

She filled them in on the bare minimum details of the weekend's events, leaving out incriminating evidence that might lead one to believe that Maxine wanted everything to do with *smoochin'* her mortal enemy.

Again.

They didn't know about the first time, and Maxine intended to keep it that way. But they sure as hell *suspected.* Rabbi Cohen watched too many rom-coms, and lately he'd been getting Marlon hooked on his late wife's romance novels. But they should know her well enough to know she wasn't romance-heroine material. She was Outrageous Friend Who Encourages the Heroine to Make Poor Choices material, at best.

"Did you at least say you're sorry to the guy afterward?" Rabbi Cohen asked when Maxine was finished recounting her lackluster tale of winning by the skin of her teeth and a whole lotta luck.

"To Hercules? Fuck no. Smarmy asshole tried to back out of the bet, but everyone shamed him until he conceded." Maxine shuddered at the memory of Hercules's vengeful glare as she'd chopped off his ponytail with a pair of dull kitchen scissors. In retrospect, pissing off the reigning champion five weeks before having to compete against him for two million bucks was a questionable choice. Hercules would be out for her blood from the get-go.

And after that practice game, even Maxine had to admit she was . . . not ready. Thus, the halfhearted training.

She held up the stack of cards. "Can we focus, please? Someone read me off a Sports and Leisure question."

"Nice try, Sporty Spice, pick a category you aren't weirdly obsessed with. And he's talking about Teddy," Marlon said.

"Sounds like he tried to offer a truce and you threw it in his face. It's a blessing you won, but do you really think it's a good idea to offend your two biggest opponents?" Rabbi Cohen took the stack of cards from Maxine and scanned the first one. "'What's the largest country, by area, that is wholly in Europe?'"

"Oh, boo-hoo, so I made some rich men sad. I'll carry the weight of my sorrow to the grave." She paused. "France. No! Spain."

"Final answer?"

She licked her lips nervously. "Spain."

Rabbi Cohen's disappointment was palpable.

Marlon visibly cringed. "Oh my god, this is so embarrassing. *Ukraine*. That's not even a hard question! How did you get this far? Have you ever *seen* a map?"

"You really want me to sit here and memorize the square mileage of 200 countries?"

"195 by the UN's count," Rabbi Cohen corrected.

"197 if you count Taiwan and Kosovo," said Marlon.

Maxine rolled her eyes. "What are you guys, the Fact Cops? Besides, the Olympic Committee recognizes 206. So technically, if you split the difference—"

"*Technically* isn't good enough for *Answers!* You can't win like this." Marlon turned to Rabbi Cohen. "She can't win like this."

"You're right, she can't. Maybe she should be training with someone who knows his geography. You know, now that I think of it, that same someone has strengths in all her weak spots."

"Yeah, and Maxine's better at betting strategy and a bunch of weird categories that fall outside the regular *Answers!* study canon. They could really benefit one another. And maybe she actually respects that someone enough to listen to him."

Maxine snarled, "I don't *respect* Teddy. What are you two trying to do right now?"

They ignored her. "You're right, she's clearly not taking this seriously."

"Okay, everyone calm the fuck down." Maxine threw back her shot, letting it scorch the memory of Ukraine's superior land mass into her esophagus.

It's just that memorizing lists of facts was so *dull.* Sure, she could go through an atlas and memorize all the US capitals and state flowers through sheer force of will, but none of it would stick past the twenty-four-hour mark. Maxine's brain simply did not learn that way. How was a learning traditionalist like Teddy going to fix that problem?

But you do remember every single thing Teddy says and does, came the unwelcome thought.

She hated that it was true. Maxine didn't like Teddy . . . but her brain did. And one surefire way to get her ADHD brain to learn something was to attach it to something *fascinating.*

"What do you want me to do? Show up on Teddy's doorstep with a bouquet of flowers and say, 'I'm sorry I spend three hours a day fantasizing about shoving you in a locker, but will you please teach me everything you know so I can beat you in the most important tournament of our lives?'"

Marlon and Rabbi Cohen said in unison, "Yes!"

"You guys are out of your minds. Why the hell would Teddy say yes?"

Dino arrived at the table with another round of drinks, which was a rare gesture. He never came out from behind the bar unless he had good reason. This was the kind of place where you got shit service and tipped generously for it . . . *or else.*

Maxine reached for her shot, but Dino didn't release his hold on the glass. "Nah, this shot's for winners. You a winner? Or you a whiner?"

"A winner," Maxine said, wishing she didn't sound so petulant.

"Then get outta here." Dino nodded at the exit. "Find your fancy guy and get him to train you."

"But I don't know how—"

"Winners figure it out." Dino released the drink. "You wanna get something you've never had before, you gotta do something you've never done before."

Maxine took the shot, slammed the glass on the table, and snatched up her backpack and coat. "Fine. But when he says no and I come crawling back from Jersey like a bad case of the clap, you all owe me. Big time!"

As she slammed the winter vestibule door behind her, she heard Marlon call out, "Don't forget the flowers!"

THE DOUBLE ANSWER ROUND

Chapter 11

IT'S A BARD'S WORLD

[Dr. Love: We'll give you a line; you give us the name of the work.]

Answer

"I would not wish any companion in the world but you; Nor can imagination form a shape, besides yourself, to like of."

Question

What is *The Tempest*?

It was past Teddy's bedtime, but he couldn't move from his armchair by the fire in his study because there was a purring cat on his lap. And Teddy didn't even own a cat.

He wasn't sure anyone owned the peach-hued creature sprawled across his thighs, luxuriating beneath regular strokes of Teddy's hand, even though the feline boasted a worn green collar and the chubby physique of a well-kept pet. Since the collar didn't have a tag, Teddy had taken to calling him Ginger Cat, in the hopes that it was generic enough not to confuse the poor thing should he, in fact, have a proper moniker. Ginger Cat patrolled the street upon which his Victorian town house stood near the Princeton campus, and could often be seen meandering from door to door in search of food and affection. Tonight, Teddy was the chosen one.

He felt very appreciative of that fact. A feline's regard was hard won.

So when the doorbell rang and a glance at the clock on his mantel showed it was approaching midnight, he was extraordinarily disinclined to answer.

Maybe I should get a security camera. It was a college town, after all, and though crime was low, there was always a risk of drunken vandalism or other mischief. His father had always said Teddy was too trusting.

The bell rang again.

Ginger Cat, having been thoroughly disturbed from his spa experience, slipped from Teddy's lap with a thud and marched toward the door as if he owned the home. He looked back at Teddy, expectant.

Teddy rubbed his tired eyes beneath his glasses and followed the cat to the door. Though he only wore his plaid bathrobe over his pajama pants and sleep shirt, he wasn't concerned with formalities. Clearly, the person who felt midnight was an appropriate time to visit wasn't concerned about them either.

The person on his doorstep was the last one in the world he'd expected to see. "Maxine?"

"Yo." Maxine shuffled from foot to foot in an uncharacteristically sheepish manner. It must have begun to rain at some point since sundown, and though Maxine wore her emerald coat, her cinnamon curls were soaked through. Aside from the small black backpack she always carried with her, she had no luggage.

It was all very unexpected and concerning. Well, it would be from someone else. It felt entirely expected from Maxine.

"Is everything all right?" he asked, just to be sure.

She held out something dark and vaguely squarish. "Oh, yeah. Sorry for showing up so late. I missed the earlier train because I had to visit three different home and garden stores to find violets. You'd think by April they'd have their perennials out."

He took the proffered gift and realized it was, in fact, a traumatized plant of some kind in a plain plastic container. "You've got me a violet plant because it's New Jersey's state flower," he said.

"Exactly!" She beamed at him.

Even soaking wet in the wan porch light, Maxine was so beautiful it made him want to fall to his knees in awe. *Careful,* his better sense warned. *She's trouble.*

By his feet, Ginger Cat's tail had gone puffy. The feline slowly backed away, never taking his eyes off Maxine.

"And *why* are you presenting me with New Jersey's state flower at midnight on a Monday?"

"It's a peace offering. Can I come in? It's pouring out here." She stepped forward as she spoke, as if she were expecting Teddy to unroll a royal carpet for her. When he didn't move, she reeled back a step. "Dude, come on. I'm sorry about the stuff that went down at Hercules's place. Is that what you want to hear?"

"You do realize you cannot simply show up unannounced at people's homes in the middle of the night, right? How did you even—" He shook his head. "Never mind, I'd like to never find out how you discovered my address because I'm confident it will irritate me. What do you want?"

She toed his welcome mat with her boot, eyeing the faded Oxford logo on it. Then she mumbled something he couldn't make out.

"Pardon?"

"Uuuuugh. Why are you making this so difficult?" Her light scuffing became a petulant kick, knocking his mat slightly off center. Teddy suppressed a smile. It was so deliciously rare to see Maxine at a social disadvantage. She always seemed to have the upper hand in their interactions, and the fact that she currently did not was positively *revelatory.* Letting her in was a foregone conclusion; Teddy wasn't the kind of villain who would leave anyone in need on his doorstep, poor weather or not. But that didn't mean he couldn't make her suffer first.

It was about time Maxine experienced an iota of the perpetual torment she caused him.

"Now might be the preferred time to avail yourself of humility," Teddy suggested helpfully. He pretended to scan the street with a wary eye. "It's late, and some of my neighbors are quick to call the authorities at the merest hint of suspicious activity."

"Okay! Jesus! I'm here because I need your help."

"With visitation etiquette? Keep your voice down."

"You were—" She huffed a breath, then switched to a stage whisper. "You were awake."

"Actually, I'm increasingly liable to fall asleep where I stand with every second of this nonsense. *What* do you need help with, Maxine?"

She looked away and mumbled, "With training for the tournament."

Oh, the elation that coursed through him! This was the very pinnacle of his existence. He wanted to crow with victory until Fiona from next door called to have him arrested.

Instead, he kept his expression as somber as he could manage. "Need I remind you we're competing *against* each other?"

"And we're *both* competing against the only undefeated *Answers!* player in history. Since as you know, our skills sets are . . . complementary and shit . . . I thought we could help each other. With our powers combined, one of us might be able to do the impossible and take down Hercules."

Teddy crossed his arms and let her squirm, ignoring the twinge of guilt he felt for leaving her in the rain another thirty seconds. "Your idea is patently absurd."

Her face fell, and the twinge ballooned into a full cramp.

She deserves it! his inner voice cried, but his gut wasn't having it. Teddy relented and stepped out of the doorway, gesturing wide at his living room. "But I'm willing to discuss it over hot chamomile tea."

Maxine curled her lip. "You got anything stronger?"

"Get inside before I lock this door in your face."

"You're so cranky at night. Is that why you're dressed like Ebenezer Scrooge?"

"Does that make you the Ghost of Manners Past?"

"Funny, I always saw myself as having a Fezziwig vibe." She swept past him, the rubber soles of her boots squeaking on his hardwood entry and leaving wet prints behind her as she headed toward the living room. Ginger Cat hissed and scrambled out of her path.

"Stop. Shoes off."

Maxine had the grace to comply without argument. But after she'd kicked her boots haphazardly next to his shoe cupboard, she was still dripping water behind her like a slug. Even her socks were wet.

She plopped into his armchair—undoubtedly soaking the expensive brocade fabric—and then had the audacity to scoot it closer to the fire. The chair's legs squealed where they dragged on the original hardwood. Teddy flinched. "Do I have to ask you not to rearrange my home, or is this the last of it?"

Maxine held her socked feet up to the fire. "Look at you with a fancy fireplace and all these leather-bound books. This is exactly what I imagined your home would look like. Grandpa chic."

Teddy bit down the urge to ask whether that made her apartment playroom chic, even though it was objectively the best way to return her jab. He did not think of Maxine as childlike in any way, shape, or form, and it would do a grave disservice to her character to suggest as much, given that individuals with ADHD are so often infantilized by well-meaning but unintentionally hurtful instructors and caregivers. And even though Maxine was the worst thing that had ever happened to his *Answers!* career and possibly even his life, she was only good to him hale and unbroken. The sight of real hurt in Maxine's eyes might end him entirely.

Without a word, Teddy went upstairs to his bedroom and returned with a neat stack of dry clothes. He noted that in his short absence, Maxine had helped herself to a snifter of his most expensive XO

Cognac, and was now inspecting the canvas world map that covered an entire wall. When she saw him notice the glass, she took a deliberate sip and held eye contact while she did it, as if daring him to chastise her.

"Put these on," he instructed, handing her the stack of clothes.

"Sweatpants? Who left these at your place?"

"I do occasionally engage in leisure activities, Maxine." He pointed her in the direction of his downstairs powder room, and then spent the next five minutes trying not to think about Maxine undressing in his home.

She emerged wearing his baggy Princeton-branded joggers and zip-up fleece. "What do you think? Can I pass for a Princeton student?" She did a deft pirouette, his loaned socks sliding on hardwood, and finished with a flourish.

"No," he said.

Teddy did not want to examine the swift arousal that hit him at the sight of Maxine in his clothes. It was a wholly proprietary feeling that was undoubtedly exaggerated by the way her bottom filled out his sweatpants in a way his certainly didn't.

"You're right, I'd never fit in at a place like this," she said lightly, and he realized she'd taken his reply to mean she lacked a certain Ivy League quality of character, rather than the fact he was technically a tenured associate professor at this university and therefore could never see Maxine as an eighteen-year-old student. The power differential was too great, and he could only think of Maxine as his equal.

A very *adult* equal.

Maxine crossed to the bookshelves and ran a desultory finger over the spines of his reference books, and the action conjured answering tingles across his chest.

Teddy quietly took a deep breath, poured his own glass of Cognac, and settled into his armchair. Perhaps there was a chance Ginger Cat would return, now that his lap was available again. "Now that you're not leaking all over my home, enlighten me as to why I should help you train for this tournament."

"Because if you can help me learn all this boring stuff that you love so much," Maxine said, "I can help you play like a champion." She ambled over to the fire and set her snifter on the mantel.

"I'm already a champion," he reminded her.

"Of an annual tournament and regular gameplay, sure. But this is the big league. You wilt under the teeniest pressure, and you bet like you're paying for every dollar with a pint of blood. You think that's good enough to beat Hercules? We only won on Friday because Zhang was high as a kite."

Teddy took a healthy swallow of his drink to quash the impulse to argue. Because she was right.

And Teddy wanted to win this tournament very, very badly.

He'd once entertained fantasies of parading into his father's study, trophy in hand, and announcing, *See? All my wins—every one of them—were real. I never needed to cheat at Quizzing League, no matter what you believed back then.*

That fantasy of winning his father's approval had swiftly withered after his first two runs on the show. If it hadn't happened yet, it likely never would. Maybe that was why Teddy had the nerve to dream of doing something else with his life if he won that prize money. Fifteen generations of Fergusons had been content to watch the world go by from their ivory-tower windows—academic Rapunzels, beholden to duty and tradition.

Then he'd spotted Maxine in the crowd below his tower, and she'd unlocked something in him. Made him crave freedom.

If only he weren't so afraid to jump.

"If I were to say yes . . . *if*," he emphasized, "how do you propose we do this? From what I've ascertained, your knowledge background is riddled with holes. And my deliberate style of play stems from a lifelong devotion to logic and caution. I'm not quite sure how you intend to change a key facet of personality in five weeks, especially with you commuting from Brooklyn. How much time do you plan to contribute to this endeavor?"

"Oh, all of it."

"All of—" He narrowed his eyes, realization dawning. "You're not staying here. My home is not a sleepaway camp. I have responsibilities. A life."

"No, you don't." Smirking, Maxine came over to his chair and leaned against it. "You extended your leave."

He scowled. "Have you broken into my email correspondence?"

"No. But I probably could. I bet you write all your passwords down in a little alphabetized notebook that you lock in your desk drawer."

Teddy made a mental note to move his password journal to a more secure, Maxine-proof location.

"I actually overheard you mentioning it to Helen at the party. But you also have a terrible poker face, which is something we'll have to work on when it comes to wagering in the Final Answer round. Lucky for you, though, I was basically raised in a casino. I can make you an excellent bluffer."

This gave him pause. He knew so little about her past. (Part of him suspected she'd been hatched from an extraterrestrial pod.) Now, he realized, he wanted to know more. "Do your parents own a gaming venue?" he ventured.

"It's adorable that your first thought is that we *owned* the place."

"Employees, then?"

"Loyal customer. So loyal that my mom dragged me and my sister down to Atlantic City every weekend to see if they had luck back in stock. Good news is I picked up a lot of slick tricks that come in handy if you ever need to compete on a game show."

"I'll decline that portion, thank you. I don't plan to go about luring my opponents into alleyways and hotel pools. I prefer to play with integrity."

Maxine spun to stand in front of him, then slowly leaned forward to place her hands on the armrests on either side of him. Caging him in. "Mister Ferguson, are you accusing me of being a dishonest woman?" Her voice was throaty and playful, but there was something sharp underneath it. "Because it really seems like you're implying I would use my feminine wiles to gain an unfair advantage."

Her proximity was alarming. Her green-gold eyes, heavy lidded and wily, reflected the flickering fire. A coil of scarlet hair slipped out from her loose ponytail and fell forward, dangling in the air before his face. Teddy clenched his fists to prevent himself from tucking it back behind her ear. For a moment, he felt strangely light headed, and then he realized he'd been holding his breath. He drew in oxygen, but that only made it worse, because she smelled like Cognac and the fruit-gum scent that haunted him at night. The one he swore he smelled when he awoke every morning after dreaming about the way her skin tasted.

"Wouldn't you?" he asked, his voice like gravel.

"Only if I knew said wiles would work. And only if you wanted me to." A tongue came out to lick her lips, and she slid her left knee onto the chair beside his right thigh, leaving the other to balance her on the floor. The move brought her close enough to kiss. Close enough that all he needed to do was pull her down, and she'd be straddling him. A pulse pounded in his low belly. How badly he wanted that.

But that was all he could ever have from her.

Maxine was an intoxicant to him—a dangerous one—and she was in his home. In his clothes.

If he let her stay, it would lead to Maxine sleeping in his guest room, exactly six steps down the hall from his bedroom. Maxine doing chaotic Maxine things all over his quiet, organized life, every minute of every day.

Panic coiled around his lungs and began to squeeze, and he wasn't sure if it was because of how much he abhorred the idea—or how much he craved it.

And so Teddy did the unthinkable: he lied. "Your wiles will certainly *not* work on me."

"Are you sure?"

"Utterly."

"So you *don't* want me to try?"

He said nothing. He only had it in him to lie once.

For an interminable moment, neither of them moved. And then, suddenly, they were devouring each other.

It happened so quickly, so violently, Teddy wasn't sure who'd moved first. He didn't know how his hand became tangled in her hair, or how Maxine's tongue came into his groaning mouth, or how she was suddenly off the floor and writhing in his lap, his grip hard on her ass to help her grind against him.

There was a roaring in his ears, and Teddy realized it was the rain pounding against his porch steps. It had begun to storm.

He couldn't get enough of her taste. It had been one year and eight days since their last kiss—an eternity. He'd imagined how well he'd kiss her if he ever had the chance to do it again. How expertly he'd tease her lips open with his own, kissing her smile, softly teasing. Then gently delving into her warm mouth. Exploring the contours. Memorizing what she liked. Listening to her gasps. Measuring the flutters of her pulse. He'd study Maxine's kiss until he'd mastered it.

But that wasn't what was happening now. This kiss was messy and hurried, wet with spit and rainwater from her hair, the pleasure sharp and their bites sharper, and what else had he expected from kissing Maxine Hart?

He couldn't think. He needed more.

Their clothes bunched and rubbed between them—an irritation—and Teddy fumbled for the zipper of her fleece, groaning. Desperate. Maxine knocked his hand aside and unzipped it herself, breaking away only long enough to fling the garment across the room and for Teddy to heave in a gulp of air, and then their mouths crashed together again, and her soft bare skin was in his hands.

He greedily smoothed his palms over her waist, gorging himself on the silken, soft feel of her. The way her waist flared out into her hips—*dear god.* This was heaven. This was hell. This was everything.

Then Maxine grabbed his wrists and wrenched them up to her breasts, and when he closed over them, his thumbs instinctively dragging over her lace-covered nipples, Maxine gave a breathless moan that made his brain waves flatten. Conscious thought, gone—

—he came back online what had to have been at least twenty seconds later and found his body had blessedly gone on autopilot, continuing their kiss while he stroked and kneaded through her bra like it was his final and sole purpose.

She likes having her breasts touched was his only thought. It was all that mattered. Her hips thrust against his. Her breath came in escalating gasps. And he didn't want to stop kissing her—ever—but he had no choice.

He found the globes of her ass and hoisted her higher in his lap, wrenched his mouth away, and closed his mouth over her right nipple, right through her bra.

"Aw, *fuck*," Maxine moaned, falling forward. Her hands came up to clasp his head to her, nails digging into his scalp like ten tiny daggers. His glasses stuck on the skin of her chest, and he paused only to remove them with a shaking hand and toss them somewhere in the direction of his side table. They clattered to the floor, and he didn't care. His mouth was back on her, laving her nipple in circles, using his mouth to suck the lace across her sensitive flesh. Using his teeth to lightly hold the peaked tip in place while he flicked it with his tongue. His other hand fondled her other breast until he felt he'd die if he didn't taste that one, too, and so he switched. And all the while, Maxine jerked her hips against him, riding the hard ridge of his cock through the fabric of their joggers.

And the frantic sounds she made, the stifled moans into his hair, the air hissing through her teeth when she gasped for breath, further and further apart as if she were holding her breath between them, he almost thought—

No. Impossible. She can't—

Lightning flashed with a crack of thunder so loud the walls shook. Maxine jumped out of his lap like a shot, her foot catching on the standing lamp beside his chair. It toppled forward, and both it and Maxine tumbled to the ground.

"Ow!" She'd landed hard on her backside.

Teddy stumbled to his feet, disoriented but determined to help. "Are you hurt?"

"No," came her distinctly embarrassed reply. She rolled over and untangled her leg from the lamppost, and Teddy reset it upright. He held out a hand to her, but Maxine merely blinked at it, her moss eyes unfocused and ringed in gray clouds of smeared eye makeup. Her chest rose and fell in great heaves, and Teddy suddenly felt like an utter pervert, because he realized he'd been openly staring at her hard nipples jutting up against sloppy wet circles of lace.

Maxine's lost gaze seemed to snag on a view of his midsection—or directly below it. Her pupils dilated, like a serpent locking in on prey. Her swollen lips parted. She said huskily, "Actually, I think I'm fatally injured. You wanna come down here and give me mouth to mouth?"

He almost did it. Teddy's muscles tensed, ready to pin Maxine down on the hardwood floor of his study and do depraved things to her until they either expired or his morning alarm went off, whichever came first.

But he remembered the last time she'd looked at him like that. *I'm going to eat you alive.*

And then she had.

"We're not doing this. I will not let you manipulate me again. I can think of nothing I want less than to have you sabotage my tournament preparations with your constant presence, spiritual disruption, and so-called *training*." He stalked over to where he'd left his Cognac glass on the mantel and drank the remainder in a single gulp, trying to sear the taste of her off his palate. He set the empty glass back down, studiously looking everywhere but at the half-naked woman on the floor of his study, then pointed at the door. "Now get out."

She blinked at him. "Out like outside, out? In the rain?"

"Yes, and now as in now. The last Dinky leaves at 1:13 a.m. You've got plenty of time to make it."

Maxine gasped. "Rude! A beautiful, delicate flower such as myself, cruelly cast out into the streets of New Jersey in a hurricane?"

"It's not a hurricane, and I distinctly recall one of your contestant interviews in which you revealed you used to teach Krav Maga classes at the YMCA." He whirled to face her, feeling very much like he'd been possessed by an unhinged stranger who could not be trusted to make wise choices, and saw she'd already got to her feet.

"That was five years ago, so I forgot all the moves and now I'm totally helpless. Besides, we both know you'd never really toss me out on the street at this hour." Maxine crossed her arms and looked at him with an expression of such scorn that Teddy fought the urge to beg for mercy. "You're a coward. Always were, always will be."

It was like a slap to the face. *All that back there on your lap—she was just getting what she wanted.* "You call me a coward, but I think you're the one who's frightened."

"That's cute."

"Is it? I think you've unconsciously tried to antagonize me because you *want* me to say no. Why is that? Are you afraid that with extended exposure to the workings of your intelligence, I'll judge you far less capable than you pretend? Will I discover that your wins were a halcyon combination of lucky categories and well-placed bets, thereby reinforcing your inner insecurity about your lack of formal education?"

"Don't try to psychoanalyze me," she snapped. "You don't want to work with me? Fine. I don't need you. But don't try to pretend the reason *you* don't want to work with *me* is because you're still horny as shit for it, except your pride can't handle the idea of slumming it in the sack with a girl like me!"

Teddy barked an involuntary laugh. He hadn't meant to. It was just so . . . *absurd.* "You don't have any idea what you're talking about."

Maxine must have taken his response for mockery. In a voice dripping with disgust, she said, "Elitist asshole."

He knew she meant it too.

Teddy stood back and scraped a hand over his face, suddenly feeling very tired. Before he could regret it, he heard himself say, "You may stay the night. Guest room is the first door to the right of the stairs. Don't go in the room at the far end of the hall on the left—that's mine. And I want you gone before breakfast."

Maxine stood primly, chin held high. "Thank you. It's the least you can do for me." She gestured meaningfully at her breasts.

He swept a hand to highlight his still-hard erection. "It's not as if I'm not suffering, Maxine!"

"Good!" She stomped up the stairs. Got to the top and called down, "Uh, which one is it again?"

"First on the right. And don't slam the—"

The door slammed.

Teddy wondered how she couldn't see it. That he'd happily let her ruin his entire life—if only she'd stay in it afterward. But what did dull Teddy have that would compel a vibrant woman like Maxine to *stay*? A sensible bedtime, a quiet life, and the promise of regular Sunday dinners with his parents? No, Maxine would be bored of his existence in the space of weeks, if not days.

He walked the empty Cognac glasses to the kitchen to hand-wash them and found Ginger Cat sitting on his kitchen table in the dark, looking rather miffed.

"You may have to get used to her," Teddy told his feline guest. "I don't think she intends to leave."

Chapter 12

ELECTROMAGNETISM

Answer

A measure of an object's opposition to the flow of electric current.

Question

What is resistance?

When Maxine came downstairs in the morning, she found Teddy in the kitchen with coffee and an egg breakfast set out on the table. She stopped in the doorway between the hallway and the kitchen, gazing around the quaint space with its breezy curtains and cream-and-blue-hued wallpaper. He'd even set her violet in a little pot on the table.

And the pièce de résistance in this charmingly domestic picture was Theodore Ferguson III, already fully dressed and groomed in a button-down shirt, olive slacks, and suspenders. He was working on a crossword and didn't look up as she hesitantly shuffled over to the table, her oversize socks gliding across the laminate floor.

His fat orange cat was nowhere to be seen. Maybe he smelled Miss Cleo on her.

"Morning, nerd," she said with as much false cheer as she could muster. It was that, or reveal she'd spent most of the night replaying their kiss—and its aftermath—in her head. She gestured to the second place setting. "Is this for me?"

"Coffee's in the pot. Cream's in the fridge, as is the bread, butter, and jam. And the eggs in the pan are still warm."

She piled her plate with a heaping portion of everything and sat down. Only then did Teddy look up at her. Before she could thank him for the breakfast she wasn't even supposed to be here for, he said, "If we do this, I want us to agree on some ground rules."

"You changed your mind about being my training partner?" Elation zipped through her—followed immediately by the urge to bolt out the door.

She really hadn't expected him to say yes. She'd planned to humor her pub-quiz teammates and maybe get an evening of entertainment from annoying Teddy. Except time had gotten away from her and so had the weather forecast, and she hadn't really planned on showing up at midnight, nor had she planned to play chicken with their mutual horniness.

Now what was she supposed to do? She didn't actually *want* to study. But if Maxine reneged now, that would make *her* a coward—and that would be worse.

Teddy took a sip of his coffee, and her gaze snagged on the way his long fingers wrapped around the mug. *Strong hands for an academic type.* She wondered what they'd feel like cupping her jaw instead of that mug, his thumbs pressing into the softness under her chin as he tilted her head back.

Maybe this studying thing wouldn't be so bad, after all.

Are you ready to learn? he'd murmur, sliding into her with a powerful thrust—

"First rule," he continued, oblivious to the filthy acts she'd been imagining them committing on the breakfast table, "I want your full commitment to my tutelage."

"Oh, I'm committed."

"I'm quite serious, Maxine. I refuse to waste my time if you won't put forth earnest effort to study and learn."

"Do you have to abide by these rules too? Because I'm not going to waste my time taking you on life-or-death excursions if you're going to bitch out."

He set down his pencil and gave her a stern look. "I'll try to commit to your instruction in good faith, but I don't agree to anything involving risk of death. Need I remind you we're training for a game show?"

Maxine gleefully chomped into her toast. "Everything involves a risk of death. Life's the most dangerous game show there is."

"*Two*," Teddy emphasized with a warning glare. "Since this is not a sleepaway camp, I expect you to contribute to the care and maintenance of this household during your stay, to my level of satisfaction, which includes meals, laundry, and the occasional errand."

"What, do you think because I grew up poor that I live in squalor?"

Teddy glanced behind himself at the counter, where she'd left out the butter with the knife sticking straight up from its center, the jam with its lid off, the bag of sugar unfurled, and two cabinets swung wide open. The empty coffeepot was still on, and she hadn't closed the refrigerator door all the way. Without a word, he reached over to nudge the fridge shut.

Right. "I was going to clean that stuff up afterward. Cut me some slack. I don't take my ADHD meds until after breakfast."

He considered this for a moment. "Fine. I'll handle breakfast, and this rule won't apply until midmorning."

She stifled a flutter of pleasant surprise. No one besides Olive had ever been that chill about the trail of disruption she sometimes left in her wake. It made her want to offer something of equal value. "When I head up to grab my stuff and my snake later today, I'll bring you some really good scotch from my collection. Maybe a couple of my sexy butt paintings, too, to replace all the pictures of the old dead people in the stairway."

"Sorry, what's this about a snake?"

"She's really quiet, you won't even notice her." Before he could issue follow-up questions, she asked, "What's rule number three? No coming into your bedroom at night and smothering you in your sleep? Because I feel like for the sake of the sacred sport of trivia, we should really set aside our vicious loathing for each other and try to, like, get along."

"No fraternization. That includes kissing or . . . other emotional distractions."

Sure, buddy . . . we'll see how long those virtuous intentions last. Maxine nodded with the expected amount of gravity. "So murder's still on the table?"

He gave her a disapproving look. "Murder is still a felony in the United States, so no. No felonies, misdemeanors, or other nefarious mischief."

"Whoa, hold on now." Maxine swirled her fork tines at him. "You're ruling out a lot of fun stuff with that addendum."

"We are preparing for a high-level crucible of skill, speed, and knowledge. Our opponents are likely doing the same as we speak, so we can't afford to waste a single minute. *Fun* isn't our priority."

"See, now that's where you're wrong. I can't learn if I'm not having fun." She tapped her fork on her forehead. "A girl needs her dopamine."

Teddy wordlessly handed her a napkin to wipe the bits of egg off her forehead.

"Thanks," she mumbled.

He got up to take their empty plates to the sink. As he washed and dried them, he told her, "There's no time to waste. As soon as you return from collecting your essentials—and I do mean *essentials*, Ms. Hart, you are not moving in permanently—we are going to the library to assess the gaps in your knowledge and check out appropriate reference materials."

Maxine made a face. Her brief childhood experience with libraries was that they smelled like old paper and older buildings, and you *definitely* weren't allowed to have fun inside them. "I can't wait to tell you about this amazing invention called the internet. You can get everything on there! Books, maps, hand-drawn pornography of Princess Kitana pegging Goro . . . you name it, they got it."

Teddy's brow furrowed. "I thought I'd memorized all the royal families of the world, but I can't recall from where Princess Kitana hails."

"Edenia."

"Where—" Realization dawned. Teddy gave an exasperated huff. "She's fictional. Of course. Tell me, is there anything you take seriously?"

Maxine plunked her coffee cup down in affront. "I take *Mortal Kombat* very seriously. I'm ranked eighty-seventh in the world in online play. And you know damn well that pop culture categories come up all the time on *Answers!*, so don't act like this is somehow less valuable information than the middle names of all forty-six US presidents."

Teddy pinched a hand to his brows and muttered something under his breath.

"What did I get wrong now?"

"It's . . . twenty-nine. There are seventeen presidents without middle names. The practice of assigning them didn't become popular until the early 1800s."

"Oh." Maxine beamed at him as she brought him her coffee cup to wash. "Thanks."

He warily took her cup. "You're not upset I corrected you?"

"I'd be upset if you didn't. I like knowing things. I just prefer knowing the boring things in bite-size pieces. If you asked me to *list* all the presidents without middle names, then I'd be upset."

She did not like the way his face lit up at that suggestion, so she scurried out of the kitchen before he could inflict this or any other tedious punishment upon her.

When she passed his open study door, her brain flashed back to a vivid memory of dry humping Teddy's lap while he went hard enough on second base that she'd been about to award him the Commissioner's Trophy in the Titty-Sucking World Series.

. . . and then he'd walked out in the third inning.

Her hopeful mood faltered. She slunk upstairs and closed herself in the hallway bathroom. Then she leaned forward and fixed her reflection with a grim stare, letting her devil-may-care mask fall so she could be real with herself for a hot second.

Pitching her voice low, she asked the mirror, "You sure this is a good idea?"

The wide-eyed girl staring back at Maxine with frizzy hair and day-old mascara smudged below her eyes looked a lot like the anxious kid who'd been kicked out of class more times than she could count. The teen whose once-loving mom had gotten so addicted to gambling that she'd been more interested in slot machines than her own daughters. The adult who'd been ghosted at the three-month mark so many times she'd started marking the calendar so she'd know when to expect it.

Sure, combining forces with Teddy *was* probably their only chance of beating smarmy Hercules McKnight.

It was also a really fast way to get her feelings hurt, and Maxine had a lot of feelings. Injuries to them took a long time to heal. What if getting down and dirty with Teddy made her catch the romance flu (despite the fact that he was her sworn foe and possibly the most aggressively boring man alive), and then he pushed her away again?

She'd always had a particularly hard time not getting sex and emotion mixed up. It didn't help that her brain just didn't compartmentalize well, which made for excellent lateral thinking and creativity but shit-poor ability to stay unaffected by upsetting things. And the idea of Teddy rejecting her was definitely upsetting, for reasons that didn't fully make sense to her since she wasn't even sure she *liked* Teddy.

But Maxine was smart. She already knew the answer to her problem.

This is how Maxine wins $2 million without getting her heart broken—what is, "Don't sleep with Theodore Ferguson?"

"Easy enough," Maxine said aloud. "You can resist the urge to bang Teddy into next Tuesday. You're fucking amazing, and don't you forget it!"

The woman in the mirror beamed back.

What? It wasn't lying to herself—it was *believing* in herself. Just because she impulsively gave into temptation all the time didn't mean that this time couldn't be different!

Chapter 13

TAKE A LOOK, IT'S IN A BOOK

Answer

On *RuPaul's Drag Race*, contestants are encouraged to "get out [their] library cards" and participate in this event involving incisive criticisms of one another.

Question

What is the Reading Challenge?

Maxine had a lot of essentials. She had so much stuff that she'd had to rent a U-Haul to drive it down, which had initially been a pain in the ass but totally paid off when she saw the expression on Teddy's face as she pulled into his driveway with the truck.

But Teddy didn't protest. Nor did he help her unload all her worldly possessions. Instead, he'd ushered her straight from the truck to the passenger seat of his car, droning on about the library closing early for some uninteresting reason, and she'd decided to humor him. Partly because the concept of rentable books seemed to bring Teddy unimaginable joy, but mostly because Maxine didn't technically have anything better to do.

It didn't take long for Maxine to regret her decision.

For one, Maxine hadn't eaten since breakfast, so she was hungry, and hunger made her feisty. And then they pulled up to a stately, humongous building that screamed "Rich People Only," and Maxine was reminded that she and libraries had a longstanding feud. In fact, she was banned from the Brooklyn Public Library for life after she'd been caught ripping out pages from the Fear Street book series (ages thirteen and up) and selling them for a penny each to the other delinquent under-thirteeners at school.

"So let me get this straight," Maxine said to Teddy as he led her through the doors. "You won over 2.5 million bucks in regular-season play, and then another half mil in the tournament, plus a professor's salary of what, another buck fifty?"

"Two ten," he said under his breath.

She whistled. "I don't even want to know what they're charging these kids for tuition. They throw in a few firstborns for your Christmas bonus, or do they save those to sacrifice on Parents' Weekend?"

He glanced around the lobby. "Can you be a bit quieter, please? This is a library."

"Right, so you have all this money, plus your grand Ferguson trust fund of gobs of inherited colonial wealth in the form of silver tureens and blood diamonds or whatever. And you drive a—"

"Will you lower your—"

She whisper-shouted, "*Nissan Leaf*!"

"I selected my vehicle for economy, not to impress you."

Teddy flashed his ID badge at reception, where he was not only recognized but greeted like a national celebrity. Which, technically, he was. Maxine, who had taken to traveling incognito in giant round shades and a scarf over her hair, was given a few questioning looks but certainly not the fond *squee*ing that Teddy garnered from the Princeton library demo.

Maxine took off her sunglasses as they entered a cavernous double-story room with sweepingly tall windows, wood floors and lots of wood bookshelves, paintings of bewigged dead guys in gilded frames, and a healthy scattering of serious students with serious notebooks. Even the air in the room felt serious. Maxine fought the urge to yawn as Teddy guided her to a nonfiction section and withdrew a notepad from his breast pocket.

"We'll start at the top and work our way down," he told her matter-of-factly, as if she were supposed to know what the hell that meant. "Philosophy?"

Maxine thought for a moment. "I'd say a toss-up between 'Get busy living or get busy dying' and 'Be excellent to each other.'"

He sighed. "I meant, how familiar are you with classical schools of philosophy?"

"And I answered you. *The Shawshank Redemption* is an exploration of Sartre's existentialism and Plato's cave analogy, and *Bill & Ted's Excellent Adventure* is all about stoicism. I mean, Socrates is literally *in* the movie. Do you know what movies are? There's these guys called the Lumière brothers—"

"I know what movies are. I simply lack time to watch them. To study for *Answers!*, I read plot summaries of the American Film Institute's top one hundred movies of all time." Teddy crossed out "philosophy" on his notepad and walked down two aisles. "Next. Religion?"

"Jewish by birth, agnostic by practice."

"I wasn't aware one could actively practice agnosticism."

"Sure you can. You just take the MTA every day. Some days, you accidentally sit in pee and you're like, 'Maybe there is no God,' and other days you're like, 'Please maybe-God, let this train come before I piss myself.'"

Teddy looked like he was about to do some praying of his own. "I need to know if this is a topic we should cover. The answer I'm looking for is, yes or no. Particularly as it pertains to the Bible, both Old and New Testaments, which are the subjects covered most frequently in the show."

"Oh yeah, we're rock solid. When I was a kid, I had this Bible-themed coloring book a nice casino security guard gave me. I used it to keep track of my mom's slot machine bets so I could calculate the payout percentage for each machine."

Teddy blinked down at his notepad, nonplussed, and crossed out "religion." He also wrote: "OK on probability math."

"What about you," she asked. "This date's starting to feel a little one sided. You a God-fearin' man, Cardinal Ferg-elieu?"

"This is not a date," he muttered absently, scribbling another note: "OK on 17th century French history."

Joke's on him, I learned that from The Three Musketeers. *Tim Curry can get it.* Although, she was pretty solid on history clues. She'd played a lot of the *Sid Meier's Civilization* computer games, in which one rewrote the history of a world empire from rise to fall while learning about its real culture, ancient wonders, and history along the way. Maxine was fond of playing as the Aztec Empire because she liked going to war with other countries just for funsies. First rule of *Civ*: either play as Montezuma, or get dicked over by Montezuma. (Second rule: do *not* let Gandhi get nukes.) Although she'd probably be more familiar with non-capital-city names if she didn't rename all the simulated ones she captured things like "Bootyville" and "Jugopolis."

"Thirty-six games," Teddy said, shaking his head. "Without a trace of preparation. How?"

She shrugged. "You'd be amazed how much you can learn when you're not paying attention to what you're supposed to be doing."

Her stomach grumbled, so she pulled the foil-wrapped bagel sandwich she'd gotten at the bodega earlier out of her coat pocket. When she unwrapped it, a piece of bacon slid out. She caught it before it landed on the carpet.

Teddy's eyes widened. With a hand at the small of her back, he ushered her down the nearest aisle. "There's no eating in here. You're going to get us thrown out. Give it to me, please."

"But I'm hungry," she said, snarfing the biggest bite she could before handing it over. He rewrapped it—along with her stray bacon slice—and tucked it back in her coat pocket. Around her bite she mumbled, "I didn't have time to eat lunch before you dragged me here, and my brain needs food to study."

"We haven't even begun studying!"

A student passing by their aisle glanced at them curiously before moving on. Maxine gave Teddy a smug look. "Lower your voice. This is a library."

A handkerchief materialized from his pocket, and he thrust it at her. "I won't have you getting grease on hundred-year-old books."

"Uh, I'm not a subway rat. I did have napkins in my pocket." She wiped her hands and then held up the square of linen he'd given her, admiring the monogram. "Is this the Ferguson sigil? Cute. I'm definitely keeping this to jerk off on."

Teddy briefly closed his eyes. "That is the noble Ferguson coat of arms, yes."

"Look, there's even a little owl, to symbolize that all your ancestors are giant nerds too. Which is ironic because did you know owls are actually the himbos of the raptor world? I had a torrid affair with a chick who works the eagle exhibit at the Bronx Zoo. She said owls are apex predators, so they don't actually need intelligence to survive, which is why you almost never see a trained owl. It's like trying to train a panda. There's just not enough gray matter per metric ounce of snuggle."

"Metric ounce," he repeated flatly.

"It's a metaphorical weight. You don't have to take systems of measurement literally, my dude. Live a little." She tugged the notepad from his hand. "Can we get this over with? What's next . . . social science? Check. Language—that's for you. Maybe we can pick up some *French for Bébé* books, hmm?"

"I'll reiterate I only missed that one question."

"Il n'y a pas de fumée sans feu." Maxine held up the list and scanned down to the bottom. "Science, math, tech, art, literature—yup, we're all good on everything here."

"The 900s include geography."

"I said we're good, as in 'I don't feel like memorizing a bunch of river names.'"

"I'll remind you that *you* propositioned *me* to teach you 'a bunch of river names.' Fortunately, I have a more complete selection of atlases in my home library than they do here," he said, looking obnoxiously proud of that fact.

"I'm stunningly aroused. Does that work on all the ladies?"

"Several of them are in rare large-format editions. So yes, if you must know, it works wonders with women who have discerning taste in geographical reference material."

"Oooh . . . who doesn't love a big, *big* book."

"Will you *please* keep your voice down."

Maxine moaned girlishly. "Yes, Professor, show me your promontory landform!"

Teddy prayed his hands in front of his face and huffed a breath. "I'm allowing this because of the correct use of *promontory*, but we need to have a word."

Then he led her, by a hand at the small of her back, to the corner at the very end of the aisle. Partially hidden from view behind a structural column was a forgotten alcove where the card catalog was stowed in well-worn teak cabinets. The alcove's overhead light bulb was out—since clearly all the tuition money went to funding their geography professors' topographical pornography collections—leaving the alcove lit by only gray afternoon light streaming in from the nearby window, which made dust motes look like silver glitter.

Maxine was delighted about her upcoming scolding. This had to be a record. Normally, it took more than fifteen minutes to completely break a man's spirit. Either she was exceptionally on point today, or Maxine's fated life's purpose was to destroy Theodore Ferguson III's will to live. Either way, she couldn't wait to get out of this library. They'd agreed on the car ride over that Maxine got to call the shots tomorrow, and she was already plotting their field trip.

Teddy steered her into the alcove, and Maxine took the opportunity to lean against the wall and stretch her arms into a full-body yawn. "Boy, did I not sleep well last night. How about you? Ooh, let me guess. Up all night, masturbating to your framed Oxford diploma."

And then, he surprised her.

He stepped forward, boxing her in against the wall, and planted his hands on either side of her head. After a furtive glance to make sure no one was around to see, he leaned forward so their faces were inches apart. In a low voice, he said, "What are you doing, Maxine?"

She blinked up at him as her body automatically switched gears. "Are we having a clandestine make-out sesh? Because I'm suddenly very on board with libraries."

"You're deliberately antagonizing me. Again."

Disappointment cooled her ardor. *Probably for the best—you're supposed to be* resisting *temptation, remember?* That probably didn't entail letting Teddy catalog her ass in the stacks. "The word *deliberate* is generous. It's not like I have to try very hard."

"Do you want me to help you train, or not? Because we can leave anytime you like. You're free to go."

She looked away, suddenly self-conscious. It wasn't a feeling Maxine experienced often. "I mean, we probably *should* train together. But the truth is, I don't think I have the patience for this boring studying stuff. I just want the results."

Teddy pulled away with a sigh, and Maxine felt a pang of loss at the departure.

He was giving up on her so easily, huh? It was silly to feel hurt by that, since she'd provoked this outcome. But inside her there was a hyperactive, troublemaking carrottop kid who'd had every other teacher in her life give up on her too.

She didn't hold it against them; there was only so much you could do with public school money, time, and class sizes. And resources for handling neurodivergent kids—especially girls, who often expressed ADHD differently from boys—had been basically nonexistent back then. It didn't help that Maxine had always been stubborn as hell, and you know what they say about horses and water.

But after a moment of thought, Teddy surprised her with a French idiom of his own. "Vouloir, c'est pouvoir." *To want to is to be able to.*

It was kind of sweet that Teddy thought he could turn her into a good student with elbow grease and a positive attitude. Still, her heart sank. "Unfortunately, inspirational 'you can do it' mantras don't work on me. It's not a lack of willpower that's the problem. Do you have any idea how much I wish that I could win two million bucks by simply . . . *trying harder*? You think if I get really psyched up about this, we'll collect stacks of reference books, raw-dog facts like we're automatons, and it'll all magically stick in my head? Because pro tip—and this is going to save us both a lot of time here—it won't work."

Then, to Maxine's utter horror, a lump formed in her throat. *Oh nooooo . . .*

It was too late. Tears welled, and Maxine smacked a hand over her eyes to hide them. "Don't look at me! I'm fine! I'm just cranky and hungry, and I don't want to be here anymore."

Teddy handled this outburst with preternatural calm. Without a word, he tucked another handkerchief into her free hand and then slid an arm around her shoulder, effectively angling them so his body blocked her from view. There was the sensation of rustling at her midsection, and when she uncovered her eyes, Teddy was holding her bagel out to her.

"Eat," he said.

Maxine blotted her tears and hesitantly took the bagel. "Really? We're not going to get kicked out and ruin your reputation on campus?"

Teddy's mouth twitched. "There is an entire wing here with my family's name on it."

Maxine greedily chomped into her bagel and gave a little groan of pleasure. "I'm suddenly pro-nepotism," she mumbled around her bite. She wanted to add that he didn't have to stand right there to shield her if there was no chance of getting in trouble, but she didn't. Maybe because eating a bagel in the crook of Teddy's arm was oddly comforting, and it was extremely rare that Maxine got to be the cared *for* one in a duo. She'd always been the capable one: the go-getter who wrote scripts to rehearse for child protective services, the innovator who figured out how to get dinner on the table when Mom had a crappy night at the craps table, the wise older sister who talked introverted Olive down from another social anxiety spiral. Yet only Maxine took care of Maxine.

When she was done eating, she took a deep breath and smiled. Everything was better with a bagel in her belly. "Thanks," she told Teddy, reluctantly extricating herself.

He nodded thoughtfully. "Perhaps it's best if we go home. I need to recalibrate my lesson plan, but I'm confident in my teaching abilities. I believe, with some research, I can determine a learning methodology that will work better for you."

"Bueno!" Maxine skipped in the direction of the exit, glancing over her shoulder at Teddy. "That means *good*."

She was starting to like the sound of his sighs.

Chapter 14

IT'S JUST A PHRASE

Answer

This hotfooted term that refers to someone subjected to a series of punishments has its origins in the old Scandinavian word *gatlopp*, whose literal translation is "street course."

Question

What is to run the gauntlet?

Teddy found Maxine on his living room couch the following morning, with the TV and video game console she'd brought softly glowing on a save screen. She'd fallen asleep with the controller still in her right hand and the other tucked under her cheek like a pillow. Wisps of coiled copper haloed her head, and in the early-morning light, as she looked barefaced and angelic in her sleep, it was hard to believe this woman was capable of making his life a living hell.

But she had.

After the library, she'd suggested an impromptu stop at a Target to collect items she deemed necessities, one of which was the board game Clue, and another was a six-pack of hideously fluffy socks. Then she requested another unplanned stop at the adjacent pet store for further necessities. And this led to a jaunt to a storied ramen shop that Maxine promised was "around the corner" but was actually forty minutes away in rush hour traffic. And by the time they came home with their cooling, gelled ramen takeaway, Maxine remembered she still had to return the U-Haul. Throughout all this, Teddy was an unwilling chauffeur, and with each passing moment he became more aware of studying that was not getting done.

His regret further solidified when he became aware of the 120-gallon python enclosure she'd placed in his guest bedroom, the video game equipment she'd set up in his living room, and the green-and-chrome motorcycle she'd asked to move into the garage next to his *perfectly sensible* car.

Teddy softly stepped into the room and turned off the TV. When he backed away, he spied a fluffy orange tail protruding from under his coffee table, and crouching to peek below confirmed that Ginger Cat had spent the evening monitoring this suspicious intruder with the utmost vigilance.

When he glanced up again, Maxine's eyes were gazing at him, heavy lidded. "Morning."

Her tone was that languid, too-familiar voice of a satisfied woman waking up after a long night of lovemaking.

He suddenly felt awkward in his own home. Standing, he replied stiffly, "Good morning."

It was an odd experience having Maxine in his home. He'd had several brief affairs in the aftermath of his *Answers!* fame, but the last time he'd had a proper relationship, he'd been twenty-six and embarking on his PhD at Oxford, and Agnieszka had been thirty-two. When she'd finished her doctorate two years later, they'd cooperatively dissolved their romantic union and remained friends to this day.

But he'd never *lived* with Agnieszka.

She'd never shown up one day with all her belongings (because surely, Maxine couldn't have more than this) and infiltrated his quiet, orderly life in the space of twenty-four hours.

Strange that he couldn't summon more than halfhearted indignation about it all.

Maxine pushed back the blanket she'd draped over herself, revealing long, pale-white legs beneath the overlarge shirt she wore, and said, "Are you stoked about running the Takahashi Gauntlet today?"

Teddy focused very hard on the wainscoting around his ceiling fan. "I don't know what that is, but the absolutely demonic tone in which you've presented it makes me certain the answer is no."

"Oh, this is going to be fun."

They arrived at a nondescript, brick-faced walk-up in Crown Heights. Graffiti tagged the beaten-up door, and they had to step over a pool of stagnant drainage water to get to the doorstep.

"It's a shame what happened to this place," Maxine said, buzzing the call panel. "This used to be a nice neighborhood, but look at how they massacred my boy! Now there's a fuckin' gelato shop on the street corner and an organic grocery across the way. You have any idea what they're charging for a pack of gum over there? It's a crime."

Teddy cast a look behind himself at his car, hoping it would still be there when they returned. Regret gnawed at him. He was certain that nothing Maxine had planned for them today would be as useful as a day spent in rigorous study, and that this foolhardy quest was going to cost him a perfectly acceptable electric vehicle that was absolutely no reflection of his character other than that he was both an environmental and financial conservationist.

They were buzzed in, and Maxine led Teddy up narrow, creaky stairs to the third floor. A tall olive-skinned man with a rather punk rock look about him waited for them in the open doorway.

"Hey, Winston," Maxine greeted him cheerily. "Teddy, this is my old pal, Winston Takahashi. He's kind of the go-to in this neighborhood for all your, ah . . . statistical needs."

Winston nodded at Maxine, then eyed Teddy. His face stretched into a pained smile before Maxine said, "Oh, you don't have to be polite with him. He's one of us."

"One of what?" Teddy asked.

"You know." Maxine winked at him. "A nerd."

Winston's face wiped clean, and his posture relaxed. "Theodore Ferguson III. You have a batting average of 0.94, first in on buzzer 0.59 percent of attempts, average take of $32,200, and average wager on Daily Duplex clues of $2,840."

Maxine winced at the last figure. "Oof."

The other man held out his hand. "Payment up front."

Teddy's foreboding grew as Maxine pulled a thick envelope out of her coat pocket and handed it over. She'd refused to tell him what this was about on the car ride over, and this entire operation reeked of Maxine's particular brand of trouble.

"This isn't one of the life-or-death excursions, is it?" he said in a low voice as Winston led them down a hallway, past a large office with several blinking computers and televisions, and a whiteboard covered in what looked like sports game odds. At the end of the hall was a dark room with a familiar three-podium setup and an even larger screen.

"No, I thought I'd ease you into the *death* part." Maxine skipped over to one of the podiums and immediately set to work on drawing her name on the touch pad.

"Brilliant. My favorite way to expire is with ease." Teddy took the podium next to Maxine's.

"We'll start by determining a baseline," Winston told them. There was a computer desk with a three-monitor display against the far wall where blackout curtains hid a window, and Winston took a seat. "Then we'll run the Gauntlet until your time is up. I also coded the player-three AI to match Hercules's profile."

When he queued up a facsimile of the *Answers!* title display on the wall screen, Teddy realized where he'd seen this before. "This is your program. You're the McKnight student who coded the simulation that Hercules showed us at his gathering on Friday."

Winston spun abruptly in his desk chair. "Wrong. Hercules stole my code. I entered this program in a science fair my senior year. I received fourth place. After MIT, I went to venture capitalists to raise investment money to turn the Gauntlet into a commercial training product, only to be told they'd already seen a nearly identical version from Mr. McKnight himself. They accused me of stealing it from him." This was all stated matter-of-factly, without the kind of anger that Teddy would expect.

It certainly made Teddy angry. He knew what it felt like to be accused of cheating when he was the one who hadn't done anything wrong.

Maxine assured Winston, "We're gonna chop his nuts off." Before Teddy could protest, she added, "Figuratively. With *trivia*. Don't look at me like that! I'm not feral."

Teddy gave her what he hoped was a glance that read, *I will not go to jail for physically assaulting a fellow* Answers! *contestant.*

If what Winston said was true, it definitely cast Hercules in a poor light. But Teddy struggled to reconcile this knowledge with his childhood idolization of the man who'd inspired his own obsession with trivia. Either way, Teddy wasn't sure there would ever be a scenario where he'd resort to an act of violence against Hercules McKnight.

Winston went on, "Hercules doesn't have this version of the Gauntlet, though. I've been working on this in my spare time for the past ten years, and I believe this is not only the most accurate way to assess a player's skill and track their progress, but also the most effective buzzer-training tool available."

Teddy raised a brow. "That's quite a claim."

"It worked for me," Maxine surprised him by saying.

"I thought you hadn't trained for *Answers!* at all. You told me this repeatedly, with great pride."

"No," Maxine said with a sly smile, "I said I hadn't *studied* for *Answers!* Knowing the answer is only half the battle, you know. I just focused on the other 50 percent."

Teddy squared his shoulders, resigned to getting this farce over with. "How is this game designed?"

Winston pulled up a starry screen with the image of a tall medieval tower floating in the center. He zoomed in, showing three square icons: headshots of himself, Maxine, and Hercules from the official *Answers!* website. "The Gauntlet is a progressive thirty-level tower tournament, where the answers get more difficult with each level you ascend. If Maxine or the AI Hercules buzzes in before you, you lose. If you get the clue incorrect, you lose."

Teddy raised a brow. "That's absurd. That requires I beat both my opponents to the buzzer on every clue, which as you stated earlier, I only accomplished 59 percent of the time during regular gameplay. And unlike in a real game, both Maxine and Hercules will be attempting to ring in every time. That means my odds of beating them both to the buzzer thirty times in a row are approximately—"

"One in 25,000," Winston said.

"And that doesn't even account for answering all thirty questions correctly! This is impossible."

Maxine held up a finger. "It's improbable, not impossible. Big difference. It's only slightly more unlikely than getting struck by lightning, and your odds of that happening are about 1 in 15,300, by the way. Higher, if you're standing on an Atlantic City beach during a thunderstorm."

"Is this meant to be reassuring?"

Winston nodded. "The Gauntlet is intentionally designed to be challenging. Only one player has ever beaten it."

Winston cued up a leaderboard screen.

LEVEL	HANDLE
30	MAXDEATH!!!!
22	taka_khan
18	*doclightning*
17	msmurrayXOXO

Maxine looked positively infernal with glee. She clicked the buzzer at him in a way that made it look threatening. "Come for the queen, you best not miss. Hit it, Winston."

"This program is impossible to beat," Teddy snapped.

"Yeah, maybe with that attitude." Maxine gestured to her name at the top of the rankings, which were still on the screen. "I did it because I believed I could."

There was a difference between optimism and delusion that Maxine didn't seem to grasp. "I *believe* that if one runs the Gauntlet enough times, one might beat it. As with all statistical probabilities, everything that can happen will, eventually, happen *if* given enough time. Which we do not have."

"Actually, that's a rephrasing of Murphy's Law, which isn't true at all."

"Am I to understand you're an expert statistician now?"

Maxine shrugged. "After my mom died in a way that some would say was the holy grail of bad luck, I spent a lot of time trying to make sense of the universe. How do some people get so unlucky? I looked into religion, philosophy, poetry, the full Britney Spears discography . . . I mean, shit got real dark. But math was the light that made everything clear. Because what's luck except probability in action?"

"Explain."

"Quantum theory tells us that, yes, all nonzero probabilities will eventually occur, given infinite time. But there are two problems with that: first, probability is subjective, since we determine probability based on prior data, so we're perceiving the universe through the lens of our human experience on this particular timeline. Because problem number two is that time isn't infinite, at least not for *us*. We'll only experience the things that *do* happen in this timeline."

Teddy rubbed his forehead. "So, your argument is that maybe everything that can happen will happen, but it will happen in other quantum multiverses."

"I mean, I didn't come up with the idea. The first guy who talked about infinite universes was probably the ancient Greek philosopher Chrysippus."

"But in essence, if I have a 1 in 25,000 chance of beating the Gauntlet, I won't necessarily beat the Gauntlet by merely playing 25,000 times."

"Exactly. Each time you play is an independent instance, which means probability doesn't stack. You toss a coin ten times, your odds of it coming up heads on the tenth flip are still one in two, even if it comes up tails the first nine times. There might be a universe out there where a version of you tosses the same coin and it comes up heads ten times in a row, but that doesn't help you in *this* universe."

Teddy mulled this frustrating tidbit until a solution came to him. "What if I were to practice tossing the coin enough times, perhaps adjusting how I throw the coin . . . ?"

"Bingo! That's what I've been trying to tell you this whole time. You can't wait out probability; you have to act on it to change it."

He scowled. "Cheating, you mean."

"Cheating, training . . . what's the difference?"

He opened his mouth to precisely and thoroughly illuminate said differences when she held up a finger and said, "Shh. That was rhetorical. The answer is that *cheating* is against the rules, and *adjusting the odds* isn't. Sure, it's frowned upon, but you better believe the best players in every game are doing it."

"I'd rather win the tournament through a fair challenge of knowledge."

"Yeah, well, *Answers!* isn't your pristine ivory tower, it's a game show—although I think calling traditional academia *fair* is laughable, since women and people of color weren't allowed to attend college in most of the Western world until the twentieth century," Maxine replied bitterly. "The point is, in an 'honest' environment, the house always wins. That's why card counting isn't illegal, but it will get you thrown out if you're caught."

Her words sank in, and Teddy groaned as the logic of her reasoning did a victory dance over his moral superiority. "So . . . if you choose to gamble against unfair odds, either prepare to lose, or adjust the odds in your favor through whatever means you have available?"

The way she beamed at him soothed the sting of defeat—slightly. "Yup! Running the Gauntlet doesn't guarantee you'll be able to beat Hercules, but it makes it more likely in *this* universe. After that . . . it's all about luck, baby."

As Winston began a ten-second countdown clock on the leaderboard screen, lead settled in Teddy's gut as it dawned on him that Maxine wasn't the only competitor who'd trained on the Gauntlet. So had Zhang Wei and Ryan Murray.

What had first seemed like a pointless exercise now seemed integral to winning.

Five . . . four . . . three . . .

"Don't worry, I supplied Winston with a list of your weakest categories."

"How did you—"

"Know thine enemy," she chirped.

The countdown zeroed out, and the first clue appeared on the screen. Teddy could feel his heart pounding.

And then Dr. Love's voice came over the speakerphones—or what must have been an AI-generated imitation of it.

This word's first-known usage has been attributed to Shakespeare, who was likely inspired by the Latin word for "reptile."

The instant the screen's perimeter lighting turned green, Teddy rang in. When his podium lit up, signaling he'd won the buzzer race, he answered, "What is alligator?"

A triumphant sound effect played. *Correct,* came AI Loretta's voice.

Teddy shot Maxine a disapproving look. "Very mature."

She grinned, dancing from foot to foot like a boxer. "That was a warm-up. Just to make sure you didn't forget."

The countdown chimed. Ding!

The Italian version of the French word for "to slide," this musical direction instructs the performer to run one's fingers over piano keys, for example.

Teddy claimed first in again. "What is glissando?"

Correct.

"Are these all clues about romance languages?" he asked Maxine.

"Wouldn't that be hilarious?"

"No." Teddy's palms had begun to sweat.

Ding! *This hockey team plays in Madison Square Garden.*

First in, again. Teddy: "Who are the Rangers?"

Maxine clapped politely around her buzzer. "Proud of you!"

Teddy stifled a look that might be interpreted as cocky and said modestly, "I live in New Jersey. I'd be remiss if I didn't know that answer."

"I know," she said gaily. "Winston, that's enough of the softballs. I think he gets the gist."

Winston tapped his keyboard, and an animation of what appeared to be a sheet of red blood slid down the screen, and the words "BEGIN THE GAUNTLET" coalesced. There was a sound effect of a woman's bloodcurdling scream, and then the words melted away.

"Do you like that?" Maxine asked. "That was my idea!"

"Very gruesome."

"Thank you! Now buckle up, buttercup, because it's go time." Maxine shifted, her chin lowering and her body sliding into a stance he recognized well. Her knees slightly bent, signaling device loosely clutched in one hand in front of her, the opposite hand holding her wrist in place. It was the position Hercules himself had used during his run, and many home-brewed *Answers!* analysts had determined that holding the buzzer hand down low increased blood flow to the appendage and reduced fatigue.

It was then Teddy realized with a sinking feeling that she hadn't been trying to ring in at all on the last three clues. She'd let him take the first three tower levels to build his confidence. As if he were a child.

Ding! *In 1891, Canadian James Naismith invented this game, which was first played with fruit baskets instead of nets.*

Teddy's thumb pummeled the buzzer for all it was worth, but it was Maxine's podium that lit up.

Immediately, there was a jarring *bzzzz!* sound effect and the screen went black. A somber tune played as the words "GAUNTLET FAILED" materialized on screen in the same sanguine font Maxine was undoubtedly responsible for.

"What is basketball?" Maxine chirped, replacing her buzzer daintily in its holster.

Winston cracked a smile for the first time since they'd arrived. "Your accuracy on that ring was 79.2. Been playing a lot of *MK11* to train those reflexes, huh?"

She fluttered her eyelashes at Teddy, even as she replied to Winston, "Every night. I finally got the lime-green reptile-print outfit!"

Teddy resisted the urge to slam his signaling device down in frustration. He was better than that—his father had taught him that a gentleman never lost his temper. In his calmest voice, he asked, "What's this accuracy measure, and how is it derived, Mr. Takahashi?"

Winston pulled up another screen, which showed a linear scale with a solid-blue rectangle labeled "Buzzer Window" in the center of the scale. At the far left of the window, his cursor highlighted a sliver of green. "That's the ideal window to buzz in. Anything within the blue rectangle is still an acceptable target, but I calculate accuracy on your proximity to the ideal window."

With a flourish on his keyboard, a series of dots appeared along the timeline. Some of them were inside the box, but most were on the edge or outside it.

"Each dot represents a time you clicked the buzzer. You were too early on most of them, so you're getting locked out for that quarter of a second, just like in real *Answers!* gameplay. See Maxine's marker? She's almost entirely in the green."

Teddy gritted his teeth. Now that he knew his problem pertained to ringing in too early, he intended to fix it. "I'd like to play again."

Maxine looked disappointed in him. "You have to say, 'I want to run the Takahashi Gauntlet.' It's, like, a tradition."

"A tradition," Winston repeated somberly.

"I really don't see—"

"Say it!" Maxine commanded. "Show respect for the Gauntlet!"

They'd been here fifteen minutes, and Teddy was already on his last nerve. He inhaled deeply, then rushed out the ridiculous phrase: "I'd like to run the Takahashi Gauntlet."

"You forgot to add a *please* in there," Maxine said. "Fifteen generations of noble Fergusons, would you believe it? And not a one of them with any respect for the working class."

Winston narrowed his eyes at Teddy. "My dad sold popcorn at the horse track to put food on the table."

"Oh, this is absurd," Teddy scoffed. He certainly did *not* consider himself above the working class, and he usually prided himself on tipping a proper 20 percent, was unfailingly polite to staff, and never issued a single word of complaint about poorly rendered food products. He paid his cleaning service above market rate and shopped at small local businesses whenever possible. Was villainizing him absolutely necessary? Not all England's peerage diaspora were heartless colonizing twats.

Teddy had a brief flashback to his stint at Oxford and revised that thought. *Most of them are, in fact, heartless colonizing twats.* But Teddy was certain that *he* was not any of those things, and this so-called Gauntlet was enough of a humbling experience as it was.

Nevertheless, they continued to glare at him in unison until Teddy relented. "I'd like to run the Takahashi Gauntlet, *please*."

Winston nodded sternly, and the countdown began. "I'm activating the AI for player three," he said.

This time, Teddy was going to—

Ding! *Otherwise known as this, sea kraits are semiaquatic and venomous.*

Bzzzz! "GAUNTLET FAILED."

Maxine gave him a pitying look, the glow of her podium casting her in an ethereal light. "What are sea snakes?"

He opened his mouth to argue how unfair it was that there was a question about *snakes*, which gave Maxine a heavy advantage, but a glance at Winston's expression said this was not the time to complain to the judge.

"Again," Teddy said. "Please."

He was out of practice—that was all there was to it. But he'd refamiliarized himself with the rhythm now.

Ding! *This actor played Spike on* Buffy the Vampire Slayer.

Bzzzz! "GAUNTLET FAILED."

Maxine gasped with affront at the glowing, empty podium to Teddy's left, from where AI Hercules ostensibly played. "That golden shit stain beat me on the ring?"

A robotic voice answered, *Who is James Marsters?*

Maxine looked so derailed that Teddy couldn't even bring himself to feel smug about it. He said to Winston, "Again, please."

To his right, Maxine shook her head and bounced a little deeper into her stance, giving herself a pep talk at the same time. "Okay, you got sloppy. Head in the game, heart to the max. Head in the game—"

Ding! *This man-made creation is the third-brightest object in the night sky.*

Bzzzz! "GAUNTLET FAILED."

AI Hercules's podium piped up: *What is the International Space Station?*

Maxine released a screech of dismay, followed by a series of curses so vitriolic—yet so *creative*—that Teddy wasn't sure if he was alarmed or aroused.

Teddy reached out a tentative hand to touch her shoulder, unsure whether he'd ever see the limb again after Maxine was done with it. Her glare arrested his action midair.

"Again," she growled at Winston. It seemed she was exempt from having to say *please*.

Ding! *This band, which was inducted into the Rock & Roll Hall of Fame in 2009, is the only musical group to have played a concert on all seven continents.*

Bzzzz! "GAUNTLET FAILED."

AI Hercules: *Who is Metallica?*

"Maybe we should take a break," Teddy suggested, raising his voice to be heard over Maxine's banshee screech.

"Again!" she howled.

This time, Winston hesitated. He glanced at Teddy for confirmation.

Teddy briefly closed his eyes, recalibrating. For whatever reason, seeing Maxine spiral made his own pulse slow down, as if his nervous system unconsciously recognized her distress and switched over to an alternate mode in which he was the protector. Her savior. A purely Paleolithic part of his brain deciding, *Maxine mad? Teddy fix.*

He opened his eyes and nodded at Winston. "If you'd be so kind."

Ding! *This country's national orchestra, called the OPMC by locals, boasts more members than its national army.*

Ostensibly about music, this was a geography question at its core—and the initialism was a giveaway. His podium lit up. "What is Monaco?"

Correct.

The tower animation moved up to the second level, and Teddy felt Maxine's stunned gaze on him. He didn't look at her. He closed his eyes again, recentering himself. *Teddy fix.*

Ding! *The origins of this term, meaning something that is cherished above all, came from the theory that the pupil was a solid sphere.*

With his eyes still closed, he used the rhythm of false-Loretta's voice to cue his buzzer press. He blinked open his eyes and saw his podium lit up. "Who is the apple of my eye?"

He realized a fraction of a second late that he'd used the wrong interrogative pronoun, but it didn't technically matter per the *Answers!* rule book, as long as he'd answered in the form of any question at all. Still, it was an embarrassing slip.

His protobrain silently answered: *Maxine.*

Stealing a glance at the apple in question, he saw she was holding her signaling device loosely, staring at him wide eyed and pink cheeked. Had she not even attempted to ring in? Had she given up trying to teach him a lesson in deference to their combined goal of defeating Hercules?

If so, disappointing her was not an option. He set to work, and the world faded away. Even conscious thought ceased. Trivia was the universe. Trivia was all.

Ding! He didn't even remember hearing the question, but suddenly his podium glowed. "What is Sagittarius A?" he answered automatically.

Correct.

After that, it truly was a blur.

Ding! "What is *The Phantom of the Opera*?"

Ding! "Who is Jon Bon Jovi?"

Ding! "Where is Gotham City?"

Ding! "What is ricotta?"

Correct echoed in his head, part of the rhythm: Ding! *Question.* Answer. *Correct.*

Maxine whispered in an awestruck tone, "You're doing it, Peter."

Peter? Teddy shook himself. She'd never once called him Teddy, but she was usually in the approximate—

Ding! *This mammal was initially introduced to the Americas in the 1750s as a form of pest control for the rodents brought over on the same ships.*

Teddy knew before he heard the sound. He'd lost the rhythm.

Bzzzz! AI Hercules's computerized voice managed to sound smug as it intoned, *What are cats?*

Winston clicked over to the leaderboard screen, then scrolled down.

And down.

And down.

"Seven levels," Winston announced with a shrug, instructing Teddy to type in a desired name. "Not bad for your first session."

Maxine seemed to deflate with a long groan. "But not good enough to win. Not even close. And that's without me trying to ring in!"

Teddy couldn't decide if he was pleased or insulted to have been right about that. He typed in "TEDDY."

"Oh, come on. You can do better than that for a gamer handle, can't you?" Maxine asked.

Teddy leveled her with a cool look. "I thought it might help my fellow contestants learn how to pronounce my name correctly." He pointedly pressed the return key, solidifying his choice for all eternity. Below his breath, he added, "Not certain where *Peter* came from."

"It's a line from *Hook*, you absolute retrograde."

Heat flared in his cheeks; he'd been envious of a fictional Peter. How pitifully childish of him. He snapped, "Am I meant to be insulted by your nonsensical use of the English language?"

"It's called being creative! Do you understand what that means, or are you only capable of coloring inside the lines?"

"The lines are there for a reason!" Apple of his eye? What had he been *thinking*? Maxine wasn't an apple. She was a reprehensible fig—deceptively sweet, filled with dead wasps. "Is this how you plan to beat our shared opponent? Because I do feel our collective time would be better spent directing this abundance of unearned vitriol you have for me in Mr. McKnight's direction."

Winston cleared his throat. "So . . . do you want to play again?"

Maxine ignored him. "Don't worry, there's plenty of *vitriol* to go around. I stocked up at the bitch store the day you humiliated me on live television."

"I'd rather say you humiliated yourself, wagering everything you had on a Daily Duplex in a category you didn't know well."

"Fortune favors the—"

"But fortune didn't favor you! You lost!" His words sounded impossibly loud in the small room, and the hurt on Maxine's face made him want to swallow the words back up. He winced. "Sorry. That was . . . unnecessary."

Maxine's face smoothed, becoming unreadable. The distance between them, which had shrunk to the span between their podiums during the Gauntlet, became oceanic. She shrugged. "It's true, though. I did lose. Thank you for the reminder."

"You still have fifteen minutes left on the clock," Winston tried again.

Teddy was about to put Winston out of his misery and answer in the affirmative when Maxine said swiftly, "Keep the change. We got what we needed today."

As Winston showed them to the door, Teddy noticed that Maxine looked troubled. But not in the hot-tempered sort of way she'd looked earlier. This was a *detective-like* sort of consternation, which was—in Teddy's estimation—far more threatening.

"By the way," she asked Winston, just before he closed the door behind them, "did you program Hercules using his old metrics, or do you have updated ones?"

Winston cocked his head. "Hercules hasn't played a single game on record since 1993."

"*On record.* But he's kept your program updated with questions from current seasons for a reason. Someone that deep into trivia doesn't quit cold turkey. What about local pub quizzes? Online matches? There's got to be something."

"I'll look into it."

Teddy had no idea where any of this was going, but he didn't like the way Maxine nodded slowly.

Thoughtfully.

Conspiratorially.

"Maybe don't bet against us just yet," she said.

In an entirely serious tone, Winston replied, "I'd never bet against you, Maxine Hart."

Chapter 15

LYRICAL SPELLING BEE

Answer

This cover of an Otis Redding song became Aretha Franklin's first number one hit.

Question

What is "Respect"?

Maxine slid into the passenger seat of Teddy's car and willed the voice in her head to shut the hell up.

You'll never be good enough to beat Hercules.

Your Answers! *streak was a fluke.*

You're a high school dropout with no direction in life, and you'll never be able to focus on the road map long enough to find one.

She wasn't even sure whose voice it was that was so determined to tear her down. It couldn't be her own, because Maxine's inner self knew exactly how amazing, hot, and smart she was. It wasn't her mom's voice, because for all her faults, Mom had been the most optimistic person in the world. *Hold for the flop, Maxie. Anyone can win with a good hand, but the best players win with bad ones.* And it definitely wasn't Olive's voice, because her little sister had a soul as pure as virgin snow. The kid didn't even do drugs, for fuck's sake!

Maybe it was Teddy. Not his voice, but his presence. Maybe being around someone who was actually a challenge (in every respect of the word) was bad for Maxine's self-esteem, and she should skulk back to Brooklyn in the dark of night with her tail between her legs.

Teddy folded himself into the driver's seat with the elegance of a court prince settling in to a plastic takeout box. With him came his nice-smelling hair and his gorgeous cheekbones and his very intense blue eyes behind tortoiseshell glasses that had made more than one unwelcome sex-dream appearance. When he fixed her with a searching look, Maxine squirmed in her seat.

Answering pleasure shot through her in response.

Oh.

Heat of battle—that's all it was. And what with all that unresolved action in his study two nights ago . . . who could blame Maxine for being hot and bothered? Maybe tonight she could convince him to take the edge off the metaphorical knives they had at each other's throats—

Hold up. Not going there, remember? Besides, she was still bothered about what had just gone down at Winston's. And even though most of her frustration was directed at herself, Teddy was the catalyst. And his low blow about her loss was a coward's move. And cowards were street scum.

"I want pizza for dinner," she told him. "You're paying."

Teddy looked like he was going to say something, but he seemed to think better of it.

They drove to the pizza shop and back to his house, ate dinner, and retreated separately to their postdinner activities—all in a weighty silence that strained at the seams with things unsaid. Because beyond the hate-lust thing they had going on, the issue of what to do about Hercules was daunting. Nothing Teddy did over the next five weeks was going to matter if Herc was as fast on the buzzer as he had been in 1993—there was no way Teddy could beat the Gauntlet in so little time. And nothing Maxine did would matter if she couldn't get her emotions under control.

Much later that night, with her belly full of pizza and her mind wearing itself out in circles over the Hercules problem, Maxine tiptoed downstairs. The lights in Teddy's bedroom were off—*he's sobbing in the dark while masturbating to the paper clip demon from Microsoft Word, probably*—and she didn't want him to know she was so bothered about today that she couldn't sleep.

Worse, that she wanted to play video games until her hands went numb and her brain went silent. She'd spent almost a thousand hours on *Mortal Kombat* over the years, executing flawless Brutalities and twenty-chained punch combos and flying kicks that shattered vertebrae straight out of her opponents' flesh like piñata candy. Her quick-trigger skills were razor sharp—yet the minute her confidence had fled the scene, so, too, had her reflexes.

And she didn't know how to fix that.

How do I make you shut the hell up? Maxine demanded of her insecurity.

It didn't answer.

The living room was across the hall from Teddy's study, and Maxine was surprised to see him at his desk, lit only by the warm glow of his fireplace and the blue light of his computer monitor. He was still in his day clothes, but he'd unbuttoned his shirt collar and rolled up his sleeves. His hair fell forward into his face, like he'd run his hands through it a time too many. Her hands itched to smooth it back. Massage the creases from between his brows.

Maxine shoved her hands in her borrowed hoodie pockets, just in case. This thing was pretty comfortable, so she'd decided to continue borrowing it indefinitely. It had nothing to do with the fact it smelled like vetiver and lemongrass.

She thought about making her presence known, but whatever he was looking at on screen had his full attention. Maybe he was googling a sense of humor.

Silent as the night in her lime-green chenille socks on hardwood, she slipped into the living room and made to shut the french doors that closed it off from the rest of the house.

"Maxine?" Teddy called.

Rats. Maxine glanced around the room and saw that orange fur ball glaring at her from the sofa, where he'd clearly expected to spend the night undisturbed. "Nooo . . . it's me, the orange cat."

A pause (she imagined Teddy sighing in exasperation). Finally: "Why are you sneaking into my living room past midnight?"

"Illegal stuff!"

"We have a busy day of studying tomorrow," he warned her.

"Too late! I promised my drug dealer we'd do insider trading tonight. Want to join?" She hated that a part of her hoped he'd say yes.

"I'm very busy."

"Cool, I didn't mean it anyway. Bye!" She closed the doors and queued up her video game. Maybe smashing Johnny Cage in the balls would make her feel less hopeless about the tournament.

Orange Cat narrowed his eyes when she approached the couch.

"I'll feed you to my snake if you don't move," she warned him.

Hiss.

"Yeah, screw you too." Maxine squeezed into the narrow spot between the cat's back feet and side cushion, then handed Orange Cat her second controller. "No cheap shots, okay?"

"Wow, you look like shit," Maxine told Teddy when she came into the study for their morning training session. He'd set out coffee and a cereal bar for her in the kitchen with a note to meet him here as soon as she was ready. She'd taken one look at that bar's "lean fiber" aesthetic and decided she'd rather die of starvation.

"Your assessment has been noted. Have a seat."

He wasn't wearing last night's clothes, but his eyes were red, as if they'd been rubbed a time too many, and there was honest-to-god *stubble* on his face, which gave him an air of danger. A little edge on his prim and proper. In fact, Maxine decided, Theodore Ferguson made *looking like shit* wholly fuckable. A brief mental detour, starring Teddy's prickly facial hair grazing her thighs en route to Pusstopia, almost—*almost*—redeemed her mood.

Until she saw the blackboard.

Maxine flopped into the armchair he'd turned to face said blackboard and glared at him over the rim of her coffee mug. A tidy list of alphabetized river names taunted her from the board's expanse.

"Is this punishment for yesterday? Because for the record, I think you owe *me* an apology."

Teddy didn't even twitch at this direct provocation, which was how Maxine knew he must really be wiped. "Through exhaustive research on the matter, I have determined that you can, in fact, memorize lists of boring river names."

"I can also roll around in a pit of magma. Doesn't mean I'm going to have a good time. Doesn't mean I'm going to survive the experience." Maxine's rotten mood was ballooning into a defiant one at record speed. The very act of sitting in front of a blackboard was sending her barely awake psyche back in time to her miserable school days. Some mornings, her ADHD was worse than others—usually when she hadn't slept well or eaten well, or was feeling a lot of negative emotions—and Maxine could always count down the *minutes* to when she'd be sent to the vice principal's office for back-talking the teacher. Might as well get it over with so she wouldn't have to sit here a minute longer.

"It's only called magma if it's below the Earth's crust. If it's in an open-air pit, it's lava."

"Thank you for mansplaining magma to me."

"It's not mansplaining if it's something you don't know."

"Oh good, now you're mansplaining how mansplaining works."

He threw up his hands. "You said yesterday you liked to be corrected!"

She did. She had. "It's seven in the morning, you're making me look at a blackboard, and you tried to feed me a horse pellet for breakfast. What do you expect?"

Teddy calmly set the chalk down. This was it. This was the moment he gave up on her and told her to leave. *Three . . . two . . . one . . .*

"Fine. Get your coat on."

Her stomach sank. *Oh.* Had she secretly hoped he'd be different? So much for that fantasy.

Maxine stood with as much dignity as she could muster. "I didn't need you anyway. Now that I know how slow you are on the buzzer, I'm confident I can take you and Hercules on my own." She snatched her coat off the hallway hook and jammed her left foot into her left boot, then looked around in vain for the second one. She'd get all her stuff later . . . or something.

But Teddy only looked confused. "I'm not asking you to leave. We're going for a walk."

"We are? Why?"

He handed over her missing boot from where it had gotten lodged behind the umbrella stand and shrugged on his own overcoat. "Because you're right. I'm trying to force you to thrive in conditions that work for me because I enjoy the structure and security of an indoor classroom environment. But I did a lot of reading on ADHD last night, and I think I understand why that doesn't work for you. That's why we're going to try something different today. And also," he said, handing her an umbrella, "those cereal bars are terrible. I haven't had time to visit the grocery. There's a coffee shop a few blocks down with excellent pastries."

Her heart leaped. "Do they have almond croissants?"

The corner of his mouth quirked. "There's the Maxine I know and l—ah, respect." He held the door open for her, and she ducked under his arm. It was pouring again. She popped open her umbrella and eagerly set off—until he redirected her to walk the other way.

"You respect me?" she asked after they'd been walking for a minute in pleasant silence, with only the patter of the rain on their umbrellas for company. The fresh air was already making her feel worlds better.

At her question, his grip tightened on his umbrella handle. When he looked at her, his expression was one she hadn't seen before. It wasn't quite *dour*, but it definitely wasn't happy. Maxine had no idea what to make of it. "Maxine, I respect you more than anyone else on this planet. You're the only person who's ever bested me at the thing *I* do best. So, if I ever gave you the impression otherwise, I'm sorry."

"Oh." His expression was too intense. She felt her skin heating, so she focused on her blurry reflection in the wet pavement as they walked. "I figured you thought you were better than me. Because I don't study."

"But you do study. Didn't you tell me you're absorbing information all the time, like a sponge? That's still studying; it's simply . . . a different way of going about it. It's my own fault if I have a narrow view of what it means to learn. It's how I was raised and taught to perceive the value of academia. Until I met you, I never thought to question that belief system."

They stopped at a crosswalk to let a school bus go by, full of bright-eyed kids. Maxine always looked for the ones in the back—the troublemakers—the ones who wanted to be the last off the bus so they wouldn't have to face another school day of being inadequate.

"So you think you can teach someone who learns like me to memorize a bunch of river names today, huh?"

"Yes, I believe so." Teddy sounded confident and adorably eager. "Not only *can* you memorize these lists, but you will *enjoy* memorizing these lists."

Maxine side-eyed him. "Why do you think you can do in one afternoon what I haven't been able to do in thirty-three years?"

He held the door of the coffee shop open for her. "It's a secret. I'd tell you, but that would ruin the fun."

"A secret?" The magic word. Like a well-kissed Sleeping Beauty, Maxine was suddenly wide awake.

It's a trap! He's luring you in with intrigue, and the next thing you know, you'll be taking a standardized test! her inner cynic warned. But as Teddy asked the barista to load a to-go box with all the pastries Maxine wanted, his tone unfailingly polite and deferential and sounding nothing at all like the arrogant snob she'd accused him of being, she decided maybe—just this once—she might loan a man her trust.

"All right, you cocky sonuvabitch. I'm in."

Chapter 16

BUILT IN THE NAME OF LOVE

Answer

This UNESCO World Heritage Site was commissioned in 1631 by Mughal emperor Shah Jahan to honor his late wife, who'd died in childbirth earlier that year.

Question

What is the Taj Mahal?

On the way back from the coffee shop, the sky redoubled its efforts to drench them. He and Maxine shed their rain-damp layers in the entryway, then retreated to the study. He'd noticed Maxine clutching her coffee like it was the only thing warding off hypothermia, so he lit a fire, then glanced at his new student to ensure she hadn't run away yet. But Maxine was right there behind him, her cheeks reddened from the brisk walk in the chilly spring morning, her expression wary but curious.

"It's a lovely day for studying," he said brightly, gesturing to the drizzly gloom from which they'd recently returned.

"Or murder," she said darkly.

"Excellent work, Detective Hart. I was about to extol the parallels between intellectual enrichment and homicide, but you beat me to the punch."

Teddy was nervous. It was a feeling he recognized as the "first day of classes" jitters, when he'd stand at the front of an empty lecture hall in his best shirt and bow tie, his name tidily written on the whiteboard behind him, hoping students would show up. Hoping they'd all laugh at his rehearsed jokes and wouldn't drop his course after the first week.

Praying Maxine wouldn't judge his teaching skills, find him an abysmal failure, and abandon him to face Hercules without her help. He'd wanted that very outcome two days ago, but the Gauntlet had shown him how poorly he'd fare on his own. The truth was, he needed Maxine.

Need? Or want?

Best not to examine the feeling too closely.

"All right, let's get this over with," Maxine said, moving to sit in the armchair again.

He held out a hand to stop her. "This lesson is interactive. I'm going to give you a tour of my palace."

Her brows found new heights beneath her damp fringe. "Is this a sex thing? Because the last time someone offered me a tour of their palace, he was talking about his butthole."

"This is not my . . ." He was a grown adult; he could say the word. He would not let her distract him. ". . . butthole," he said.

"Mmm. Too bad." Maxine took a sip of her coffee, but her eyes crinkled at the edges in an all-too-pleased manner.

He went on, ignoring the flicker of heat she'd lit in his belly. "It's called a memory palace, and it's a metaphorical device that helps an individual retain long lists of information by visualizing the items you wish to learn on a three-dimensional map, and then imagining yourself walking through said map when you need to recall this information. Our brains are specifically wired to recall places we know well."

"I hate maps."

"But you do love using your imagination," he pointed out.

Maxine still looked skeptical, so he added, "Did you know, this was the technique Hannibal Lecter used to memorize the intricate details of his patients' records in the horror novel *Hannibal*? I think you mentioned in a contestant interview that that was one of your favorite movies, even though that particular detail was never translated to screen."

"Sold. Walk me through it."

"We're going to start here, in North America." He gestured all around. "You're standing in the middle of the room—in Kansas. But if you walk over here"—he strode to the far-left corner of the room, where the window looked out onto the front porch—"this is Alaska. This entire wall of bookshelves is Canada, this corner is Greenland, and then we come down to the East Coast—that's the fireplace—and my desk? Florida. We'll loop around to Mexico and Central America on this wall with the map, and then—"

Maxine pointed at the doors leading out to the entryway and said, "West Coast."

"Exactly! Excellent work."

Was it his imagination, or did Maxine stand up a little straighter at that comment?

Note to self: Maxine responds well to praise.

"Now what? Do I just visualize a bunch of rivers in this room? I hope you've got flood insurance."

He started to say no, then stopped himself. "If that works for you," he said with care. "But here, try this. Go stand by Alaska."

Maxine dutifully joined him at the window and peered out. "This gray weather is really setting the Alaskan mood. In fact, I think I see a grizzly bear. You ever gamble on Katmai National Park's Fat Bear Week? My big boy Otis was robbed this year."

Once again, Teddy caught himself before scolding her for getting distracted. The key with this exercise was to teach her to use her imagination to her benefit, not treat it like a detriment. "That's absolutely right, Ms. Hart. Bears like Otis enjoy fishing for salmon on the Naknek

River, which originates in Naknek Lake and flows out into Bristol Bay. But the Naknek is likely too small to be subject to a clue on a general trivia show like *Answers!*, so we'll move Otis farther north, to the most significant river in Alaska: the Yukon. So, if you look now"—Teddy internally winced at what he was about to say—"Yu-kon *see* Otis enjoying this river, which originates in British Columbia and empties into the Bering Sea."

Maxine set down her coffee and leveled him with a very serious look. "Theodore Ferguson . . . did you make a *pun*?"

"I did." He avoided her gaze by reaching up to tap the curtain rod over the window. "Now, let's discuss the longest river in Canada, the majestic Mackenzie, which we can represent with this long rod—"

He felt a tug on the front of his shirt, and when he looked down, Maxine looped her hands around the back of his neck to gaze up at him with a wondering expression. "Teddy, you made a *pun*. But you dislike wordplay of all kinds."

"Anything for the pursuit of geographical education," he murmured, entirely distracted by the fact her warm body was pressed against him.

In fact, her proximity was so disorienting that it took his brain several seconds to register she'd called him Teddy. Not Theodore. Not Professor Pudding or whatever other nonsense names she liked to bestow on him.

Teddy.

Kissing her was inevitable.

Her lashes fluttered shut as he cupped her cheek, running his thumb over her soft skin before his hand slid around to cup the back of her head. Her exhale tickled his chin, and he pressed his lips to hers, with all the slowness and intention that he'd lacked before. His brain was wide awake for this, fully conscious that kissing Maxine was exactly what he wanted to be doing in this instant.

Her lips tasted like the cream and sugar she'd doused her coffee with, and he wanted to savor her sweetness. Wanted to imprint the nape of her neck to his palm. Wanted to memorize the smell of her exactly like this: rain, coffee, fruit gum, the herbal cigarettes she stashed in her pocket.

And as he kissed her, the world around them hushed. Muffled by the pattering of rain and the sheer paleness of the light streaming through the curtains. The steady *shhhshhs* of his pulse was deafening in comparison. He nearly forgot to breathe until Maxine leisurely parted her lips for him, but even then, he didn't ask for more. Didn't want to claim her mouth, hoist her up to ride her thighs around his waist and ravish her against his bookshelf. (Oh, but he did want that—so badly the desire sharpened with each inhale.)

This moment, though . . . it was too precious, too far removed from base lust, too real. He wanted the stillness of this moment to last forever.

When he finally pulled away, it wasn't because he wanted to stop. It simply felt right, to set her lips free and gaze down into her face, to watch her eyes drift open and see her pupils contract against the light. Her irises reminded him of a murky, wooded pond being illuminated by a perfectly angled ray of sunlight, revealing the lush, hidden biome flourishing below the surface.

"Wow. That was . . ." Maxine blinked a few times, seemingly at a loss.

Teddy wasn't sure what to make of it either. "Yes. That was." Though it pained him, he unraveled his hand from her hair and set her free.

Maxine withdrew with equal reluctance. "I thought rule number three was no kissing."

Teddy briefly closed his eyes. "It . . . was."

"Bad *boy*," she purred. "What are you doing later? You want to go rob a bank?"

"In my defense, I've had three hours of sleep."

"We probably shouldn't do that again."

"Why not?" He didn't like how petulant he sounded. Why was Maxine suddenly the voice of reason?

"Because I don't think we're going to stop at second base next time. You kiss me again, we're going all nine innings. You know what I mean?"

"I understand how baseball works."

"Because I'm talking about choking up on that bat and playing *ball*—"

"The analogy is crystal clear, Ms. Hart." He took off his glasses and rubbed at his eyes, trying to dispel the imagery said analogy had inspired. There was a limit to his willpower. "And you're absolutely right. We need to stay focused on studying."

Maxine's nose wrinkled. It made him want to kiss the creases away.

Instead, he said, "What's wrong now? I thought you were enjoying today's lesson."

"You could have put up a little more of a fight, you know. At least pretend you're sad we're not gonna bang out home runs for the next five weeks."

"Jesus, Maxine." What was he supposed to tell her? Unlike everything else in his carefully ordered life, he hadn't charted a course for Maxine's presence. He hadn't planned to fall in love with her within minutes of meeting her. He didn't *want* to lie awake at night, tortured by thoughts of her. And now she was here, in his home for the next five weeks, brightening every damn room she entered, and he was supposed to pretend this wasn't killing him?

"I mean, *look* at me! I'm so hot!" She spread her arms, and he looked at her in his oversize sweatshirt she clearly had no intention of returning, her skin bare and her curls clipped in a haphazard pile on top of her head, and he'd never been more attracted to anyone in his life. Her gaze sparked with challenge, and it set him on fire.

He wanted to fuck her in that sweatshirt. Over and over, until every time she wore it, he was all she could think of. Months from now, long after she'd grown bored of him, he wanted her to press the sleeve to her mouth to smell his lingering scent and imagine how he felt inside her.

She asked, "How can you possibly keep saying no to this?"

Something snapped inside him. With deliberate movements, he tucked his eyeglasses into his pocket and stepped forward until Maxine was forced to retreat. Three more steps and she was backed up against one of his bookshelves (Geology, Earth Sciences, Explorers' Early Maps). Her hands shot out to stabilize herself by gripping a middle shelf, but he didn't stop there. He stepped between her legs, wrapped an arm around her waist, and took her mouth with all the voracious need he'd worked so hard to suppress.

And she kissed him back with the same intensity, like she'd been goading him into doing exactly this.

He didn't care. She could have it.

Her hands came up to his shirt, fumbling at the buttons. Blood rushed in Teddy's ears. *Yes, touch me,* he wanted to say, but it came out as a groan against her lips. One button, then two, and her hand slid into the pocket she'd created, her touch searing the bare skin over his sternum.

The simple touch nearly undid him. It was intimate and possessive—and dangerously close to his heart.

It made him want to keep her. Forever. He wanted it even more than he wanted to win the tournament. But unless he was wildly mistaken, Maxine despised everything about him *except* the way he kissed her, and he wasn't giving up $2 million just to be used and discarded—no matter how much certain parts of him wished he would.

Teddy tore away from the kiss, breath heaving. "What do you want from me? Teaching or sex? Choose," he demanded.

The irises had been swallowed by darkness, leaving only a mossy ring. "Why can't I have both?"

"Choose."

Her throat worked. Teddy imagined he could see reason returning, the clouds in her gaze dissipating. Then, quietly: "Teaching."

Disappointment stabbed through him. He forcibly ignored it. "That means absolutely no baseball whatsoever."

"What if it's to save my life? Like if you have to give me mouth to mouth?"

"That's an obvious exception." At the thoughtful expression on her face, he added, "Promise me you will not spend valuable brainpower and study time inventing loopholes to this agreement."

She rolled her eyes. "Fine. I promise."

He patted the bookshelf and gave her a stern look. "Good girl."

The way her eyes widened at that almost made him forget everything they'd just agreed on. But they'd made a deal. He was a man of his word.

"Let's continue on our geographical journey to the Saint Lawrence River, which emerges from Lake Ontario and drains into its eponymous gulf in the Atlantic Ocean . . ."

Chapter 17

OH, CAPTAIN!

Answer

In a season three episode, this "bold" *Enterprise* space captain says to his first officer, "The best defense is a good offense, and I intend to start offending right now."

Question

Who is Captain James T. Kirk?

They'd built a map of North America in Teddy's study, until they'd run out of pastries and Maxine's stomach had growled for an early dinner. She couldn't believe how pooped she was by 4:00 p.m. Who'd have thought building a river palace was such hard work? Those poor beavers.

Maxine had barely mustered the energy to order takeout. "I'll cook next time," she promised, in deference to rule number two (*Maxine must pretend to be a contributing member of society,* or some other bullshit).

But as they sat down to takeout and Teddy started to quiz her on the legion of river names she'd ostensibly memorized, Maxine had the startling realization that she had, in fact . . . memorized them.

When Teddy asked, "Río Conchos?" Maxine would think, *"Conchos" comes from "concha," the Spanish for "shell," because the river used to have a lot of endemic mussels in it, which were overfished due to the pinkish-purple pearls they made,* and the image of a mussel shell appeared in her mind—black and shiny—and she was able to mentally walk through the study until she found the shiny black feet on his study chair. *Chair* sounded like *Sierra*, as in Sierra Madres. "It flows down the mountains, through Chair-huahua, and into the Río Bravo del Norte," she answered.

"They'll also accept Rio Grande," Teddy reminded her.

"Rio Grande," she murmured, and it called to mind the image she'd placed of a grand giant, lounging in that same chair, wearing a golf shirt. "It empties into the *Golf* of Mexico."

"Excellent work!" Teddy toasted her with his can of soda water, which made her insides glow like a pinkish-purple pearl.

After dinner, Maxine went to her room to call her sister and tell her the good news (Maxine was a genius, she lived in a palace, and maybe she stood a chance against Hercules after all, et cetera—none of which happened to mention any kissing, because Olive would say, *I told you so*, and Maxine wasn't ready to come down from her ego high). Meanwhile, Teddy had told her he was going out to the gym, which shouldn't have surprised her as much as it did, given that she'd felt his lean muscles close up three nights prior. The thought of those very muscles made Maxine flush.

Stop thinking about him. It was hard enough to fall asleep on a regular day because her brain took so long to wind down. If her mental gears locked on the way Teddy's thighs went rigid beneath her as she straddled him, she'd never get to sleep.

In a vain attempt to distract herself, Maxine showered under water so hot her skin went lobster red, brushed and flossed her teeth so thoroughly even her dentist would be impressed, and repainted her nails a vivid green. Then she threw on Teddy's hoodie, snuggled into bed in Teddy's guest room, cued up a podcast episode about Rio Grande water rights, and got out a deck of cards to work on her sleight of hand card tricks. Finally, after an eternity, the front door softly opened and shut.

It's not like she'd been waiting for him to come home.

Through the door of her guest room, she could hear Teddy's footsteps creak up the stairs. Then the footsteps stopped, as if deciding which way to turn.

If he turned right, he'd come into her room. To the left, his room.

Maxine held her breath, the ace of hearts tucked between the fingers of one hand, the rest of her stacked deck in the other. Anticipating that he'd do the responsible thing and turn left, aching for him to do the opposite.

He turned left. The door to his room closed seconds later with hope-dashing finality.

Maxine let the deck of cards spill out of her hand. Then she angrily unzipped his sweatshirt, flung it across the room, and flopped back against her pillow. A tug on the bedside lamp's pull cord threw the room into darkness.

This was fine. She could definitely withstand five weeks of this. No problem. Sin problema. Pas de problème. Méi wèntí.

♡

She gave sleep an earnest effort. Three full hours of lying in bed with her eyes closed, a murder-mystery podcast droning on her portable speaker that she'd set to the quietest volume. She did a relaxing yoga routine. She walked herself through her river palace until she knew North America's water flows as well as she did the MTA subway map. And when that didn't work, she got out her vibrator and got herself off to a vivid fantasy of Teddy fucking her against one of the *Answers!* podiums, but that almost made her problem worse, because the release wasn't enough. It wasn't an orgasm she needed—those were a dime a dozen with modern technology and a skilled hand—it was Teddy.

Which made her angry.

And Maxine had the perfect outlet for anger.

Maxine threw on the sweatpants and hoodie he'd loaned her and was halfway down the steps when she noticed the blue glow of her television in the living room. "Damn it," she whispered. "I swore I turned it off."

But when she came to the bottom of the steps, she saw Teddy sitting on the sofa. He wore a pair of black sweatpants and a faded tee that read "London Jazz Fest 2012," and he was squinting at whatever was on screen with his brows scrunched together like he was trying to solve differential calculus equations using mental math.

Her stomach did an inexplicable loop de loop. Was it the "I'm just a normal guy" costume? The fact he was up past his draconian bedtime and holding her gaming controller? Whatever it was, he looked vulnerably, utterly human.

He was so focused on the screen that he didn't notice her until she'd plopped down next to him.

Teddy startled, nearly dropping her top-of-the-line controller.

"Careful with that thing," she warned him. "If you break it, you have to let me win the tournament so I can afford to buy another one."

Teddy shifted, trying to make space for her. But the couch was a two-seater, and with all the god-awful throw cushions involved, there was no way to avoid her thigh and hip pressing against him. Her skin felt fragile, oversensitized with pent-up need, and a part of her wanted to avoid touching him at all. It was chilly, though, and Teddy radiated heat. Maxine tucked her legs up to her chest and pulled her borrowed hoodie down over her knees, making herself into a pod, and tentatively sank into the softness of the couch—and Teddy's side.

"You ever played this before?" she asked, noticing he'd queued up the *Mortal Kombat* launch screen.

"No," he said gruffly, handing over the controller. "I couldn't sleep. I thought that maybe . . . after the Gauntlet . . . well. I should have asked if this was all right. And it doesn't matter, because I don't know how to use this thing. I wasn't allowed to have a gaming console as a child." His sheepish expression made her heart squeeze.

She laid a comforting hand on his knee. "You poor, unfortunate soul. I'll call first thing in the morning and have your parents reported for cruelty. Were you also forced to eat all your peas?"

"And the carrots."

"Immediate imprisonment without possibility of parole."

She selected the player-customization screen and returned the controller to him. "Use the little knob by your right thumb to scroll through the characters and find one who speaks to you on a spiritual level. But you can't have Kitana, because she's mine. You can also choose an outfit. I've unlocked, like, thousands of bonus costumes."

She watched him instead of the screen because she could see the reflection in his glasses anyway. He was so focused on his task that he didn't seem to notice. Seeing Teddy like this was like running into a celebrity with all their makeup off. *Academic aristocrats: they're just like us!*

"Actually, my parents are lovely," he said after a moment. "They live close by, you know. I see them every Sunday for dinner."

"Can't wait to meet them. I'll start practicing my curtsies." When Teddy didn't respond, Maxine added, "Watch some Guy Ritchie movies to brush up on my accent." Still nothing. "Buy a very large decorative hat?"

Teddy looked like he was suppressing a smile at the last one, but he was quiet as he scrolled through Liu Kang's wardrobe. Maxine wondered if she should tell him how fitting his choice of fighter was, given Liu Kang and Kitana's romantic canon.

When he'd finished picking a monkish gray-toned outfit for Liu Kang, Maxine showed him how to queue up a practice match with the AI. "This mode lets you test your moves without getting hurt. Want me to show you?"

He moved to hand the controller back to her, but she stayed him by placing her hand on top of his, laying her thumb across his thumb. The simple touch sent a shimmer of electricity up her arm. His skin was hot. The veins on the backs of his hands stood out in shadowed relief from the game screen's colored glow. The urge to trace her fingertips over them made her mouth water.

She swallowed. Dragged her focus back to the game. "You can't learn by watching, this is all muscle memory." She guided his thumb to the action buttons. "We'll start simple. *X* is punch, and *A* is kick. They do other stuff, too, when you combo that with moving or jumping, but you're like a fresh baby deer right now, and you're going to get slaughtered if you don't defend yourself. Do you know what the best defense is?"

Teddy hesitantly executed an on-screen punch. "Preparation?" When she didn't answer, he stole a glance at her appalled face. ". . . not preparation." He tapped out a few more punches into the empty air, half a screen away from his dummy opponent.

"*Offense*, dude. The best defense is a good offense." Maxine muttered under her breath, "Jesus, five weeks is not enough." Then she added, "Go ahead and walk your guy closer to Sonya Blade using that joystick, then do the punch again."

"I'm not sure it's appropriate to punch a woman."

"First of all, this video game is a fictional tournament to save Earthrealm by way of gruesome violence, and gruesome violence is inherently gender neutral in the natural world. You ever seen hyenas hunt? They're matriarchal, they're vicious, and they can digest *bones*. Second, Sonya's character is purely military-industrial complex propaganda, so you should feel absolutely no remorse helping her die valiantly for the cause when you kick a watermelon-size hole in her sternum."

Was Teddy looking vaguely green, or was that the glow of the screen? Nevertheless, he walked Liu Kang across the screen and, after a brief wince, socked Sonya right in her all-American mouth.

"How'd that feel?" she asked.

Teddy looked at her morosely. "I'm a monster."

"You wanna do it again?"

"Yes."

Maxine walked him through the rest of the basics, of which he was a delightfully quick study. Not that she was surprised to find out Teddy was good at something. When he focused on a task with such determination and focus, like he was now, he was a prodigy.

She set him up with a few easy matches against the AI and watched him learn to pick himself up when he got knocked down. Coached him on how to interact with the environment to trigger bonus attacks. And before she knew it, he'd won his first match.

"Nice job, buddy," Maxine said, patting his bicep. Then she yawned. The hour hand on the grandfather clock in the corner crept toward two.

"I want to try that again. I've almost mastered the timing of the dropkick. I must jump precisely a half instant before pressing the kick combination."

"How long is a half instant?" she teased him.

"Half the length of a full instant," he answered without hesitation. The corner of his mouth quirked.

Adorable. Maxine let her head rest on his shoulder. He was so warm. So huggable in his Normal Human clothes. Like a giant teddy bear.

He queued up a new match, muttering the combo attack pattern under his breath.

"Mmm. You'll get it." Her lids were heavy, so she let them rest for a moment, and she murmured, "Vouloir, c'est pouvoir."

Maxine didn't remember falling asleep. But she did remember dreaming about Teddy carrying her upstairs to the bedroom. The hard planes of his chest against her cheek. The laundry-fresh scent of his cotton shirt.

The tender kiss he laid on her forehead before leaving her tucked into her bed, warm and relaxed beneath the juniper velvet duvet she'd brought over. Everything was lovely.

Maxine even dreamed Teddy was in love with her, and in her dream she didn't mind. It didn't scare her, like it would have if she'd been awake. Dream-Teddy would never disappear when she needed him most. He'd never make her feel like she was *too much*. Or worse—*not enough*.

It was a good thing she'd dreamed all that, because Maxine didn't know what she'd do if he really was in love with her. Freak out and run back to Brooklyn, probably.

Besides, even if he was in love with her today, he definitely wouldn't be after what she planned to do to him tomorrow.

Chapter 18

SCIENCE FICTION AUTHORS

Answer

In *Parable of the Talents*, this author writes, "Kindness eases change. Love quiets fear."

Question

Who is Octavia Butler?

"I'd like a little more clarity about why we're approaching a skydiving venue," Teddy said, turning onto the gravel road the GPS had instructed. Teddy was no Oracle of Delphi, but he was starting to have a bad feeling about today's "excursion."

Technically, the bad feeling had begun the second Maxine had come downstairs in a black Lycra jumpsuit, taken a look at Teddy's button-down and trousers, and asked if he might feel more comfortable in clothes that were more "aerodynamic." A savvier individual might have assembled the puzzle right then, but in Teddy's defense (and he did suspect a jury of his peers would understand), Maxine was wearing a *Lycra jumpsuit*. The shiny black material stretched over her tall body made shadows under the tiny swells of her breasts and valiantly strained against the S curves of her waist and hips.

Even then, he'd still had the wherewithal to wheeze out a final interrogation about their stated destination, since he'd been assigned to drive, to which Maxine had responded cheekily, "It's a secret. I'd tell you, but that would ruin the fun."

This deferral didn't satisfy him in the slightest, but (Your Honor, I beg you to consider the extenuating circumstances) Maxine had subsequently bent over to put on a pair of tennis shoes, the action managing to strain both the jumpsuit's bottom seam and the front of Teddy's trousers in one go, and Maxine had said something like, "This bodysuit feels so much tighter than it used to be," and Teddy's brain had asphyxiated from sudden blood displacement.

And now here they were. Stepping out of his exceedingly reasonable car that said absolutely nothing about his character or account balance, into a chilly and overcast—but delightfully dry—day, the light breeze whispering of boundless traumas yet to unfold.

Maxine led him into a squat building, where she was greeted like a beloved soldier returning from war, and Teddy hung back in the waiting room, warily eyeing stock photos of humans suspended against the cerulean sky by a flimsy scrap of nylon.

When Maxine handed him a clipboard hosting several documents with bolded, underlined warnings with the words "DEATH" and "DIE" and "MORTALITY" and "WAIVE ALL LIABILITY" in them, Teddy thrust the clipboard back into her hands.

"Categorically, unquestionably, exhaustively no."

She cocked her hip and pouted. "Teddy, you promised."

"You don't have permission to call me Teddy while you're luring me to my death." He withdrew a miniature crossword book from his coat pocket. "I'm perfectly content waiting here while you perform this pointless, unreasonably dangerous exercise."

Her eyes narrowed, the playful pout evaporating, and Teddy's pulse sped faster.

If someone asked Teddy whether he had any addictions, he'd lie and say he enjoyed everything in moderation. But the truth of the matter was that Teddy was wholly addicted to the light of challenge sparking in Maxine's eyes. She was the Dr. Frankenstein of his soul, and he lived and breathed by the electricity generated when their minds clashed in opposition.

She snapped, "I went along with your memory palace, and you have to go along with my excursions."

"There is no world in which flinging myself from a plane is a remotely useful training exercise for a trivia game show. Is this supposed to teach me about aviation? The physics of gravity? Because I assure you, I'm well versed in these subjects."

"It's meant to teach you to stop being a little bitch whenever you wager on a Daily Duplex clue."

"This *little bitch* won seventy-six games wagering exactly three thousand dollars on Daily Duplexes, and exactly one-third of my total score on the Final Answer!"

"That's odd. I could have sworn it was seventy-seven—oh, that's right, you lost that game because you didn't bet it all on the Final Answer, even though the category was Crossword Clues." She flicked his crossword book with a finger, and it tumbled from his hand and onto the floor.

Teddy glanced down at the book, then up at her. "Very mature."

"Yeah? Well, this *immature* player took your ass to the cleaners and hung it out to dry like a jockstrap that's been fermenting in a gym bag for three weeks."

"Thank you for that vivid imagery."

"You're welcome. Now, listen up, because for a smart guy you can be a real knucklehead when it comes to recognizing your own flaws." Maxine flipped over his death waiver and scribbled the numbers "$24,000" and "$17,000" on the paper in her chaotic scrawl. "I had $17,000 going into the Final, which was about 71 percent of your score of $24,000. So according to *Answers!* wagering strategy, your cover bet should have been $10,001. A mature player would have given you the benefit of the doubt, assumed you would make the smart wager, and only bet $3,000—enough to cover you if you'd gotten the question wrong." She scribbled the math on the paper as she spoke.

The memory of it made his stomach clench. *Coward.* He gritted out, "I'm well acquainted with this information, no need for a review."

"But I, as you helpfully pointed out, am not *mature*. I am a shameless, low-down hustler who purposely let you underestimate me. I knew you'd count on me following the rules and only betting $3,000, which would allow *you* to make the conservative wager of $8,000, which was exactly one-third of your score. Because you, Theodore Ferguson III, are *superstitious*. That's why you had to have your special powdered chocolate doughnut that morning, wasn't it?"

He pursed his lips. "I like consistency. It's reassuring."

"I'll bet it is. Why leave the safety of the nest, right? Why risk flight? Why alter the strategy that won you seventy-six straight games, just because I was the only player who'd gotten within striking distance of you? You always bet one-third of your total score for the Final Answer clue. Every. Single. Time."

"True," he admitted.

"That day we first met, I sat in the audience while they filmed five of your games. I saw you make that bet five times in a row, so I gambled all my gold that you'd done it seventy-six times before, and that you'd do it a seventy-seventh time too. But it wasn't even that simple. If I'd gotten that Final Answer wrong, I wouldn't have just ended up in second place. I'd have ended in third, with half as much prize money. So not only did I have to trust my brain to get the clue right, I had to trust that my instincts had gotten *you* right." She handed him the clipboard with the number "$34,000" circled so hard the ballpoint ink shimmered like a knife. Her final score—she'd gone double or nothing. "That's why I won, Teddy. Because I was ready to leap from the metaphorical plane. And you weren't."

She might as well have stripped him naked. He wished she had done so instead. But she was right.

He reluctantly took the clipboard, flipped the paper back over to the waiver side, and took the pen from her outstretched hand. "Fine. I'll admit you have a point. But I still don't see why we have to be so . . . *literal* . . . about this lesson."

"Oh, well, that's easy." She watched with a hawkish eye as he tidily signed the document and handed it back to her. Then her face broke out into a smile that was truly spine chilling. "Because it's fun."

After an instructional tutorial full of safety tips and assurances that his odds of plunging to a final rest whilst skydiving were significantly lower than the odds of being struck by lightning—a statistic that seemed suspect, given that one scenario didn't involve *volunteering* to laugh in the face of death—he was stuffed into a humiliating red jumpsuit, fitted with a harness and backpack, and herded onto a cargo crate with wings.

As Maxine had paid for a private session, it was only she and Teddy inside the plane with the instructor—a very tanned white man with dreadlocked blond hair, whom Maxine had introduced as Starfall by shouting over the roaring *put-put-put* of the engine.

Teddy didn't know if he felt comfortable jumping out of a plane in the arms of a man with *fall* in his name.

In fact, he decided, as the single-engine craft climbed higher into the sheet-white sky, his commitment to doing any such jumping was waning with dramatic speed. Teddy slowly slid forward to rest his head between his thighs, squeezing his eyelids shut.

He heard Maxine's conversation with Starfall go silent a second before he felt a cool hand on the back of his neck. Then her lips pressed against his ear, the smell of fruit punch enveloping him. "Do you want some gum?"

Teddy shook his head.

"Do you get motion sick?"

"This is less gastrointestinal, more of a last rites situation," he mumbled, even though he knew she couldn't hear him.

Maxine moved so she was crouching between his legs, her hands splaying on his thighs. And since Teddy was definitively facing his last moments on this earth, he allowed himself to revel in the fantasy that she was about to perform hot sex acts on him. And it would have been even hotter if he'd been remotely able to get an erection while in such a state of despondency.

"Tell me what you're afraid of."

"Death!" he shouted, levering up on his elbows to stare at her. "You absolute madwoman! You're luring me to my *death*."

Maxine nodded slowly, as if this were a revelation. "Don't worry! Going splat is relatively painless! It's living with regret that hurts!"

She grasped his hands between hers and kissed his fingertips. It was a tender, surprising gesture. His heartbeat slowed.

"Want to know a secret?"

"Is it horrifying?"

"Yes!" She leaned in close again, her lips touching his cheek so he could better hear her. "I'm scared too."

Teddy fix. "You don't have to do this. I'll tell Starfall—"

She stayed his hand before he could raise it. "It's okay! I like to be scared. It's a sign I'm doing something bold. Something worthwhile. Life's scary, dude! We're hurtling through space on a rock protected by a fragile shell of atmosphere, and none of us know what the fuck we're doing here. That's terrifying!" She pulled back and shrugged. "Embrace the fear. Accept that it's always gonna be there, under everything else, and *get busy living*."

"And what if my parachute doesn't open?"

"There's a backup. And then there's an autodeployment sensor in case of user error."

"There's still a chance of disaster!"

"There's a chance of disaster in everything we do! Did I ever tell you how my mom died? It's a funny story."

"Maybe now isn't the best time!"

"Remind me later! Hey, I think we've reached altitude. Come on." She stood up, holding out her hand. "Would you rather die like Pliny, saving your best friend from Mount Vesuvius, or would you rather live, knowing you could've been an *Answers!* ultimate champion if only you'd risked enough?"

Starfall came up beside them and began adjusting Teddy's harness. Teddy said, "Why are those the only two options?"

"You're thinking too much!" Maxine lowered her goggles and slid behind him, and he felt her breasts press tightly against his back. It took him a moment to realize *she*—not Starfall—was being strapped to him.

"What are you—"

"Didn't I tell you I'm a certified tandem-skydiving instructor?" Her lips grazed his ear again, and a bolt of desire shot through him. *Is this really the time?* he demanded of his body, half-delirious with adrenaline.

Starfall tested their harnesses one last time, then hauled open the side door. The air gusting into the cavity stole the breath from his lungs and, along with it, the last-ditch plea for mercy on his lips. Maxine reached up to grab a horizontal bar to steady them in the open hatch, and he could feel the hard points of her nipples pressing into his back—was she not wearing a *bra* with that jumpsuit?—and his brain spun. His eyes registered that he was extremely high up in the sky, and the ceiling of white clouds above was as uncomfortably close as the patchwork earth below was far away, but his mind and body were consumed with Maxine's closeness.

Why am I thinking about this right now? What's wrong with me? Why am I jumping out of a plane to impress a woman who can't stand me?

This was a pattern of questioning that had likely fueled the poor choices of men since the dawn of civilization. And it was in that very moment that Teddy's brain unlocked the epiphany that should have been so obvious: Pliny the Elder hadn't sailed his troops into the arms of an erupting volcano to save a mere *friend.*

"Ready?" she asked him. "I'm going to count down from three!"

A preternatural calm came over him. If he died, at least he'd be spending the rest of his short life in Maxine's arms.

"Three . . ."

Teddy thought about his parents. He was their only child. Who would take care of them when he was skilleted on a blacktop in northwestern New Jersey?

"Two . . ."

He thought of the tournament. Who would beat Hercules, when—

Maxine let go, and suddenly he was flying.

He screamed, "One? Where's the one?" but it came out like, "Aaaaaahhhhhh!!!!"

Maxine's bubbling laughter filled his ears, and Teddy stopped screaming. Mostly because he'd run out of air, but partly because his body finally caught up to his eyes.

He gasped in a breath.

Atmosphere rushed past him, buffeting his body, and it was . . . soft. The air was *soft.* He'd expected his stomach to drop the way it did when an elevator descended quickly, but it wasn't like that at all. This was like emerging from the dark, climate-controlled library into a windstorm and being caught up in a sudden gust. It was surprising, and it made his muscles brace, but it wasn't . . . it wasn't *frightening.* The sky greeted him like he was a long-lost child.

Welcome back! said the wind. *This is where you belong. Why were you inside so long?*

The entire earth stretched out below him, so infinite and gloriously green and lush. Had he spent the past few days grumbling about the rain? Because that same rain had watered all this land and given it life. And when his eyes watered—surely from the wind, despite the goggles—the landscape blurred and became Maxine's eyes.

His worries fell away; his daily trials seemed so mundane. *Hurtling through space on a rock protected by a fragile shell of atmosphere.* In that instant, Maxine's words crystallized and made immaculate sense. How had he ever thought luck was a farce? Somehow, he'd found *her*, out of nearly eight billion others. Stratospherically impossible odds.

"Look!" came Maxine's voice in his ear.

He blinked until his vision cleared and saw her finger directing him to see a V of Canada geese directly below them. *Below them.*

How had he lived his whole life only seeing migrating geese above his head? His entire perspective had been so limited. But now, he could see there was so much more. It wasn't that he'd craved that singular experience—geese hardly crossed his mind at all—but he was now aware of an endless host of things he'd yet to experience with what remained of his life (he was thirty-five, so by all accounts, he was approaching the halfway marker), and he was filled with the exhilarating urge to do them *all*. He wanted to watch the sun never set from the North Pole in July. He wanted to swim in equatorial water. He wanted to touch the bottom of Lake Baikal and float in the Dead Sea. He wanted to lose his breath in a crowd at Shibuya Crossing and catch it at Point Nemo. He wanted to tell Maxine he loved her and—

The parachute erupted from their backs and puffed up overhead, and Teddy came back to reality with a startling jerk of the harness around his midsection.

The world tilted as Maxine rocked him upright. Their euphoric plunge became a leisurely, meandering glide with the ground in mind, and the wind had gone quiet, so he could feel his heartbeat thundering in his ears.

"How you feeling?" Maxine asked him, and she barely had to raise her voice to be heard.

It took several seconds for Teddy to trust his own voice to answer. "I've decided to live, after all."

Maxine's laugh sparkled through him.

During the tutorial, they'd told him the free fall portion was only meant to last thirty seconds, but the drift to the ground after the chute opened would take three to five minutes. Teddy had lived an entire lifetime in those thirty seconds, and now he felt like he'd only just blinked, and suddenly they were on the ground.

Teddy's legs collapsed. Maxine tumbled them to their side, and the red parachute drifted over them like a dome, casting them both in a filtered haze of scarlet. He had a sudden flashback to the magic moment in American gym class, when he'd first experienced Parachute Day. For sixty seconds, the world had faded away under that rainbow bubble of nylon, and everything was magical.

Maxine unclipped herself from him, giggling something about having landed slightly off target from the drop zone, but Teddy wasn't listening.

He rolled onto his back, grasped Maxine by her Lycra-clad waist, and dragged her to straddle him. She let out a gasp of delight and fell forward, burying her hands in his sweat-dampened hair. He was breathing like he'd finished a marathon, and so was she.

"Maxine," he said between panting breaths. "That was . . . I—" He had to tell her what he'd discovered while he was flying, but it was hard to articulate with the endorphins flooding his brain like a burst dam.

"I know," she breathed into his neck. "Trust me, I *know*."

He didn't think she did. But then she was kissing him, their lips meeting amid her tiny pants and his shuddering gasps, and what remained of his revelation fled from his mind. This was the revelation: his hands skimming down to dig into the soft globes of her ass and drag her hard against the ridge of his cock, eliciting whimpers from low in her throat and spearing him with pleasure so acute he thought he might expire.

Dimly, he recalled, *We agreed not to do this.*

But then she did something with her hips—something obscene—that involved arching her low back and gyrating as if he were a mechanical bull, and intelligent thought fled. He choked out a tortured "*Christ almighty*" because he was so turned on he saw spots against the underside of the parachute, then shuddered beneath her as she moved back and forth, again and again, building a rhythm of friction that made his balls tighten in warning.

He tried to stay her movements by gripping tighter. "If you don't slow down—"

"No time. We've got about three minutes," she whispered—though *why* she whispered, when they were alone in what appeared to be an overgrown field in the middle of nowhere, he didn't understand.

And then everything spiraled out of control.

Her hands found his forearms, tugged his grip free of her body, and pinned his arms over his head. Nor did he understand why she was unbuckling his harness and unzipping his jumpsuit with the speed and tenacity of a race car pit technician.

There was no way she intended to get them both undressed. It was impossible. She wore boots that laced up to her shins and a skintight spandex suit that would take five miracles and a prayer to remove, and beneath his own jumpsuit he still wore his trousers and button-down, and he couldn't fathom an acrobatic way around this conundrum in three minutes.

"Have you gone mad?" he asked as she splayed his jumpsuit open and reached for his fly. His cock, throbbing in anticipation, was desperate for it to be true.

"When was the last time you were tested?" Maxine asked as she undid his zipper. He tried to lift his head to see what she was doing, but when her hand slid between the placket of his trousers, closing over the length of his cock through his briefs, his skull thunked back against the grass.

Nothing. *Nothing* had ever felt as good as Maxine's hand on his cock. He had no recollection of what she'd asked him, but dear god, he didn't want her to stop, so he did his best. "Ah—what's the . . . what are you—?"

"Teddy?" she prompted. "Have you been tested since your last sexual partner?" Her hand slid under the waistband, and his cock bolted into her palm, his precum making the path slick.

"Yes," he wheezed, his brain finally assembling enough neurons to answer coherently.

"Fantastic. Me too." She suddenly rotated, swinging one thigh over his shoulder, then another, until she hovered over him. Her Lycra-clothed pelvis was at eye level; her mouth, dangerously close to his cock. "Do you want to see? I have a screenshot on my phone."

But before he could answer that he didn't give a rat's ass whether she had the goddamn black plague itself because he would die for her in a heartbeat if she asked him to, he felt the flick of her tongue on his sensitive head, and he could only groan in utter agony.

He wanted his last moments on earth to be exactly like this. *Bury me in searing ash, Mount Vesuvius.*

Maxine's free hand slid between her legs and fumbled at the seam along her crotch, and he had the startling realization that there was a folded slit there, hiding a delicate zipper that traversed the length from front to back.

"I had it modified so I could pee without stripping naked," she panted. And praise the heavens, because she wasn't wearing a damn thing underneath.

"You are the most brilliant woman alive," he lauded her, and he meant every word.

And then, because he'd decided to stop hesitating when there was so much yet to do and so little time with which to do it, he dragged her soft hips down and buried his face in the pillow of her salty heat. He parted her labia with his fingers and plunged his tongue inside her wet pussy, letting her grind her clit against his chin.

He'd only begun to establish a rhythm when he felt her shift forward again, and even though he knew what was coming, he wasn't ready. The feel of her mouth closing over his cock, angling it so deep it slid down her throat, made his eyes roll back in his head. As long as he lived, he'd never be *ready* for that.

The effort to not buck his hips wildly required his entire concentration, and he didn't even realize he'd lost focus on his side of the bargain until Maxine released his cock with a wet *pop* and moaned, "Don't stop. Don't fucking *stop*."

He heard the noise of a wild animal, realized it had come from his own throat, and devoted himself to her pussy like he was starving and this was the only sustenance that would sate him.

He tongue-fucked her tight passage with passion.

He devoured her clit with fervent adoration.

And his efforts were rewarded. The bite of her nails dug into his hips, holding him in place with ten points of pain, and she redoubled her efforts. Her mouth slid down his shaft, and once it was firmly lodged against the roof of her mouth, she curled her tongue against his tender flesh, torturing him with searing, wet strokes.

Teddy thought he could survive it. His self-discipline had always been an iron fist around his base urges. But when Maxine moaned, and he felt the vibration of her throat like electricity down his shaft, he gasped for air—for a shred of control—but there was no reprieve. Only Maxine's heady scent, her salty taste, filling his mouth and lungs.

Can't hold back—

He tried to warn her. But she moaned again, and her hips bucked against his mouth, and his plea was muffled, absorbed by her swollen pussy. Stars burst down his spine and coalesced in his balls, just as he felt her delicate inner muscles clamping down on his tongue.

They shattered together. Exploding into a thousand brilliant spots of light against his eyelids. He felt her inner walls pulse against his mouth, and he breathed in her orgasm as he came harder than he'd ever done in his whole life, his cum filling her mouth until it spilled over. When she swallowed and lapped the stray rivulets from his still-throbbing cock, he saw the entire universe.

She collapsed, her body going slack and landing atop him with a heavy yet comforting weight. Teddy was ready to give himself over to the afterlife, but seconds before he felt himself begin to pass out, she tumbled over to the side, freeing his passageways to draw air again.

In his mind, an eternity had passed while they lay like that, wheezing for breath in a sweaty tangle of limbs, clothes, harness, and parachute. In reality, it was likely thirty seconds.

A car's engine sounded from the distance.

Maxine pushed up onto her elbows, tenting the red fabric that blanketed them. "The cavalry is here. I'm about to act my ass off, so play it cool and don't sell me out."

With colossal effort, Teddy gathered the strength in his limbs to zip up his fly before collapsing back in defeat. "Cool as the East Antarctic Plateau."

Her face appeared in Teddy's vision as she hovered over him. "Coldest recorded temperature on earth?" Her lips were shiny and swollen, her cheeks pink and sweaty, her nipples diamond points poking through her jumpsuit. There was absolutely 0 percent chance the skydiving crew would believe Maxine's story, even if she gave the greatest performance in the entire history of the Academy.

He grinned, reaching up to tuck a coil of hair behind her ear. "Most brilliant woman alive," he repeated.

Maxine kissed the tip of his nose. "Most brilliant *person* alive," she corrected him. "And I'll prove it at the tournament."

The tournament. The rosy haze cleared from his vision. That's all this was to her—a training exercise. Only one of the two of them had experienced a life-altering epiphany today. Nothing had changed for Maxine; she still thought of him as her rival to beat, and everything else that happened between them was simply . . . fun.

I love you beyond reason, Teddy thought.

"It'll be an honor to defeat you," he said instead, because that was what she wanted to hear.

If only he could tell her it meant the same thing.

Chapter 19

BIG BANG THEORY

Answer

This ancient Greek geographer, known as the father of cosmology, not only published the first-known world map but also posed the theory of apeiron, in which all matter derives from an infinite void of chaos.

Question

Who is Anaximander?

Maxine thought it was a done deal. You jump out of a plane with a guy, sixty-nine the brains out of each other in some random field, and then get hoagies afterward—you were basically in a serious fucklationship.

Sure, they'd made a *no kissing* deal . . . but that was obviously off the table now that they'd sixty-nined in a random field. (Cue up Muse's "Supermassive Black Hole," because baseball was back on the menu.)

Oopsy-daisy, my bad, Maxine thought to herself during the weighty silence of the car ride home, in a vain attempt to feel guilty about what she'd done.

Except she didn't really feel that bad, did she? Consequences were a problem for future-Maxine. Present-Maxine was about to get her freak on and explore her not-so-latent professor-student kink for the next few weeks.

Or so she'd thought.

When Teddy failed to close the deal that night—nor had he even opened negotiations, for that matter—Maxine was confused. And when Maxine was confused, Maxine was angry.

It didn't help that despite their shared orgasms earlier that day, she was still sexually frustrated, which made her angry too.

(In fact, most emotions entering the maze of Maxine's brain rerouted to anger except, ironically, anger itself—which rerouted to either sadness or horniness, depending on how much sleep she'd gotten and whether she had the option to eat shredded cheese straight from the bag while standing over the sink and sobbing.)

He'd gone to the gym again, which seemed excessive to Maxine, but what did she know? The idea of running in place without a reward in sight made her skin itch. Someday, she was going to open a zoo gym where humans could pay to be chased by big cats. Enrichment for the tigers, motivational cardio for the humans. The cats would even get to catch the ones who didn't pay their monthly fees!

Maxine was lying in bed, writing this very idea in her Notes app to pitch on *Shark Tank*, when Teddy's footsteps sounded on the stairs.

She set her phone down and fluffed her hair. Anticipation prickled her skin. A favorite Sherlock Holmes line rang in her mind: *Now is the dramatic moment of fate, Watson, when you hear a step upon the stair which is walking into your life, and you know not whether for good or ill . . .*

He turned left. Again.

God dammit, Teddy! She flung aside her duvet and burst into the hallway.

Just in time to see the door to his room click shut.

Maxine hosted a brief, violent war between her worst impulses—*bang on his door until he bangs you!*—and her only slightly better ones—*mope in self-pity tonight and punish him with indifference tomorrow!*

No one was more surprised than Maxine when she did neither of those things. Instead, she went back to her room and opened up the lap-size book of country flags he'd made her check out from his "library" (replete with a little Ferguson coat of arms rubber stamp on the checkout log and several unenforceable threats about overdue fees, damage reparations, and what he'd do to her if she followed through on her proposal to draw hidden dicks on every flag). She popped in her earbuds, queued up an Urdu language lesson on double time to keep her company, and tossed her scrunchie across the room for Orange Cat, who had been waiting expectantly for her to resume their fetch game for the last several minutes.

"Do you think all this studying is actually going to make a difference?" Maxine asked her feline companion.

Orange Cat snatched the scrunchie from the air and growled.

Maxine sighed. "Yeah, me neither."

At least it gave her something to do for four more weeks until the tournament. Besides, it seemed to bring Teddy joy to help her memorize these useless facts, and that man definitely needed joy in his drab life. She thought of the rapturous expression on his face as they'd landed under the parachute this morning, and her stomach went fizzy.

Kind of the way it did when she saw a teeny-tiny baby snake inspecting a flower. Or like how she felt when Olive called her to gush about a test she'd aced. It was an odd feeling she couldn't quite pin a name on, but it was a light and safe one, because it was in her stomach, not her heart. Her heart feelings were the heavy, painful ones. Those were the ones that made her want to turn to violence and cheese so she wouldn't shatter from the weight of emotion.

What is this feeling? She could feel her subconscious poking at the puzzle box in the background, trying to figure out how to open it. No dice so far.

Well, whatever the fizziness was, Maxine liked it, and if making Teddy smile was the cause, then she'd do what needed to be done to get more.

She always wanted more of a good thing.

But he'd better have something else in store for her than building memory palaces for the next month, or she, Orange Cat, and Miss Cleo were going to stage a revolution and ensure the prolific Ferguson line ended with Teddy . . .

♡

Teddy pressed his back to his bedroom door and inhaled deeply to steel his resolve.

He'd panicked when she'd come out of her room, so he'd hidden in his. After all, she'd told him he had a terrible poker face; what if she saw that the reason he'd gone to the fitness center and abused himself on the erg machine was because he was trying to purge his lingering feelings for her?

But now he felt like a fool. He might be an enthusiastic apostle of academia, and he might have the bleeding heart of a poet, but Teddy was not a saint.

He and Maxine were going to have sex.

It had ceased being a mere possibility—if it had ever been only that—the second she'd shown up sopping wet on his doorstep Monday night. And still, he'd agreed to her bargain, knowing she'd delight in upending the carefully ordered outline of his life story and flounce into the footnotes afterward.

"Never give all the heart," the poet Yeats had written after a rejected proposal. When Teddy had experienced his first heartbreak at seventeen, after Brittany Bauer had turned down his invitation to prom, he'd done what any sensitive, intellectual boy would have done: plundered his mother's first-edition poetry collection, glommed on to Yeats and

Byron, and sulked about the house being wretchedly maudlin and cynical for an entire summer.

Thankfully, his mother had discovered his hoard of misanthropic literature and put a stop to his otherwise-inevitable slide into insufferable self-absorption that all too often terminated in late-stage virginity, prosaic misogyny, and having one's own podcast. She was the one who'd introduced him to Butler and other brilliant feminist, antiestablishment authors.

"If you want to earn a woman's love at some point in your life, you must first understand her rage," she'd said, followed by the sly warning: "Don't tell your father about these."

Maybe Teddy didn't fully understand Maxine's loathing for him—nor could he ever, having grown up privileged and well educated—but he didn't begrudge her for it. It was unfair of him to claim he loved her yet treat kissing her like it was a mistake he regretted.

He was running away to protect his own heart—at Maxine's expense. But by waiting for her to love him back before being honest about his desires, he was being a coward. Something he'd sworn he wouldn't do any longer after today's flight.

He stepped back into the hallway—but Maxine was already gone. When he peered into the guest room through the crack in the door, he saw her hunched over the book of flags, unruly locks tumbling around bare shoulders and her lips pressed together in concentration.

His hand, curled into a fist to knock, unfurled at the sight.

She was the most beautiful thing he'd ever seen, and he'd never been prouder to see her studying on her own.

And also: *fuck*.

He couldn't interrupt her. Not now.

Teddy retreated to his bedroom, unsated desire burning in his belly, and cued up an incognito window on his laptop browser. He'd gotten as far as typing "sexy redheads" into the search engine before slapping the computer closed and flopping back onto his bed. It was no use.

There was no substitute for Maxine.

With a long, miserable exhale, Teddy went to sort out his frustrations on a video game.

The next morning, Maxine woke up early, and she woke up determined. There were few things that could get her out of bed before the crack of dawn, but subterfuge was number one. Second was sex.

Third was . . . well, it would probably be someone telling Maxine she absolutely *shouldn't* wake up before dawn, because nobody told Maxine what to do, and she'd show them! (Spite: the breakfast of champions.)

Maxine went silent as a cat into Teddy's study, helped herself to his office chair, and snooped through his desk until she found his tidy, ridiculously detailed day planner, written in his slanted cursive. She flipped back through his agendas, trying to ID what he'd planned for her training days, and was disappointed to find nothing relevant. *He must keep track of that somewhere else.*

She knew she should close the planner and keep looking, but she was fascinated by his color-coding scheme. Another puzzle to decode!

Orange-highlighted items appeared to be personal chores: dry cleaning pickups, haircuts, and the like. Pink was for family—tomorrow, he had a standing five o'clock appointment that read, "Dinner at Mum and Dad's." Yellow was for work-related things. And then there was green.

There were only a few activities coded in this color, and Maxine couldn't parse a theme among them:

—Poetry Reading

—Lyrid Meteor Shower

—Call Katharine

Maxine snapped the planner shut. *Who the fuck is Katharine?* Her brain supplied a highly unwelcome image of Teddy in the arms of a buxom, brunette librarian type. *Oh, Theodore, show me your enormous atlases.*

"May I help you, Ms. Hart?"

Maxine's gaze snapped up to see Teddy leaning against the door-frame, expression impassive. He wore a dark-gray, pin-striped version of his usual suspender-accented outfit, which complemented both the rainy weather and the faint circles under his eyes. He'd forgone the bow tie today, leaving the collar of his shirt open to flaunt the hollow at the base of his neck, which was suddenly the sexiest thing Maxine had ever seen.

God, I need to get laid.

"Well, aren't you looking very 'Tim Burton protagonist' today," she said archly, sitting back in his chair like she owned it. "I was just getting a head start on our exciting lesson plan. Who's Katharine?"

"That's private," he answered calmly. He strode to stand in front of the desk and placed his hands flat on the polished surface, leaning forward to tower over her. "Our lesson plan is the notebook in the center drawer."

Maxine retrieved the item in question, recognizing it as the same green leather-bound pad he'd brought to the library. She opened it to today's date and pretended to scan the items on the page as if she still cared about what was written there. "I think, since I've had your balls in my face, I have the right to know if there's someone else."

Teddy glanced at the ceiling, as if summoning patience from the heavens. "Have you considered a career in poetry?"

"Absolutely, I've always wanted to be rich and successful. Answer my question, Teddy."

"No, I'm not currently sleeping with anyone else." He slid his finger down the planner and tapped on an item. "Today, we're covering bodies of water, subtype, saline."

She hadn't turned on the lights when she'd snuck in, and the watery dawn streaming in through the windows wasn't bright enough to read Teddy's expression through the shadows of the room.

Maxine narrowed her eyes. "You're very specific with that word choice."

"Saline?" Teddy's brow furrowed. "You're right. I'd meant to cover oceans and seas, but 44 percent of the volume of landlocked water in geographically defined lake regions contains a salinity content greater than 0.05 percent sodium chloride—"

"I meant *currently*," she interrupted. "Because you should know, I'm highly territorial."

Teddy fixed her with a look she didn't quite understand—something almost amused, but not quite. "Would you prefer an exclusive dating arrangement?"

"Are you serious right now? Dating, like, 'make you my boyfriend' dating?" Maxine's heart skipped a beat.

"Something like that."

"You and me? Theodore Ferguson III, heir to the throne of academia, dating Maxine Hart, heir to gambling debt and a fondness for cheap thrills? *Dating* dating, as in buying each other stupid little greeting cards for special occasions? As in, exchanging 'miss u, sexy' texts while we're apart like we don't actually hate each other's guts? Are you serious?"

Teddy raised his brows, awaiting her answer.

Her brain howled: *No, no, no! Dating's the gateway to uncontrollable emotion feelings!* Maxine had seen what happened to a woman with ADHD who fell so despondent with heartbreak that she had to go on gambling binges every weekend just to get enough dopamine to numb the pain. Easiest way to end up just like her mom was to give someone else the keys to her heart—so they could unlock it from its protective cage and chuck it into the trash can once they'd really gotten to know her.

Maxine had already learned from many, many failed dating attempts that she was the kind of woman who was easy to become infatuated with, but impossible to fall in love with. No one ever wanted *all* of her.

She was like a stick of gum: those fun, fruity quirks her dates gobbled up lost their flavor the longer they chewed. Complimentary descriptions like *fun*, *irreverent*, and *adventurous* quickly morphed into critical ones like *annoying*, *messy*, *fickle*, *immature*, and *adrenaline junkie with an attitude*.

"Don't be ridiculous," Maxine scoffed. "We can't stand each other, remember? I don't care if you date other women—or any other gender—I'm only thinking about safe sex protocols. I'm not coming back from Jersey with the clap again, that's all I'm saying, so if you start sleeping with someone else, then you have to let me know."

He nodded very seriously. "Unquestionably in agreement." He held out his hand for her to shake.

She took it, still feeling mulish for some reason. "Also, I lied when I said I forgot all my Krav Maga. I can pop out a pair of eyeballs faster than you can blink."

"This critical information will be taken under advisement. Would you like some coffee and breakfast before we begin?"

Maxine trudged after Teddy into the kitchen, wishing her brain didn't itch so much. *Stop thinking about Katharine's hot librarian body, and start thinking about cold saline bodies.*

But it was a foul way to start the day, and it put her in a grumpy mood that failed to inspire her imagination. By noon, she could tell Teddy was on his last nerve with her, and there was a part of Maxine that spitefully enjoyed that fact.

". . . and you can remember the Black Sea is named thusly not because of the color, but because the ancient Turkic peoples used color navigationally, with black representing north, and that is how you might remember the Black Sea is north of Turkey, and—are you paying attention?"

Maxine raised her head to see an upside-down Teddy glaring at her from his position in front of the wall map at the head of their study "classroom." She let her head flop back, having draped herself horizontally over the chair in the center of the room, her arms and legs dangling. It gave her a nice core stretch.

"Nope," she answered cheerfully. "I'm bored."

"I thought you enjoyed the memory palace."

She yawned. "That was two whole days ago. It had the gleam of novelty attached back then. It's gone now. This is very hard, repetitive work, and I don't like it."

"'One should imagine Sisyphus happy,'" Teddy quoted.

"Camus can suck my dick."

"Thank you for that riveting intellectual analysis."

Maxine rolled her eyes. "Okay, let me put it in fancy Teddy speak: Camus's essay *The Myth of Sisyphus* was an explanation of absurdism as it relates to suicide, and after a lot of masturbatory whining about how life sucks, he eventually decides that nothing matters, so we should just have fun with it. And right now, I'm not having any *fun*."

She didn't need to see his face to know he was at the end of his rope with her. "Do you need food? Fresh air? I can open a window. Or we can do this lesson walking around the neighborhood, if you'd prefer. The rain looks as if it's about to let up."

As if to rudely contradict Teddy, the downpour pelting against the window began to clink as it turned to hail. Maxine lolled her head to the side so she could give Teddy a smug look. "I need motivation. I'm a very reward-based learner."

"Is our shared goal of defeating Hercules not enough? Is the additional prize of $2 million not motivational?"

"That's a long-term goal," she explained, deliberately, like she was speaking to someone with a minimal grasp of her language. "I need regular infusions of dopamine to keep me stimulated."

"I see." His voice was flat. "And how does one keep Maxine Hart *stimulated*?"

Maxine hoisted herself up to sitting and held up three fingers. "Firstly, the promise of conquest. Ya girl needs a good challenge."

"I challenge you to put forth a modicum of effort beyond complaining."

"*Secondly*, a reward for achieving said conquest."

Teddy opened his mouth, and Maxine rushed to add, "And it can't be, 'learning is a reward for its own sake.'"

His glower darkened. "And what's third? Please say it's fear, because I'm this close to instilling it by turning you over my knee."

"Thirdly—" Teddy's words registered. Her mouth went dry, her words evaporating, as a spear of desire pinned her in place. *Yes, Professor.*

He raised a brow. "Third?"

She shifted in her seat. What was it about this particular kink that appealed so much to Maxine? Was it that she'd never been to college, so it was already a forbidden fantasy? She cleared her throat, but her words still came out raspy. "Lots and lots of positive reinforcement."

"Very well." Teddy paced back to the blackboard and pointed at his handwritten list of *Europe's Top 20 Bodies of Water, comma, Saline.* "You have fifteen minutes to memorize the location of each of these. I'll print out a blank map for you, and you'll fill them in."

Maxine sputtered, "That's not enough time!"

The heartless bastard shrugged. "Do it in fifteen, and I'll tell you who Katharine is." And then, without waiting for her to respond, he strode out of the room.

Maxine gaped at the empty doorway for a solid ten seconds, still trying to wrap her head around the fact he expected her to memorize something in a mere fifteen minutes that they'd set aside half the morning to learn. Then she bolted to his desk, snatched a ballpoint pen from his pen cup so she could draw a cheat map on her palm, and whirled—right into Teddy's chest.

He caught her wrist, spearing her with his intense blue gaze from behind tortoiseshell glasses. "There's no cheating in my classroom, Ms. Hart."

Maxine dropped the pen, her cheeks heating. "Are you going to punish me?" she asked breathlessly.

His hand tightened on her wrist. The too-fast rise and fall of his chest told her that he wasn't as unaffected as he pretended. "No," he said softly. "But do it in ten, and I'll tell you you're a good girl."

"Positive reinforcement," she whispered. And suddenly, Maxine was so wet she'd created an entirely new body of water (comma, saline). A whimper slipped out of her throat.

At the sound, black swallowed Teddy's irises.

"I'll be watching from my desk, to ensure a rigorous standard of integrity." He released her wrist, then settled into his rolling chair and placed the kitchen egg timer on the desk's surface facing her. "Your time begins now."

The timer started with a hushed whir. There was no other sound except for the clatter of mixed hail and rain, and Maxine's own breathing. Teddy gave her an expectant look. "Well?"

She swallowed. "Don't look at me. It's making me nervous."

"All right." He withdrew the green lesson planner, uncapped a pen, and began scrawling notes with the studied focus of a teacher grading papers. *What's he writing about me?*

She craned her neck to read, but his eyes flicked up at her, the pen halting. "I don't advise procrastinating, Ms. Hart. Time is precious."

She waited until he'd gone back to writing before mouthing a mocking, *Time is precious, mew, mew, mew.*

"Fourteen minutes," he warned without lifting his eyes from the page.

Maxine dragged her feet over to the wall map and stood in front of it, arms crossed.

Black Sea, north of Turkey, because "black" means "north." She had *mostly* been paying attention earlier, not that she'd wanted to admit it. Give a mouse too much credit, and he'll ask for a glass of milk, and it was good for Teddy to stay thirsty. Humility leveled the playing field.

Her eyes scanned the map. There had to be a faster way. A shortcut. What if she stared at it for fifteen minutes without blinking so the reverse image would be imprinted on her eyelids? No, the text labels would still be too small.

A glance at Teddy showed him scribbling away in his dorky Maxine diary, unperturbed by her inner turmoil, and it irritated her that he'd be so cavalier about dangling such a high-value carrot on a stick that was impossible to reach. He knew she was bad at maps!

Why was she so bad at maps? Most people with ADHD were excellent visual learners and handled auditory input poorly, but Maxine's brain had decided to operate in the reverse. Wasn't she the specialest snowflake. Everyone wanted to be the quirky side character until they understood the price of being so goddamn quirky. The modern world was a palace built for typical brains.

Well, screw that. And screw Teddy and the high horse he'd ridden in on! Maxine would simply build herself a palace that worked for her brain. An auditory palace.

Glancing at the blackboard to make sure she knew the list, she closed her eyes and let her brain pick a song. Perhaps she chose the song she did because Teddy had seeded her subconscious with Camus, which made her think of *The Stranger*—a story about a man facing execution and regret after an impulsive murder—and then at the same time her eye had landed on England. Or, perhaps, she was simply horny and Freddie Mercury's sweet 'stache did it for her.

Either way, what came out in a murmur under her breath was: "North of the Baltic, it's very, very arctic . . . Gulf of Finland, Gulf of Riga, Gulf of Bothnia and-the-Norwegian Sea, oh-oh-ohhh" to the tune of "Bohemian Rhapsody." Working her modified lyrics into the song she knew by heart, she traced a route on the map.

And it worked.

When the timer dinged, Maxine primly sat in the brocade armchair and said, "I'm ready for my test, Professor." She hadn't done it in sub ten, but the way his brows rose when she scrawled in every label with perfect accuracy was almost as rewarding.

When she was done, she walked the test over to his desk and placed it square in front of him. Batting her eyelashes, she said, "Who's Katharine?"

Teddy didn't even glance at the paper. He leaned back in his chair, leveling her with a thoughtful expression. Then his mouth crooked in a way that made her insides glow with heat. "Very clever. You created a mnemonic device using a familiar song, thereby linking your working memory—the area most affected by your ADHD—to your long-term memory, which is quite strong, given your natural capacity for intelligence. Sort of like accessing an external hard drive to save a large file."

"Wow, is that hard drive where I keep all the fucks I can't find right now?" Maxine smacked her hands down on the desk and leaned forward, much like Teddy had done to her earlier in the morning. She growled, "Who. Is. *Katharine*?"

"She's my agent."

Maxine blinked. "Like a secret agent? Are you working for the FBI? Ew, I should have known you were a narc, what with the suspenders and all. My mother always said you can't trust a man who wears suspenders."

"What on—why—" Teddy rubbed his temples, then shook his head. "Katherine is my *writing* agent. I'm exploring a . . . career transition."

"Oh, cool." Maxine's relief at learning Katharine was not a smokin'-hot date eclipsed all curiosity, but she felt obligated to ask, "So am I your guinea pig? Are you writing an educational book about how to train depraved redheads in the fine art of kicking your ass on a game show?"

"No."

"Huh." Well, *now* she was curious. "Is it—"

He stood up. "Are you ready to do East Asia next, or shall we do Africa?"

"We're still doing this?" Maxine's mood soured again. Her victory felt too short lived after how hard she'd worked for it. She hadn't even gotten a *good girl.* And she'd earned it, no matter how long it had taken her!

Teddy rounded the desk to stand beside her. "Yes, Maxine. We are still doing *this*. We're doing *this* for four more hours today, and we're doing *this* every other day for the next four weeks until the tournament." He took her chin in his hand and said in a low voice, "That's what we agreed upon."

Desire kicked her in the gut. "What's my reward?"

"Is this the game you want to play?" His grip tightened on her chin.

A challenge. How the hell was she supposed to resist that?

In answer, she bit his wrist.

He snatched his hand away, chuckling darkly. "You want your reward? Earn it. Start by walking over to the map and putting your left hand on the Arabian Sea, the right on the Bay of Bengal."

Her limbs felt heavy as she walked, desire thickening the air. She found the spans of blue in question and spread her palms flat against the printed canvas. "Like this?" She peeked over her shoulder.

"Face the map. Don't look anywhere else."

Maxine rolled her eyes at the Tibetan Plateau. "Is this a learning—"

"Quiet." His voice cracked in the air.

The rest of her words sucked back into her lungs with a sudden inhale. Slow, forbidding footsteps came up behind her until the hair on the back of her neck lifted with his proximity. Static attraction.

"We'll begin with the Caspian Sea." His finger traced the bare skin between her collar and chin, then tucked her fall of hair over her shoulder to leave her cervical vertebrae unguarded. When he spoke again, his breath was hot against her neck. "The largest lake in the world. Five times the size of Lake Superior."

His left hand came around to cover her left wrist, his long fingers stroking feather light across the backs of her own before threading between them. Locking their hands together. He closed her hand into a single pointed index finger and tugged, dragging it upward along the map. She watched helplessly as their bound hands traversed the length of Iran, settling the tip of her finger on the swath of blue shaped like a coiled cobra waiting to strike.

"Repeat it," he instructed.

"Caspian Sea." Her voice trembled. Her nipples were aching points. "Largest lake in the world."

"Good girl."

An involuntary gasp left her. Wetness pooled between her legs, and she arched her back, pushing her bottom back against his hardness. She was only a few inches too short to make it work—her shoes were off. Still, Teddy let out a quiet hiss, his hand tightening over hers.

"Don't move."

She nearly cried out when he moved away, but he was back a second later. Something hard smacked the ground—an atlas. He dropped two more atop it, and then used his foot to slide the stack against her heels. "Up," he ordered.

Carefully, she lifted herself up, and in response he gripped the indent of her waist and fitted himself behind her. Now, it was the perfect tessellation of parts. Through his pin-striped slacks, his hard cock nestled like a ridge of steel against her ass. *This is why they're always wearing those plaid miniskirts in porn,* she thought, regretting her choice of faded forest-green sweatpants.

"Professor, I have a question."

"Yes, Ms. Hart?"

"Why is it called a sea if it's a lake?"

"An excellent query." His right hand slipped under the hem of her shirt and came to rest under the swell of her breast, trailing fire across her skin. "Geologically, it shares properties of both a lake and a sea because it's actually a remnant of the prehistoric Paratethys Ocean, as are its sisters, the Mediterranean and the Black Seas. But it is currently considered a lake politically, which is important in such a politically fraught region, because lake governance is divided only among bordering nations and seas are governed internationally by the UN's Law of the Sea. The *Answers!* clue writers consider it a lake, so that is what I'm teaching you."

His fingers slipped under the band of her bra to cup her breast. He smoothed his palm over her beaded nipple, sending currents of pleasure down her nerve endings.

"Fascinating," she breathed.

"Next, the Aral Sea." He slid their joined hands east to a smaller spot of blue. "When we were born, this was the fourth-largest lake in the world. It is now the world's youngest desert. Ecosystem collapse as a direct result of human activity."

Maxine gasped. "That's horrible. Don't tell me this sad stuff while I'm trying to learn."

He kissed her temple. "To learn without involving emotion isn't fully learning at all. We aren't computers. Human intelligence is part knowing, part feeling. You can't be afraid to hurt, Maxine." Without warning, he pinched her nipple hard enough to spike pain, and she cried out. "Pain makes the pleasure sweeter."

When he let go, pleasure bloomed hot and viscous where the pain had been. The cartilage in her knees went liquid, and she wobbled precariously on her stack of atlases. "Holy shit. If you don't fuck me soon—"

He roughly pulled her tighter against him, the imprint of his cock digging into her backside, and she forgot what she'd been about to say.

"We're not finished yet." He pressed her left hand hard against the wall, as if to stick it there, and then slid his now-free hand beneath the front waistband of her sweatpants, into her damp underwear, and between her slick folds. Yet he stopped short of circling her aching clit. "Reach up with both hands as far as you can go toward the Arctic Circle and the three Siberian seas."

Her hands trembled as they skimmed up the wall until both her arms were overhead, with Teddy's strong arm beneath her shirt binding her in place.

"The Kara, the Laptev, and the East Siberian," he murmured against her ear. As he spoke, he traced three tight ovals exactly where she ached most. His finger slid down and plunged into her slick channel. "The Sea of Okhotsk."

Maxine moaned, her head falling forward to rest on the wall as his finger stroked, in and out, with such excruciating deliberation. She bucked against his hand, hungry for more.

"Look up at the map. Your lesson isn't over."

She tilted her head back, arching to see more clearly, and he worked a second finger into her. His right hand, still on her breast, worked a steady pattern of pleasure-pain over her nipple. "Sea of Japan." His left thumb worked at her clit. "The Yellow Sea. The East China Sea. The South China Sea."

Pleasure spiraled fast. Her skin was hot, her pulse throbbing in her neck as she breathlessly repeated Teddy's words. She was so close—

"Don't come yet. We're not finished."

"But I can't—"

"You *can.*" His fingers withdrew, and an unwilling sob escaped her.

"Wait, go back," she begged.

"We're only going forward." He roughly dragged her waistband down. Cool air teased her buttocks, her upper thighs. In a gruff voice: "The Philippine Sea."

His hand jerked against her skin as he unbuttoned his pants. "The Sulu and the Celebes Seas."

The heavy weight of his cock slapped against her left cheek, and he guided it down between her legs. Without prompting, Maxine arched her back farther. She was ready. She'd been ready since the day he'd first challenged her.

Still, he paused there, the blunt tip pressed against her wetness.

"Maxine?" The arm holding her steady was, perhaps, less steady than it had been before. He wanted to be sure of her.

She reverently pressed her cheek to the map and gazed at the pattern of blue. The crisscrossing of meridians and jagged whorls of islands and delicate inlets, seeing the beauty of it all through Teddy's eyes. This was his passion; that was all that mattered. Softly, she said, "The Banda Sea."

He groaned and thrust into her, forcing a moan from her throat. "Arafura."

"Timor."

He withdrew and plunged into her again, and again, until she came on her toes, bracing her forearms on the wall to hold steady. "Bismarck," he grunted.

She could feel the climax building, unstoppable. "I'm . . . um . . . ," she tried to tell him, but in that moment his fingers found her clit again, and she could only gasp for air. The map blurred.

"Not yet." He withdrew his cock until only the tip was inside her, then placed his palm flat over her vulva. She rocked against it, desperate for relief, but he gritted out, "Four more."

Maxine blinked, willing her eyes to refocus, but her brain had already disconnected. She was drunk with pleasure, able to see and feel yet incapable of comprehending what was there.

His lips skated over her pulse, feather light. "Solomon Sea, all the way to the east," he rasped. "The Java Sea." He thrust back inside her. "The Gulf of Thailand, and . . ."

Maxine felt her body seize without her permission, her pussy spasming helplessly around his thickness. Over her cry of pleasure, he said, "Andaman Sea," and groaned. Then he pumped into her again, and again, fucking her into the wall until she came to balance on her tiptoes, her thighs shaking so hard he had to lift her entirely upright, and Maxine's nails clawed at the map—until she heard a tiny rip.

Her eyes flew wide with dismay, and she flexed her fingers free of the punctures, but Teddy didn't seem to notice. With his face buried in her neck, he groaned long and pained, and came with a final anguished shudder.

They collapsed against the wall. Atlases slid out from beneath her feet, and Teddy came to his knees, still inside her, and cradled her against his heaving chest.

Sweat beaded their skin, sticking them together. Maxine let her limp arms collapse by her sides and allowed her head to loll up to look at her instructor.

"Do I get an A?" she panted.

Teddy swiped a hand down his face, removed his fogged glasses, and blinked in the manner of a man recovering from a concussion. "Top marks. Flawless victory, as they say."

Maxine felt as if she'd die of joy. Her pride ballooned to cover the earth. Reaching up to cup his cheek, she smiled up at her new favorite person. "I've never been more enthusiastic about attending class. Why don't you go get a towel and clean up, and we can start on Africa and South America?"

He hesitated. "We should talk about this."

Panic spiked. "Nope." She shook her head like she could dislodge her own reservations from her skull that way. "You promised to help me learn, and this is working. If you keep training me like you did just now, I'll have world geography down cold by Tuesday. Think about it: beating Hercules is almost impossible, but this new learning strategy is super effective. We just might have a chance against him now."

Teddy's brow furrowed as he considered this and absently toyed with one of her curls. "How does this help me?"

"Besides getting to touch my boobs whenever you want?"

He instantly dropped the curl and did exactly that. Against her back, his chest hummed with approval, "Unfortunately for us both, your breasts, while absolutely spectacular, won't win me $2 million."

Maxine thought fast. When she really wanted something—especially something she *shouldn't* want—her brain did its most creative work. "This is how you learn to get comfortable with risk," she told him. "We agree this could blow up in our faces. But it could also win you the game. So for once, don't play it safe. Take the gamble. Let's bet it all and just . . . see what happens."

She held her breath.

He was quiet for so long she thought he'd fallen asleep, but when she peeked over her shoulder, his eyes were open. Staring down at her with that same odd expression he'd given her several times before, he finally nodded.

She discreetly released her breath. "You're all in?"

"All in. Max heart."

Maxine clapped her hands with delight—and prayed she hadn't just lost them both the whole game.

Chapter 20

I MELT WITH YOU

Answer

Surrealist Salvador Dalí explained that the melting watches in his most famous work, entitled this, were not inspired by the theory of relativity but rather by Camembert cheese melting in the sun.

Question

What is *The Persistence of Memory*?

The next three weeks slipped by so quickly that Teddy didn't notice it happening.

They'd fallen into a rhythm with their studying: Teddy's tutorials one day, Maxine's excursions the next.

On Teddy's days, they memorized facts and defiled all the surfaces of his home, his lovely and sensible automobile, and eventually, his bedroom, to which Maxine had slowly but surely annexed into her territory. By the end of April, she'd acquired the rest of his home, the garden, and the neighborhood cat. Teddy wasn't even sure *when* he'd lost half the shelf space in his bathroom medicine cabinet, but he had the sinking feeling his possession over the remaining 50 percent was gravely endangered.

On Maxine's days, they either visited Winston to run the Gauntlet and track Teddy's sluggish progress toward the top-ten rankings, or they went on a variety of excursions that Maxine deemed vital to developing an enthusiastic sense of valor in battle. These included—but were not limited to—attendance at a Krav Maga class; a visit to a tattoo shop; multiple ventures to a sex-toy store; participation in an illegal street-racing motorcycle meetup; an extremely regretful evening at a karaoke bar that served a dangerous alcoholic concoction by the name of "Pussy Wussy," which Teddy had (reportedly) recommended to several patrons with enthusiasm prior to projectile vomiting said Pussy Wussies onto the sidewalk and then proudly declaring that he was "no longer a pussy wussy"; and finally, a trip to Atlantic City—a venture in which Teddy was ostensibly to work on his poker face but mostly entailed losing uncomfortable sums of money and guarding Maxine while she stuffed takeaway containers with mozzarella sticks from the buffet.

At night, Teddy cooked or Maxine ordered in. After dinner, they retreated to their own activities until one of them (usually Maxine) appeared in the other's line of vision, scantily clad and suggesting all manner of vice. Other nights, Teddy challenged Maxine to *Kombat*, and he allowed her to tuck her bare feet under his thigh while her reptile-clad avatar pummeled his shirtless Liu Kang into a pulp. And afterward, Maxine slid into bed with him like she belonged there, commandeering most of his duvet and leaving copper strands all over his linen pillowcases. Most nights, Teddy would lie awake to watch the steady rise and fall of her shoulders as her soft-backed earbuds whispered podcast stories to her, and he'd wonder what he'd done to deserve such good fortune. Here was the woman he'd dreamed about for well over a year, never daring to hope she'd spare him a second glance—one not filled with disdain, anyway—and now she lay curled in his arms like a seashell.

He knew he was losing his mind; the neatly sewn pattern of his life had slowly begun to unravel, and there was a troubling tangle growing around the unrequited love in his chest. But he couldn't bring himself to care.

Hell, he barely even cared about the *tournament* anymore. In the back of his mind, he was aware that Maxine was progressing with flying colors, while his reaction time and courage on the stand had improved in equal measure. Even if they could beat Hercules—what would happen when it came down to him versus her? (Would she resent him forever if he won?)

But this only became a worrying concern on Sunday nights, when he visited his parents and remembered why winning was so important. The rest of the time he was able to inter those worries in a temporary holding cell far removed from the taste of Maxine's skin on his tongue.

He was on extended vacation. A sabbatical from reality.

The rhythm of their time together became so comfortable that before either of them recognized it, they'd composed a whole song. And suddenly, a month had passed since that fateful midnight storm when she'd arrived on his doorstep and demanded they join forces.

It was Maxine who'd noticed first. They'd been lying in bed in the middle of the afternoon, lazily tracing notable mathematical equations on each other's skin in ballpoint ink, when Maxine had glanced at his Bibliophile wall calendar and said, "You get to flip it to May tomorrow. I bet the quote is like, 'May your heart be an open book and your book be an open heart' or some sappy bullshit."

"They're not that bad."

"Teddy."

He glanced at April, which read: *April showers bring . . . more time to read indoors.* "In my defense, this was a gift from my mother."

"Mm-hmm." Maxine finished outlining a cone on his right bicep. "The tournament starts filming next Monday. So are you inviting me to dinner tonight, or what?"

He inwardly winced. Maxine hitting him with a one-two punch was exactly her agile fighting style. Gently reminding him that their time together was almost through, and then inviting herself to dinner with his parents.

He thought he'd been discreet about devising myriad excuses for why *this* particular Sunday wasn't the best to have another guest to dinner. Or the next Sunday, or the one after. He should have known that with Maxine, it was never a question of *if* she'd catch on to a ruse, only a question of how long she'd allow him to think he'd got away with it.

The best defense is a good offense. "Am I coming to Trivia Night at your pub on Tuesday, then?"

Maxine snorted. "You don't want to come to Dino's."

"And you wouldn't enjoy dinner at my parents' home."

"Why? Are you embarrassed about introducing your aristocratic parents to a filthy commoner like me?"

"Are you embarrassed about *me*?" he rejoined.

He expected her to swiftly deny it. When she didn't say anything, he pushed himself upright. Maxine rubbed at a stray spot of ink on the sheets, refusing to look at him.

"You are. I don't believe it. *You're* ashamed to be seen with *me*." He laughed in disbelief.

Now she sat up, too, her green eyes narrowing into slits. "Why do you say it like that? Like it's supposed to be the other way around?"

"I've no idea what you're talking about."

"I think you do, *Theodore*." She poked the cap side of the pen into his chest. Not enough to hurt, but enough to get his attention. "I think you're ashamed to be seen in high society with your grubby, uneducated, uncivilized mistress." She pushed the pen into his sternum for emphasis.

He snatched the pen and flung it across the room, disarming her before she accidentally performed open-heart surgery. There was no telling what would spill out of his chest cavity if she punctured it.

"Maxine," he said in a gentle tone. "Don't insult my uncivilized mistress by calling her grubby and uneducated."

Now it was Maxine's turn to give him an exasperated look. "Don't try to distract me with humor."

"How would you prefer to be distracted? Because I'll warn you, I've been developing excellent stamina in my right hand with all this buzzer practice." He made a lewd gesture, as if he hadn't already had his fingers buried deep inside her today.

Maxine looked like she was about to pummel him, which turned him on. It didn't help they were both already naked. When she noticed the effect she'd had on him, she tossed a pillow into his chest.

"I'm coming to dinner," she told him before magnanimously adding, "You can come to Dino's for Trivia Night. But don't wear something dorky. I have a reputation to maintain."

Teddy sighed. Maxine did not like being told no, and the more he tried to put her off the venture, the more she'd want to go.

He almost told her the truth about why he hadn't wanted her to meet his parents. In retrospect, he should have briefed her ahead of time. He'd had ample opportunity to dispel the fantasy she'd built about his background, but he'd played into it instead. Maybe a part of him had liked pretending.

Except now, when he opened his mouth to tell Maxine about his father, nothing came out. The feelings that Arthur Ferguson conjured were too complicated. In fact, outside of Sunday dinners, Teddy tried not to think about his father at all.

Despite all Maxine's efforts to fix him, part of Teddy was still a coward.

"*This* is the grand Ferguson estate?"

Maxine had changed three times before deciding on green plaid pants and a yellow silk shirt with a pussy-bow collar. She'd run an internet search for "what to wear to visit your boyfriend's snobby parents so they don't think you're a cheap floozy," but the results had reeked of misogyny and triggered her thirst for the blood of the patriarchy. She'd have worn her "SLUT" baby tee and cut-off shorts if it weren't still so unseasonably cold for early May.

But now, seeing the unassuming two-story home with its overgrown lawn and Kia Soul out front, she felt overdressed. At least Teddy was in his usual Professor Plum costume, so they matched.

Teddy parked and came around to open the door for Maxine, which always made her feel like a princess.

She asked, "Who drives the Kia?"

"I bought it for my mother. She's fond of the hamster commercials."

Maxine blinked, once again revising her expectations.

Teddy escorted her to the front door, his posture rigid. His skin was drawn tight over his cheekbones, and Maxine realized he was nervous.

"Don't worry." She patted his arm. "Parents love me. I'm super charming."

Before he could answer, the door swung open and they were greeted by an elegant, fawn-brown-skinned woman with long graying dark hair. Teddy embraced her warmly, then made introductions.

"Maxine, this is my mum, Suravi. Mum, this is Maxine."

Maxine panicked, torn between offering an air-kiss, a handshake, or a hug—or a curtsy, maybe?—when Suravi made the decision for her by enveloping her in a hug. "I'm so delighted to finally meet you. Teddy hasn't stopped talking about you since you met on the show!"

"Oh, *really*." Over Suravi's shoulder, Maxine made eye contact with Teddy and raised a brow.

He had the grace to look sheepish. "Mum, could you please wait to embarrass me until after I've had a glass of wine to soften the sting?"

They were shown into a modest kitchen with faded floral wallpaper. The air smelled of basil and bread, and Suravi proudly announced they were having homemade margherita pizza, because Teddy had once mentioned how much Maxine loved pizza.

"I've been watching these cooking shows on TikTok!" Suravi explained before directing Teddy to the garage to pick out a bottle of wine. When he was gone, leaving Maxine alone in the kitchen with his mother, Suravi lowered her voice and said with a conspiratorial smile, "He didn't tell you he was adopted, did he?"

Maxine flushed. Had she made her surprise so obvious? "No, I . . . I think I had a very different impression of Teddy's origin story."

Suravi winked and plucked a scrap of shaved parmesan from the plastic container before offering some to Maxine. "It's those bow ties. He dresses like his father! Wait until you meet Arthur, then it'll all make sense. He's down the hall in his library, if you'd like to go meet him."

Maxine hesitated, glancing at the stairs Suravi had pointed to. "I can just wait for him to come to dinner."

"Oh!" She patted Maxine's hand. "No, he's probably not up to dinner, darling. He's . . . well, Arthur is a great deal older than I am."

"Oh. Is he sick?"

The older woman's smile faltered. "Did you know I met him when I was a graduate student at Oxford? He was a distinguished professor from a well-to-do lineage, and I was merely a naive scholar of poetry from an immigrant family. But from the moment I first saw him in that library, I knew I loved him." She sighed in dreamy remembrance. "I had to pursue him relentlessly until he admitted he loved me back, which he did, of course. So much so, he allowed his family to disown him for marrying me! Now, that's devotion. A woman should never settle for less."

Well, that explains why Teddy's family doesn't live in a mansion. She inwardly cringed at how many times she'd accused Teddy of being some loaded English lord. It must have stung every time to be reminded that his branch had been so callously lopped off the family tree by a grandfather who *really was* an elitist dickweed.

Maxine followed Suravi's directions to the room at the end of the hall, still unsure what she'd find there.

The "library," as she'd called it, was really an L-shaped area with built-in bookshelves covering every square inch of wall space. A scarred desk, piled high with ancient tomes, sat in the center of the room. In the nook around the corner was a medical bed—though it appeared the bed's inhabitant was currently in a wheelchair parked in front of an outdated television. And in that wheelchair was an ancient man wearing a bow tie and vest.

Well, not *ancient*. But if Maxine hadn't seen his frail, hunched back moving up and down with breath, she'd have thought he was Halloween decor. His hair was ice white and attached to his head in sparse puffs. His white, liver-spotted skin was so pale she could trace the pattern of veins crisscrossing his skull. But his eyes, blinking at her from behind thick glasses, were still sharp. For an instant, Maxine imagined he was seeing right through her skin, into her soul, weighing it against a feather and finding her wanting.

Maxine had never given a single shit what people thought of her, but now she was nervous about impressing Arthur Ferguson. *I stole the cigarettes in my pocket even though I can afford them,* she wanted to confess. *I dropped out of high school after my chemistry teacher caught me cheating on a test. I begged your son to come on my face this morning in the shower.*

"Come in! Come in!" Arthur called, squinting at Maxine in the doorway. "My office hours are closed for the night, but I've always got time for the intellectually curious."

Her steps were hesitant, but he patted the chair situated next to him, so Maxine sat. "Hi. I'm Maxine."

"Oh, lovely! I do remember you, Marlene. Marlene Wheaton, of the Bedfordshire Wheatons." He tapped his head with a bony finger, watery eyes twinkling. "I may be getting on in years, but I never forget a name. What can I do for you, Miss Wheaton? Have you come to check out further reference material on blacksmithing? I came across the most fascinating record you might find of great interest in your studies!"

His hands scrabbled at the arms of his wheelchair, as if he meant to attempt standing up, which seemed impossible at best and fatal at worst, so Maxine rushed to reply, "No, no, please don't get up." There didn't seem to be anything to do but play along, so she slipped into her best approximation of an English accent. "I've actually finished defending my dissertation on gargantuan swords and their versatile applications in the medieval practices."

"Ah, medieval practices." Arthur nodded. "Pray tell, which ones in particular?"

"Oh, you know . . . brandishing. Beheading. Bisecting." Maxine made a random flourish that seemed like something a posh intellectual would do to imply: *and a bunch of other bullshit.*

"Absolutely brilliant, my dear. I may not be an expert in that realm, but the confidence with which you speak of your passion assures me *you* are the true expert. Never lose that passion, even after you've moved on from your studies here. Oh!" With a shaky finger he directed her attention to the TV screen. "My boy is on this show. Do you see that fine young man on the left? That's my boy, Theodore."

And there he was. Whatever channel Arthur watched was airing a rerun of one of Teddy's early episodes. Even though Maxine had seen them all—several times—it was still a trip seeing Teddy on screen. It had only been a year and two months since his run had started, yet he looked so . . . different. So serious, so stiff, so *young*. The Teddy she'd first met in the greenroom that day had been arrogant and relaxed, so sure of his place in the world. But that was the Teddy who'd just won seventy-one games in a row and become a multimillionaire in the space of weeks; hard not to let that kind of thing go to one's head. Maxine would have suffered the same overinflated confidence during her run if her ego hadn't already been at max capacity before she'd started.

She'd never known this before-Teddy. This shy, anxious nerd with too-short hair and a crooked bow tie, clutching his buzzer to his chest as he shifted from foot to foot.

"*I'll take Capital Ls, please*," said before-Teddy.

Loretta's dry reply: "*Should I pick which one, Mr. Ferguson?*"

"*Ah—sorry, for four hundred, please.*"

Maxine winced in sympathy for poor fresh-faced Teddy, who still seemed bewildered to be on *Answers!* at all.

"That's my boy," Arthur said.

A sound in the doorway made Maxine look up to find Teddy watching them from where he'd leaned against the doorframe, his brow furrowed as he looked at his father.

"Is that for me?" Maxine asked, nodding at the second glass of red wine in his hand.

"Yes." He came to her side to deliver the drink and rested a hand on her shoulder. "This was my third game, I believe. The Final Answer clue was a triple stumper, but I carried a narrow lead into the finish and wagered conservatively."

"You? A conservative wager? I don't believe it."

Arthur looked up at Teddy. "That's my boy on screen, you know."

Teddy's hand tightened on Maxine's shoulder, but his voice was calm. Kind, even. "He's doing very well. You must be proud."

"I always worried about him. There was an incident during his school years, you see . . . I worried I hadn't instilled the right values in him. Hadn't taught him to appreciate the pursuit of learning for learning's sake. But we all go astray sometimes, don't we?" He glanced at Maxine and frowned. "Remind me, what was your name again?"

Maxine swallowed past the tightness in her throat. "Marlene. Of the Bedfordshire Wheatons."

"Ah, Marlene Wheaton." He tapped his temple. "I never forget a name."

Teddy cleared his throat. "Would you like to join us for dinner, Dad? I can help you down the hallway."

There was a brief flash of confusion on Arthur's face. A scrunch of his brow, a dulling of spark. He looked up at Teddy as if only now becoming aware of him. "Oh, Theodore, you're home." Then his expression grew very somber. "I wish you hadn't done that quizzing-team business. We sent you to the finest academy, and, and . . . a man's integrity is all he's got, you know. You've always got to do what's right, even when it's quite hard."

"I know, Dad. I'm sorry."

Arthur nodded, his gaze drifting back to the TV. His brow smoothed as the on-screen Teddy correctly guessed the Daily Duplex clue. "That's my boy," the old man murmured.

Quietly, Teddy guided Maxine out into the hallway. "His nurse feeds him early on Sundays so he can catch *Answers!* reruns at six, so it'll just be us at the kitchen table tonight. Do you like the wine? It's a Montepulciano red blend that should pair nicely with the pizza."

He didn't seem interested in addressing the elephant in the room, so Maxine continued to play along, albeit in a different play. "How's my accent, though?"

"Atrocious. If you do that in front of my mother, you'll be walking home."

"It's, like, a thirty-minute walk, and that's a normal distance to walk to the grocery store in Brooklyn, sooo . . . pip-pip! Cheerio!"

He sighed. "Fine. What's your price, wench?"

"Oi, guvnah!" Maxine tapped her fingers together with devilish glee. "Five shillings."

Teddy fished his money clip out of his pocket and handed her a dollar. "That's about four times as much. Keep the change."

"Damn it. Five shillings always sounded like a lot."

"You're thinking sovereigns, which were the equivalent of a pound and made of gold, and you'd get twenty shillings to a sovereign."

"Bollocks." At Teddy's glower, she relented. "Okay, okay! I'm done."

Dinner was otherwise a delightful and uneventful experience. Teddy had clearly acquired his artistic talent from his adoptive mother, who made a surprisingly decent thin-crust pizza (for a home without a proper pizza oven), even if he hadn't absorbed her social skills and effusive charm. The only problem was that Suravi was obviously under the impression that Maxine was Teddy's girlfriend, and this notion made the woman so damn happy that Maxine didn't have the heart to correct her. Especially once it became clear that Maxine was the first woman to ever be presented at Sunday dinner. Poor Suravi—she must have been convinced her only son was doomed to die a bachelor and, along with him, all dreams of grandchildren.

As they were gathering their coats to leave, Suravi asked Teddy if he wouldn't mind fetching her favorite pink cardigan from the upstairs closet. After his footsteps had faded, Suravi tugged Maxine into the tidy office off the foyer. "It'll take him a minute to realize no such cardigan exists, but I'd like to ask you to do me a favor." She handed Maxine a manila envelope. "Put this on his desk. Convince him to sign the paperwork, if you can. He refuses to take it from me."

The envelope was thick in the way important shit always was. "What is it?"

"Before my father-in-law—Theodore II—passed, he wrote Teddy into his will. He didn't want a dime of it to go to us, but he had no other heirs, so he wanted the Ferguson line to continue, or some bollocks."

"Absolute bollocks," Maxine agreed with the gravest expression she could muster.

"There's quite a great deal of money involved, and an estate, all of which he claims he'd like nothing to do with out of loyalty to his father. It's all being held in trust for him until he assumes ownership. I know it's a lot to ask of you, especially because you know how stubborn that man is, but I've never seen him so smitten before. I have the feeling you might be the only person on this planet who can challenge his conviction—and I mean that in the most complimentary way."

A great deal of money involved. The envelope burned in Maxine's hands. If she convinced Teddy to accept his inheritance, maybe he'd drop out of the tournament . . .

As soon as the thought crossed her mind, her whole body recoiled.

What the fuck is wrong with you? Thoughts like that were vestiges of who Maxine was before she'd trained with Teddy. They came from a place of resentment at her lot in life and insecurity about her own self-worth, and Teddy had helped her let go of both.

Or so she'd thought.

Besides, this visit had made it painfully clear why winning this tournament was so important to Teddy—and it had nothing to do with money.

Guilt made her stomach turn. She'd been so judgmental about Teddy's background, when she hadn't even known his whole story. How could she have made so many assumptions about his motivations for competing?

She'd been so . . . childish. So wrong. And admitting that to herself was harder than anything she'd done these past four weeks.

Maybe the right thing to do is to let Teddy win.

But that thought, too, felt wrong. It wasn't just about her pride. *What about setting an example for other neurodiverse kids? What about seed money for a school? You've worked so hard—are you really going to give up now?*

"Are you all right?"

Maxine forced a bright smile. "Don't worry, Mrs. Ferguson. I'll make sure this gets taken care of."

She tucked the papers into her backpack and tried not to think about the very serious conflict of interest taking her heart hostage.

AND NOW, A QUICK WORD FROM OUR SPONSORS . . .

From: Nora Stallone

To: Answers! Ultimate Tournament Participants

Subject: *IMPORTANT* Taping Schedule & Reminders

Dear Participants,

Happy Monday! We're excited to see you all again back here in exactly one week. We hope your past month has been full of rest and trivia!

I've attached the official tournament bracket to this email. Later today, we'll be posting this on the official website as well as on our social media for fans to view and fill in their bracket picks, but we wanted you to all have a first look! As with our annual tournament, there are 18 players in the quarterfinals. Winners of each of the six quarterfinal games from Day 1 will go on to compete in the semifinals on Day 2.

And, of course, our top three ranked champions are automatically slotted into each of the three semifinals matches. Our three semifinals winners will compete on Day 3 in our final game.

Taping Schedule

Day 1 (Monday):

8:30 am—shuttle arrives at hotel

9:00 am—arrival

9:15-10:15 am—hair & makeup

10:30 am—practice games & sound checks

11:00 am—begin filming QF games 1-6

1:00 pm*—lunch break

6:00 pm*—wrap-up, shuttle back to hotel

**approximate times, dependent on filming delays*

Days 2 and 3 will have the same arrival times, but will likely wrap shortly after lunch unless there are unforeseen delays.

As a friendly reminder, I'll be acting as de facto social media liaison for the tournament, so I'll be filming behind-the-scenes shorts throughout the tape days. This is a great engagement opportunity for fans, and we encourage you to post on your own accounts, with a gentle reminder about avoiding anything remotely spoiler-y, since the tournament won't air until August.

See you all soon!

Cheers,

Nora Stallone

Executive Producer

PS. Wardrobe would like to remind individuals that small-patterned prints (i.e. reptile scales) do not look good on camera and to please bring alternate wardrobe options.

PPS. Our Health & Safety director has issued yet another warning regarding registered service animals, which are always welcomed, and we will work with contestants to accommodate disabilities. However, *unregistered* emotional support animals, including but not limited to snakes of any size, are prohibited on set.

PPPS. In response to one contestant's many emails regarding the matter, I'm afraid we are upholding the policy that $69 and $420 are unacceptable wagers. However, in the extremely rare event that a contestant has at their disposal enough money to do so, the judges will accept a wager of $69,420, and may God save your soul.

Answers! Official Line-Up for the Ultimate Champion Tournament

<table>
<tr><th>Quarterfinals
Winner of each game advances to semifinals</th><th>Semifinals
Winner of each game advances to finals</th><th>Finals</th></tr>
<tr><td>GAME 1
Tarrah Prince (10)
Andrea Hsu (11)
Trey Sambu (18)</td><td rowspan="2">Hercules McKnight (1)
Winner of Game 1
Winner of Game 2</td><td rowspan="6">Highest score wins
1st place: $2,000,000
2nd place: $500,000
3rd place: $100,000</td></tr>
<tr><td>GAME 2:
Sikander Shaw (6)
Jay James (9)
Rayla Woods (15)</td></tr>
<tr><td>GAME 3:
Ryan Murray (4)
Colin Julias (16)
William Broad (20)</td><td rowspan="2">Teddy Ferguson (2)
Winner of Game 3
Winner of Game 4</td></tr>
<tr><td>GAME 4:
Zhang Wei (7)
Matt Cricket (12)
Mi-Kyung Hwang (17)</td></tr>
<tr><td>GAME 5:
Helen Kaur (5)
Rutger Bradley (13)
Tom Damiota (19)</td><td rowspan="2">Maxine Hart (3)
Winner of Game 5
Winner of Game 6</td></tr>
<tr><td>GAME 6:
Zola Mattick (C*)
Jeff Jones (8)
Cristal Lunnpo (14)</td></tr>
</table>

(n)—player's rank

(C*)—College Tournament champion, Fan Favorite poll winner

Chapter 21

MYTHOLOGICAL RIVALRIES

Answer

Chaoskampf is a motif that arises repeatedly across cultures and religions and usually involves a battle between a winged hero and this beastly representation of chaos.

Question

What is a serpent?

[Dr. Love: We'll also accept dragon.]

"I said *bollocks* to your mom."

Teddy held the vestibule door to Dino's open for Maxine and then followed her into the dingy pub. "Why are you telling me this now?"

The instant they entered, they were greeted by a smattering of cheers and hollers. Maxine smiled and waved to the other trivia enthusiasts gathered at the tall round booths in the back of the bar, and said to Teddy through her teeth, "Because I don't want us to act too cutesy-wootsy."

Teddy rubbed his brow, already regretting having fought so hard for this invitation. "I didn't think that was a danger where you were concerned."

"It's you I'm worried about. Can't have you ruining my reputation as the Baddest Bitch in Brooklyn, subtype, Bar Trivia."

"Is this a self-ordained title, or are you required to defend it annually?"

"I host a pageant in the mirror every morning, okay, smart-ass? How about you consider this practice for the tournament next week, because if anyone suspects we're fucking, it'll invite a bunch of questions about collusion and shit."

"Nothing we've done is against the rules." Teddy had made sure of that. Repeatedly and thoroughly. The thought of even *bending* the rules made him nauseated. During regular gameplay, the show went to great lengths to ensure contestants with prior acquaintance didn't compete against each other, but the rules for elite tournaments made necessary exceptions to that rule. At this level, it was expected that players not only knew their opponents but had often developed professional friendships or—in particular cases—bitter rivalries.

"I'd rather not deal with questions, either way. You know Nora is champing at the bit for a juicy subplot for her little social media videos."

Teddy reluctantly agreed. As much as it rankled to treat their relationship—such as it was—like an illicit secret, she did have a point. Teddy disliked the idea that lowbrow gossip might overshadow their intellectual achievements. *Answers!* should remain an elegant celebration of trivial knowledge and the noble accumulation and recall thereof.

Maxine led him to the bar, where the grizzled bartender Teddy recognized from before had already poured two shots of amber liquid. Maxine said under her breath, "And definitely don't look at me like that."

"Like what?"

She gestured to his face, as if he could see himself in the invisible mirror she drew in the air. "Like you're in love with me."

But I am in love with you. Teddy reached for one of the glasses, but the bartender waved him away.

"These aren't for you."

"Aw, Dino, you're so sweet." Maxine tossed back both shots with expert finesse and beamed at Teddy. "Isn't he sweet?"

"Call me *sweet* one more time and you're drinking Jäger for the rest of the night."

Maxine didn't seem remotely concerned. "My gentleman guest will have your finest glass of red wine."

The bartender—Dino—gave Teddy a long, assessing look. Then poured a shot of whisky. "This one's on the house. You been spending a lot of time with our girl here."

It wasn't clear whether Dino said it with gratitude or condolences. Teddy opened his mouth to politely decline, because he really did want that wine, when the press of a boot heel into his toe made Maxine's warning clear. Instead, he thanked the man and followed Maxine toward a table in the back area of the bar, where television screens hooked up to a host's laptop advertised "Dino's Tuesday Trivia."

"Don't ever turn down a shot from Dino," Maxine told him once they were out of earshot. "It's an honor to be chosen."

"I think he feels sorry for me."

Maxine gave him a narrow-eyed look. "Not sorry enough."

"Kindly refrain from making come-hither eyes at me in this upstanding place of business, unless you'd like me to take you out back for a formal apology."

"Stop flirting and start acting like we can't stand each other," Maxine said through her teeth. They approached a table inhabited by two men—a bearded, middle-aged white man in a kippah and a reedy Black man with thick-framed glasses much like Teddy's own. "Rabbi Cohen! Marlon! Look who I brought to help us take home the trophy tonight. Be gentle with him, he's still sober."

Her teammates welcomed Teddy with thinly veiled delight, the likes of which told Teddy he was a popular topic on Tuesday evenings.

Maxine had told Teddy her bar-trivia friends were entirely in the dark about their *thing*, and thus—per Maxine's threatening instructions—Teddy dutifully played the role of the insufferable heel, even though the shoes didn't quite fit the way they used to.

Teddy had never played bar trivia, but he was surprised to find it challenging. Unlike *Answers!* clues, the questions were less about general knowledge and more about oddly specific, niche factoids. Things like, "What is the only letter that doesn't appear on the periodic table?" which involved a lot of arguing between Maxine and Marlon and Rabbi Cohen—"What about *Y*?" countered with "Ytterbium, dinklehead!"—while Teddy silently and methodically went through every element in his memory. The arguing produced a result faster, and Maxine lunged toward the judge with their *J* scribbled on a scrap of paper, barely beating out longtime foes, the Mice Men.

"They call themselves Steinbeck superfans," Marlon told Teddy, rolling his eyes as he said it. "Maxine, sweetie, get us another round!"

Maxine flipped Marlon off but dutifully went to the bar. Teddy, who lagged on his drinking performance, took a halfhearted sip of his whisky.

Rabbi Cohen leaned in, eyes crinkling at the corners. "Now we've got you alone. Tell us the truth: You gonna make an honest woman of her?"

Half his whisky went down Teddy's windpipe, and he sputtered. The rabbi patted his back—more forcefully than necessary, by Teddy's estimation.

"You think I should propose?"

The rabbi's brows shot up. "Propose? I'm talking about the tournament! Thought maybe you'd have spent this time teaching her how to play trivia on the straight and narrow. None of this Takahashi Gauntlet, all-or-nothing-wagering bull crap. That girl will run around in wild circles to avoid believing in herself. But sounds to me like there's more than teaching going on between you two."

Marlon swirled his Chardonnay. "Mm-hmm. Called it."

"It was my idea to send her to his house. You think I didn't know the score, the way she went on and on about how much she couldn't stand him?" Rabbi Cohen looked hard at Teddy. "Question is, if he's got the chutzpah to pull it off."

"For her? Ha!" Marlon eyed Teddy over the top of his glasses. "I'd pray for you, but I think even God's afraid of her."

Teddy glanced at the bar to make sure Maxine was still out of earshot, his ears stinging with heat. So much for his fine acting skills. "I regret to inform you both that any romantic aspirations on my end are unrequited on hers."

Rabbi Cohen said to Marlon, "He's smart enough to be an *Answers!* champion, but not smart enough to read between the lines."

Marlon added, "Maxine's like one of those trick trivia questions. You think she's complicated, but the answer's hidden in the clue."

"How so?" Teddy asked.

"She's got a great poker face, but then she gives away the game with her mouth," Marlon said. "She'll be all like, 'What, you think I'm afraid of birds? Give me a break,' and that's how you know she's deathly afraid of birds."

Teddy processed this. "Maxine fears birds."

The rabbi threw up his hands. "Kiddo, she's afraid of *love*."

"Well, she's also afraid of birds," Marlon said. At his teammate's sharp look, Marlon conceded, "And being vulnerable. She's a total marshmallow on the inside, and she gets her feelings hurt really easy. That's why she likes snakes so much. Because when you think about it, they don't have any arms or legs, which puts them at a disadvantage in a one-on-one fight—and they're all soft and delicious. Bird food. So they dress up in these bright colors and do all this scary hissing and rattling and slithering . . ." Marlon demonstrated by swaying back and forth in the manner of a snake.

"Exactly like that," Rabbi Cohen said. And then he, too, started swaying. Together, they looked like a pair of wacky inflatable car-dealership tube guys, and Teddy was having a hard time keeping a straight face. "You just gotta prove to her she can trust you. Only then will she let down her guard and admit she's got feelings too. But it's gonna be tough."

Marlon added, "I'd say give it time, but you don't have time—if she sees it coming, she'll slither right back into the safety of her cave."

"Metaphorically," Rabbi Cohen explained, clearly under the impression that Teddy was a bit dense. (And to the rabbi's credit, Teddy *had* been dense—it was all so obvious now that he was ashamed of himself for not seeing it earlier.) "I don't think you can romance Maxine the way you play trivia. I think if you really want to win this one, you're gonna have to go all in."

Marlon gasped. "Are you thinking what I'm thinking?"

In unison, they said, "Grand romantic gesture!" and then they waved their arms over their heads and continued to sway back and forth with glee.

Teddy's gut was equal parts bubbling hope and knotty worry. If they were wrong and Teddy confessed his true feelings, he'd ruin the tentative friendship he'd established with Maxine. And even if it wasn't everything he desired, wasn't it better than nothing?

That's the coward talking, he recognized. The Teddy who'd jumped out of a plane and got a miniature green heart tattooed on his right buttock (done up discreetly and with class, mind you) was ready to risk it all for love.

Theoretically.

A grand romantic gesture really was the riskiest move in the book, though. Was it really necessary to go to such drastic lengths to win Maxine's trust?

Perhaps he could do a medium romantic gesture.

Or a conservative, platonic wave from a safe distance?

"The fuck is going on here?" Maxine said, appearing in front of the table with a round of drinks clutched between her hands. "I leave for one minute and you two start acting like a bunch of jabronis in front of my esteemed rival?"

To their credit, neither Marlon nor the rabbi deflated a single inch in response to her jab.

"We're showing Teddy a hot new dance on the clock app," Rabbi Cohen answered smoothly. "Come on, join us."

Teddy mouthed *Help me*, but he knew he was grinning.

Maxine gestured for her teammates to scoot in. "As much as I'd *love* to sit in Teddy's lap right now, they're about to put up the next clue and I'm not about to let the Rescue Rangers over there make two *Answers!* champs look like *Answers!* chumps."

While Maxine busied herself getting settled, Marlon waggled his eyebrows at Teddy. *She gives away the game with her mouth.*

"What are you looking so smug about?" Maxine accused Teddy when she looked up. "Do I have something on my face?"

"Yes," he lied, reaching across the table to brush an invisible speck off her cheek. Her skin was soft as velvet under his thumb, and he lingered next to the corner of her mouth. "There. Think I've got it."

For an instant, her mask faltered, her mouth parting like it would if they were alone, and Teddy fought the depraved urge to slide his thumb between her lips in front of everyone in the bar.

Instead, he drew back, leaving her to hastily wipe the desire off her face before anyone noticed. He'd promised to uphold her reputation, and he couldn't betray his oath to her now.

Especially now that he knew winning her trust was the key to winning her heart.

They walked away from Tuesday Trivia as champions, but as Maxine watched Teddy run the Gauntlet the next morning, she wasn't sure she'd be celebrating when she walked away from the set of *Answers!* in Culver City next week.

Bzzzz! "GAUNTLET FAILED."

"Level twenty-seven," Winston announced.

Maxine applauded. "Wow, amazing work! Only three levels away from beating the Gauntlet."

Even though she beamed at Teddy with the appropriate amount of delight in his success, she wanted to snap her buzzer in half. Teddy's reflexes had gotten good—really good.

He could actually beat me. Maxine shoved the thought aside. Thanks to his diligent tutelage, Maxine had systematically filled in nearly all her trivia weak spots, and combined with her aggressive play style and impeccable buzzer timing, she'd improved just as much as Teddy had. Between the two of them, Hercules would get a run for his money.

But there can only be one winner . . .

Winston pulled up Teddy's stats for review, and Maxine made herself busy packing up their things so she wouldn't have to see, in crystal clear math, the monster she'd brought to life.

The worst part was, she couldn't even be annoyed at Teddy if he beat her. She'd been so excited to see him improve—her brain so scrambled by intimacy and sex—that she'd orchestrated her own downfall.

"Winston, I think we're good for today," Maxine said.

"You're already a half hour over time," Winston muttered.

But before they left, Winston pulled Maxine aside. "You know that thing you asked me about? I have some info for you."

Maxine sent Teddy to go get the car, then met Winston in his front office, where he conducted his official bookie business. She sat on the edge of his desk, fiddling with the box of cigarettes in her coat pocket while he pulled up something on his computer.

"Remember how you wanted to know whether there was any updated buzzer data on Hercules?" Winston asked.

"Tell me you got some."

"I started thinking about it, and I realized the original program code for the Gauntlet linked back to a cloud-based server where I stored all the *Answers!* clues. Based on the info you gave me about the game he ran with you guys a few weeks ago, I suspected that Hercules was still accessing that same database with the code he stole from me. Sure enough, I asked the server to track who's accessing the data, and I got several pings from a single computer in Louisiana. Guy's not even using a VPN." Winston shook his head.

"So you hacked into his computer through the backend firewall?"

Winston gave Maxine a flat-eyed look. "Please don't use computer terminology you learned from a Hollywood movie." He paused. "But yeah, basically. I changed the settings on his—*my*—program so that it sent summary data of all the practice games played on that machine back to the cloud database instead of storing them on the local hard drive."

He printed out a sheet, and Maxine eagerly plucked it from the printing tray. She scanned the stats. Her pulse notched up at what she saw there:

52.77% first in on buzzer

21.05% first in on rebound

15.8% incorrect rate

Maxine thrust the paper back at Winston. "No. These can't be right. Maybe there weren't enough data points. Maybe he had other people playing practice games on his computer. There's no way the guy that was undefeated in 1993 is now answering one out of every seven questions incorrectly."

Winston gave her a hard look. "Are you calling my methodology into question? You know I ran everything through my prediction model. Every one of the practice games he played plots well within the standard deviation. I can say with 99.8 percent accuracy this is the same person playing every time."

"So either someone else is playing on Hercules's computer . . . or he sucks now. I mean, only 21 percent on rebound clues? That's horrendous." Rebounds were when another player answered incorrectly, and the other two competitors had a chance to ring in for the opportunity to answer. The timing was always harder on rebounds because the rhythm was less predictable than on a normal clue read, but the average player only lost about 10 percent accuracy on rebounds—not over half.

Could Hercules have been relying too *much on the Gauntlet to train his buzzer timing?*

"There is a third option, you know. For why he did so well during his original run."

"What could—" And then it dawned on her. She gasped. "He *cheated.* He somehow had the answers already. That's how his correct-answer rate back then was over 80 percent. But how? They've been so paranoid about scandal ever since the Van Doren trials. Rigging a game show is a federal offense! How the hell would he have gotten away with it for so long?"

"I only said it was a possibility," Winston reminded her. "It could be that he's simply out of practice. He hasn't competed in thirty years."

Maxine's hunger for answers to this new mystery was all consuming. She paced in front of Winston's desk. "Why would he do this at all, then? He can't be hurting for money. He's a billionaire."

"All I'm saying is that something doesn't check out. There's an error somewhere in the Hercules code, although I haven't figured out what it is yet."

Maxine wondered what to do with that information. Report it to Nora? She had no real evidence aside from Winston's printout and a hunch—it would be her word against his.

Hercules was a beloved and well-respected public figure with Teflon PR.

Maxine was not.

She supposed she could always go to the cops with her suspicions, but the thought made her shudder. Her mom had trained her and Olive to never trust law enforcement. In retrospect, it was probably because their family was on the wrong side of the law in the first place, but the aversion was still deeply ingrained, and there was plenty of evidence in the news to support it.

A honk sounded from outside. *Teddy.*

Winston said, "The good news is that if I'm right, your training partner there is your only real competition. Assuming all three of you advance to the finals, of course."

"You saw his stats. Teddy's better than I am now."

"I've seen your stats too. Strange, how they've declined so much in such a short period of time. In fact, it's so improbable I had to exclude your data from the algorithm so it wouldn't skew my model." He gave her a knowing look. "You don't want him to know that you're his real competition, not Hercules."

"Unless Hercules plans to cheat again."

"Either way, the odds don't look good for your friend Teddy. Are you planning on telling him?"

Maxine plucked a cigarette out of her box and rolled it between her fingers, inhaling the herbal smell that usually soothed her nerves. Winston was right: she'd been holding back. Teddy had helped her far more than she'd benefited him. He'd handed her the card she needed, and now she had a complete set: buzzer timing, wagering gusto, and a broad repertoire of trivia knowledge. All she'd given him was a confidence boost, an introduction to Winston, and a cute tattoo on his butt.

Now, Maxine was good enough to beat Teddy—except Teddy didn't know that.

All the times they'd run the Gauntlet together, she'd intentionally missed buzzes. Whenever he'd tested her memory of what she'd learned the day prior, she'd pretended to forget things. Convincing her opponents to underestimate her was how she'd always gambled, and she'd done it out of habit—an instinct of self-preservation. Because at the end of the day, Maxine trusted two people: herself and Olive.

The only problem was that if she did win this tournament, Teddy's dad wouldn't see his son triumph—and she suspected that was a huge motivating factor. Why else would Teddy want to win so badly? He couldn't possibly need the money; he'd already won millions on the show, and it wasn't like he'd spent it all on flashy cars.

But what was the alternative? Play poorly so Teddy wouldn't feel bad? That was ridiculous. She'd beat him once without remorse, and he'd done the same to her in return.

A voice whispered, *He'd do it again in a heartbeat.*

Wouldn't he?

She shrugged. "Teddy's going to play *Answers!* the same way, with or without that knowledge. He's all about proving that stupid integrity of his."

Winston gave her a long look but said nothing. She had the distinct impression he was judging her and finding her wanting, which was ridiculous, since she and Winston shared the same mindset about money—it was morally right to cheat a rich person to get it. As teens, they'd made a lot of money at the horse track with that philosophy, scamming the hotshot finance bros who came to show off their seersucker suits and flash their luxury timepieces.

But you're not a poor kid anymore, her conscience reminded her. *And Teddy's not a hotshot finance bro.*

Maybe it was time to stop treating Teddy like her enemy, because now that she'd really stopped to think about it . . . it seemed an awful lot like he'd never been her enemy in the first place.

Chapter 22
CELESTIAL ROCK

Answer

Robert Plant refuted claims that this popular song's mystical lyrics were inspired by *The Lord of the Rings* and said he actually drew inspiration from an occult book called *The Magic Arts in Celtic Britain*.

Question

What is "Stairway to Heaven"?

Maxine felt compelled to be particularly nice to Teddy when they got back home that night after the Gauntlet. She offered Teddy effusive compliments on his driving, didn't ask him to make a single superfluous stop along the way home, and even offered to make dinner—from scratch.

Yet even as they sat down to eat in the kitchen, Maxine could only muster the enthusiasm to poke at her lasagna.

"A toast," Teddy announced, his eyes crinkling at the edges. "To worthy competition."

Despite everything, the sight of Teddy looking so damn pleased with himself made it impossible not to smile back.

"To $2 million," she said, raising her glass.

He winked with the cocky confidence of a man who thought he had a win in the bag. "To the victor go the spoils."

The red wine Teddy had picked was probably perfect, but when she took her sip, all she could taste was guilt. "How's the lasagna?" she asked, even though she knew it was burnt to within an inch of Hades. She could have sworn she'd set a timer, but two hours later she discovered she . . . hadn't. *Oops.*

"It's abundant with cheese and effort," Teddy said diplomatically.

"You don't have to lie to me. I know it sucks."

"Did you know lasagna was actually invented by the English in the 1390s?"

Classic Teddy—using trivia as an olive branch. He was always so damn considerate of her feelings. "Someone's trying to get lucky tonight."

Teddy's mouth quirked. "I'm only adjusting the odds in my favor, like you taught me." Then he licked the fork clean, his tongue curling around the tines with deliberate care. Maxine melted, wax under his blue-hot gaze.

Maybe she could keep him around. They definitely didn't mind each other's company, did they? After all, Teddy had given her the best sex of her life—every day, and in multiples and variations she'd only dreamed of. And then he'd held her afterward in bed, and not like he was counting down the minutes of the cuddling quota, but like she were an elevation map he was determined to memorize with his hands.

The thought of going back to her lonely loft apartment after five weeks of this arrangement was suddenly unappealing.

Who would make her coffee in the morning, or tell her cool facts about everything they did together, or keep her feet warm while they played *Mortal Kombat*? Who would patiently stick around even on days when she hadn't slept well and her ADHD was especially itchy in her brain, making her more impulsive and emotional? Who would make her feel capable of anything, even when age-old insecurity rotted away at the foundation of her sturdily constructed confidence?

More important, how was she expected to go about her day without Teddy's lopsided half smile to come home to? How was she supposed to enjoy anything at all without knowing what trivia Teddy had to share about whatever they were doing? Where was the joy in creating a tempest of chaos without Teddy's calming, steady presence to anchor her at its center?

It would end eventually, she recognized, even though Teddy had a higher tolerance than the average man for her unique brand of personality. But it was no use hoping for a different outcome. When she was in her early twenties, she'd tried stuffing herself in a box to suppress her more "unlikable" traits and become the ideal bonsai girlfriend—and all she'd done was make herself miserable. Inevitably, she'd outgrow the box, and they'd leave anyway.

But why rush the process when she and Teddy were both still enjoying it?

"Teddy," she began, with an awkwardness she wasn't used to. "What are you doing after this?"

"You, I hope. Have we explored the geography of the solar system yet?"

"I mean after the tournament." She shaped the square of burnt cheese in front of her with the edge of her utensil.

He took a sip of his wine before answering. "If I win, I may resign at Princeton and seriously pursue writing full-time."

Katharine is my writing *agent,* he'd told her. Maxine tried not to let surprise show on her face. "I didn't realize you were serious."

He gave her an arch look. "Because I'm simply so whimsical."

She continued poking at her cheese. "I mean, why can't you be a writer now, if this is what you really want? You already won over two and a half mil."

"Would you believe me if I told you I spent it all?"

"On *what*?" She'd assumed he was hoarding it in the bank, or in complicated investments, or whatever else old-money people did with wealth. She gestured around his kitchen. "Vintage appliances from the nineties? Suspenders? Cat food?"

Orange Cat looked up at them from where he sprawled on the back-door welcome mat, clearly hoping this was his invitation to the halcyon world of singed mozzarella. When no cheese appeared, he lowered his head with an air of dramatic sorrow.

Teddy sighed. "If I tell you, will you promise not to mock me for my naivete?"

"But Teddy, you know there's nothing I adore more than delighting in the folly of suckers! What happened, did you get worked over by one of those internet doms who shames you into sending all your money because you missed being financially dominated by me on *Answers!* so much?"

"Maxine."

"Fine, it's a big ask, but I, too, am looking to get lucky tonight, so I accept your terms."

"Very well. I donated it to science. Specifically, I funded a memory-based study that may have dramatic impacts on our understanding of dementia, Alzheimer's, amnesia, and other conditions that degrade memory function."

Maxine set her fork down and stared at her plate, her rib cage squeezing so painfully she felt like she was going to be sick. Vaguely, she registered that she'd formed her cheese crust into a crude heart shape.

Oh, motherforking shirtballs, I'm in love with Teddy.

"Oh," she said, because she didn't trust herself to say more without her voice—or her heart—cracking.

"It's a ten-year study, so there won't be results for a while. But early data is promising."

His dad was old, and ten years was a long time. Teddy had to know that this study wouldn't be able to restore his parent to the man he once had been . . . yet, Teddy had still chosen to spend his winnings that way.

To help other people. He might be the most purehearted person she'd ever known. How could he possibly feel the need to defend his integrity? Teddy was *good*, down to the nucleus of every atom in his body.

Maxine's throat ached with the effort not to cry. Why did feelings have to *hurt* so much? Why couldn't she be like other people, whose emotions didn't consume them from head to toe? There was no such thing as suppressing them once they started; that's why she avoided situations where she'd be required to feel. No sappy movies. No love songs. No *poetry*. Only fast-paced action! Horror and gore! Big, exciting, fast! Exclamation points on everything—flood her brain with dopamine to drown out everything else!!!

But now it was too late. She'd let her guard down, and *bam!* She loved Teddy so keenly that it was causing her physical pain.

Adrenaline spiked in response to the pain, her fight-or-flight instincts going haywire. Her brain automatically charted an escape route—bolt from the kitchen, grab her cell phone and backpack, call a rideshare back to Brooklyn, withdraw from the tournament, apply for citizenship in Timbuktu (*Mali, near the Niger River,* her brain automatically supplied, because Teddy had taught her the rivers of Africa while he tongue-fucked her on his kitchen counter), and live out the rest of her days under an assumed name and identity.

Because it was either that or shatter into a thousand pieces when Teddy dumped her.

She knew exactly how that would go down. Her ADHD mom hadn't really been addicted to gambling; she'd been addicted to love—and when Maxine's dad (and Olive's dad and every man who'd come before and after) had gotten sick of the chaos, they'd peaced the fuck out. For Mom, gambling had been the next best thing to romance; at least you had better odds of hitting the jackpot when you played.

But at the end of the day, the house always wins. Maxine would be damned if she'd let herself get addicted to anything—especially not love.

Teddy's hand covered hers, warm and steadying, and she realized her own was shaking. "Are you all right? Did I upset you?"

She squeezed her eyes shut and shook her head. *Fight or flight*, and Maxine wasn't the running kind. All she knew was how to turn the pain into anger and fight.

"Your mom gave me some paperwork the other night after dinner, and I didn't tell you," she blurted.

Her backpack was on the hook in the entryway, so she went and retrieved it, using the space to take several deep breaths. Each one hurt like she'd inhaled razors, but Maxine tried reminding herself she liked pain. Pain was *exciting*, right? If she could memorize a bunch of river names, she could do this.

To want to is to be able to.

By the time she came back into the kitchen, her pulse had slowed to a reasonable aerobic rate. She wordlessly handed Teddy the manila folder, then busied herself with cleaning dishes while he read through the documents. When she was sure Teddy wasn't looking, Maxine dangled her mutilated heart cheese down by her knee. Seconds later, a silent assassin made the evidence disappear.

"I've already told her I didn't want this," Teddy said gruffly, setting the papers down. "Why did she give these to you?"

Maxine scrubbed at the burnt noodle clinging to the side of the pan. "Because she thought I could convince you to take it."

"I see." Teddy stood and, with deliberate steps, came to stand beside her. He placed a hand on the counter, angling himself so she had no choice but to see him out of the corner of her vision. "I gave my father my word I wouldn't have anything to do with his family."

"Is that why you keep all those hankies with the Ferguson coat of arms in your pockets? And the embossed lighter you carry around even though you don't smoke that's clearly a family heirloom? And all those books about Ferguson family history in your study?" She turned off the water, dried her hands, and faced him, raising her chin. *Fight with me.* "I think you secretly want everything to do with it. I think you'd love to have all this money, and a grand, history-filled estate from which to write your sexy sci-fi novels."

He raised a brow. "You think a lot of things about me. Should I be flattered I occupy so much of your working memory?"

"Deflecting instead of outright denying—that's the mark of a guilty man."

"Perhaps you should be the one considering a career change, Madame Investigator. Who said my books were going to be sexy sci-fi?"

"Aren't they? I've seen what you really read, when you're not poring over reference material. All the good stuff is on the bookshelf in your bedroom."

"You're spending entirely too much time looking at my books when you're in my bed," he said darkly.

"Then keep me busier," she challenged.

Teddy threaded his hand into her hair at the base of her neck, then tugged her roughly against him. But he didn't kiss her. Instead, he pulled her face close until their lips brushed, and growled into her mouth, "I can see what you're doing. Stop."

"Why? You don't like me calling you out on your bullshit anymore?" Her voice came out breathier than she wanted, and he swallowed her carbon dioxide with a kiss that sucked the rest of the air from her lungs too.

Maxine bit his lip, tasting copper.

He broke away, but didn't let go of her. "I'm not fighting with you."

"Why not? It's fun. I like fun."

His tongue flicked out, capturing the bead of blood that had welled on his lower lip. Blue eyes searched her face, narrowing when they found whatever they'd been looking for. "You're afraid of something. What's wrong?"

"Don't be ridiculous." Maxine's hands found the top buttons of his shirt and worked to undo them. "I'm only afraid you're not going to follow through on fucking me."

He watched her systematically undo buttons, his nostrils flaring as she bared his chest. When she slid her hand down the front of his pants, feeling his hard erection, he warned her, "You can't fight or fuck your way out of every serious conversation."

"Watch me."

He caught her hand and dragged it away from his cock, pinning it to the counter behind her instead. "I always am. That's the problem, Maxine. I'm always watching you. And do you know what I've observed? Your so-called poker face isn't as impermeable as you think it is."

"Go to hell." Maxine shoved off him, making for the hallway. She didn't like where this was going. He was dangerously close to peeling back the anger and seeing the raw wound underneath. She wanted to run into her room and slam the door so she could scream her anguish into her pillowcase before it started bleeding out. Did he think she *wanted* to love him?

Heavy footsteps followed her. "Now who's the coward?"

Maxine whirled at the base of the staircase, gripping the banister so hard her knuckles whitened. "How dare you?"

A lock of his sandy hair fell forward into his face, and standing there in the unlit hallway with his shirt undone and his chest heaving, it gave him an air of an impassioned and slightly deranged movie villain. "How dare *I*? You've invaded my entire life, pushed me to bare my family secrets, probed at the hopes and desires I've never spoken of to anyone else, and I've *let you*. But when I ask for reciprocity, you won't give me a single, *fucking* scrap of the real Maxine!"

It was still a shock to hear him swear in anger. The Teddy she'd gotten used to was so polite, so well tempered. She choked out past the tightness in her throat, "This is the real Maxine. I'm the most likable, adorkable, fun person on earth until you get to know me and realize this is all there is. This isn't a cute persona I wear during the day, only to turn back into a normal pumpkin at midnight. This is who I am. You don't like it? Well, join the club, because most of the people I've dated feel that way." She spun and rushed up the steps.

She made it to stair three.

Teddy's arm closed around her waist, and she fell forward with an outraged gasp. He came down with her, catching both their falls with his free hand on the banister.

"Let me go!" she cried, even though she could easily wrest herself free if she wanted to. So why didn't she?

More gently now, he lowered them both to their knees. "I never said I didn't like it." His voice was rough, as if scraped over brimstone. "I do like it. I like it so much I lie awake at night while you sleep, wanting it more than you can imagine, wanting *more* Maxine. Wanting so badly I've considered writing terrible, miserable poetry in your honor. You'd love that, wouldn't you? If I abased myself in more humiliating ways just to have the privilege of pretending this means something to you while you dismantle me, piece by piece?" He buried his face in her neck, his mouth closing over her pulse.

Why was she trembling? "I'm sorry for ruining your life," she whispered, her eyes falling shut as his tongue worked against her artery as if he were envenoming her, injecting heady desire into her veins. Golden warmth pooled between her legs. Without thinking, she arched back against him, intensely grateful that today she was wearing the plaid skirt with only her 40 denier black tights beneath.

With a hiss, he lifted her up and flipped her onto her back, and her body responded without her brain's permission. Her legs came up to wrap around his waist, her arms reaching up to spread his shirt lapels wide and feel the hard heat of his chest.

In the darkness, he gazed down at her with a feverish glower, the barest light from the kitchen glinting in the ink of his eyes. Then his expression suddenly hardened with resolve. "I want you to destroy my life, Maxine."

Before she knew what was happening, his hand was sliding up her thigh. Up and up, to the elastic waistband of her tights. He roughly tugged it down until the band stuck around the widest part of her spread thighs.

She was vulnerable. Exposed. Heat thrummed from the pulse between her legs.

"Do you understand me? I built my old life so carefully. I existed to accumulate knowledge and pass it on, but I wasn't *living*. You've come into my life like a meteor from the heavens, destroying my quiet, my peace, my organizational system, my schedule, my routine, my sense of direction, my ego, my goddamn sanity—but I've never been more fucking . . . *alive*! And now you want to leave me in shambles, to rebuild without you? *No.*"

She whispered, "It's only a meteor if it burns up before hitting the ground. Otherwise it's a meteorite."

"Don't," he growled. "You think you can taunt me into fucking you so we won't have this talk? You're about to learn I can multitask." He clenched his fists around the center of the elastic waistband.

"You'll never tear those. They cost eighty bucks, and they're made of a special reinforced fiber—"

He tore them right down the seam with the brute strength of a man who'd spent night after night rowing until exhaustion. "I'll buy you ten more pairs." He dropped the fabric, and now she wore only modified thigh highs. "Tell me why you're running away."

Maxine whimpered as cool air swirled around her bare skin—her unclothed sex. She curled her nails into her palms, trying to generate enough pain to distract from all the terrible *feelings*. It was like trying to dilute an ocean with a cup of tap water. "I'm not obligated to explain myself to you."

Instead of an immediate answer, he jerked his suspenders free and flung them aside, then worked the fly of his pants open. His movements were short, his jaw tight, like he was holding something dangerous at bay. Then he interlaced his fingers with hers and locked her in place, eyes blazing down into hers like she was a collected moth: wings spread, pinned down for dissection.

"You want to leave?" he said, at last. "Fine."

He lowered himself over her, cupping the back of her head with one hand to cushion it from the wooden staircase, and Maxine hissed an inhale because she knew what that meant. She was about to get *fucked.*

"Please," she begged, tightening her legs around his waist.

Teddy thrust inside her with a grunt, slamming her against the stairs, and it was the best thing she'd ever felt in her life. Her eyes rolled back. The air in her lungs rushed out between her clenched teeth.

"Fine," he repeated, thrusting again. *"Leave me."* Another thrust. "But if you're going to break my heart, I deserve to know why." He plunged into her again, and again, mouth parted with heaving breaths. A vein pulsed at his neck, his muscles and tendons standing out in shadowy relief.

He hadn't given her time to adjust, and now he felt enormous inside her, thrusting deep enough to make her inner muscles clench of their own accord. After four weeks of daily fucking, he knew how she liked it, and she couldn't pretend otherwise, or he'd see right through it. He knew the angles, the pressure, the movements that made her moan; worse, he knew the sounds she made. He knew when her whimper was code for *more*, when her keening meant *faster*, and that her guttural gasps meant *I'm close*. It was like he'd built a memory palace in his mind and filled it with her.

He overwhelmed her defenses, inside and out, and she couldn't fight it anymore. Her vision blurred, twin tears spilling onto her cheeks.

Teddy's movements instantly slowed, and his eyes filled with concern. "Am I hurting you? I'm sorry. Darling, I'm so sorry." He began to withdraw, but she tightened her calves around his backside, holding him in place.

She shook her head. Her trembling hands came up to his face, and she smoothed his cheekbones with her thumbs. "I'm just catching feelings, and it sucks, okay? It sucks. I don't want this." The words spilled out, and they kept coming. "I don't want to feel so good now, because when this ends, it's going to feel so, so bad."

His forehead fell forward to touch hers. "I'm not going to hurt you. I'd rather burn every book in my library. If you only knew—" He closed his eyes, biting off his own words.

"You won't be able to help it. You'll eventually get sick of me. I'm meant to be enjoyed in small doses."

"Never. I will never get sick of you. I may become frustrated, or exasperated, but it's never at *you*." He pressed a kiss to her nose, then another to each of the tears on her cheeks. "I don't want you to change. I don't want you to go away. I want you to stay, for however long you'd like."

She let out a sob, and now her sorrow was at the helm. Her chest shuddered as tears became a continuous stream and she made ugly animal noises. Her nose ran, and she sniffed helplessly, and when that didn't work, she tried swiping at it with her sleeve. Teddy gently nudged her hand away and retrieved another handkerchief from his back pocket.

And that, of all things, broke through the tears. She snorted a laugh as she blotted her face with the cloth. "Where do you keep getting these from?"

He gave her a wry smile. A quirk of his lips that managed to look so tender, her heart responded with another squeeze of fuzzy joy-pain. "My mother had ten of them made for me when I went to Oxford. Perhaps she expected I'd be very homesick."

"Were you?"

"Of course. Cried my pussy-wussy heart out for the first three weeks."

Maxine tried to laugh, but it turned into tears again. Through sniffles, she told him, "I'm sorry. I—I just get like this sometimes. I don't emotionally regulate well."

"Shh, please don't apologize." He slid his arms around her back and lifted her up, withdrawing from between her legs and switching places with her so he sat on the steps and she straddled his lap. His cock was still hard, but he let it rest against her pelvis, seemingly unbothered.

Gently, he urged her to lean against him, and he stroked her hair in a soothing rhythm.

"I feel like Ginger Cat," she mumbled against his shoulder.

"I regret to inform you I don't have a furry fetish." He leaned back to look at her, tilting his head to see beneath her fall of hair. "Although, you would look very fetching in cat ears."

Maxine scrunched her nose. "I'm team cold-blooded reptile, and never forget it."

"Darling, I don't know how to deliver this tragic news, but you are anything but cold blooded."

Maxine looked up at him through her wet lashes and offered a sad smile. "God, you're going to regret saying that when I break your heart."

"I thought you'd already decided *I'll* inevitably break *your* heart. I'm not the skilled detective you are, but your story has already contradicted itself."

He had a point. Maxine pouted. "I'm not thinking straight right now, okay? There's lots of"—she swirled a hand around her head—"*stuff* in here."

Teddy's eyes searched hers, and for once, Maxine didn't feel the compulsion to look away. What was the point? He'd already seen her hot mess of a soul dribble out all over her face. So quietly she thought she'd imagined it, he said, "I love you."

She expected the words to sear like holy water, but they didn't. "Yeah. I could tell," she replied softly. "I . . ."

He waited for her to say something else, but no matter how hard she tried, the words wouldn't come. Not yet. Not when it was still too raw, too humongous and unfathomable.

Wriggling closer on his lap, she arched into his hard member. Sure enough, he was still ready for her, so she guided his length back inside herself, slowly lowering herself down his shaft until she couldn't go farther.

I love you too, she tried to tell him with her body, since she couldn't say it with her mouth. "I'm sorry that I can't . . . that this is all I can give you right now."

"I know, and that's all right." He cradled her to his chest while she rode to an orgasm that crested like a gentle wave, sweeping warmth through her limbs from head to toe and leaving her spent. When his orgasm followed shortly after, he shuddered and spoke her name into the muffle of her hair. It was bittersweet bliss.

After some time, they managed to gather themselves enough to stumble upstairs and into the shower, where they could only muster the energy to sit on the tile floor while they rinsed their sweat and tears away. If it were her own shower, she'd have balked, but this man scrubbed his bathroom to oblivion after every use.

Teddy had turned the water as scalding hot as he could make it, just for her, and now he let her lie back against him as he wiped the rest of the mascara from her face and kneaded conditioner into the lengths of her hair.

"You have to comb it out with your fingers while it's still wet," she directed him, her voice sounding so languid she tried to remember if she'd drugged their wine.

"It's so long," he marveled at a length of wet curl. He ran it through his fingers, seemingly fascinated by how it trailed down past her breast, and his expression was so wondrous that Maxine once again questioned herself. But no, still no drugs. *Teddy would never let you defile his Louis Jadot Beaujolais-Villages like that, silly.* It was true; he'd complain she was ruining the flavor profile.

"Curly hair shrinks about 30 percent when it dries," she offered.

"Fascinating."

Maxine ran her hand through Teddy's hair. It was longer than most men kept it, and she finally asked him something she'd been wondering. "Why did you grow it out? It was so short early on in your run."

Was he blushing? "Dr. Love told me I looked like an elongated version of the man who played Jaime Lannister on the *Game of Thrones* show."

She gasped in delight. "First of all, put some respect on Nikolaj Coster-Waldau's name. Second: you *do* have a crush on Loretta! I knew it!"

"Absolutely not," he sputtered. "I was flattered to receive a lovely compliment, nothing more."

"Teddy and Loretta, sitting in a tree, F-U-C—"

"For the love of all that is literature, I beg you to cease."

"K-I—"

He tried to stuff a hand over her mouth, but she easily dodged his attack, gleeful laughter bubbling from her chest.

"Krav Maga, motherfucker, you'll never take me alive!" She squirmed out of his lap and rose to her knees.

"Oh, I'll take you alive," he growled, dragging her back down into his lap. Unbalanced, they tumbled to the side and sprawled on his shower floor in a chorus of his low chuckles and her playful squeals. Once he had her good and pinned—which she generously allowed—he added, "I'll take you alive, I'll take you in the shower, I'll take you when you're being lovely, and I'll take you when you're at your very worst. I'll take you when you're ancient and when you're sick, I'll take you when you're terribly sad, and I'll take you when you're impoverished because you've spent all your money on board games and pornography."

This was disgustingly romantic, and she was so drained of sadness that the only emotion she managed to summon was that warm fuzziness. "It's adorable you think I'd pay for pornography. No one pays for that."

"I do. I believe in supporting the creative arts."

Maxine bit her lip. "So, like, will you take me even when I'm hungry?"

"Is this your way of telling me you're hungry?"

"Well. I mean." She sat up and gave him a wide-eyed look that she hoped conveyed the tragicness of her plight. "I barely ate any of that delicious lasagna."

Teddy grinned up at her, and he looked so content that Maxine wondered if she'd imagined the torment on his face when he'd confessed his feelings, knowing she couldn't bring herself to say the words back. "Maxine, I'll take you however you are. Always."

"And?"

"*And*, I'll go make us some scrambled eggs."

Teddy and Maxine spent Saturday night in his bed, lingering over each other's bodies, reluctant to sleep. They both knew it was their last night together before the tournament because they couldn't risk the scandal of being caught in the same room, given that the show put up all the contestants in the same hotel.

By unspoken agreement, they avoided discussing the fraught subjects of Wednesday night: his feelings, the inheritance, or what their post-tournament future held.

Part of him wanted to push for more from Maxine—like a promise they could keep seeing each other after the tournament, at the very least. Best-case scenario, she never went back to Brooklyn at all. Another part of him was simply relieved she hadn't run away after he'd confessed his feelings, and was afraid that he'd already risked too much.

Half the gamble was that so much depended on the results of the tournament. If he won, the world was their oyster—they could go anywhere they liked. But if Hercules won, then Teddy would keep his current position, and what would Maxine do with her days here in Princeton when they didn't have a trivia competition to train for? For that matter, he wasn't quite sure what she'd done with her days in Brooklyn prior to this.

What if their lives weren't necessarily compatible? It was a thought he didn't like to dwell on.

On Sunday, they took separate flights to Los Angeles so they'd have time to get two full nights of sleep and be rested before the tournament—a factor known to improve reaction time. He was proud of her for taking the tournament as seriously as he was. Still, it was the first time he'd seen Maxine so uncharacteristically reserved.

She was nearly silent as they drove to Newark airport, staring out the window at the smokestacks and rubbish lots as if lost in the fascinating annals of her brain.

Teddy, who normally preferred quiet contemplation, was suddenly in the odd position of carrying the conversation. "Are you sure taking different airlines is necessary? I doubt anyone will find it odd we took the same flight, since we live so near to one another."

"Better safe than sorry, right?"

Teddy blinked. "Who are you, and what have you done with my beloved risk-taking Maxine?"

"Don't worry. My flight is actually at eleven a.m. and not at noon. I told you it was later so you wouldn't lecture me about cutting it too close, but I wanted to sleep in."

Teddy glanced at the dashboard clock: 10:07 a.m. "I stand corrected. Only you would have the audacity to test your luck with Newark's security line."

When he dropped her curbside several minutes later and helped her with her bags, Maxine gave him such a long and tender kiss that Teddy had to fight the urge to shove her into the terminal. "Please, go. They'll close the cabin doors fifteen minutes before the departure time."

"I'm just trying to leave you with some romance before we have to spend the next three days pretending to hate each other. I've queued up some really solid trash talk, so you better get ready to bring the heat. We're gonna sell this rivalry like we're going out of business." Her eyes sparkled, but there was something else in her expression that Teddy couldn't place.

Teddy kissed her forehead. "If one of us can somehow win against Hercules, we *will* be going out of business. That prize money is enough to embark upon my writing career and be able to continue supporting my parents."

"So we're still not discussing the inheritance option?"

The phantom glare of fatherly disappointment made Teddy's shoulders tense. "Not yet." No matter how tempting it was. If he won, he wouldn't have to make that choice.

"What about if I win? You know that's still a possibility. I've learned a *lot* of boring shit."

Dutifully, he replied, "Of course you have, darling. You are a fearsome foe in possession of a mind positively resplendent with a vast array of knowledge." Teddy thought for a moment before answering her question. Maxine hadn't mentioned any specific life goals, and he realized, belatedly, he'd never asked. He'd assumed she wanted to play for the thrill of competition. Surely, this prize money couldn't matter as much to her as it did to him.

He winked at her. "If you win, you can finally begin to pay for pornography!"

"Yeah, totally." Maxine opened her mouth as if she was going to say more, but she didn't. After a strange pause, she said, "I really should go."

"You absolutely should."

She marched toward the sliding doors, turned, and blew him another kiss.

"I am about to vomit from anxiety about whether you'll make your flight."

"Okay, I'm going! Jeez!" She turned back around—and generously let a large family pass in front of her, cackling with delight at Teddy's groan of impatience.

Against all odds, Maxine texted him a photo from her seat at 10:52 a.m. with the cheerful caption: Technically, the flight was at 10:55 am! See you in LA, enemy mine.

Teddy breathed a sigh of relief. This tournament week was off to a good start. A sign of good things to come, he decided.

He didn't know how terribly wrong he was.

THE FINAL ANSWER ROUND

Chapter 23

FIRST MOVES

Answer

The Ruy López, the Sicilian Defense, and the Italian Game are all classic opening moves in this popular board game.

Question

What is chess?

Day 1: Quarterfinals.

The next time Teddy saw Maxine in person, it was Monday morning. Since he, Maxine, and Hercules weren't competing until the second day, he arrived well rested and full of the same confidence he'd felt that cold March morning when his life had changed forever. Now, he experienced the déjà vu thrill of walking into the greenroom and locking eyes with a redheaded hellion at the coffee station.

In deference to their bye for the quarterfinals, she wore reptile-patterned Converse and a cropped T-shirt emblazoned with "Dino's Trivia Night" beneath a loose-fitting green blazer. But she'd done her makeup and wore a flippy miniskirt that showed off the fantastically long legs he'd watched her bronze with some sort of bear-paw mitt on Sunday morning, and it was suddenly as if he'd been punched in the face with a reminder: *she's stunning.*

It didn't matter that they'd exchanged lascivious text messages the night before from their respective hotel rooms, or that he'd had her voice purring into his ear while he came by his own hand. Whenever he saw her for the first time on any given day, he fell in love again as forcefully as if he'd never met her before.

His brief walk past three tables and a handful of fellow contestants was an interminable voyage.

"Well, well, well," she purred, slowly stirring her coffee like a cat flicking its tail at the sight of prey. "If it isn't Theodore Ferguson III."

"The one and only Maxine Hart," he replied coolly.

She popped the stir stick in her mouth, sucking the last drops of coffee free as she locked eyes with his, desire flaring between them. For an instant, the compulsion to kiss her bloodred mouth annihilated reason. When she flicked the stick into the trash and licked coffee off her lower lip, he nearly combusted.

Then someone clapped a hand on Teddy's shoulder, and Ryan Murray drew alongside them, bright eyed and oblivious. "You two play nice," Ryan teased.

"Boo," Tarrah's voice chimed in. Their curvy, plum-haired competitor sidled up to the coffeepot. "Fight to the death! Then there'll be an extra spot in the semifinals. You do karate or something, right, Maxine?"

Maxine's mouth curled. "Oh, I don't need to kill Teddy to take him out of the running. Just give him a sports clue, and he'll *run* all the way back to New Jersey."

"That's quite the distance. But perhaps you're confusing my home state's location with another's. I know maps can be rather confusing."

Tarrah sipped her coffee, wide eyed with glee. "Oh, this is good."

Maxine sauntered over to the doughnuts. Teddy retrieved coffee, then followed.

So did their growing audience, which now included several other contestants gathering at the coffee station, pretending not to eavesdrop.

Maxine said to him, "What I *am* confused about is why you bothered to show up. I mean, since you sucked so hard during the practice game at McKnight's place."

"Me?" he sputtered, temporarily forgetting this was only a ruse. "Have you acquired amnesia?"

"Denial ain't just a river in Egypt."

"Well done, you've learned your rivers."

"Oh, you have no idea." She plucked a doughnut from the stack and inspected the white powder atop it. "Did you know it's titanium dioxide that makes the powder so white?"

He reached for the doughnut. *His* doughnut. "You don't even like chocolate."

"But I do love the smell of victory," she said, waving her hand over the confection like a perfumer wafting a fine scent toward her nose.

They were interrupted by a voice coming on over the loudspeaker: "All contestants in games one and two, please report to hair and makeup."

Amid the shuffle as Tarrah and the rest of the first two groups lidded their to-go cups of coffee and hurried off, no one paid attention to Maxine handing Teddy the doughnut on a paper plate.

Thank you, he mouthed.

Maxine winked at him, then used a powder-tipped digit to swipe a crude drawing on the black lapel of his jacket.

"Must you?" he groaned, reaching down to brush it off—until he saw what she'd drawn.

With a finger wave, she departed. "See ya later, el lagarto."

He sipped his coffee to hide his smile of satisfaction. She'd marked him with a little white heart.

He'd watched the first game from the front of the audience section, as did most of the other players. Contestants weren't required to watch the other matchups, but it was not only tradition to do so (and good sportsmanship to cheer on one's fellows), but an opportunity to assess the performance of one's potential competition in the semifinals—just as Maxine had watched him play that very first day.

Maxine slunk into the audience only a few minutes before the game started, slipping into the last row of seating without making eye contact with Teddy. He tried not to feel a pang; this distance was what they'd agreed on.

The game itself was only of moderate interest to Teddy, however. Eleventh-ranked Andrea Hsu and eighteenth-ranked Trey Sambu competed against Tarrah Prince, whom Teddy and Maxine had already played more than once now. Andrea was known for aggressively going after the Daily Duplex clues, but Trey found the first-round Double—only to get it wrong—and Tarrah found both in the second round, missing one and barely recovering her lost money with the second. It was a low-scoring game with particularly challenging clues, and no one performed all that well. The three players each guessed the Final Answer clue incorrectly, with Tarrah winning by a lackluster margin.

But he still missed Maxine—and since audience members were highly discouraged from using cell phones during tapings, he couldn't even send her a suggestive text note.

In his dreams, they'd be sitting here side by side, with Maxine whispering snarky comments about everyone's wagers, and Teddy catching her eye when someone missed a clue that they really *should* have known.

The second match of the day was, at least, exciting enough to take his mind off his secret romance. Sikander Shaw was the favorite to win this contest; he was up against the unmemorable Jay James—the medium-brown-haired man who'd interrupted them in Hercules's library—and Rayla Woods, a soft-mannered Canadian who played in a cautious but steady manner of which Teddy wholeheartedly approved.

Sikander dominated in the first round, clearing an Olympics category as well as a category about *Twilight*, of all things.

("My wife is a fan," Sikander had answered stone faced when Dr. Love posed the question during the interview break, to which Dr. Love had replied, "What a dedicated husband you are," in such a tone as to imply that even the most devoted marriage did not impart one with the knowledge that Robert Pattinson's glittering abdominals had been brushed on with makeup.)

But Jay, who'd never stood out to Teddy as anything but an above-average player, was a dark horse in the second half, coming from behind to claim both Daily Answers and narrowly edge Sikander out of the lead going into the final. In the end, Sikander signed his own death warrant by betting everything—and getting it wrong—which allowed Jay to capture an unlikely win.

See? Never bet it all on a Final Answer category as deceptively simple as Epitaphs, Teddy would have said to Maxine, were she sitting next to him. The clue asked contestants to identify whose gravestone read "I'm a writer, but then nobody's perfect," which required that one know the quote was a paraphrase of the final line of *Some Like It Hot*, and then doubly required one to know Billy Wilder cowrote and directed that movie.

Imaginary-Maxine would have turned to him and said something like, *If you got that wrong, I'd revoke your jazz-enthusiast card.*

And Teddy would have replied, *I most certainly knew the answer, but the category wasn't Jazzy Movies, was it?*

Finally, it was time to break for lunch. Teddy leaped from his seat and made his way to the greenroom, fighting the urge to push his way past the rest of the contestants and audience members who crowded the narrow walkways. Maxine was already seated when he arrived, and the pizza delivery she'd sprung for made her table a popular destination for the other contestants. There were only two chairs left, but if he could snag one on the pretense of wanting pizza—

Hercules appeared in his path and clapped him on the shoulder. "Why, Teddy Ferguson! Just the gentleman I'd been hoping to encounter."

Tarrah took one of the two remaining seats.

Teddy forced a polite nod. "Mr. McKnight." He didn't want to speak to the trivia world's greatest champion and hadn't done so since he'd seen Maxine prance out of his party with the man's ponytail in a plastic bag. It didn't help that Teddy had spent the last five weeks of training against HercAI, who was a massive twat—computer-wise—and now Teddy had the strongest urge to tell the man he'd once idolized to get the hell out of his way so he could eat pizza while stealing longing glances at one of his competitors.

"Would you care to join me for lunch off campus? My treat."

"Thank you for the offer, but unfortunately . . ." Teddy trailed off as Zhang Wei claimed the last seat.

Teddy shook himself. He was being ridiculous. What was he going to do, play footsie with Maxine under the table?

Hercules lowered his voice. "I've acquired some terribly fascinating information regarding your time at McKnight Academy. I think it'd be wise to discuss it before tomorrow's matches, wouldn't you say?"

Teddy's blood became ice; then it sublimated into vapor. *Why does that sound like blackmail?* Maxine had repeatedly called Hercules a scam artist, but he'd written it off as part of her general dislike for rich people. Had she been right, all along?

No. He had to be imagining things. Hercules McKnight was a respected trivia champion, with an abundance of wealth and power at his disposal. It made absolutely no sense that he'd risk doing something *illegal* over a game show.

But what if Hercules had found out that it was Teddy who'd discovered the cheating in the first place? That it was Teddy who'd sent an anonymous email to the National Quizzing League Board, sparking the scandal that had begun the McKnight Academy's decline? And what if, now, he planned to use this information to have Teddy disqualified from the tournament? It was one thing to have attended a school long ago; it was another to have tipped off a nationwide scandal involving said school—*that* could be construed as a serious conflict of interest.

Would it matter at all that Teddy had attempted to do the right thing and withdraw? Or would Teddy's face flash across his father's television news screen under the headline, "*Answers!* Tournament Marred by Scandal"? It would surely break Arthur Ferguson's heart and forever tarnish what little lucid memory remained of their relationship.

"On second thought, I'd be delighted to have lunch with you."

Teddy tried not to feel the weight of Maxine's stare as he left with their competitor. *Focus—you can't worry about Maxine's judgment right now.*

He tried to reassure his nerves that if Hercules had already reported it, Teddy would be in Nora's office, not en route to lunch.

"My driver's parked by the main gate, and I've reserved a table at the Peninsula," Hercules told him as they strolled out the studio doors into the sunlight. "We'll be back in time for the second half of game three, if you care to watch the others play."

The way he said *the others* reminded Teddy of the way his wealthier Oxford classmates had jokingly called students attending on scholarship *the commoners*. Although Teddy had been bothered by Hercules's mockery of Maxine during their prior encounters, the full scope of the man's elitism was starting to dawn on him. As Maxine would say: this guy sucked.

And maybe—just maybe—Teddy had missed all the clues because there'd been a vestigial part of him that related to the feeling of *better than*. He hadn't fit in with the other New Jersey public school kids, so he'd decided to style himself in the lofty image of his Ferguson ancestors—as if any of *them* hadn't been hugely elitist twats. His snobbery had only worsened when he'd gone to Oxford.

To add insult to his humiliating self-realization, his memory supplied a reminder of the time he'd first met Maxine and demanded to know where she'd gone to university. And then he'd called her an *uneducated nobody*.

God, I'm an idiot. I owe Maxine several apologies for the way I've acted.

As Hercules's driver held the door of a black sedan open for them, Teddy's phone buzzed. Out of habit, he swiped open his screen to see a text from Maxine: wtf????

He looked up to see Hercules watching him, eyebrows raised, and Teddy realized he'd made a huge mistake—he hadn't bothered to tilt the screen away.

And above her most recent text were the photos they'd sent each other the night before. Blood rushed to his face.

Never once in his entire life had he had reason to worry about something inappropriate popping up on his phone, but now he did, and Maxine would murder him if he'd given away their affair with his naivete.

Teddy hastily shoved the phone in his breast pocket.

"Oh, I didn't see a thing," Hercules drawled, lips curling with smug satisfaction.

Fuck.

This day had gone from bad to worse.

Chapter 24

OTHER STAIRWAYS TO HEAVEN

Answer

The extremely steep staircase at this UNESCO World Heritage Site in Cambodia is said to represent the difficulty of ascending to the kingdom of the gods.

Question

What is Angkor Wat?

Between the fifth and sixth games of the day, Maxine leaned against the stucco wall in the smoking area, absorbing vitamin D into her pale cheeks.

Her eyes were closed. The cigarette she toyed with was limp from being rubbed back and forth between her fingers. It had been a long time since she'd actually smoked one; the taste and smell of a live stick were repulsive to her, and the nicotine buzz wasn't worth it.

Lowest ROI of all the drugs out there, Maxine liked to tell people who asked—and people always asked. Nonsmokers and smokers alike were suspicious of a woman simply holding a cigarette.

What was she supposed to say to them? That she sometimes felt horribly alone and wished her sister weren't away at med school, and that the familiar smell of tobacco was the next-closest thing to a hug from her dead mom?

Now, though, she wished she had a lighter. Even the rare caress of warm sunshine wasn't doing jack shit for her nerves.

Why hasn't Teddy replied to my text?

Doubt gnawed at her. Tiny, insidious fangs, attached to a lifetime of trust issues. There was absolutely no way that Teddy—the obsessively honest, by-the-book man she'd fallen in love with over the past five weeks—was going to get involved with Hercules's shady, game-rigging business.

She tried to dismiss her nagging suspicions. Getting lunch with the guy didn't mean anything. And maybe Teddy still had his phone on airplane mode and wasn't checking it between games.

Maybe.

"Well, well. I didn't take you for a fumigator, Miss Hart."

Speak of the devil. Maxine didn't have to open her eyes to recognize that smug drawl. "Eat a dick, McKnight."

There was a distinct snick, then the bright, acrid scent. "As generously liberated as I am to the concept, I'm merely here to enjoy my vice, same as you. No need to get feisty. You can save that for Wednesday."

She cracked an eye and inspected her opponent. Hercules McKnight wore all black—a black tee, black slacks, and black dress shoes. It really made the Valencian hue of his skin pop. "Nice haircut."

Hercules leaned back against the same wall and took a long, long drag. His hair in question had been cut further after Maxine's intentional hack job, and he'd slicked it back with enough gel to run a Slip 'N Slide party off his scalp. Smoke curled around his exhaled words: "You'll regret that, you know."

"Oooh, are you threatening me?" Now both her eyes were open, her pulse thrumming. This was exactly the excitement she needed to take her mind off the fact she hadn't been entirely forthcoming with Teddy about the man in front of her right now. And maybe—just maybe—she could taunt Herc into giving her clues about whatever shady shit he'd been up to in 1993. (Make no mistake: a man didn't apply that much hair gel unless he did *shady shit*.)

"Why, Ms. Hart! A man like me has no need to *threaten*. The word itself implies fearmongering for the sake of achieving a desired goal, and there's nothing you have that I desire." He tapped ash onto the pavement between them. "I'm merely informing you of facts. Thought you'd appreciate facts, from one practitioner thereof to another."

"Here's a fact for you, then: I think you cheated in your original run."

Hercules paused, cigarette halfway to his lips. "Whyever would you make such a preposterous statement?"

Not a denial. Maxine pretended to inspect the tiny tear she'd worn in her own cigarette's wrapping. "Call it a hunch."

"Mmm." He nodded thoughtfully. "I know your kind, my dear. So much raw intelligence, but no guidance to shape it. It's a shame, really. Had you been a McKnight student, we could have made something of you. As it is, you're merely . . . wasted potential."

"That's a funny thing to say to someone who won thirty-eight games on this show."

"Oh, I saw your episodes. I was impressed: I've never seen a bull charge into a china shop and not break a thing." He exhaled smoke in her direction. "You won't be so fortunate this time. You've got better odds of being struck by lightning."

Maxine refused to flinch. She held her breath until the smoke cloud dissipated, then responded calmly, "I'm going to win this tournament."

"That requires you to win your semifinal match, doesn't it? You, of all people, know anything can happen on this show." He pushed off the wall and stepped into Maxine's personal space, blocking the sun like a malevolent eclipse. In a low voice, he said, "I could help you, you know."

"I'd rather share a stadium hot dog with Margaret Thatcher's rotting corpse."

"Such an angry, bitter woman. What *does* Theodore see in you?"

Betrayal sliced through her gut. Hercules looked so certain. So smug.

Teddy wouldn't have told Hercules about our affair. He knows how much I hate that guy.

But her memory supplied an image of Teddy and Hercules standing there during Maxine's teaser interview five weeks ago, laughing like chummy rich boys at a polo match. And she distinctly recalled a contestant interview during his run in which Teddy had credited Hercules as the inspiration for his own interest in trivia.

It didn't matter.

If Teddy had spilled the juice to earn Hercules's favor, she'd cut his heart out and feed it to Miss Cleo—but that was between her and her man. It wasn't any of this scumbag's business.

Maxine locked eyes with Hercules. Slowly, she plucked the cigarette from his fingers and dropped it on the ground. Sparks danced between their feet, and Maxine crushed the butt beneath her boot.

"He goes by Teddy," she said. "Not Theodore."

But before he could answer, James (or was it Jay?) popped out of the stage door and gave them a cheerful wave. "So this is where all the cool kids are hanging out! Is there room for one more?"

Hercules stepped back from Maxine and swept a hand in elegant welcome. "By all means."

Jay ambled over to them, patting his khaki pockets before giving them a sheepish shrug. "Can I also bum a cigarette? My wife's been trying to get me to quit, but I swore I had a couple stashed away."

Hercules offered his pack to the other man with a polite smile that didn't reach his eyes. "You played quite the surprising match," Hercules said.

It wasn't a compliment, but Jay seemed to take it like one, his eyes lighting up in starstruck delight. "Thanks! Boy, no one was more surprised than me. I guess luck was just on my side. Huge fan, by the way.

Man, I can't believe I'm standing next to the legend himself. Can I get a photo with you later to send to my Chrissy? Y'know, butter her up before she finds out I snuck a couple smokes?"

"Why, I'd be delighted." Hercules did not look like he'd be delighted. Nevertheless, he allowed himself to be posed for several shots with the other man.

Maxine used the opportunity to slink back inside. *Not retreating from battle—only regrouping,* she told herself. It was better than letting McKnight see that he'd gotten under her skin.

The hallway was sparsely populated, with only Maxine and a stray crew member dashing toward the backstage access doors. There was only a fifteen-minute break between tapings, and from the sound of applause coming from the auditorium, they'd just begun the sixth and final match of the day. Maxine supposed she should be watching, since whoever won this match would compete in the third semifinal game tomorrow against her and Helen Kaur, the purple-haired librarian who had won game five. But she needed a minute in private to gather herself. To mute the insidious voice of distrust in her head.

She was halfway down the hallway to the greenroom when she saw Teddy exit from the emergency stairwell to the second floor, where Nora and other important people to the show kept their offices. It was an area strictly off limits to contestants during taping—or so the *Answers!* contestant coordinators had said. He held a manila envelope under his arm, tucked tight against his chest.

Her heart plummeted. *The evidence stacks up, and it's not looking good.*

Teddy turned, visibly startling. "Maxine. What are you doing here?"

"Well, well, if it isn't Sir Fergalicious," she called, sauntering the rest of the way to meet him at the stairwell door. She glanced over her shoulder, making sure no one was behind her, then lowered her voice to an urgent hiss: "What the hell are you doing?"

Please have an explanation for this. Maxine had never wanted to be wrong more in her life.

Teddy clutched the envelope tighter, but his face was a perfectly schooled blank mask—something he'd never have been able to do five weeks ago. "I had a meeting."

"A meeting," Maxine repeated flatly.

"Yes."

"What the *fuck*—" She took a calming breath, then grabbed his arm and pushed him ahead of her into the dimly lit stairwell. "We need to talk. Alone."

A single fluorescent light buzzed quietly on the second floor ceiling, one of the two tubes having burned out. When the door shut behind him, she walked him against the cement wall so that they were out of sight of the rectangular window in the first floor door.

He went willingly. "I know this looks suspicious—"

"Looks? *Looks?* Teddy, when I said to turn the odds in your favor, I didn't mean you should get caught red handed committing a federal crime." Maxine snatched the envelope from under his arm, embarrassed to note her hands weren't steady. Whether she shook from fear or rage, she couldn't tell anymore. She stared at the "CONFIDENTIAL" sticker sealing the envelope shut, and then slowly looked up to meet Teddy's shadowed blue eyes. "Tell me what's inside here."

She knew the answer, but she needed to hear him say it. If he told her the truth . . . that would be better than nothing.

There was a long, pregnant silence before he answered. "I know what it looks like," he said slowly. "But it's not that. Please trust me."

"Why?" When he didn't answer, she repeated her question. "Give me one reason I should believe you, Teddy, because it sure looks like you let that shithead convince you to steal tomorrow's clues for him."

His nostrils flared, as if her words had hurt, but Maxine didn't care. Her own hurt was an enormous lance through her heart. She'd thought about *moving in* (for real) with this man. She'd believed he was a good person.

Yet all it had taken to break him was the slightest pressure from his childhood hero.

"I can't tell you more, no matter how badly I wish I could."

Maxine could open the envelope. Tear the sticker and make it known that someone had looked inside and seen all the clues for tomorrow's semifinal games. They always had backups, in the event the first set of clues was compromised, but the fact Teddy had even gotten into the office where they were kept under lock and key was incriminating enough to disqualify him from the tournament. That's *if* they didn't report him to the feds to cover their own asses.

The envelope burned in her hands, and suddenly she couldn't be holding it anymore. She shoved it against his chest.

"I should report you right now." Maxine had never snitched before in her life, but suddenly she wanted to hurt him. Make him feel what she felt.

"I can't tell you what's going on because I signed a legally binding agreement, and if something goes wrong, you don't want to be involved." He placed his hand over the one of hers that held the envelope to his chest. "Look at me, Maxine. You know me. I'm still the same person who jumped out of a plane with you. The man who irons his sweatpants and sorts all the chocolate pieces out of the snack mix for you."

"Oh. I thought you'd found snack mix that didn't have chocolate in it."

Teddy held her gaze. "Give me your trust for twenty-four hours. That's it."

Maxine stared at the man she'd spent nearly every moment of the past five weeks with. The rival she used to dislike primarily on principle. In her mind, she ran through the viable scenarios.

Scenario one: She reports Teddy. Maxine imagined Nora making the somber announcement; the press release that would follow; the possible follow-up where Teddy gets taken away in handcuffs by the feds . . . the look of betrayal and hurt on his face as he passes her in the audience. The Fergusons watching this go down on TV, Suravi sobbing as Arthur asks, "Why has my boy brought shame on our family . . . again?" Then, Maxine going back to the house to get her things. Orange Cat would be standing in front of the locked door, having awaited their return, only to discover that Teddy was not coming home. (*I smell a rat,* Orange Cat would meow, glaring at Maxine, because unlike dogs, cats would never work with the cops and could ID a dirty, rotten squeaker like nobody's business.)

Scenario two: She doesn't report Teddy. He gives these answers to Hercules. Hercules wipes the floor in the semifinals. Teddy sheepishly explains to Maxine that he was guaranteed a disgusting sum of money, or that Hercules was holding the Fergusons at gunpoint. The latter seems more forgivable, so Maxine goes with that, although she breaks up with Teddy anyway, because how could she ever trust him again after this? Maxine returns to Teddy's house to get her stuff, but he's already there with a new woman: a busty librarian named . . . Batharine. ("Oh, Teddy, I love your big atlases . . . and all your immorally acquired money.") Orange Cat sits in Batharine's lap, purring. Batharine doesn't smell like a rat.

Maxine was miserable in both scenarios. But at least in the latter scenario, Orange Cat was happy, and so were Teddy and his parents. Batharine was going to end up in the East River if she harmed a single hair on Teddy's head, though.

Be excellent to each other. She hadn't lied when she'd told Teddy this was one of the two philosophies by which she tried to live.

Maxine was selective in who she loved; who she brought into her circle of trust. But once she'd chosen someone, they were *hers*, and she'd protect and love them until the heat death of the universe.

Sure, she'd been screwed over by a lot of people she'd dated. But deep down, Maxine knew that those people hadn't passed her gut check. They weren't meant to be *hers*—she'd simply wanted to be chosen by someone. To prove she wasn't the broken, annoying, utterly unlovable person she believed she was, deep down, underneath all the layers of confidence she wore over it.

Unlike all those bozos, Teddy had passed her intuition checkpoint time and again, despite having put up with more than his fair share of Real Maxine (TM). He'd essentially been waterboarded with her full-strength personality in a condensed span of time, and if that wasn't enough to make him run for the hills, there probably wasn't anything else that would. And he hadn't merely put up with her. Teddy had not only helped her feel like she was worthy of being chosen; he'd made her feel like she was whole. Perfectly lovable, exactly as she was. Even after this ended, that feeling was a gift she'd keep forever.

She took a deep breath. Teddy was one of her people, and she'd be excellent to him.

"Okay. I trust you." As soon as she said it, a calm fell over her. A weighted blanket of *rightness.* She released the envelope.

"Really?" Teddy searched her face.

"Yeah."

The tension melted from his posture, and he swept her into a hug, clutching her against himself like she'd float up the stairwell if he let go. He buried his face in her hair and inhaled. "Thank God. I thought I'd lost you."

"You'll have to work harder than that to get rid of me," she mumbled into his chest. Maxine let him tighten his grip and squish her nose into his white shirt, even though it was certainly going to leave a foundation stain. When he was done, she pulled away and gave him an assessing look. Sure enough, there was a pale-peach smudge on his collar.

"Lesson one of lawbreaking: hide the contraband."

She gestured for him to turn around, then took the envelope from him and shoved it halfway into his waistband. She dropped his blazer over it and smoothed it down over the evidence.

"Lesson two: create an alibi."

She steered him back around to face her. Then she dragged his head down to hers and frenched the living bejesus out of him.

At first, Teddy seemed too stunned to react, but it didn't take him long to realize what was happening and kiss her back with fervor. He kissed her like it had been years since the last time, even though it had been thirty-eight and a half hours, and it was a pure shock of pleasure. Nothing had ever been so good. Maxine was an addict, and this was her first hit after withdrawal.

He clutched her backside, dragging her against his growing erection, and a whipcrack of electric need coursed through her. A throaty moan escaped her, only to be swallowed, hushed by his mouth. For that utopian instant, nothing existed outside their kiss. Then, suddenly, the wall was at her back.

Ripping his mouth free of hers, Teddy sank to his knees in front of her and said her name like a prayer. His hands slid up her bare thighs to glide her modest boy shorts down until they pooled at her ankles. Maxine bit her lip and clutched at the wall behind her for purchase so he could prop her left leg on his right shoulder.

He traced a line back up that same leg, parting her with his fingers. Maxine had to silently whistle a slow breath to stay in control as a single digit slid inside, pressing with expert precision against her G-spot. Her inner walls clamped down: *More.*

He responded as if she'd spoken aloud. He gave her more—he pressed a reverent kiss to her clit, then opened wide and wielded his tongue with the precision of an expert swordsman. Flicking back and forth, sweeping around to ply her most sensitive parts, and all the while he worked her dripping pussy with his fingers, until she was hissing breath in and out through her teeth to stop herself from moaning, bucking against his hand. Even still, the lurid, wet sounds of Teddy's fingers echoed in the tall stairwell, amplified by concrete.

She panted in an urgent whisper, "Hurry."

She'd meant to give him a plausibly deniable reason for being rumpled if anyone noticed them exiting—not actually get caught midcunnilingus. And there was only so long both of them could be missing before others took notice.

His mouth came free of her clit with a vulgar slurp. "Trust me," he rasped. "I know how to make you come."

"Oh, no. No, no . . ."

"Shh . . ." He held eye contact. Slid his fingers out of her pussy and inserted them into his mouth, sucking her juices off his fingers. His tongue curled over each one, his eyes briefly closing as he gave a quiet hedonist's groan. When he was finished with his profane display, he slicked his own spit over his middle finger and replaced it beneath her skirt.

But not where he'd been before.

Desperation took hold. She clapped a hand over her mouth, so her own breath wheezed out between her fingers, but she didn't know if it would be enough to stifle her moans.

She felt the lightest touch glide over the tight entrance, swirling a teasing circle around the puckered skin. Her nerve endings lit up, sparking up her spine and tingling the back of her tongue.

His own tongue set back to work on her sensitive clit, redoubling his efforts, and suddenly her orgasm was right there on the horizon, barreling down the track too fast. Maxine scraped a hand into his hair, her nails curling into his scalp, and the hand holding her hips steady spasmed. Teddy *loved* having his hair pulled. His muffled "*Fuck*" vibrated against her swollen tissues.

She was so close. So fucking cl—

His middle finger eased into her back entrance, gently stretching. Her muscles reflexively relaxed, then tightened back around this foreign invader, the sensation so intimate and erotic and wicked that Maxine's eyes rolled back, her head fell against the wall, and her body seized with an orgasm that exploded through her body. A gravelly moan came ripping out of the depths of her lungs, and it was all she could do to keep her hand in place, to crush it back into her mouth.

She pulsed against his mouth and finger until her standing leg gave way, and Teddy broke free to steady her.

"Are you all right?" he whispered.

Maxine finally let her hand fall to her side, freeing her voice. "Seriously?"

"I meant, can you stand?"

She managed a nod.

With expert skill, he withdrew one of his signature hankies from his breast pocket and wiped his fingers clean. Then he tugged her underwear back up her legs, smoothed her skirt down, and came to his feet. With a kiss on her forehead, he stepped back and leaned against the opposite wall.

"You'll have to go out first." He gave a meaningful glance at the obvious erection straining his pants.

Maxine gave him a dazed nod and swiped at her hair. "Right. Um, do I look somewhat decent?"

Teddy raked a glance up her body, mouth quirking at one end. "Not in the slightest."

"Well, at least your alibi is rock solid."

"Among other things."

"Don't look at me for pity. You'll still have a lot of explaining to do when this is over." Maxine cracked the door, ensuring the coast was clear. Before slipping out into the hallway, she reminded him, "Twenty-four hours."

QUARTERFINAL RESULTS

Quarterfinals Winner of each game advances to semifinals	Semifinals Winner of each game advances to finals	Finals
GAME 1 Tarrah Prince (10) ~~Andrea Hsu (11)~~ ~~Trey Sambu (18)~~	Hercules McKnight (1) Tarrah Prince (10) Jay James (9)	Highest score wins 1st place: $2,000,000 2nd place: $500,000 3rd place: $100,000
GAME 2: ~~Sikander Shaw (6)~~ Jay James (9) ~~Rayla Woods (15)~~		
GAME 3: Ryan Murray (4) ~~Colin Julias (16)~~ ~~William Broad (20)~~	Teddy Ferguson (2) Ryan Murray (4) Zhang Wei (7)	
GAME 4: Zhang Wei (7) ~~Matt Cricket (12)~~ ~~Mi-Kyung Hwang (17)~~		
GAME 5: Helen Kaur (5) ~~Rutger Bradley (13)~~ ~~Tom Damiota (19)~~	Maxine Hart (3) Helen Kaur (5) Zola Mattick (C*)	
GAME 6: Zola Mattick (C*) ~~Jeff Jones (8)~~ ~~Cristal Lunnpo (14)~~		

(n)—player's rank

(C*)—College Tournament champion, Fan Favorite poll winner

Chapter 25

LOVE AND BASKETBALL MOVIES

Answer

This actress's character, Gloria, spends most of *White Men Can't Jump* studying for a trivia game show called *Jeopardy!*

Question

Who is Rosie Perez?

Day 2: Semifinals.

The air in the *Answers!* studio the following morning smelled like Lysol, cheap coffee, breath mints, and Helen Kaur's patchouli-based perfume, but Maxine's nose also picked up undertones of tension and whatever the fuck had crawled up Nora's ass to die.

The executive producer's rock 'n' roll mullet was flat, her mouth pinched. As eight of the nine remaining contestants milled about the greenroom post-hair and post-makeup, Nora greeted them with a distinct lack of her usual dry New Zealandian charm.

"Quick announcement about a schedule for today," Nora called out, tapping her clipboard on a tabletop to capture everyone's attention.

Maxine looked up from the breakfast burrito she'd been wolfing down.

Tarrah and Ryan sat at Maxine's table, gossiping about last night's after-party. With no next-day competition hanging over their heads, everyone who'd lost in the quarterfinals had gone out on the town to celebrate, and someone had thought it was a good idea to bring up the age-old debate about whether the *Iliad* or the *Odyssey* fucks more. Shit had gotten so out of hand that Sikander Shaw left with a black eye, Rutger Bradley was now banned from Wingstop, and apparently Rayla Woods was seen going back to Andrea Hsu's hotel room.

Elsewhere in the greenroom, Teddy ate his special doughnut in stiff silence at the same table as the *J*-named dude who wasn't the Jay who'd crashed Maxine's showdown with McKnight yesterday in the smoking area.

At another table, Zola Mattick, Helen Kaur, and Zhang Wei quietly reviewed study material.

Hercules, who was too important to be corralled in the greenroom with the proletariat, was doing an "important work call" from an empty office across the hall that was sometimes used as a lactation room. When Maxine had passed by earlier, she'd heard Hercules asking for a *sepia-toned desert aesthetic* and determined he was either on a call with his interior designer or his personal tanning salon.

"Due to a personal matter, Jay James has been delayed this morning, so we'll be reversing the taping schedule," Nora went on, her tone as miserable as a newscaster reporting that Godzilla was, in fact, no longer on our side. "Game three will be first up with Maxine, Helen, and Zola. Then game two, with Teddy, Ryan, and Zhang, and then we'll record Hercules, Tarrah, and Jay after lunch."

"Sweet," Tarrah said.

Maxine tried to catch Teddy's eye, but he was busy dissecting his doughnut, a troubled expression on his face. Was having her compete first part of the plan? Had McKnight intentionally sabotaged another contestant—poisoned his cigarette, maybe? Maxine's mystery-obsessed brain had spent all night twisting itself into the same knots it was trying to unravel.

Maybe McKnight's plot was as simple as: steal the answers, hope to beat everyone to the buzzer, and talk smack to Maxine to throw her off balance.

Or maybe there was nothing sinister going on at all. What if Teddy's envelope had contained top-secret recipes from the cooking show they filmed in Studio 8?

One way or another, Maxine was going to find out today.

Don't make me regret trusting you, she thought in Teddy's direction.

Before she knew it, they were all being herded backstage by the contestant coordinators. "Time for the practice game and sound check," Paul announced.

Maxine placed herself strategically within the herd, so that when it came time to select the first three contestants to play a few test clues, she and Teddy would be side by side.

She glanced at him from the corner of her eye as one of the sound techs clipped a lapel mic onto her tyrannosaurus-printed blouse, trying to read anything at all from his body language, but Teddy didn't look at her at all. He was like a diluted version of himself—Teddy Lite.

The intimidating Dr. Love was perched behind the podium. She'd stopped standing during taping a few years ago, when a minor stroke had left her with weakness on her right side. But Maxine secretly suspected the elegant older woman enjoyed lording over contestants from the velvet, throne-like stool they'd procured for her.

Maxine was surprised to see her at all, given that usually Paul or another coordinator ran the practice round. Perhaps it was a sign that Loretta was as invested in this tournament as everyone else was.

"First three victims, step up to the podiums," Dr. Love commanded.

"Contestants," Nora corrected.

Dr. Love merely gave Nora a look over the top of her cat-eye reading glasses. Nora may be their new executive producer, but everyone knew who really had the final say around these parts.

Maxine, Teddy, and Ryan stepped up to their podiums.

"You all know the drill," Loretta told them. "Ten questions, standard rules apply, scores don't matter. Problems with your mic, the buzzer, the touch screen—now is the time to let us know. Any other problems unrelated to the technical equipment, tell someone who cares. Probably that guy over there."

Paul waved at them.

"I'd ask if you have any questions, but that's the entire point of the game. Ready? Ms. Hart, you have control of the board, if not your sense of fashion."

"Thank you, Dr. Love. I'll take Foods That Start with the Letter Q for eight hundred."

Maxine could have played soft and started with a $200 clue—none of this really mattered. But it was clear that Teddy's head wasn't in the game, and there was only one thing she knew would spark his competitive spirit—a warm-up ass kicking. And thus, she started with the column second from the left, four rows down, where the round's Daily Duplex clue was statistically most likely to appear.

Dr. Love read: "'This game bird can be easily distinguished from its distant pheasant relatives by its topknot-like head plumage.'"

Not a Daily Duplex, but an easy clue nonetheless. Maxine hit the buzzer, and the row of red lights on her podium—which faced Maxine so only she and not the audience could see—lit up, indicating she'd gotten to the question first.

"What is quail?" Maxine answered.

"Correct."

She took the time to cast a smug glance at Teddy. *See? I'm not going easy on you just because we're in love. Get your head in the game.*

"Same category, six hundred."

The dulcet synths of the Daily Duplex sound effect chorused through the set's speakers.

Dr. Love made the go-ahead motion. "Wager?"

Maxine rested her elbow on the podium, directing her answer to Teddy. "A bajillion dollars."

On her right, Ryan could be heard snickering, but Maxine only had eyes for the man on her left.

Below his breath he asked her, "What are you doing?"

"Play," she gritted between her teeth.

"It's only practice," he gritted back.

Dr. Love sighed. "For a bajillion imaginary dollars . . . 'In his precursor to the encyclopedia *Natural History*, Pliny the Elder wrote that this "golden apple" is an emblem of Venus, the goddess of love.'"

"What is a quince?"

"Correct. For a bajillion and eight hundred dollars."

Maxine called for the $1,000 *Q* clue.

"'This location-named variety of savory tart is made with cream, eggs, and bacon.'"

She buzzed in, but her red lights didn't blink on.

Teddy's voice rang out, "What is quiche Lorraine?"

"Good," Dr. Love said. Was it Maxine's imagination, or was there a note of approval in that tone? It seemed the legendary host wanted a lively rematch of rivals in this tournament as much as everyone else did.

By the end of the practice round, there was finally a tiny spark of life in Teddy's ocean eyes, Ryan hadn't managed to buzz in on a single answer, and the two had tied 5–5. Not that anyone was keeping score.

Except—based on the excited whispering from the other contestants and staff—everyone *was* keeping score. Maxine hoped to hell that both she and Teddy would make it to the final match, because a lot of people were going to be disappointed if their long-awaited face-off never came to fruition.

Ryan raised his hand to call Paul over, then held out his buzzer for analysis. "I think something's wrong with my signaling device."

Paul looked like he was fighting a grin as he inspected the item in question.

As Maxine cleared the stage for the next round of practice contestants, Tarrah gave her a high five. "Hottest foreplay I've ever seen. Don't stop, I was almost there."

You and me both. "We'll finish you off in the finals, baby."

Truth was, she'd forgotten how thrilling it was to battle wits with Teddy when they were both switched on. She felt flushed, a buzz running below the surface of her skin. And this was just from ten questions. Imagining a full sixty-one-clue game made Maxine breathless.

After that, she watched from the audience seating as the remaining five players ran through their practice tests, paying special attention to Hercules.

Unfortunately, the *Answers!* legend didn't reveal anything useful, only bothering to ring in for one practice clue. Every now and then, he even set the buzzer down to slick his hair back with a hand like an old-timey gangster, as if he cared more about how he looked than anything else. He leaned against the first podium with such a studied air of cool indifference that Maxine expected him to don a pair of aviators and depart the stage on a motorcycle.

When Hercules lingered onstage to flirt with Dr. Love, Zola Mattick, who sat to Maxine's left, said under her breath, "Ew. What a paper cut."

"A paper cut?" Maxine asked. She made a mental note to remember this hip new terminology.

Zola gave her side-eye. "Don't write that down, it's not Gen Z slang or anything. I just said it because paper cuts are annoying."

"I didn't write anything down."

"Uh-huh."

Maxine fought a smile. "You'd get along well with my younger sister."

"She hot?"

Maxine thought about it. "I think Olive pulls in a 'take a seat while I finish my math homework' sort of attraction."

Zola gave a thoughtful nod. "Olive . . . is she coming to see you compete?"

Maxine's heart uttered an involuntary thump of sorrow. "No. I invited her, but she's in med school and can't afford to miss class."

Maxine didn't understand why her sister couldn't voluntarily skip a seminar she'd paid hundreds of thousands of dollars for, but what did Maxine know? She hadn't even attended classes she'd paid zero dollars for.

"I'll fly out to watch it with you on TV when it airs," Olive had vowed apologetically. "You can pay for my flight, since you'll be a double millionaire. Again."

Maxine returned to the dressing room to do a final lipstick check, and then next thing she knew, Paul was hustling her backstage again.

Someone tested her lapel mic.

Someone else blotted Maxine's forehead with powder.

Even though her view of the audience was blocked by a black curtain, she could hear the studio audience starting to file in, the atmosphere charging with anticipation. It was finally sinking in that she was participating in the biggest *Answers!* tournament the show had ever put on in its forty-three-year history.

"You're at the first podium," Paul whispered, lining her up in front of Helen and Zola. He pointed at Helen. "You're second. Zola, third."

They all nodded. This wasn't anyone's first time onstage, but a glance at her fellow contestants said they were all feeling the adrenaline rush. Helen fiddled with the fringe on her silk scarf. Zola rolled out her ankles, then her wrists, then her neck.

Paul pointed at the three of them. "Okay, you're on in three . . . two . . . one . . ."

"Please give a welcome to our first set of players!" came longtime announcer Gilbert Johnson's booming baritone.

Ten strides, and she was onstage, the glossy black floor clicking under her booted heels.

Maxine stepped up to her podium and gazed out over the set, taking in the experience in all its halcyon glory. The color-changing lights and backdrop, the thirty-five blank screens that made up the clue board, the sea of shadowed faces in the audience where the stage lights didn't reach. The audience clapped and cheered with enthusiasm far beyond a regular show taping, and Maxine wondered if Teddy's mother was among the crowd.

Don't think about him. Maxine dragged her mind back to the here and now. Threw her shoulders back and situated herself beneath a crown of confidence. *You are the most badass, capable, fearless player to ever walk on this stage,* she reminded herself. *You've spent five weeks training harder than you've ever trained before, and you are unstoppable. This is your palace of trivia, and you are its queen. Never forget why you're here and what winning means to all the neurodivergent kids who don't believe they have what it takes to do something like this. Show no mercy, you foxy fucking bitch.*

On her touch screen, Maxine inscribed her name: "MAX ♡." Then she picked up her signaling device and prepared to take it to the max.

Zola and Helen were good players, but they weren't anywhere near Maxine's buzzer skill level, and neither of them bet like she did either. Maxine would angle to keep librarian Helen away from literature questions and engineer Zola away from science and math questions. She knew she'd have this in the bag as long as she could keep control of the board and find those Daily Duplex clues. Wager big, pull ahead early, close out the second round with an unstoppable lead and a lock on the win.

Except nothing went the way it should have.

Chapter 26

IT'S GRAMMAR TIME

Answer

The motto "all for one, one for all" is an example of this rhetorical figure in which two or more clauses are repeated but in an inverse grammatical structure.

Question

What is a chiasmus?

Maxine wanted to punch something.

By the first commercial break, she'd only successfully rung in on one out of fifteen clues. Helen and Zola were murdering her on the buzzer. Zola had even cleared an entire category about the French Revolution.

The studio stayed relatively quiet during the break, as these interludes were used to rerecord any misspoken clues or introductions from the previous segment. While Dr. Love argued with Nora and some of the question writers about the correct pronunciation of *Abbé Sieyès*, contestant coordinators brought Maxine, Zola, and Helen bottles of water and a lively pep talk.

"You're doing great, hon," Paul said, opening the bottle's lid for her.

Maxine waved away the water and thrust her signaling device at him. "Something's fucked with this."

Paul's look of sympathy only made her see red. Did he really think she was like every *other* player who'd blamed their timing problems on the buzzer? "You're just a little slow on the clicker. Try hitting it a skosh earlier, okay? There are still a lot of clues left. Tons of money to make up in the Daily Duplex round."

"No, listen to me, Paul. I could ring in on time in my sleep, okay? This isn't about timing." She showed him by clicking the buzzer. "Test it yourself. Something's off."

Paul motioned for her to lower her voice. "Take a deep breath."

"Please! Just look at it."

Annoyance flashed across his face, but he accepted the pen-shaped clicker from her hand and looked it over. Then he spritzed lemon-scented cleaning spray on a microfiber towel and wiped it clean before returning it to her. "Maxine, we test the signaling devices right before the show starts for a reason. Three separate people used this buzzer and had no problem. And on our end, it's just showing you're ringing in a fraction of a second late. There's no connection error, everything's plugged in . . . you're good, honey. You know how this works."

The set director called out, "All right, back on in ten."

As he left with her rejected water bottle, Paul said, "If it's still giving you trouble, we'll swap it out at the next break."

The audience applauded on cue, and Dr. Love began the interview segment with Zola, who used the opportunity to gush about how it was Dr. Love herself who'd inspired her to get into trivia.

Savvy move, buttering up the host, Maxine thought, but she had a hard time bringing herself to pay attention to the rest of it. The sickly-sweet voice of doubt had wheedled into her synapses.

You're not as good as you thought you were.

How could you ever compete against people like Helen and Zola? Helen's got two degrees! Zola graduated from Medgar Evers College! At her age, you were busy getting fired from a petting zoo for "accidentally" letting Miss Cleo the ball python "escape." Hercules was right: you got a high dose of luck before, and now you're all out. Boo-hoo.

The buzzer in her grip felt cursed. She thought about how Hercules had lingered after the last test round, holding this exact buzzer. He'd been the last person to touch it.

She rolled the device between her fingers, but it looked normal to her. No sign of fuckery. It was Maxine's gut that sensed something was off, not her eyes.

It doesn't matter, she told herself. *Anyone can win with a good hand, but the best players win with bad ones.*

Paul had told her she was ringing in late? Fine—she'd kick the football to wherever the goalpost moved.

Except that strategy wasn't working either. Without knowing exactly how long the delay was on her trigger, Maxine could only guess. The mechanical rhythm she'd painstakingly honed on the Gauntlet was useless because it relied on her subconscious reflexes, and those reflexes were trained to ring in at the "normal" time, not a quarter of a second early.

Her fury grew as the round continued at an abysmal rate for Maxine, and by the end of it, her screen read a grand total of $800.

Helen had $4,600. Zola was in the lead at $5,200.

When Paul came back up to check on her and offer water again, Maxine demanded he switch out her buzzer. "I won't play with this thing anymore."

With a put-upon sigh that indicated he thought she was trying to sell him on sour grapes, Paul called for one of the techs to get the backup device.

Eternal minutes later, as the audience, Dr. Love, Nora, and Maxine's two competitors all awaited this switch out with varying degrees of irritation or curiosity, the tech returned to the stage empty handed. "The backup is missing."

Paul swore under his breath. He called Nora over, and there was a terse discussion in hushed tones. Finally, Nora came up to Maxine's podium.

"All right, we've got two options. We can scrap the game and delay a day or two until we can get in a replacement buzzer, or we can move forward. What do you want to do?" The answer they wanted was clear: delaying the game would inconvenience everyone who worked on the show, and anyone still competing would probably have to reschedule their flights home. They ran on a tight schedule. Did Maxine really want to be a problem child?

Doubt and rage whispered in opposing ears, and it was so, so difficult to resist the urge to cry. She'd worked so *hard*. She'd played by the rules!

Without thinking, Maxine looked out into the audience, trying to find Teddy. She needed to see the look in his eyes that said, *I believe you because you're the most brilliant person I've ever met.*

But Teddy wasn't there.

Nor was Olive.

And there was no one else. Maxine was alone, and the only person she could count on was herself. Just like always.

Before she could stop it, her vision blurred.

Horrified, Maxine shielded her eyes with a hand. Look what falling in love had done to her! Love had poked holes in her shell, and now it didn't seal tight anymore. Her impulsiveness, her emotional reactivity, her insecurity—it was spilling out on a national game show in front of a live audience. Forget about losing to Teddy during the annual tournament; *this* was now the most humiliating experience of her life.

A hand fell on her shoulder. It was Helen Kaur's. "There, there. Take your time. We're already ahead of schedule. Paul, be a dear and get some tissues, will you?" A pause. "And Claudia from makeup."

Maxine swallowed hard. "Sorry," she mumbled. "I'm being a big, stupid baby."

"'Crying does not indicate that you are weak. Since birth, crying has always been a sign we are alive,'" Helen quoted. "Ms. Charlotte Brontë had no tolerance for the patriarchal view that intelligence and emotionality are distinct and oppositional concepts. I, for one, believe they are two halves of a whole. That's why you are so good at playing this game show, you know."

Zola came around to the other side of Maxine's podium. "Hey, Ms. Hart? Did I ever tell you that you're my hero? Not, like, from your run on the show. But because you used to tutor my brother. Zakai said you're the only reason he didn't drop out."

Their encouraging words were like a heavy blanket settling over an out-of-control fire.

"Thank you," Maxine said quietly. They didn't have to console her; her competitors could have let Maxine flounder in a pit of her own bitter rage and used her breakdown to their advantage. It's what Maxine would have done—before she'd fallen in love with Teddy. Guess that wasn't very *Be excellent to each other* of her old self, was it?

Zola shrugged. "Us nerds have to stick together, okay? We're all here because we love trivia. You're one of us."

Then, unexpectedly, Dr. Love approached and held out a hand, palm up. "Let me see the signaling device."

Maxine winced and clutched the buzzer to her chest. "It's fine. Really. I'm just imagining a delay. Paul already looked at it—"

"Ms. Hart, I've been with this show since the day of its inception. Do not presume to advise me on how my equipment works." She took the buzzer gently from Maxine's hand and clicked it—once, then twice. Dr. Love raised her hand to call over a stage tech. "Bethany, go get me some rubbing alcohol and a Q-tip."

"Is there something wrong with it?" Maxine asked.

Dr. Love held the buzzer up to her nose and—of all things—*sniffed* it. "Mm-hmm. Here, tell me what you smell."

Maxine closed her eyes and sniffed. With her nose still drippy with emotion, it wasn't easy.

“It smells . . . like dirt.”

“What kind?”

Come on, she coaxed her nose. She’d trained at one of the world’s premiere perfumeries; surely her sniffer had to be good for more than recognizing Teddy’s vetiver and lemongrass hair product.

Like maybe . . . *recognizing Hercules’s hair product?*

Her eyes flew open. “Metal-based dirt, like volcanic ash. Maybe a bentonite-clay-based hair pomade.”

“Very good,” Dr. Love said, as if Maxine had answered a clue correctly. “And bentonite clay expands when it comes in contact with water. Or in this case, the water-based disinfectant we use to wipe everything down between matches. Swipe a bit of the pomade around the sides of the button, and it’ll get pressed down into the cracks, where it’ll gum up resistance on the very sensitive spring that compresses when you press the button. A very improbable series of events, but luck is a fickle mistress, isn’t she?”

Maxine recalled how Hercules had stroked his hair while he’d flirted with Loretta during the practice round. She cast a furtive glance into the audience, but Hercules was pretending to be preoccupied with his cell phone. Was he really so cocky he didn’t think they’d discover his sabotage?

Well, he’s gotten away with cheating before, she reminded herself. Three decades of getting away with his crimes could do a lot to shore up a scam artist’s ego. Especially when his entire plan hinged on plausible deniability, like this one had.

The tech scurried back with the requested materials, and Dr. Love withdrew from her blazer pocket one of those small screwdrivers found in eyeglass repair kits. She then removed the outer casing of the device and cleaned out the gunk herself. In all, it took less than five minutes, but because no one in the audience could see exactly what they were doing, a buzz of confusion had swelled by the time the show’s host handed Maxine her buzzer.

Maxine cleared her throat. "Thank you. Seriously. Not just for this, but for . . . believing me."

Loretta took in her tearstained face and tapped the top of Maxine's podium—something the host only did when she approved of something the player had said or done. "Remember, this is a game show, and we're here to entertain. Do your best to have fun up here, will you?"

And when the second round began, Maxine did.

Teddy watched from backstage as Maxine claimed her semifinal victory, the tension in his rib cage easing slightly at the sight of her glowing with joy.

Hercules came up alongside him. "That was unexpected."

Teddy glanced around before replying. They stood far enough away from everyone else that they wouldn't be heard over the stage music. At that moment, the lights in the set rose so the audience could use the restroom and have a brief break, and Nora stayed onstage with the three semifinalists to take photos and conduct postgame interviews.

No one paid Teddy or Hercules the slightest attention. Still, Teddy cast his voice at its lowest register as he said, "Sabotaging her buzzer wasn't part of the plan."

The barrel-chested man chuckled, low and dark. "Careful, now. That sounds like an accusation. And didn't we have a nice talk about the kind of accusations we could make of one another? *I* heard a certain someone has a history of *cheating* at Quizzing League. And cavorting with another contestant? Why, that could be construed as downright *collusion*."

Teddy flexed his balled fist, imagining Liu Kang's flurry of blows from *Mortal Kombat*. If only such vengeance were as simple as *press X, repeatedly*. "I'm also assigned to the first podium, based on my rank. Was this sabotage meant to affect my game play too?"

"Oh, Theodore, don't be so dramatic. Technology breaks all the time."

Teddy was glad he'd never trusted Hercules. This cretin would stab his own mother in the back.

"Just remember our deal," Hercules said softly. "All silence comes at a price, dear boy."

When Maxine walked offstage, it took every last ounce of Teddy's willpower not to wrap her in his arms. Seeing her crying from backstage but knowing he was helpless to do anything for her . . . it had nearly broken him.

He tried to catch her eye as she exited the stage, but she avoided looking at him. *Does she think I had something to do with this?*

The thought made his stomach revolt.

"How are you doing?" Paul asked him. The contestant coordinator inspected Teddy's face. "Claudia, do you think you could do a little bronzer here? He's looking a tad *wan*."

From the corner of his eye, Teddy saw Hercules slip away.

Focus on the game, he reminded himself. He'd done everything he could do for the Hercules problem; the outcome was now out of his hands. All he could do was hope his gamble would pay off.

Fortune favors the bold.

Despite everything else going on behind the scenes, Teddy was able to parse out a narrow win in his first match. Ryan Murray and Zhang Wei were solid opponents, but each had areas of weakness that he was able to exploit.

Ryan, who was ranked fourth, had been the one to beat. His breadth and depth of knowledge were impressive, but Teddy realized in the Single Answer round that Ryan did best when he had control of the board, gaining confidence as he cleared categories from top to bottom. It was exactly how Teddy used to play, which meant his job had been to unsettle his opponent by bouncing around the board seemingly at random, hunting for the Daily Duplex clues and preventing Ryan from gaining steam in a single category. Such unpredictability used to give Teddy a headache, but time spent in Maxine's company had made him comfortable with adapting to frequent course changes.

Zhang Wei, on the other hand, was still lightning fast on the buzzer, but he answered incorrectly on several high-value clues. He remained in third place throughout the game but had enough money to play the spoiler for Ryan in the final round, requiring strategic betting from all three players. Fortunately for Teddy, the final category was 18th-Century Poetry, and he was able to begin writing his answer four words into the clue: "'In this beastly poem . . .'" ("The Tyger," William Blake).

Jay, the final missing player, arrived at the lunch break with apologies about an unavoidable work emergency, which meant the afternoon's planned schedule was still on track.

Teddy briefly closed his eyes in relief. Had there been a delay in taping, it would be yet another twenty-four hours before he could hold Maxine. The need to do so was starting to feel urgent, as if he were going to crawl out of his own skin.

He wondered if this was how Maxine felt most of the time; she'd once described boredom as a feeling of intense suffering that filled her with a driving impulse to seek relief at all costs. At the time, he'd struggled to imagine an intangible need so visceral it had the power to overrule logic.

But that was before he'd discovered love.

Not the infatuation that had consumed him after their first meeting—real love. The solvent that had unstuck him from his rigid patterns, swept his neural pathways clean, and made space between his ribs to breathe in joy.

Maxine had taught him to worry less about inconsequential details and more about whether he was having fun. Her love was sunlight streaming in to the darkest corner of a library, murmuring in dust motes against his cheek, *All this collected knowledge is wonderful, but have you been outside lately?*

She brought the pages of his world alive, and without her, he was only an atlas drawn upon a flat page—a two-dimensional re-creation of Teddy Ferguson III. Concentric squiggles mapping the highs and lows of his existence.

Across the greenroom, Maxine laughed at something Tarrah had said. It was only when her gaze snagged on his that Teddy realized he'd been staring.

Her smile faded, and she tore her gaze away.

Panic clawed at him. Everything hinged on this afternoon, when this absurd high-stakes poker game with Hercules would come to its conclusion. But what if she still didn't forgive him, even after the truth came out?

I can't let her go.

All this time, he'd wanted to compete in this tournament because of the $2 million prize. Then, he'd decided, his future would be secured. But what was a future without Maxine? If there was a prize to be won in this battle of wits, it wasn't the money—it was her.

Teddy knew what he needed to do tomorrow.

But first, there was something even more important he'd forgotten. Something he should have done days ago.

He picked up his phone and sent a single text to Maxine . . .

Chapter 27

GOOD ADVICE FROM BAD GUYS

Answer

During an 1805 battle, this general is quoted as having said to his marshals, "Let us wait twenty minutes; when the enemy is making a false movement, we must take good care not to interrupt him."

Question

Who is Napoleon Bonaparte?

As the final game of the day got underway onstage, Maxine sat in the audience, clutching her phone against her breast like it was a bouquet of flowers.

Teddy: Miss u, sexy.

He'd remembered. Romance really wasn't dead, after all.

Unfortunately, something else was looking fully unalive, and that was Tarrah's and Jay's chances of beating Hercules. Despite the fact that the *Answers!* legend wasn't buzzing in first on every question, by the end of the first two rounds, his correct-answer rate was 100 percent.

Any hope Maxine had harbored that maybe the Envelope of Doom contained something other than the clues Hercules was acing had long since dwindled.

"The final category today is Sports History. Contestants, make your wagers." Dr. Love smiled into the close-up camera until the stage manager announced the cut; then the host's smile instantly dropped. At the podiums, Tarrah, Jay, and Hercules bent over their touch screens. They'd have been given a pen and paper to handwrite their wagering math, but no one had to do any calculations—Hercules was going into the final round with a runaway lead.

"Someone bring me a potent potable," Tarrah called out, which received a lively response. Since no one on the production side tried to stop her, Tarrah then asked of the crowd, "What do we think? Should I bet eighty bucks?"

There were cheers in the affirmative. Tarrah had a grand total of $500, after barely clawing her way out of the hole on a Daily Duplex question. When they cut to commercial, Nora spoke into the producer's mic, "Just a reminder, Ms. Prince, any wagers resulting in off-limits values will be disqualified. I *know* you read my emails."

Tarrah shrugged. "Always wanted to go out in a blaze of glory."

"We'll cut away from the screen and rerecord the entire bit," Nora threatened.

"Oh my god, I'm kidding." Tarrah waited until Nora had turned away to speak with a PA who'd come darting into the studio with a flurry of urgency, then gave the audience an exaggerated wink.

Then Maxine saw something she hadn't seen before, at least not during her taping experiences: Nora went up onstage to say something to Dr. Love, and after a tense exchange, they both disappeared backstage.

There were murmurs in the audience, but only a few. Most of the crowd here hadn't been to a taping before, so they didn't know it was strange to have such a long delay before the Final Answer segment.

"You know what's funny?" Zola asked, returning to the seat next to Maxine after stepping out to use the restroom.

"What?"

"There's, like, a bunch of extra security in the hallway right now."

Her heart stage-dived into her stomach. *Please don't let them be here for Teddy.* Had they caught him stealing those questions?

Reputation be damned—Maxine leaned forward in her seat, trying to make eye contact with her lover at the end of the first row in front of her, but it was no use. All she could see were his long, tweed-clad legs stretched out before him, ankles crossed, and his broad shoulders straining his matching blazer as he sat forward, elbows on his knees.

After an interminable delay, Dr. Love took her place at the host stand and presented the Final Answer: "'The 1919 World Series was plagued by an infamous scandal when eight players from this team were caught colluding to throw games in exchange for bribes.'" Maxine knew the answer right away, thanks to Winston: the Chicago White Sox. The event was known colloquially as the Black Sox scandal, and the fallout resulted in increased scrutiny of the sports-betting realm for the rest of the twentieth century.

Hercules appeared to be as confident as he had been the rest of the game. He had plenty of time after setting his stylus down to grin and give a thumbs-up to the cameras that panned across the contestants while the tense thinking music played.

When it came time to reveal the answers, Tarrah went first. Except instead of writing the answer, she had just written: "I had fun After party at the Rainbow Room tonight!" She had wagered zero dollars.

Next up was Jay, who correctly guessed the White Sox, and since he had a lock on second place, he hadn't wagered anything.

Dr. Love said, "Hercules, you've had a perfect game thus far. Let's see if you can maintain that. Did you know the answer was the White Sox?"

Hercules's face had taken on a distinctly greenish cast, and the blue background lights weren't helping.

Then his answer was revealed: he'd written the Chicago Cubs.

It shouldn't have mattered. Hercules already had a lock on the win with a score of 53,600. With Jay's score at a measly 12,100, Herc had room to bet up to 41,499 and still win the match. So why did he seem to care so much that he'd gotten it wrong?

"Congratulations," Dr. Love said. "We know that answer is incorrect, but you didn't need to bet anything to win. How much did you wager?"

The LED panel below Hercules's podium revealed the bet he'd written in bombastic, cursive loops, swollen with ego. The television facing the audience showed a close-up of the same view, and everyone watching at home would see the same thing on their screens. Which meant that everyone realized at the same time what Hercules had done.

He'd wagered it all.

Gasps rang out from the audience. He'd been so confident . . . so certain he knew the answer. And it had cost him the game.

Even Dr. Love's brows rose, as if she couldn't believe what she was seeing. "53,600 points," she read aloud, shaking her head. "You bet everything. And now you have lost it all. It seems your overconfidence has cost you the game, and a seat in the finals." The host turned to the camera. "A legend has fallen, my friends. A historic day here on *Answers!*, and I suspect there will be more surprises for us in tomorrow's final match. We'll see you there."

Maxine still didn't understand what had happened. She'd just seen Hercules answer nearly every single question correctly. Teddy *had* to have given him that envelope with the clues. There was no other way.

But then why had he gotten the Final Answer wrong? It didn't make any sense.

Hercules appeared equally stunned.

The close-out music began to play, but the hair-gelled champion waved his hands. "Stop! There's been a mistake. That wasn't the answer I—"

He stopped himself, but it was too late.

Dr. Love narrowed her eyes. "Wasn't the answer you *what*? That you saw in advance?"

Nora darted onto the stage, approaching Hercules's podium with her hands raised like she was trying to show a wild animal she meant no harm. "Please calm down, Mr. McKnight. We can discuss your concerns—"

He slammed his fist on the podium. "This game was rigged!"

"First you attempt to cheat, and now you *dare* insult my show?" Dr. Love dismounted her podium seat, as if she planned to disembowel Hercules in front of the studio audience.

Nora flagged down Paul, and there was a tense conversation, probably along the lines of: *Get the audience out of here before this turns ugly.*

Paul gave an order over his headset, and suddenly the ushers were very quick to start herding bodies out of the theater. A voice came on over the loudspeaker and advised the crowd: "Due to a routine maintenance procedure, we aren't able to offer photo opportunities in the studio today. We're asking friends and family to greet your contestants outside at the main studio-lot entrance."

When the audience seemed reluctant to go, the ushers redoubled their efforts. "Please make your way to the studio-lot entrance! Let's go, people!"

Maxine and some of the other contestants moved to get up, too, but Paul had come out into the section where the contestants sat, and he motioned for them to sit back down. "Sorry, folks, we need you all to stick around."

"What's going on?" Maxine asked.

Paul gave her an apologetic look. "You'll see."

Onstage, Hercules had begun to yell at Nora. "This is bullshit! You'll be hearing from my lawyers! You hear me, you New Zealand bitch?"

Zola asked, "Where'd his accent go?"

Suddenly, there was a commotion at the entrance. Onstage, Hercules's eyes widened. Breaking off midconversation with Dr. Love, he backed away from the podium.

And that's when Maxine saw the stream of six navy-clad officers making their way toward the stage. The backs of their jackets were emblazoned with glaring yellow "FBI" lettering.

Tarrah cried, "It's legal in California!" before bolting for the stage exit, where she was stopped by another pair of feds who'd appeared there.

"Ma'am, please calm down. We're not here for you."

Tarrah threw her arms around the man's neck. "Oh, thank God! I was so scared."

The agent seemed unsure what to do about the woman clinging to him like a barnacle, so he hesitantly patted her back.

Since she was still miked up, everyone could hear Tarrah murmur into the agent's chest, "Do you do CrossFit?"

Meanwhile, Hercules paced the back of the stage like a cornered boar. His face was still red with fury, but he'd reclaimed his fake-ass Louisiana accent. "Now, Officers, I think there's been a mistake . . . I'm Hercules McKnight, founder of the McKnight Academy. Is there someone in your directorial department I might have a word with about this grave misunderstanding?"

Then, in the most unexpected twist of all, Jay—the human embodiment of one of Teddy's high-fiber cereal bars—stepped into Hercules's path, producing a badge from his back pocket. "Hercules McKnight, you're under arrest for conspiring to fix a game show, which is a federal crime under chapter 5 of US Code title 47, section 509 . . ."

As Jay continued to read Hercules his rights, two more agents emerged from the backstage entrance and handcuffed him.

After that, the afternoon was a whirl of interviews, affidavits, and one-on-ones with Nora and an army of lawyers. Every contestant was asked to sign documentation saying that they were unaware of the behind-the-scenes fixing operation that Hercules thought he'd masterminded—oblivious to the fact that he'd been under investigation for years.

Nora had given everyone involved in the tournament a brief summary of events leading up to Hercules's arrest, but it was Paul who later filled in Maxine on the real juice. ("I should have been a priest; people love telling me things.")

After last year's *Answers!* kerfuffle, the bureau had reached out to Nora, promising to get off the show's back and waive the fines from last season's nepotism-lite scandal if the *Answers!* execs helped bring Hercules in.

At first, the feds had been trying to pin Herc on illegally bribing college-admissions officers to get McKnight Academy students bumped up the acceptance list, but their hunt for clues had sputtered because they hadn't been able to find a single witness who was willing to testify.

"You think he bought people off?" Maxine mused.

"Or blackmail," Paul said. "Rumor is he keeps files on all his students. Spyware on Academy-issued laptops."

Maxine made a face of disgust. "Heinous."

She had to begrudgingly admire the detective who'd woken up one morning and thought to himself, *You know what cold case I should look into with our department's limited resources? That guy who won a fuck ton of game shows thirty years ago.*

And Jay being a fed was a twist that shouldn't have surprised her as much as it did. He was so nondescript that she'd struggle to place him in a lineup, but now Maxine felt like a sucker. She'd fallen hook, line, and sinker for his dweeb routine. Guess that had been the point of the FBI recruiting him after his original run on the show. It didn't hurt that Jay had told her he had three brothers in the military; this was a naturally bookish man who had waited his whole life to be chosen for something more exciting than khaki fits and spelling bees.

So, it turned out the entire tournament had been a setup from the get-go—although the prize money? That was still real. And they still planned to tape the final episode tomorrow, except they'd replaced

Hercules with Zola, who'd finished with the third-highest score in semifinals.

Which meant Maxine still had to defeat Zola—and the man she loved—in order to win the $2 million grand prize. But before their third and final showdown, there was one thing Maxine still needed to tell Teddy.

When she finally got back to the hotel that night, she slipped an envelope with instructions under Teddy's door, and hoped he'd follow them.

♡

At exactly midnight, the elevator doors to the rooftop pool slid open, and Teddy stepped out into the deck illuminated only by the LA night sky and the aqua glow of the pool.

Maxine had left the gate open a crack, and he quietly shut it behind himself. He approached the water where she floated in silhouette, her lower body distorted by ripples where she treaded water.

"Come on in—the water is heated."

At the familiar words, the knot in his chest loosened. He removed his shoes, then approached the edge. "And if I'm afraid of getting in trouble?"

Maxine dived under the surface and reemerged beneath him in the water, a scarlet-haired naiad beckoning him to drown in her arms.

"Want to know a secret?" She grabbed the side of the pool and levered herself up, water sluicing down her pale arms. Her nipples were dark buds beneath translucent ocean-blue underthings. When she beckoned for him to crouch down, Teddy obeyed without a thought, and she whispered, "I don't think you are."

He plucked a damp curl from her cheek and tucked it behind her ear. "Why do you say that?"

"Because you risked losing me to do the right thing. You're the bravest man I know."

"I've never been more terrified in my life," he admitted.

"I know. That's what makes it so badass."

He lowered himself to sit on the pool's lip, letting his trouser-clad legs dangle in the water on either side of her. "When I first went to Nora to report that Hercules had tried to blackmail me into stealing the clues, I thought she'd disqualify me too. But they'd already been looking for a way to set him up. You have no idea how many documents the legal team made me sign—"

"Shh." Maxine pressed a finger to his lips. "Tell me that stuff later. I have to say something first. Well, several somethings. But first, get in so you don't catch a cold."

"It's not that cold—"

"Oh my god, Teddy, I'm trying to have a cinematic moment. Just get in the pool."

Fighting a smile, he pushed off the edge and slipped into the water, letting her warm body glide against his on the way down. He slid an arm around her waist, and she immediately hooked her legs around his. "Happy now?" he murmured into her ear.

Her smile lit up the night. "Yup."

"If you keep rubbing yourself against me like that, you're not going to have a chance to speak."

"I'll be fast, I promise." She punctuated her claim with a roll of her hips that nearly made his eyes roll back in his head. Had it only been seventy-two hours? Desire locked him in a vise.

"You've got ten seconds," he warned.

"Okay, first of all . . ." Maxine's voice was breathy. "I'm sorry I ever underestimated you. You're not a coward. You never have been, and you've taught me that bravery is a lot more than just accepting every risk the universe offers."

A droplet of water traced a path down the side of her neck to her collarbone. Unable to help himself, he bent down to lick it off. "Go on," he said when he was done.

"Second, I wanted to thank you for everything you taught me. For letting me stay with you and take over your life. For trusting me with your heart. For everything." She swiped her tongue over his bottom lip, but when he pulled her back for a full kiss, she dodged away. "Wait, I'm not done yet! This is important."

A sound came from his throat that felt a lot like a growl. "Don't *lick* me if you want to be allowed to finish. What could be more important than this?"

"Before I eat you alive tomorrow on that stage, I need you to know . . ." She searched his face, suddenly hesitant. "I love you."

His heart ballooned to twice the size of his chest, but he managed to hold it together. Given the choice between crying in gratitude and kissing the living hell out of Maxine, he knew where his priorities lay. He pulled her close to himself and cupped her face.

"Prove it," he murmured against her lips.

"I intend to."

"No. Right now."

So she kissed him, and he tasted tropical fruit and chlorine on her lips, and this time when her mouth parted and the kiss ratcheted to a fever pitch, Teddy didn't turn tail and run.

And neither did she.

Chapter 28
GAME THEORY

Answer

An early version of this familiar two-player game was known as *shoushiling* during the Han Dynasty, and used hand gestures to represent a frog, a slug, and a snake.

Question

What is rock, paper, scissors?

Day 3: Finals.

Maxine wore white to her final battle on the *Answers!* stage. Her suit was tailored to perfection, crisp and clean lines up front—a metallic-green snake embroidered on each lapel, and a chain mail corset peeking out from beneath the deep-cut blazer.

Her foe was already in position when she stepped up to the second podium. "So we meet again, Turd Ferguson."

Teddy's lips twitched as he glanced at her from the corner of his eye. He set his stylus down, having written out "Teddy" on the first podium screen in his lovely slanted cursive. "Really?"

"What? It's a funny name."

"Great," came his exasperated reply. Teddy wore a dark evergreen suit with a matching brocade waistcoat and a tiny bronze lapel pin with the Ferguson coat of arms.

"You look rich," she observed.

"Would Elton John like his coat back after taping?" Teddy returned smoothly.

"No, not at all. This was a gift." In a stage whisper: "He's a fan."

"Did you know he composed a Broadway original called *Lestat*, which closed after a mere thirty-nine days?"

"Did *you* know his birth name was Reginald Dwight? *Elton* and *John* were the names of two of his bandmates."

Zola made a disgusted noise from the third podium. "Get a room."

She sputtered. "What? Ew. Teddy? Ha! Never."

The younger woman only rolled her eyes.

Teddy shot Maxine an *I told you so* look.

Claudia from makeup came up to dab powder on Maxine's nose. Another tech came to double-check the signaling devices for a third and final time.

Then Nora came up to all of them. "We're all ready to put yesterday behind us and have a fun time, yeah?"

Teddy adjusted his cuff links. "The funnest."

Maxine hid a smile. "Stoked."

"Beyond," Zola added.

Nora gave the three of them a look that said she wasn't sure if they were messing with her, which was fair. But after this wild ride of a tournament experience, the exec producer deserved a little good-natured ribbing.

Then, to Maxine's shock, a familiar voice called from the audience seating: "Maxie!"

She squinted into the dimly lit crowd and saw a tall, powerfully built redhead waving at her from the first row. Behind her were Marlon and Rabbi Cohen, who waved their hands wildly over their heads.

"Max heart! Max heart!" Marlon called out.

Rabbi Cohen made her signature heart shape with his hands. "We're here on behalf of all of Dino's to wish you luck!"

Maxine rushed to the edge of the stage, making the heart shape back at her Dino's trivia teammates. Then she gestured for Olive to meet her for an embrace. Audience members were absolutely not allowed to come up on the stage like this before the show, but Maxine dared anyone to stop her. She hadn't hugged her little sister in months.

"I thought you were busy with classes," Maxine said into the other woman's shoulder.

"Did you really think I'd miss your triumphant revenge? Besides, I know you like surprises." Ollie pulled back, inspecting Maxine with an assessing eye. "You look suspiciously . . . content."

"Never. I'm a restless soul, never satisfied, always on the move."

Olive looked unbearably smug. "Uh-huh. I called it, didn't I? You're in loooove."

Habit made Maxine want to deny it so Olive wouldn't worry about her if things with Teddy fell through, but instead she forced herself to nod. "I have a lot to catch you up on. Can you stay after the show?"

"I booked a room in your hotel for the night, so you can regale me with all the details about how right I was about you getting lucky with you-know-who. That reminds me . . ." Olive pressed a cool round disk into Maxine's palm—Mom's lucky casino token, which she'd saved from her first big win. Maxine and Olive mailed it back and forth for whoever needed it most. It wasn't superstition, exactly, but it did make her feel like her mother was influencing Maxine's odds from the great slot machine in the hereafter.

Bittersweet joy welled at the thought. Their mom hadn't been the best parent on paper, but Maxine had always known her mom loved them. On the rare nights she'd won, she'd returned to the motel room bearing gifts for her daughters. *Told you luck was coming our way, girls!*

She'd always been so optimistic; nothing had ever made their mother lose hope. In those moments, Maxine had always believed it was true.

Holding this coin made Maxine feel that way again. Like luck was right around the corner—even if, for her mother, that luck had meant being struck by lightning while standing on a beach eating a snow cone. That was still luck, wasn't it? Adjusting the odds only got you so far. Whether you ate your powdered doughnut or mastered buzzer timing, at the end of the day, chance made the final call.

Maxine gave her sister one last hug of thanks. "Now, go sit down and gloat, brat. I have $2 million to win."

"I like your Eurovision costume!" Olive called after her.

Maxine blew her a kiss that ended in a surprise middle finger. God, she loved that woman.

She retook her spot at the podium and cast Teddy a final glance.

"One of us three will determine the outcome of this tournament. The fate of millions depends on us," she said.

His lips quirked. "Let *Mortal Kombat* begin."

Everything that happened next would forever feel like a dream to Maxine.

The lights and music came on, and Dr. Love's introductions were a blur. All Maxine remembered was the moment the first five categories were revealed and she knew, beyond a doubt, that she was meant to win this tournament:

ANCIENT CIVILIZATIONS	RIVERS IN REVERSE	IT'S A MYSTERY	SNAKES AND ADDERS	. . . AND OTHER BOARD GAMES

Then the longtime host announced, "Zola, you won the random drawing to have control of the board first," and the game was underway.

Zola eased in with Ancient Civilizations for $200—a straightforward clue about the earliest known writing system, credited to ancient Sumerians (cuneiform). It was a gimme clue, but the early questions tended to be audience friendly. Maxine picked that one up easily, then bounced to Rivers in Reverse for $800.

"'Completion of a canal in 1900 resulted in this river artificially changing direction.'"

Maxine knew it was the Chicago River, thanks to her memory palace in Teddy's study, but Teddy rang in first with the correct answer, which meant he had control of the board.

Oh, hell no. Maxine couldn't allow him to snag the only Daily Duplex in the round.

Luckily, it was Teddy, so he predictably stuck with rivers and went back up to the top, where the Duplexes were least likely to hide. Maxine snagged the next clue, about the Amazon (which reversed direction after the creation of the Andes), and then she kept control of the board up until the first commercial break.

"You know your rivers . . . backward and forward," Teddy said to her as he sipped bottled water. "Well done."

"I've become a passionate fan of maps."

Teddy studied the board. "These categories are randomly chosen long before the final contestants have been selected. What are the odds all of them are so perfectly attuned to your strengths?"

Maxine thumbed the coin in her pocket and stifled a grin. "About the odds of being struck by lightning."

"I fail to see what's so funny about that statement."

"I'll . . . explain later." Mom had clearly cut a deal with fate on her behalf, but now wasn't the time to explain the morbid irony of that fact to Teddy. He'd be understandably horrified.

"We're back on in ten," someone announced.

Maxine fluffed her hair. "Try to ring in this round, Fergalicious. It's lonely at the top."

Zola cleared her throat. "Y'all know it's not just the two of you up here, right?"

Maxine gave Zola an apologetic moue. "You're absolutely right. It's rude of me not to trash-talk you too."

Zola straightened her spine. "Thank you."

"Thank you, *and* . . . ?"

"Bring it, Millennial Carrot Top."

"Oh, it's already been brought-Zed."

Teddy's groan was cut off by the theme music as the break ended.

Dr. Love approached their podiums with her note cards, which usually contained the contestant-provided fun facts to use as talking points, although Maxine knew they were blank this time. It was *Answers!* tradition to allow contestants to use the final game of a tournament as the equivalent of an Oscars thank-you speech, albeit with far less time to gush and—in most cases—fewer people to thank.

Zola thanked her parents, her Quizzing League coach and teammates, and her dog, Zero.

"Maxine Hart," Dr. Love said, approaching the podium. "The floor is yours."

Maxine recited her boilerplate thanks to Olive and their mom (*RIP, thanks for teaching me to gamble*), as well as the Dino's crew, then took a breath. Up until this very second, she'd intended to keep it short and sweet—but impulse took hold. If this was her final time on this stage, then she wanted to make it count.

Go out in *style*.

"There's one more person I want to thank. When I first came on this show, I thought I had all the answers already. But during my annual-tournament run, the guy on my right taught me I still had a lot to learn. Not just about trivia, but about what I was capable of achieving. It's because of him that I'm standing here now." She turned to face Teddy, locking eyes with ocean-blue ones that had gone wide behind his glasses. "So, thank you. Thank you for being the Moriarty to my Holmes, the Creed to my Rocky, and the Sub-Zero to my Scorpion. They say to love your enemy, and I never understood what that meant until I met you. I love you, Theodore Ferguson III. That's why when I defeat you today, I'll make it quick . . . consider it a professional courtesy."

The audience didn't normally applaud during the contestant-interview portion, but they applauded now.

Dr. Love, whose eyebrows were nearly lost in her towering updo, muttered, "We're going to have to cut most of that for time, you know."

"This is a game show, Dr. Love." Maxine gave her a beatific smile. "Is the audience not entertained?"

"Mmm." Dr. Love tapped her note cards on Maxine's podium before moving on to Teddy. Maxine might have been imagining it, but there was the faintest smile on the host's lips.

Maxine had never expected that Teddy would upstage her—but she'd never been prouder of him for doing so.

Like her, Teddy began by thanking his family. Then he turned to face her, just like she'd done to him. "Maxine Hart, you are my worthiest adversary—and my most worthy ally. The Bard once wrote, 'Cowards die many times before their deaths; the valiant never taste of death but once.' And the day I met you, I ran from fear and met death for what I pray will be the penultimate time. You've taught me not to hesitate, to place my trust in fate, and to leap into the unknown with my mind open. You've taught me to go all in. To bet it all. To give my maximum heart.

"So, it is with everything I have to wager that I ask: Will you marry me?"

Chapter 29

AN OLD-FASHIONED WEDDING

Answer

Scandinavian lore suggests it was tradition for wealthy Vikings to give their new brides one of these prized creatures, like the ones Thor gave to Freyja to pull her chariot.

Question

What is a cat?

Three months later.

Here was a fun trivia fact that Teddy hadn't known until recently: if one helped bring in the best viewer ratings that a network game show had ever seen, it was quite easy to obtain permission to be married on said game show's set.

Another fact he'd learned: his newly acquired fiancée had no compunction about obliterating his trivia prowess on television in the Daily

Duplex round despite having been proposed to by him during contestant interviews.

But none of that compared to what he'd learned about Maxine during the Final Answer question.

"There she is!" crowed Marlon when Maxine finally burst into Dino's like a whirlwind of fiery hair and summer heat.

"We thought you were going to miss the grand finale," Rabbi Cohen added, patting the open spot on the bench next to him. The bar was packed with engagement-party guests, and he and Marlon were forced to squeeze tight into their usual booth.

Maxine scoffed. "Please, and miss the look on Teddy's face when—"

"Shh!" Olive whispered, gesturing to the gathered crowd, who'd been rapt during the tournament screening thus far. "Not everyone was there—we agreed, absolutely *no spoilers*."

Maxine cast a dismissive glance at the empty seat next to Rabbi Cohen, then primly planted herself in Teddy's lap. He wrapped an arm around her waist and politely suppressed the urge to test the softness of her bare thighs beneath her flouncy, grass-hued dress. Not while her sister—and Teddy's parents, who sat two booths over, for that matter—were in attendance.

Maxine waved at the elder Fergusons, and his mother waved back. She'd been beyond delighted to have Maxine as her future daughter-in-law, and even more thrilled when Teddy had returned a certain package of signed documents to her for transfer to his father's solicitor.

His father, who sat in his wheelchair next to his medical attendant, pointed at the midcommercial promotional teaser that featured Teddy, Maxine, and Zola. "That's my boy!" he declared.

Tarrah returned from the bar with a tray full of what appeared to be radioactive waste in martini glasses, and squealed when she saw Maxine. Teddy's future wife deftly took the tray from her friend's grip and set it behind her on the table before accepting an enthusiastic embrace.

"I want to talk bachelorette party ideas, because your sister said ixnay on the strippers dressed like famous historical figures."

Olive shot Maxine a very nonplussed side-eye. "Britney Spears is not a famous historical figure."

"Um, rude?" Tarrah flipped her hair over her shoulder. "Maxine, final verdict? I do want to point out that there was going to be a giant boa involved."

"Feathered or scaled?"

"Definitely the second one, but now that you mention it, also definitely the first one."

Maxine sipped her toxic waste, expression pensive. "Olive's right that it makes absolutely no damn sense. The snake's compelling, though." Then she wrinkled her nose. "What the fuck is in this?"

"Yellow Chartreuse and VitaQuila," Tarrah said. "Liquor smarter, not harder! Teddy, do you want one?"

"I would rather have every word on my gravestone misspelled." He pulled out his phone to remind himself to follow up on his email to their corporate team. "I have sent multiple explanations of how they might correct their grammatical errors, and still they refuse to remedy their advertising."

Maxine patted his arm. "Want me to mail them a box of dead cockroaches?"

Rabbi Cohen asked, "Where are you getting all these dead cockroaches?" His tone was curious, yet not disapproving.

"I mean, they're not dead *yet*."

Teddy said, "No, but thank you for the offer, my very hot but strange darling." He knew Maxine well enough to know he wouldn't have to wait very long before an explanation was revealed to him—whether he wanted it or not.

She kissed his cheek. "You're welcome, Teddy Bear."

"Aww, you guys are disgusting," Tarrah said cheerfully.

Then someone shouted, "Everyone quiet! We're back from commercial!" and the familiar *Answers!* theme music rang out through the bar.

In Maxine's ear, Teddy whispered, "You're just in time for the final. I assume the location you inspected was worthwhile?"

She whispered back, "It's perfect. It's actually an old McKnight Academy building that went defunct years ago. It's failed to sell due to an, um . . . infestation."

And there it is. Teddy sighed. "The collective noun for a group of cockroaches is an *intrusion.* And I assume the removal cost is astronomical?"

She beamed at him. "Cockroaches are from the order Blattodea, which is derived from the Latin *blatta*, meaning 'one who shuns the light.'"

"I love you too."

And then, from the TV: *"Welcome back to* Answers! *Our final category is Poetry."*

The screen panned across all three contestants, showing Zola's score at 7,200, Maxine's at 32,400, and Teddy's at 22,000. Although Maxine had dominated in the first round, where she'd been smiled upon by the categories, both Teddy and Zola had elbowed their way into ringing in on a fairer share of questions during the Daily Duplex portion.

Teddy had known Maxine would go all in; his only hope to win would have been to bet everything, since it was a category he would almost certainly know the answer in, and hope she got it wrong.

But how could Teddy have wagered against believing in Maxine? It had always been clear that she was the superior player; he simply hadn't been able to see it until she'd dragged him—and his antiquated views of education—out of the darkness and into the light.

"*The final clue is . . . ,*" Dr. Love said. *"In his tenth eclogue, Virgil wrote, 'omnia vincit amor,' or this 'conquers all things.'"*

To this day, Teddy would never know whether that had been the original clue chosen for the Final Answer. Maxine swore upon every last cent to her name that Nora had lobbied for a last-minute change in order to pander to the as-yet-unanswered marriage proposal from earlier that episode, but Teddy was highly doubtful the *Answers!* legal team would have allowed such tampering after the dramatic events of the day prior.

All Teddy was certain of was that if he were given the opportunity to redo the entire match, he wouldn't have changed a single thing.

When the thinking music wound to a close, Dr. Love began with Zola's answer.

"Zola Mattick, our College Champion and Fan Favorite, you played admirably well tonight against our two highest-ranked players. What did you put as your answer?"

Zola smiled into the camera as her answer was revealed: "WHAT IS LOVE?"

"That's correct. Virgil wrote, 'Love conquers all things; let us too surrender to love.' And your wager? 7,200 points—all of it, for a total score of 14,400 points. Will it be enough? Let's move over to Teddy, who came into finals in second place. Teddy Ferguson, did you know the answer was 'love'? I suspect you do, after the grand romantic proposal we witnessed earlier this episode."

Teddy remembered the feeling of utter calm as his answer was revealed. The gasps from the audience, which were now echoed from those members of the crowd at Dino's who hadn't been in the audience that day.

"Teddy, you wrote . . . 'WHAT IS MAXINE?' That is, while a lovely sentiment, not an acceptable answer. What did you wager?"

Another round of gasps.

Dr. Love hesitated before reading: *"Twenty-two thousand points . . . all of it. You wagered everything."*

"*Yes*," he said, and nothing more.

On screen, Maxine had covered her mouth with both hands.

"Maxine Hart . . . I suspect that, based on your reaction, we're in for a surprise as well. Did you write the correct answer?"

Maxine slowly nodded, and her screen was revealed.

"YES, I WILL MARRY YOU."

The screen cut to Dr. Love's face, which featured an extraordinarily rare moment of befuddlement, then back to Maxine's wide-eyed shock.

"Do I dare assume . . ."

Maxine let her hands fall away as her wager was revealed. Quietly, she confirmed: *"To the max. All in."*

Teddy said, *"I thought that you—"*

At the same time as Maxine said, *"I didn't expect you to freaking—"*

Someone cut the audio to Teddy's and Maxine's mics, and Dr. Love announced, *"Congratulations, Zola Mattick, you've just won the Ultimate* Answers! *Tournament."*

The screen cut to Zola's absolutely thunderstruck reaction as it dawned on her that she'd just won $2 million. This filming decision also ensured that the camera wasn't recording how Maxine leaped into Teddy's arms and began kissing him with a wholly broadcast-inappropriate fervor. All Dino's erupted into a chaos of cheer and shock.

Teddy winked at Maxine. They'd managed to keep their personal twist ending under wraps for three months, and it had been worth the effort to see their friends and family react at the same time as the rest of the country.

Winston, who reigned over the corner booth, was suddenly inundated with Dino's regulars who'd made regrettable betting decisions—despite Maxine having done her best to discourage everyone she knew from gambling on the tournament without spoiling anything.

"You know it's all over for you guys now that it's public," Dino warned as he delivered a tray of celebratory whisky shots to Maxine and Teddy's table. "You better not be bringing paparazzi in here for Tuesday-night trivia, snooping and getting their grubby paws on my bar top."

"Don't worry," Maxine said. "We're retiring from the trivia world for a little while. This time, I really mean it. We've got a wedding to plan, I've got a school program to develop, and Teddy's got a sexy sci-fi novel to write."

"I never said it was sexy," he grumbled.

Later that night, long after most of their guests had stumbled into taxis, Teddy found Maxine upstairs in the old storage room, where the muggy summer air was only marginally lessened by the breeze from the open window.

He joined her in kneeling on the old banquette so they could gaze at the city, side by side. The sky was heavy with bruised clouds, and across the East River, the top of One World Trade Center disappeared into dark mist.

"We should head back soon," Maxine said. "Orange Cat is probably wondering where we are."

He hid a smile. "We're not putting *Orange Cat* on the adoption papers. He's a dignified gentleman, and he shall go by Ginger."

Maxine whipped her head around, eyes wide with delight. "We're adopting Ginger?"

"I don't think we have much say. Redheads seem to move into my house without asking my opinion about it. And since he's not chipped and no one has responded to our postings, I think it's settled."

Maxine threw her arms around him for a kiss so fervent that he was halfway to unbuckling his pants when she broke away with a breathless "Not here. It's too dangerous."

"What are you talking about?"

"Dino will murder us."

Teddy took a moment to assess his future bride, with her pupils dilated and lips swollen, her hair a haphazard mess around her damp cheeks, and her nipples outlined by the thin material of her dress, and decided to never care about propriety ever again. "Hasn't anyone told you life is the most dangerous game show of all?"

Maxine pouted. "I'm retired from game shows. We're going to live responsible, tame, ordinary lives. I'm going to have a skin-care routine . . ." She began counting on her fingers. "A calendar that I update more than once a month, I'm going to learn how to fold a fitted bedsheet—"

Teddy groaned with arousal. "You filthy tease. Come, have a seat on my lap and regale me with trivia instead."

Maxine eyed his lap warily. "This is a trap."

"You're damn right it is." He patted his thigh.

She dutifully swung a leg over to straddle him, palms coming up to caress the flat of his chest. "Here's a trivia fact for you. Did you know that brain scans of people in love show increased activity in the dopamine-reward-system region? So being in love is actually beneficial for my ADHD."

Teddy hummed in approval as he slid his hands up her thighs. Her skin was smooth and hot under his palms. "Then I vow to thoroughly activate your reward system, as often as needed."

"And the same scans showed decreased activity in the amygdala, which is where all your fear comes from."

"Then I'm going to be an extraordinarily brave man going forward, because I love you quite intensely." He shifted under her, fitting their bodies more tightly together, and she fell forward until her forehead rested against his.

"Oh, Teddy. You're already the bravest person I know." She traced a heart on his chest. "And I love you so, so much. Like, to the max."

His hands slipped higher on her thighs, thumbs tucking under the elastic around her hips. From the way her breath hitched in response, he knew this wouldn't take long at all.

"I think it may storm tonight," he murmured.

She fanned herself. "If we're lucky."

"I suspect we're the luckiest two people alive."

When Teddy took her mouth in a kiss, a silent flicker of lightning lit up the skyline.

And thus, the greatest rivalry in the history of trivia concluded . . . in love.

HOW CAN I GET ON A SHOW LIKE *ANSWERS*!?

I'm going to preface this section with the disclaimer that unlike Maxine and Teddy, I've never competed on a trivia game show, even though I'm such a hard-core fan that I wrote an entire romance novel centered on one. Up until I started researching for this book, I didn't think I ever *could* compete on a show like *Answers!* Like Maxine, I have ADHD, so a lot of her insecurities about her ability to study and retain information in the "traditional" way were pulled directly from my own experience. But I don't think that feeling is exclusive to my neurodivergent brethren either—I suspect the majority of you reading this are thinking, *Well, this was a fun story, but Teddy and Maxine are fictional geniuses. There's no way someone like* me *could compete on a trivia show. Heck, I barely remember what day it is.*

But I spent months poring over every single *Jeopardy!*-related book and study guide out there, and you want to know the sneaky little secret I uncovered? *Anyone can become a trivia game show champion.*

Yes, *you* can probably study your way onto *Jeopardy!*, no matter how "smart" you think you are. (If it wasn't already clear from this book, I think traditional ways to measure intelligence are kind of BS. They're usually a narrow measure of highly specific skills that have been deemed useful by a bunch of people who happen to also be good at those specific skills, and those people all look awfully similar to one another.)

There are entire books and serious websites dedicated to this topic, so the list I'm about to give you isn't really a competing study guide—it's just meant to give your inspiration a jumping-off point. I chose to highlight these specific strategies because they're the most interesting ones for *my* style of learning with ADHD (keeping in mind that everyone is different and YMMV).

All right, that's enough of the foreplay. Let's play baseball!

Here's a list of things you could do if you wanted to train to get on *Jeopardy!*:

1. Watch the show. (*Bonus points*: practice using a ballpoint pen's clicker as your buzzer, and answer in the form of a question, which was how Ken Jennings practiced for his original run.)

2. Read children's reference books on broad categories. These often distill broad topics into memorable trivia, often with accompanying visuals. (This is one of champion James Holzhauer's study techniques.)

3. Go wiki walking. Find one topic on Wikipedia, then follow links in the article down whichever rabbit holes your interest takes you. (Champion Amy Schneider credits this method for her success.)

4. Read *Moonwalking with Einstein*. This book explains how to build a memory palace, like the one Teddy teaches Maxine, among other techniques that have been proven to help learn long lists of information. (This isn't the only book out there on memorization techniques—pick a different one if you prefer!)

5. Quiz yourself (or each other!). The show has an official game app you can download, but devoted fans have compiled a database of nearly every question ever used on the episode at J! Archive (https://j-archive.com). What's a hotter way to spend the evening than exchanging *Jeopardy!* clues with your special someone?

See? None of these things are boring, "sit down and memorize a bunch of river names" nonsense. These are all things you can do in your spare time, and they can be pretty fun—you know, if you like to get down and nerdy like that.

All I'm saying is, don't count yourself out just because someone or something gave you the wrong idea about what being "smart" means. Vouloir, c'est pouvoir.

PS If you want to know more about Jeopardy! *the show from a noncompetitive standpoint, I highly recommend* Answers in the Form of Questions, *by Claire McNear, which will take you through the history of the show and behind the scenes on set. For a deeper dive into the world of trivia beyond* Jeopardy!, *I recommend Ken Jennings's book* Brainiac, *which also gives you the juicy firsthand account of his record-setting run (by which Teddy's run was heavily inspired).*

ACKNOWLEDGMENTS

This is my third time doing this, so I should be able to knock this out before the *Jeopardy!* thinking music for the final round stops playing, right? Let's see how I do.

As always: My writing support group, the Ponies. You've all had my back this year more than ever before, and I couldn't have done this without you incredible women. Alexis, Kelly, Kate, Jo, Elle, Lin, Jas, and Mel—you all have my loyalty forever. Call me if you ever need to bury a body. (Since the Pony who's a lawyer is glaring at me while she reads this: I'm kidding! You all know I don't have the upper-body strength to bury anything!)

Superhuman gratitude to my crit partners, Jo and Kate, who got the first draft of this book [redacted] days before it was due and still turned around top-notch feedback in record time. Lin also came through for me on that round—I owe you one!

On the business side of the mullet: My agent, Eva Scalzo, freaking rules. Also, she flew across the country to support me for my *Midnight Duet* book release at the Ripped Bodice (shout-out!). Can you say Best. Agent. Ever?! My acquiring editor, Alison Dasho, whom I finally got to meet in person this year, is the coolest, and I remain eternally grateful that she believes in me and I get to publish books with her blessing. My dev editor, Krista Stroever, is an impossibly patient genius and mind reader, and I'm not sure how I'd ever manage without her guiding my books from their "kinda sorta almost there" drafts to their "OMG, this is a real freaking book" final forms! Alicia Lea, whatever they're paying you for copyediting, they should double it for so patiently putting up with my BS and utter lack of respect for grammar, *Merriam-Webster*, *The Chicago Manual of Style*, and the English language in general. Bill Siever, I'm honored to have a fellow *Jeopardy!* nerd on the proofreading game; thanks for catching those nuanced (and sometimes *not* nuanced) errors to ensure this book is so polished it could even withstand a withering once-over at the podium with the late, great Trebek himself. And once again, to everyone at Montlake who made this book possible, including Karah Nichols on production management (a.k.a. the unenviable job of corralling cats), Kris Beecroft on art direction, Stef Sloma on marketing, and Allyson Cullinan on public relations.

Special shout-outs to fellow rom-com author Nellie Wilson (if you like my style of humor, check out her books!) and the other former *Jeopardy!* contestants who generously shared their behind-the-scenes experiences on the show with me so I could add elements of realism to the *Answers!* taping scenes. I inevitably took wild liberties with reality for plot and fashion reasons (*Jeopardy!* prefers that contestants don't wear white, for example), but as Maxine would say: knowing the rules is the first step to breaking them on purpose.

Oh god, the music is winding down. Quick, scribble something in!

Friends: Kyle, thank you for taking such good care of the pets and listening to me with eternal patience while I complained about the same things all the time. Katie and Virginia, thank you for the food delivery and emotional support while I was deep in the trenches with this one. Tara and Anna, I hope Tarrah Prince's character was a proper tribute to your collective awesomeness. Anchi and Kimiko, thank you for always finding the time to be there for me when I need it, no matter how busy life gets. Cindy and Percy, thanks for helping Taiga and me get outside. Jason: "I'm really feelin' the fuck out of this nerd." (Risky inclusion here, but Maxine would approve.)

To all my foster pets this year, who have reminded me how to love again after heartbreak—Flower, Princesa, and Saturn—you deserve all the happiness in the world. I'm so glad I got to meet you. And to my dog, Taiga, and my cat, Kitana: you're my favorite unlikable heroines, and I'd die for both you bitches.

Maximum heart. ♡

ABOUT THE AUTHOR

Jen Comfort is originally from Portland, Oregon, and dabbled in astrophysics before spending a decade working in restaurants in New York City and Portland. Now she writes romantic comedies about hot nerds with very cool jobs. She spends her free time growing plants destined to die before their time, playing video games, and encouraging her cat and malamute-husky dog to become internet famous, with zero success.